MYS JOR
Jordan, Oakley
Death's parallel

Rainbow Books, Inc.
FLORIDA

A Rainbow Book

DEATH'S PARALLEL

Oakley Jordan

RAINBOW BOOKS, INC.

Published by Rainbow Books, Inc.
Highland City, Florida 33846-0430 USA

3 5 7 9 10 8 6 4 2

PUBLISHER'S NOTE

This is a work of fiction. Names, characters, places and incidents are either the product of the author's imagination, or are used fictitiously, and any resemblance to actual persons, living or dead, business establishments, events or locales is entirely coincidental.

Library of Congress Cataloging-in-Publication Data

Jordan, Oakley.
    Death's parallel / Oakley Jordan.
       p.cm.
    ISBN 1-56825-078-9 (alk. paper)
       1. Assisted suicide--Fiction. 2. Serial murders--Fiction.
    3. Physicians--Fiction. I. Title.

PS3570.O7613 D4 2000
813'.6--dc21

                                                         00-046031

This book is printed on acid-free paper.

Printed in the United States of America

DEDICATION

To my guardian angel.

There is a defining moment in every life, and it is the inevitable and merciless end of the human process.

Death is a tragedy I witness daily, but this man's defining moment was too much for my trained mind. My soul bled of the faith he'd taught me. My shaken spirit prayed for an answer, but science gave me no clue. A metastasizing pain crippled his proud flesh. His strong faith fought a heartless fate. Unselfish tears tempered his cries of pain. A forced smile was the legacy of his never-ending love. His strength, now mine, I will cherish until I see him again, and again I will. "I will be with you in spirit until I see you face to face," he whispered and then was gone. A horrible ending to a wonderful life, he deserved better.

"I love you, Dad."

CHAPTER ONE

A sudden gust of wind chilled the kitchen and a clamoring shutter banged against the open window. The ebony maid turned quickly, securing the shutter, then she stared outside, transfixed by the orange and gold of early fall. A leaf spiraled to earth and a robin plucked a worm from the rich soil, hidden by multicolored leaves swirling in the breeze.

A faint voice broke the maid's reverie. She cocked an ear toward the bedroom. "Geraldine . . . Geraldine, where are you?" called a thin voice.

"Mrs. Taylor, I'm in the kitchen, ma'am." The maid heard the weary footsteps approaching but her eyes feasted a moment longer on the autumnal glory outside. "I love this time of year with them changing colors," she said aloud.

A silver-haired woman slowly made her way into the kitchen. "Oh, yes," she half-whispered and joined her maid at the window. Together they surveyed the beauty beyond. "This was my Henry's favorite time of the year," she softly whispered.

"Oh, yes, ma'am," Geraldine sighed. "My favorite, too." The maid moved from the window. She prepared to leave and reached for her purse. "Now, Mrs. Taylor, you promise me that you'll keep your appointment tomorrow. You know your daughter is going to be very upset you've missed your therapy. This is the second treatment you've missed this week."

"I know, you're right," responded the elderly woman, "but I feel so tired afterwards." She paused and her eyes strayed toward another room. "I stare at Henry's picture on the piano. I hear his voice telling me to be strong." Her thin, shaky hands slowly reached for the window shutters, closing out the brilliance of the late afternoon sun and darkening the room. "I know you are always right when it comes to my well being." She smiled warmly.

Geraldine returned the love with a caring grin. Mrs. Taylor raised her arms to embrace Geraldine, her sadness momentarily vanishing as Geraldine gripped her tightly with a loving grunt. "I love you, Mrs. Taylor," she said.

"And I love you, my sweet Geraldine. Now you go on and get home to that wonderful husband of yours. You're very lucky to still have him. Cherish each moment because it will be over before you know it."

"We all love you, Mrs. T.," said Geraldine. She held back a tear knowing how ill Mrs. Taylor had become. She had been with the Taylors for more than twenty years. She had seen their daughter grow and been there when Dr. Taylor died. "Keep those treatments going, ma'am. Don't cheat us. Your Henry would want you to fight. And here, don't forget these pills to help your pain."

Thinning hands grasped the vials. "Morphine and more morphine," she sighed deeply, "but it really doesn't help. And, yes —" her tiny voice filled with exasperation "— I know Henry would want me to fight but —" She tossed the vials onto the counter and her brow furrowed. "But if he knew how horrible I felt, well, I'm not so sure he would push me."

"I know, Mrs. T.," whispered Geraldine softly. "He was a great man and a wonderful doctor. They don't make them like him anymore."

Mrs. Taylor nodded. "I feel him with me all the time and I miss him so. It's just —"

A dark hand caressed the aged face. "I've got to run. Got to pick up some groceries on my way home. See you tomorrow." At the rear door Geraldine paused. "Oh, I almost forgot. Remember, your daughter is on her way over with her kids. She's in a hurry, so be looking for her. Now you go to the couch and rest yourself, Mrs. T." Geraldine spoke while slowly backing down the steps waving good-bye.

"I won't forget, Geraldine," mumbled Mrs. Taylor, managing a slight wave, then her frail hands closed the screen door. "My, my," she sighed, resting her back against the door, closing her tired eyes. "Henry, my love," she breathed quietly. "My dearest Henry, it's almost time, my darling." Glancing upward, a broad smile swept her tired face.

Mrs. Taylor walked through the large house. In the living room she paused. She slid a delicate finger over the grand piano. She lifted a gold framed picture to her lips and placed a gentle kiss upon the glass. The frame held the image of a smiling, gray haired man, her precious Henry, embracing his wife tightly. She gently set it down and brushed a tear from her cheek. Unsteadily, with shuffling steps, she made her way to the front hall. She opened the massive carved door with great effort. On the porch she stood in painful silence. Her failing vision scanned the landscaped grounds.

The bright sunshine and fragrance of fall refreshed her spirit. A cascade of memories flooded her thoughts. She turned to her beloved home, her refuge and sanctuary, then she suddenly gasped. The picture in the window took her breath. Death had taken her husband and now a terrible illness cast a shroud over her once proud self. She leaned her frail body against a white pillar. She sighed. The sensitive scar reminded her the mastectomy had failed to stop the spreading cancer.

It was time.

The car was filled with the children's boisterous voices.

Sarah darted a reproving look to the back seat. "Both of you, quiet down!" She fumbled for a cigarette. "I bet your father's already at the school wondering where in the heck we are. I don't know why on earth your grandmother needs to see you before the game. So here we are late again." She glanced in the rear view mirror as the two children continued to fight and scream. "Thank God, we're here!" she practically shouted, pulling into the drive.

"There's Mama Dear on the front porch. Now both of you, listen to your mother," Sarah commanded. "We need to hurry." She tugged at her daughter's tee-ball uniform. "Madeline, if you hit him one more time we're going home!"

Entranced by the colors of the changing season, Mrs. Taylor smiled at the birds gliding from tree to tree, then she heard the car approach and car doors slam.

"Mama Dear, Mama Dear!" the children yelled, running up the long sidewalk and steps. They stood proudly in their red uniforms.

"My babies!" exclaimed Mrs. Taylor, delight in her eyes. She bent slightly to give them a hug. "I was watching the robins make a winter nest in that tree." She pointed.

Sarah sulked. "Mom, I have no idea why we had to come by now. You know we're late for Trey's tee-ball game. We could have come by later and stayed longer."

"I know, Sarah, but it was something I needed. You know your mother when she gets her mind set on something."

"Boy, do I know that."

Mrs. Taylor clasped a small hand in each of hers. "You two have grown so through the summer," she smiled.

"Now," ordered Sarah, "give Mama Dear a big hug and kiss. We'll come back after the game. Mom, how do you feel after your therapy today?"

"Didn't go today," answered Mrs. Taylor, giving a last hug to both children.

"Mom," complained Sarah, with such disappointment, the children turned. "You promised me you wouldn't miss anymore."

Mrs. Taylor stood erect. "Daughter, this will be the last time you'll ever have to scold me about missing a treatment. Now give your mother a hug and a kiss and be off with your children."

"I love you, Mom." The hug was brief, then she descended the steep steps.

"And I love you, my sweet baby girl. I look at you and still see a child walking around with a —" she laughed "— a droopy diaper."

The grandchildren laughed wildly. Sarah frowned.

"Oh, don't get mad. I see so much of your father's lively eyes in yours . . . and his temper. I think —"

But Sarah was already leading her children across the wide driveway. Mrs. Taylor's sad look returned. She raised her arm in a grimace and waved good-bye. A smile masked deep pain. With a honk the car sped off, the children waving from the back window.

The elderly woman stared until the car disappeared. She began to hum a lullaby. High above the blue sky was touched with a feathering of clouds, soaring fast to a destination unknown, far beyond the horizon they went. A string of geese flew gracefully in a straight line. Wild songbirds chanted. A robin caught her gaze. Perched on the lawn, the bird scratched at the earth. She reached out as if to touch it. The bird danced magically, then raised its wings and was lifted aloft by the fall wind.

A dark automobile rolled in front of the home. It slowly pulled into the drive. Rays of the sun flashed against steel and chrome, momentarily blinding Mrs. Taylor. She caught her breath and her heart raced. The afternoon sun shone on the salt and pepper hair, brightening a handsome face. In his hand was a dark suitcase. She felt an instant warmth comfort her agony. The tall figure waved. He was a man in his mid-sixties. But the years had been kind; time had yet to etch its mark. With a broad smile he came forward, ascending the steep steps with a sureness of purpose.

"Benjamin." Both of her small hands reached out.

"Helen, how —" He hesitated.

"I'm ready, Benjamin," she said in a soothing voice.

The large suitcase was placed beside her, then their hands locked.

"You're certain?" he asked. "How do you feel?"

"I'm still in constant pain. The therapy is making me sicker than this damn cancer," she intoned with anger. "I'm so nauseated that I can't even look at food. I thought dying would be the worst thing ever, but now I know that trying to stay alive is even worse. I'm getting weaker and weaker and hurting more."

He nodded. The anger and frustration were evident. He had seen the same pattern in hundreds of patients. There was no hope for Helen Taylor. His face was caring as he listened. He embraced her lightly. She looked up in his understanding face.

"I've spoken to God and Henry about it. Both are waiting. God knows how much I love Him and he knows more than anyone the pain I feel. He wants me to be at ease." She paused, then spoke with deep emotion. "I know God understands and no one can tell me different." She stamped her foot on the pavement. With great effort she pushed the door open. He gripped the suitcase and followed.

The spacious room was filled with expensive antiques and priceless paintings. A marble bust of Dr. Taylor rested on a gold leaf Chippendale table. It was bathed in sunlight, glowing with color in the somber room. Her small hand turned a light switch and overhead beams brightened the lovely paintings which graced the walls. But still Benjamin's gaze was on the marble bust.

"Remember all the good times we had when my Henry was alive?" she reminisced. "And all the parties in this room."

His eyes swept the room, then he pointed to a bookcase. He laughed loudly. "Henry and I never did figure out who took the silver cat that New Year's Eve."

Mrs. Taylor's hands fluttered and she laughed with a small musical voice. Her hands patted the bust excitedly. "Oh, it was Jane Mitchell," she smiled. "She was drunk. Dr. Mitchell came over about two weeks later. He was so embarrassed. He had found my precious cat under their bed!" The large room filled with harmonious laughter. "Dr. Mitchell begged me not to tell. And I promised. Henry paid over twenty-thousand dollars for the cat when we were in Paris. He would have banned Jane from our home forever. I just told the old boy my cat had been returned through an ad in the Sunday newspaper." She placed her fists on her hips and said coyly, "Henry believed that tale."

"You rascal," said Benjamin. "I always suspected Dr. Peterson. He was always over-billing everybody and swiping my stethoscope."

Mrs. Taylor took small steps toward a nearby bookshelf. With both hands she lifted a silver cat and unsteadily handed it to Benjamin who placed it on the Chippendale table. She returned with small silver kittens and carefully set them beside the beautiful silver cat, snarling with claws ready to scratch mercilessly.

"Henry bragged that cat belonged to Marie Antoinette."

"Is that right?"

"So he told me," answered Mrs. Taylor. "And that's what I told my bridge club," she laughed. "And were they jealous!"

Benjamin reached for a framed baby portrait.

"You and Henry practicing medicine together and us having the time of our lives. Remember when I found out I was pregnant with Sarah?" Her voice stifled a sob and her eyes moistened. Benjamin walked slowly to her side and placed a comforting arm around her shoulder.

"Ben, you will look after Sarah and the children, won't you?"

"She's my godchild, Helen. She's like family. She's my Terry's best friend, too."

"I know you will," she whispered, planting a soft kiss on his cheek. "I know, Junior," she whispered.

Benjamin smiled.

"I can just hear Henry now. He loved to goad me with that junior partner stuff. He was what, ten years older?"

"Age does make a difference, Ben. I'll be seventy my next —"

She halted. "Now, Benjamin, I've decided I'd like you to play my favorite song while I go to sleep. You know the song. It was Henry's favorite, too." He nodded. Mrs. Taylor eased into a brown leather wing chair. Her small frame seemed ever so tiny in Henry's favorite chair.

Helen was always such a beautiful woman, thought Benjamin. Well educated and charming, she had been a leader in cultural and philanthropic events. Though socially prominent and quite wealthy, Helen was remarkably down to earth. For years she had graced the newspaper, her classic face and luxuriant brown hair, arranged in a chignon, brought both admiration and envy. But those who knew her loved her, and all realized the Taylors were a perfect match. Benjamin had been surprised that she allowed her hair to turn white. Then after the breast cancer was diagnosed, she had aged tremendously. The sparkling eyes faded. The regal bearing was burdened by illness.

He knelt. He opened the suitcase and began placing the canisters on the thick carpet. There was a lifeless quiet filling the room. He connected a long black hose to a plastic mask, then noticed his patient standing at the piano.

When Helen turned toward him, she held aloft a framed photograph, displaying a laughing couple embracing. She pressed a button and the fireplace flamed. She practically collapsed in the leather chair, breathing deeply. "I'm so tired," she sighed.

As Benjamin stood a machine hummed. "Ben, would you sing? Henry always admired your voice. 'Sing something, Junior,' he'd say."

He wagged a finger. "You tell Henry I'm senior now."

She laughed and Benjamin returned to the equipment, carefully examining the mask on the carpet and the odorless vapor which filled it. His face betrayed his heart. "Benjamin, please don't be sad. This is what I've been praying for. I love you for this."

He turned a knob and the humming machine grew louder. She gazed upward with grateful eyes. The photograph of the

Taylors, vibrant and in love, was cradled in her lap. She patted his cheek affectionately as he slipped the mask over her face and adjusted the headband behind her soft white hair. He turned the knob of the small tank at the side of her chair. The whir increased.

"I love you, Helen."

A pair of thin fingers gently touched the mask at her lips and a kiss came his way.

At the piano now his hands swept the keys and an arpeggio sounded. He glanced over his shoulder and Helen smiled. She gave a little wave.

"You are my sunshine . . ." he half spoke and sang. Then his deep voice filled the room. Before him were Henry and Helen, dozens of friends, champagne and joy. He sang for Helen and for himself. And he remembered the best of times. After several minutes that seemed like hours he stopped. He closed the piano. The picture had now fallen to the thick carpet.

Lifting the mask from the sleeping face he witnessed a freedom from pain and an eternal calm. Helen was now at peace and Ben felt relieved. He turned off the machine. Closing her eyes with a soft stroke he observed that the wrinkles of pain were gone. He kissed her forehead, then slowly walked across the room, easing himself onto a long golden sofa. He wiped his eyes and waited. His breathing became steady. He dialed 911.

"I'd like to report a death," said Dr. Benjamin Pritchitt.

CHAPTER TWO

The ambulance pulled away from the home in silence. No siren wailed; only emergency lights flashed. But there was no emergency. Curious neighbors hovered, whispering in the descending twilight.

Benjamin Pritchitt answered the last of many questions. Detectives closed their notebooks, then strode away, leaving him alone on the large porch. He made certain the home was locked, then walked to his waiting car, meeting the stare of onlookers. "That's him!" he heard a woman say excitedly. As he lifted the empty suitcase into the trunk, he took a last look at the antebellum mansion, once the site of so much happiness. It was his last visit and he had lost a good friend. A dark curtain had descended.

Benjamin Pritchitt was a prominent Memphis physician. As chief-of-staff at Memorial Hospital and Director of the Department of Surgery, he was revered by thousands of patients. Pritchitt was a caring husband, honored parent and loving grandfather. Throughout his decades of practice a deep sense of responsibility to alleviate human suffering was the essence of his life. His dedication and concern were so great that his actions had led him to the brink of professional and personal ruin. In only a few months the esteem and respect had crumbled, as his life changed forever. Once acclaimed for his medical expertise, he had suddenly become controversial, praised by some, cursed by most, reviled as the doctor aiding in the suicides of the terminally ill. Helen Taylor was the seventh patient whose death he had hastened. But she was more than a patient. Continued pleas to end her suffering had finally won him over. With the seven deaths, justification had come from his heart. For decades a line had been drawn by the ethics of the medical community. He had now crossed the line. But Pritchitt knew he was hardly alone. In fact, many physicians felt as he did but few had the courage to act. Breast cancer and it's ugly metastasis had riddled the body of Helen Taylor, creating excruciating pain which only drugging to near unconsciousness could ease. He had no regrets. The local and national medical community had been thrust into the midst of a furor created by his unashamed deeds. Pritchitt was already under indictment. District Attorney General Jeremy Bates had announced that Dr. Pritchitt was a monster who must be stopped. His trial was only weeks away and a court order forbade any further suicide assistance. Memorial Hospital had suspended him as chief of staff. The likelihood of losing all staff privileges and even his medical license was evident. His family, shattered by his sudden fall from grace, had been unable to convince him of any wrong.

The moral dilemma had festered within him for years until he could no longer ignore the suffering he so often witnessed. He was convinced he had a moral obligation to ease the pain of the terminally ill.

With the searing controversy his private life had been mercilessly scrutinized. But reporters found few skeletons. He was recognized as a brilliant Harvard graduate with a devoted wife, two children and two grandchildren. He was a gracious man of a quiet nature, not one to seek the limelight. A physician of commitment, not only to patients, but also to the young doctors and medical students he had instructed over the years. He was a church-going, God-fearing man, now ostracized from his congregation, shunned by the clergy. Editorials in religious newspapers had denounced him for "playing God." There was even a comparison with the Nazi physicians whose horrific treatment of captive patients had been condemned by the world. He had been shocked when his wife had handed him an article which said he was but one step behind the notorious Dr. Mengele. "First assisted suicide," it warned, "then euthanasia, then death camps for the unwanted . . ." Press reports had stated his family was bitterly opposed to his "mercy killing."

All who knew of his professional reputation were shocked and puzzled. Was he mentally ill? they wondered. Why else would such a distinguished physician purposefully destroy his career? But Pritchitt knew his most vicious critics had not looked into the despairing eyes of those whose end was certain. As a younger doctor, he had been unable to prevent the agonizing deaths of his parents.

He was haunted by his father's demise. Suffering from prostate cancer his father had pleaded, "Either end my pain or put me to death." And he could do neither. Finally, a troubled conscience and deep compassion had convinced him which path to take, no matter the cost.

Memorial's ER entrance was, as usual, crowded with ambulances and blue cruisers. Police vehicles were common since crime victims received the best emergency treatment there. Pritchitt by now recognized the familiar faces of the men in blue. And they knew him. He drove slowly into his reserved space, near an ambulance, intending to slip in a side entrance. Bright lights suddenly engulfed him. A television camera team came charging behind him. A crowd surrounded the entrance. He resisted the impulse to run.

"Dr. Pritchitt! Dr. Benjamin Pritchitt!" shouted a woman approaching. "This is Dorothy Cohen reporting live," she blurted breathlessly, "at Memorial Hospital where, according to police reports, Dr. Benjamin Pritchitt has assisted in yet another suicide." Just as Pritchitt made it to the entrance ramp a security guard blocked her way.

"No media inside!" the guard shouted.

As Pritchitt struggled to push through a sea of blue uniforms the reporter's voice exploded, "You've seen it here, live on Channel 8, a special breaking news story. Dr. Benjamin Pritchitt, suspended chief-of-staff at Memphis' largest hospital has again aided in the death of a patient while under indictment by the District Attorney's Office. There are unconfirmed reports that number seven is a Helen Taylor, widow of Pritchitt's deceased partner —" Her voice trailed off as he finally pushed his way through the throng.

Chaos reigned; not the usual bedlam of emergency rooms, but the focus of a national controversy, creating a sensational atmosphere which overshadowed the painful cries and concerned voices. Hospital staff stood and watched in the narrow corridor, awestruck as Dr. Pritchitt slowly walked behind the stretcher carrying the covered body of his dear friend. Someone was now walking beside him.

"Benjamin, are you all right?" asked Dr. Lane Powers, medical director of the emergency room.

"I'm fine, Lane."

"Why, Ben?" asked Powers, taut emotion in his voice. "Why are you throwing yourself to the wolves? Your whole career, Ben, why?" Pritchitt said nothing, and Powers fell behind, trailing the sad procession. Powers was truly shocked. He had studied under the master, and was revulsed by the public spectacle of a revered physician destroying his reputation. "They're going to die anyway, Ben. What's the point?"

Pritchitt suddenly wheeled, his eyes wide, but he contained his anger. "Lane, I'm going up to my office. When Sarah Taylor comes in, call me!"

Realizing his emotional state, Powers calmed himself, placing his hand on his mentor's shoulder. "I hope everything works out for you. I really do."

"Thanks, Lane. I appreciate your concern." Pritchitt turned toward the elevators at the end of the corridor.

The Department of Surgery offices were strangely quiet.

The mood of the staff had been tense for weeks after the indictment of their respected director. The buzz through the hospital had already spread the news of another assisted suicide.

Dr. Pritchitt stopped at his secretary's desk. "I'm expecting a call from Dr. Powers." He could read the fear in Patsy's eyes. "I'm all right," he assured her.

"Oh, doctor, I —" she stammered. Her voice choked with emotion. Dr. Pritchitt was the man she had served for all the years of his practice at Memorial. The door to his office closed behind him. The secretary shook her head over the latest death.

Minutes passed as Pritchitt sat in his chair. He stared aimlessly at the stacks of medical files on his desk. His eyes focused on a note in Patsy's precise handwriting. "Telephone your attorney." He stood and walked to the window. The bridge linking Memphis to Arkansas was aglow in the roseate hue of the setting sun. The river became molten. In the falling darkness tiny colored headlights flickered as traffic crossed the bridge over the Mississippi River. The steel girders in the shape of an *M* suddenly brightened making him catch his breath. He stepped back, and saw his reflected image in the window, with an *M* emblazoned on the once renowned Dr. Benjamin Pritchitt. Was it the mark of Cain? Was he a murderer?

The door burst open.

"For the love of God, Benjamin, what is happening to you?" Dr. James Peters glowered. He slammed his fists on Pritchitt's desk and records toppled to the floor. "Do you want to go to prison? Is that it?"

Pritchitt picked up the medical records and tossed them on his desk. He eased into his large leather chair and stared into Dr. Peters' fiery eyes. Peters was the temporary chairman of the Surgery Department. As Dr. Peters ranted, Pritchitt frowned inwardly. He's going to be a rotten chairman, thought Pritchitt. There was no room for error in Dr. Peter's unrealistic approach to life . . . and death. Yet, his steely, unyielding manner had made him the likeliest replacement. There would be no surprises for the hospital's board of directors.

"James, you're a bit wound up, aren't you?"

Stunned by Pritchitt's calmness, Dr. Peters was silent.

"Sit down, before you have some kind of a heart attack and we find ourselves autopsying you."

Dr. Peters paced before the large desk, then jabbed a finger, "You know you're becoming a humiliating embarrassment to the hospital and this entire damn department."

"That's funny," smiled Pritchitt.

"And what's so funny about all of this?" shot back Dr. Peters.

"Just that . . . when I was chief the department wasn't damned."

"Oh, bullshit! Pritchitt, how can we gain the respect of interns and resident doctors with the former department chief going around committing murder?"

"That's enough!" Pritchitt shouted. "I'm not a murderer." Peters was startled by the outburst, stumbling backwards into a chair. "Now get the hell out of my office!"

"You'll be sorry, Dr. Pritchitt. You will not address me in that tone. I'm the chairman of the department now and —" he stood menacingly, "and I'm going to make certain your ass is banned from the hospital — permanently!"

Acting head, Pritchitt thought, and a poor acting job at best. Peters turned with a huff and stormed out the door.

The moment Peters left Patsy rushed in. "Dr. Pritchitt," she said in a tense voice, "Dr. Wiseman is here to see you. He's come to your office three times today. He says it's very important."

"Do I know this Dr. Wiseman?"

"Dr. Bernie Wiseman, surgery resident," she reminded.

There was a soft knock against the open door. It was Dr. Wiseman. "Dr. Pritchitt, I'm sorry to disturb you but it's important, so I know you'd want me to tell you today and not tomorrow."

Pritchitt remembered Wiseman, a small talkative fellow

who came with the reputation of a slightly eccentric genius. "Sit down, Wiseman."

Wiseman closed the door, observing the wounded spirit in Pritchitt's face.

"Are you all right, Dr. Pritchitt?" asked Wiseman, seating himself.

"That seems to be the ten million dollar question around here. What do you think?"

"I don't think you are, sir."

"Bingo. Right answer, Bernie. Now what is it that brings you to this criminal's office, knowing if you stand too close you may just see yourself on the evening news?"

"There's something very strange going on, Dr. Pritchitt. I mean really quite strange. At first, I didn't think anything of it, but now— ? Every morning this week I've been finding the most peculiar fax messages here in your office when I get to work. I'm usually the first one here each morning. Routinely, I check the fax machine for messages from different departments. All this week, however, I've been finding messages that make no sense at all." Wiseman held a small stack of faxes.

"That happens all the time, Dr. Wiseman. Some crank gets a fax number and begins to send all kinds of crazy things over those damn machines. They're like computers, everyone wants to play on them."

"I think there's more to this, sir. I believe —"

The telephone beeped. A brief pause was interrupted by the secretary's anxious voice over the intercom. "Dr. Powers on line three. And Dr. Wiseman I know you slipped past me and you are on my bad list."

Pritchitt punched a blinking red light.

"She's here," spoke a voice through the intercom.

"Thanks, Lane. I'll be right down."

Pritchitt stood, his face somber, his voice flat and serious. "Dr. Wiseman, I have an emergency situation and must go down. You understand?"

Wiseman rose, nodding. "But please read these messages."

Pritchitt opened the door.

"Sir," spoke Wiseman respectfully. "I just want you to know I hope everything goes well with you. If I can be of any help —"

"Of course, Dr. Wiseman, thank you. Now, young man, I must hurry." Then he was gone.

Bernie Wiseman walked to the window. Night had fallen on Memphis and evil deeds transpired at night, knew the young doctor. How many gunshot victims tonight? he wondered.

Lt. Lori Bordeaux inhaled deeply, then flicked ashes from the car window. It's going to be a bad night, she had thought earlier and, sure enough, only an hour into her shift there was an emergency call. Seeing two squad cars ahead she turned off the siren and tossed the cigarette butt through the window. She pulled into a narrow alley and parked. As she exited the car, she was met by two policemen.

"Lieutenant, we found her over there," said an officer, pointing to one of the tall garbage containers supplied by the city. The trio hurried across the street. Curious bystanders huddled near the container. "Get them back," ordered Lt. Bordeaux, and a young policeman barked a command. "Where's the kid?" she asked, lighting a cigarette.

"Over there, with his mother."

Lt. Bordeaux turned and stared. "Not a pleasant thing for a boy that young to find," she said, lifting the lid of the garbage container.

"About the same age as the other girl we found last month," said the policeman.

Bordeaux stared at the open eyes of the lifeless face, nestled between empty cereal boxes and tin cans.

"Damn she stinks or else the garbage does," said a nearby officer with revulsion.

She glanced at his badge. "Gee, Officer Billingsly, I think it's both. If you keep getting smart like that maybe you'll make detective. By then I'll probably be so damn sick of this shit you can have my job. What's that on her neck?"

"Some kind of tattoo. Looks like a snake but it's hard to tell with that cereal box in the way."

"Well, don't touch anything until the coroner arrives. Have y'all questioned the boy?"

"No, sir. I mean, no ma'am," the officer stammered, embarrassed by his mistake. "We were waiting for you."

"Well, how about us moving our butts across the alley and try to learn something." Lt. Bordeaux approached the boy. He had his arms wrapped around his mother's waist. She smiled and crouched to talk. The policemen stepped back and listened.

Lt. Lori Bordeaux was a 10-year veteran of the police department and the only female detective in homicide. She was a honey blonde, tall, attractive and hardened. She was recognized for her undercover prowess, changing her appearance when necessary. Her professional demeanor was strictly business. Her style was deliberate, blunt. There were grumbles that she was a cold-hearted bitch. She spoke with a pronounced twang that suffered few fools. Lt. Bordeaux was a young widow with no family other than her job. She kept her private life far from work. Her partners found her aloof, distant, but good at what she did. Lt. Bordeaux, dressed immaculately in a blue tailored suit, could have been mistaken for a businesswoman, an attorney or a real estate agent. A slight hint of perfume added a warm touch. But her green eyes were penetrating, withering and cold. This was now her territory. Like a lioness on the prowl, she was the dominant force. Lt. Bordeaux exuded confidence and control. She was seething within.

This was the third young girl in a month found murdered in a garbage container. Not a lead had surfaced in the bizarre killings.

Lt. Bordeaux stood. "He didn't know much," she told the two policemen. "Didn't anyone see anything?" she asked.

"Nothing," said Officer Billingsly. "We questioned those people milling around," added his partner, pointing.

"Well, guys, I want every door in a two block radius knocked on." She reached for a pack of cigarettes, then returned

to the garbage container. She gave a cold frown and lifted the lid
and peered inside. Slamming the lid shut, she began studying
the alley. The coroner's ambulance screeched to a stop. There's
a pattern here, she told herself. A serial killer was weaving a
blood-dripped tapestry. There was a key. She had to unlock the
mystery. Like a tigress stalking her prey, Lori Bordeaux began
her hunt down the alley.

Memorial's Emergency Room was crowded but Pritchitt's
mind was oblivious to the noise. Dr. Powers sat behind a messy
desk.

"Where is she, Lane?"

"Ben, I don't think it's a good idea for you to see her right
now," he cautioned, rising. "She's very upset."

"I held this child in my arms when she was less than five
minutes old. Now where is she?"

"She's not a baby anymore, For God's sake, man,
remember you helped her mother kill herself."

"Lane, I've got to see her." There was a pleading tone in his
words. A frantic look came over Pritchitt. He rushed toward the
door. Powers begged him to return. But the plea went
unanswered as Pritchitt raced toward the morgue. Through a
window in a swinging door he saw Sarah, her head cradled in
her husband's chest. She rocked in pain standing near the
covered body of her mother. A nurse led the children quietly
from the room, passing Pritchitt in the doorway. "Sarah," he
said calmly.

She slowly lifted her head in recognition. Her red eyes
widened. "You murderer!" she screamed. Tearing herself from
her husband, her fists hammered Pritchitt's chest.

"I understand how you feel, Sarah, but —"

Her cheeks were tear stained as she looked him square in
the face. "Why, Mom?" she cried. "Uncle Benjamin, she loved
you." Pulling away from her husband's grip she slapped
Pritchitt across the face. "I hate you, you bastard!" she
screamed. "You killed my mother." Pritchitt clung to her
tightly. She struck his back with a feeble blow, then her anger

subsided.

"I love you, Sarah. I loved your parents like my brother and sister."

"I didn't get to say good-bye," she cried, her voice barely a whisper and her face twisted in grief.

Pritchitt held her hands and looked her in the face. "Sarah, your mother was in such pain. She had lost over thirty pounds in just six weeks. She was taking six morphine pills a day and dozens of other pain pills. Nothing was helping her. I— " His voice broke and tears filled his eyes. "I wanted her to live as much as you, but she begged me and looked into my soul for help."

Looking into Pritchitt's eyes, she could barely form her words. "I'm going to miss her so much. I don't remember if I told her how much I loved her when I saw her this afternoon. I was too worried," she began sobbing, "about getting to a damn tee-ball game." She buried her head in Pritchitt's shoulder. "Why didn't she tell me?"

Pritchitt had regained his composure. His voice was steady. "Sarah, your mother was my patient. It's what your mother wanted. She prayed about it. Now listen to me," he said, holding her at arm's length. "It's time to go home. Your husband and family need you . . . and you need them." Her husband nodded and escorted his wife from the room. Pritchitt hovered near the body of Helen Taylor, hiding a wisp of silver hair beneath the sheet.

"Ben, I hope you know what you're doing," offered Dr. Powers.

"I pray that I know what I'm doing, Lane, and one thing is sure."

"What's that?"

"Helen Taylor is no longer in pain."

Powers supportively tapped his friend's shoulder and walked away.

CHAPTER THREE

On the fourth ring Terry Mercer rushed into her office and snatched the receiver.

"Assistant District Attorney Mercer speaking." She caught her breath, searching for words. "Yes, I just saw the news. Everybody in Memphis knows by now. We've all talked to him until we are blue in the face. Yes, he knows he could go to prison. He's not stupid," she said with impatience. She slammed down the telephone in anger. She took a deep breath; the phone rang again.

"Of course I'm upset. It's not every day your father aids in a suicide." She sighed. "I appreciate your call but I don't feel like talking anymore."

Terry Mercer was shattered by her father's actions. The District Attorney's Office was vigorously prosecuting the case. Her boss, Dist. Atty. Jeremy Bates, had obtained an indictment and vowed that Dr. Benjamin Pritchitt would be convicted. He had violated state laws which banned assisted suicide.

Bates issued a statement that "the diabolical apparatus" which Pritchitt had constructed emitted deadly carbon monoxide gases, and was designed for a single purpose: to kill innocent people, confused in thought due to illness. "The

Supreme Court has ruled on this issue and it's my duty to prosecute."

After the indictment, Bates had rejected Terry's offer to resign. She was a good attorney and needed in the office. However, she was to avoid the Pritchitt case, as a conflict of loyalty was apparent. Terry kept the resignation letter in her purse. There was no question she would have to resign, but her primary duty was to complete the case which obsessed her. There was a serial killer to be caught.

Justin Nash, the Executive Asst. D.A., had urged her to stay on. Nash was in charge of the serial case and was being hammered daily by the public's terror and demand to apprehend the maniac. Duty dictated that she remain and help Nash. As an attorney, Terry Mercer had a strict sense of justice. Now she was tormented by her father's actions. The indictment. The publicity. The worry. Sleepless nights had led to exhaustion. Her own marriage was near its end. Even her estranged husband was supportive of his father-in-law, and they had argued bitterly over his conduct. Now, with Helen Taylor's death, thoughts of resigning her position returned.

The telephone rang. She sighed and reached for the receiver. It was her brother. She listened to his angry words. Tyler Pritchitt was a forensic pathologist at the university. He and his father had once been very close, sharing a world of medicine but now the distance between them was immeasurable. Tyler was unable to reach his father.

Terry understood the pain in her brother's voice. "God knows I love him," he lamented, "as much as a son can love a father but Terry, I don't know him anymore. He won't talk to me. It's as if God himself had told him what to do and with that, he doesn't give a damn about anything else."

Terry noticed an attorney approaching her and she abruptly ended the conversation. "I'll meet you at the house later. I've gotta go." She was handed a police report. It detailed the recent victim found in Audubon Park. Nauseated at the grim description, she sat.

Tyler Pritchitt would most likely participate in the autopsy. He was the best in the mid-south and the Coroner's Office always had him assist their own staff in times when violence was rampant. Terry Mercer knew all too well the viciousness of the human race. She was sworn to uphold the law. She opened her purse and unfolded the resignation letter.

From the desk drawer Benjamin Pritchitt removed a half bottle of scotch. He lifted his glass. "To you, Henry and Helen. My good friends, may you rest in peace and, wherever you are, wait for Ruth and I." He emptied the contents, then poured another shot. His eyes fell on a note attached to a folder. They were the fax messages Wiseman had referred to earlier.

Each fax began with "Simon says" and included a conversation between two doctors who talked of sin and filthy garbage. He leafed through the sheets, then stuffed them back in the envelope. The ranting of a disgruntled nurse or orderly, thought Pritchitt. Hell, it could even be a doctor with a few loose screws. He smiled inwardly.

"Maybe we can go into practice together," he laughed aloud. "Everyone seems to assume I've crossed the bend anyway." He tossed the envelope onto his desk. It was time to go home.

Terry Mercer was the last to arrive. Smoke drifted through the air. Justin Nash sat at his desk, puffing his distasteful trademark. When Terry entered the conversation quieted. The staff hovered respectfully near the irritated stance of the boss, District Attorney Jeremy Bates, a bald, heavy-set figure.

All eyes fixed on Terry. "Glad you could make it," said Bates, with unusual courtesy. "We're all concerned about you and your family."

She nodded and took a seat beside Lt. Lori Bordeaux who pulled out a chair for her.

Bates began pacing, then pointed at Justin Nash, the real power behind the throne.

Nash was an imposing figure. In his mid-fifties, quite striking with a classic face, light gray at the temples completed the appearance of a powerful man. He was respected in the legal community. His work was his life and his was considered one of the sharpest legal minds in Memphis. His family was of old Memphis with roots stretching back to the Nineteenth Century. He had long received invitations to join the corporate law firms but was content to remain in the D.A.'s office. Nash was the *go to* guy who ran the department on a daily basis. His mood swings had become legend. Brilliant but intense, observed his underlings.

Nash and Bates had a mutual dislike of each other. Bates, with his expanding waist and bald dome, was a portrait of the political boss of old. His smiles were frequent and his jokes corny, while Nash had a natural scowl and was all business. There was talk Bates had his eye on a political seat, either governor or senator, but he kept his cards hidden. At the present, Bates had one consuming thought: to send Dr. Benjamin Pritchitt to prison. Nash was determined to catch a vicious serial murderer.

Justin Nash opened a black leather briefcase. "This report is from the Coroner's Office, specifically from Dr. Tyler Pritchitt and is the break we've been looking for," he said. Terry Mercer leaned forward, hearing her brother's name. Nash glanced at her, continuing in a somber tone. "There is a common thread between all three dead girls. They all had abortions within twenty-four hours of their deaths."

Murmurs swept the room.

Terry began to speak. "Justin, do you mean to tell us you think this killer is giving these girls abortions before murdering them?" she asked incredulously.

Bates interrupted. "The autopsy results are startling. Your brother has determined the victims have undergone abortions, either voluntarily or otherwise. He has given us something to go on," said the chief, glancing at the report. "It could even be a doctor we're looking for." Eyes glanced at Terry. Her frown turned to disgust.

"What? You think my father killed these girls, too?"

"Terry," said Bates in an even tone, "no one said that. Besides, we cannot discuss Dr. Benjamin Pritchitt in your presence, remember?"

Terry stood, reaching for her purse. "I think it's time for me to resign."

"Terry, wait." Justin Nash's voice was even and supportive. "There's no conflict as long as you're excluded from the Pritchitt case. We need you now on this serial murder. And —" he emphasized, "if you do resign before the Pritchitt trial begins, it won't look good for you or your father." Terry sat.

Nash strolled around his desk, puffing on the ever-present half-burnt cigar. "Why don't we all use the brains the good Lord gave us and think."

Staff Attorney Tim Bauers made a feeble attempt at raising his hand. Nash suddenly stopped. "What is this, a third grade classroom? Mr. Bauers, what is it you so dearly want to say?"

"Start with the abortion clinics, right away," he offered. "It's someone with a medical background. Someone who understands the procedure."

"Good idea, Bauers," agreed Nash. "We'll ask the police to query the clinics and place them on alert. We'll ask if any strangers have been observed, watching women enter or leave the clinics. Maybe even assign an extra police patrol around the clinics." He paused.

Could it be the young women were stalked by the killer, Terry wondered. Her head bowed in prayerful thought.

"Or," added Bates, deliberately avoiding Terry Mercer's eyes, "maybe it's a sicko who forced abortions on them. A doctor maybe. The police have a sex crimes file."

Terry's stomach churned. She wanted out of the room. She realized how much she hated her boss, Jeremy Bates. He was going to disgrace her father and send him to prison.

"You're sure the second body was in Tennessee?" asked Bates.

Nash removed the cigar. "Sir, it was in a ditch right on the Tennessee and Mississippi state lines. But the troopers agree with us it was in Tennessee . . . by inches."

"We don't need the Feds to interfere," interjected Bates, with venom in his voice. "Hell, they're still fighting the cigarette manufacturers. Now they're gonna regulate nicotine. More drunks kill people than cigarettes."

"Bullshit!" Heads turned. It was Lt. Bordeaux. "Cigarettes kill many more people than drunks. Anyway, what's the damn point, Mr. Bates? Are you saying we should have Prohibition again?" fired the defiant Bordeaux.

"I'm not advocating any such thing," Bates shot back.

"Me neither," said Nash, exhaling a cloud of smoke. He removed his cigar. "For God's sake, we've got more important things to talk about, people."

Bates reached for a file stamped "Helen Taylor." He focused his gaze toward Terry. "You're dismissed," he coldly ordered.

It was now late evening. Pritchitt was emotionally drained. How many times had he defended his actions today? Those who suffered terminal pain understood his deeds. He slipped a cassette in the tape deck. The drive home was longer than usual. Classical music soothed his jangled nerves.

Pulling into his drive he recognized both his children's cars. He didn't want more arguments, for this was his family. He felt guilty about inflicting pain on them. Through the window his wife was pacing, a drink in her hand. Her face contorted as she shouted. There were no words heard but he knew the subject. The children were trying to calm her. The alcoholic binges, almost a distant memory, had returned. He entered the side door, desperately hoping to slip upstairs quietly. His wife's voice seared him. "He's lost his mind!" she slurred. "He killed Helen, for God's sake, she was my best friend. You know your father has lost his mind and he's driving me crazy."

She began crying. "Terry, do you think the devil has poisoned his thoughts?"

Pritchitt stepped quietly toward the den.

"Dad didn't exactly kill anyone," said Terry.

"Absolutely true," answered Benjamin, walking into the den.

Terry threw her arms around her father. "Why, Daddy?" she cried. "Why all of this?" Staring into his exhausted face she waited for an answer. As a child her father had always been delighted to answer any questions. He knew everything. But this time he was silent.

"Hitler's home at last," shouted Ruth, raising her glass in a toast.

"Dad, we all need to talk," pleaded Tyler.

"I think we all need to sleep," Pritchitt said, turning back toward the door.

"Dad, please, we have to talk," insisted his son.

"That's it, Son, be nice to your daddy. Hell, let's fix a picnic basket and go to the park like the Brady Bunch. We can just sit around and chit-chat. Is that what you want?"

"I told you he was mentally ill," Ruth barked, slouching her unsteady body into a chair, spilling her drink on her blouse. She licked at the blouse, sucking the precious nectar, then licked her lips. "Excuse me," she slurred. "I'm not my charming self tonight."

Pritchitt stared at Ruth. He could barely stand the sight of his wife's decline.

He closed his eyes, shutting out his wife's fierce stare.

"The Butcher of Memphis," she half-shouted. "That's what everybody's calling the great Dr. Benjamin Pritchitt."

"Mom, that's not true," said Tyler.

She downed her drink. "It is true! My husband, your father. Benji and Claire's grandfather. And, oh, please don't forget, Sarah Taylor's godfather." Ruth began licking the blouse again.

"Mother, you've had enough," said Tyler.

"You bet! I've had enough of all this crap," she fumed, jumping up from the chair and stumbling backwards.

"You need to sleep," said Benjamin, "you don't know what you're saying."

"That's a lie, Benjamin Pritchitt!"

"I thought you had stopped drinking," he responded in an accusing tone.

"And I thought you had stopped killing."

Terry took her mother's hand, trying to lead her from the room, but she pushed her daughter aside.

"I'll make you a deal, sweetheart," she hissed. "I'll go back to AA if you stop killing people."

"Go to bed!" ordered her tired husband.

"No! Let's watch the news," she said, switching on the remote control. She slumped in a chair; her face was pale.

The anchor newscaster launched into the headline story. Benjamin collapsed onto the sofa. It was just what he expected. He watched himself being followed to the emergency room entrance. ". . . he was formerly a pillar of our community," the reporter was saying. "Now the same man has been indicted and faces imprisonment. It is now a growing story of a man's moral conviction and his apparent self-destruction." Sarah Taylor appeared on the screen. Accompanied by her husband and children, she rushed past the newsmen.

"Friends wonder when Dr. Pritchitt will end his crusade." The close-up was on the newscaster's face.

"It's not a crusade!" Benjamin shouted angrily.

"See, kids, your father was the big story," said Ruth.

Once again the room quieted and eyes fixed on the newscast. A microphone was thrust in the face of Dist. Atty. Jeremy Bates as he shook his head. "I have no comment at this time," he said, a media smile on his face.

Coverage of what had become the Memphis serial murder story followed. The camera showed attendants loading a plastic body bag into an ambulance.

"Terry, they've got your case, too. What a record for the family scrapbook," Ruth Pritchitt mocked.

The reporter explained that the young woman had been killed like the others, strangled with a plastic bag around her head. Justin Nash appeared on the screen. "Our office is working around the clock to nab the serial killer. We have a significant lead but that is confidential for now," he added with assurance. His face was typically unemotional.

The telephone rang.

"It's your lawyer, Dad," Terry said. "He's furious you've defied the court's order."

Benjamin said nothing.

"He wants you in his office tomorrow morning."

Benjamin nodded.

Tyler sat beside him unable to speak. He tried to understand why his father had changed from a healer to something or someone he didn't know.

Benjamin gazed apprehensively at his son. Physically so like himself when he was in his thirties, yet philosophically vastly apart on the issue of assisted-suicide for the terminally ill.

He rose. "I'm going to bed."

"Say a prayer for your victim," said Ruth.

"The only thing that made Helen Taylor a victim is the blind society we live in," Benjamin responded.

Ruth began crying. Her eyes closed and she slid down in the chair. "Your father cares more about his suicide patients than his own family's welfare."

"That's not true, Ruth," he shot back. "I love all of you more than you'll ever know, but I have moral obligations to my patients. I have to live with my own conscience. I have to —"

Ruth struggled to her feet. "I've had enough. Good night."

Benjamin helped his wife. Terry held her arm. She hugged her husband. "I do love you," she whispered. "But for the love of God I don't know you anymore." Then she and her daughter mounted the stairs leading to the bedrooms above.

Only father and son remained. The tension between them was evident.

Benjamin clicked on the TV and began surfing the other channels for news. "For God's sake, what are you doing, Dad?"

"There's something," said Benjamin, frowning. He studied a report from the earlier broadcast.

"Dad, that's about the serial killings. What the hell does that have to do with anything concerning you?"

Benjamin stared at the television, then with an abruptness he grabbed his jacket, turned quickly and walked from the den.

"Dad, where are you going? We have to talk. They might be coming to arrest you at any time. The police are going to have to take you downtown and book you again —"

"There's something back at the office I have to check, son. Tomorrow is Saturday. We'll have lunch and talk. I promise." He disappeared through the front door.

"If you're not in jail we might have lunch!" Tyler shouted after him.

Frustration swept Tyler. Back in the den he paced.

"Mother's asleep," Terry said, walking into the den. "Where's Dad?" she asked.

"He's gone to the hospital. He said he had to check on something that couldn't wait."

"He's . . . having a breakdown. He needs to see his lawyer," gasped Terry.

The door bell rang, followed by two loud knocks. Terry stared through a window as Tyler rose. She saw a blue police cruiser parked in the drive. She opened the door. There stood Asst. Dist. Atty. Tim Bauers flanked by two policemen.

"Hello, Tim," she said calmly.

Bauers said nothing. He looked embarrassed. "We're here with a warrant for your father, I'm sorry to say," he finally mumbled, clearing his throat.

"He's not here," Tyler answered.

"Where is he?" asked an officer.

"Just wait until he returns," said Terry. "He's not running." The men stared at one another.

"You know the rules, Terry," Bauers responded. "Jeremy Bates wants him now, and if we don't bring him back, we're going to have an already pissed off boss breathing fire, Terry. We gave him all afternoon to take care of business and now it's time for him to come with us."

"He went to his office," Terry said defensively. "But he'll be right back."

Not a word was spoken. Bauers and the two officers turned and hurriedly made for the police vehicle in the driveway.

Terry closed the door. She hurried to the telephone. "I'd better not. It might be construed as obstructing justice," she said aloud, then slammed the receiver down.

"Come on, Tyler. We've got to go to Dad's office. He'll need us to be there when they arrest him." It took a minute to secure the house, then they hurried out the door.

CHAPTER FOUR

The alley was abandoned. Only the yelps of a barking dog pierced the quiet night. The car pulled to a stop in the shadows. The door opened and the driver stood, studying the dark alley. The trunk popped open. A limp body stuffed in a bag was hoisted over the shoulder of the silhouetted figure. Just a few steps away, the bag was lifted and stuffed into a garbage container. The trunk was gently closed. A growl and furious barking broke the dead silence. The car drove quietly down the alley and vanished. A scent of death permeated the darkness.

"What's all the barking about, Susie? You senile old dog," scolded an old man. He leaned over the fence and saw the fading red lights of a car as it turned onto a dimly lit street. "Nobody's back here, girl." He opened a gate. "What a guard dog you turned out to be. Barking at the dark." He struggled with a plastic garbage bag. "Tomorrow's pickup day and Mother said if I missed it she'd divorce me after a half century of putting up with her."

The dog growled and stood on its hind legs, jumping

nervously. The old man strained with the weight of the garbage bag. "What is it?" The old man turned his head suspiciously. "You crazy old dog. You gettin' as senile as Mother and you ain't even seventy-five yet, barking at the dark and all." He opened the lid of a garbage container and hoisted the bag with a straining grunt. The garbage bag wouldn't fit. He stood in the darkness trying to push the bag into the container. "This damn thing is full," he mumbled. "Mother told a fib, Susie. She said she hadn't emptied any trash all week. Well, if that's the case, then tell me why this thing's so cotton-picking full," he fumed. He left the bag atop the garbage container, the lid hanging open. With a shuffling step he crossed the alley and opened the gate. "Come on, old girl, let's go to bed. I'm too damn old to fight with a garbage can."

Dark medical offices lined the hall of the professional building. Pritchitt walked alone down the long corridor. His steps echoed into the emptiness. He fumbled with his key as growing impatience swept his already exhausted mind. He finally opened the door and hurried inside. Moonlight flooded the lonely office. He flicked on the light switch. On his desk was the envelope. He pulled sheets out and onto his cluttered desk. He lit a small desk lamp and eased into his executive chair. He hurriedly searched through the papers, then stopped. "Good God!" he exclaimed. He read aloud: "'Mr. Audubon has a surprise for you. It's not fully wrapped but it's boxed.'"

Pritchitt leaned back in his chair. He massaged his temples where the blood pounded. Was this a coincidence, he wondered. Or did Wiseman have something. He thought back to the newscast. The body had been discovered in Audubon Park. He rested his head on his desk for a moment, quietly pondering the curious messages. He straightened himself, then removed a pair of reading glasses he kept in his desk. Sheet by sheet, he scrutinized the bizarre fax messages.

"Dr. Pritchitt," a voice called from the outer office.

Startled, Pritchitt's body flinched in panic. He looked up sharply. "My God, Wiseman. You scared the hell out of me."

"You've read the fax messages?"

"Yeah," sighed Pritchitt. "Sit down, Bernie, and tell me what you know."

Wiseman sat before Pritchitt and leaned forward. "You saw the news tonight, didn't you?"

Pritchitt nodded.

"It was Audubon that brought you back?" asked Wiseman.

"Yeah," said Pritchitt, "Mr. Audubon. Do you think all of this is connected?"

"I do," said Wiseman. "Hand me those."

Bernie Wiseman began studying the messages and jotted notes on a piece of paper.

"You're supposed to be brilliant," remarked Pritchitt.

"No, I'm just Wiseman," he said, peering mischievously over reading glasses perched at the tip of his nose.

Pritchitt laughed. "You're just like your mother."

"You know Mama?"

"Everyone knows your mother."

Abundant energy and intelligence were evident, acknowledged Pritchitt. Bernie Wiseman was going to be a good doctor. He was a first year resident, having just completed his internship. He yearned for the day when he would have his own practice. He lived at home with Mama Wiseman in midtown, where the family owned a popular breakfast stop, Mama's Bagel Shop. Bernie was simple and friendly. He rode to work on a yellow motor scooter. His inquisitive nature aided his sharp mind when it came to medicine and anything else he studied.

Wiseman leaned back. "Dr. Pritchitt, let's look back and see if it all fits." With that Wiseman removed a folded sheet from his pocket. "This is where the other two victims were found." He placed the map under the desk lamp. Their eyes locked.

"The streets," gasped Pritchitt, "they're named on the faxes. It's where the bodies were found."

"That's what I wanted to tell you this morning."

"You already figured this out?"

"Right," said Wiseman. "Dr. Pritchitt, what you have here

is a psychopathic killer, telling you by fax where his victims can be found."

"And they are all addressed to me?" whispered Pritchitt, his throat suddenly parched. This was yet another burden for his troubled mind.

"Look here," said Wiseman excitedly. "Look at this conversation. Wiseman's finger slowly moved across a page as he read. "It says, 'Mr. Barksdale,' 'Yes, Mr. Harbert.' 'I had a vision from God. Simon says it must be done.' 'Another one?' 'Yes, Mr. Barksdale, another vision and another woman of sin. She is to be taken out with the other garbage of this life. Simon says it must be done.'"

A dreaded silence filled the room, as both pondered the evil thoughts inherent in what Wiseman had read.

"We've got to get this to my daughter."

"This Simon, or whoever, may well be the maniac murdering these girls." Pritchitt stood and motioned for Wiseman to follow. "My daughter's with the D.A.'s office. She's assigned to the serial killer case."

As Wiseman and Pritchitt exited the building, a dark trio appeared out of the shadows. They briskly crossed the moonlit parking lot. "Dr. Pritchitt!" a strong voice yelled.

The envelope of fax sheets was slipped into Wiseman's hand.

"I'm Officer Evans. You're under arrest. It is your right to remain silent until in the presence of your attorney."

"What's the charge?" a flustered Wiseman asked.

The second policeman waved a warrant. "Violation of state law to unlawfully assist in the death of Helen Taylor."

"Hello, Tim," said Pritchitt, recognizing Asst. Dist. Atty. Bauers, an associate of his daughter. Handcuffs were locked on his wrists. Bauers said nothing.

A fast moving car moved across the lot and screeched to a stop. Terry and Tyler hurried from the car. "Why the handcuffs?" yelled Tyler. Bauers, saying nothing, opened the door of the police cruiser.

"Don't worry, Dad," pleaded Terry, "I'll telephone your lawyer."

"Everything will be okay," assured Tyler in a strong voice, but his pale face betrayed his words. As the car drove off Benjamin Pritchitt glanced through the rear window.

"He's in deeper than ever," sighed Terry, stifling a sob.

"You're his daughter?" asked Wiseman.

"Yes, and who are you?"

"I'm Dr. Bernie Wiseman, your father's surgery resident this month." He handed her the envelope. "This is for you."

In Dr. Pritchitt's office, they huddled over the messages. Beyond the window a menacing rain began to fall. It tapped at the glass, interrupting their concentration. Terry sat in stunned silence. She read and re-read the dire messages.

"Thank you for helping my father," she said with an appreciative stare.

Wiseman nodded. "I admire him," he responded. "I know he's very proud of his family."

"He's . . . a special man," Terry acknowledged.

Outside the rain swept through the parking lot. "Doesn't the man upstairs know I've got a scooter?" sighed Wiseman. He declined the offer of a ride home. "I'm not going home," he said. "Anyway, what's a little rain? Our body is made of about 70 percent water, right?" He bolted for his yellow motor scooter.

It was nearly 2:00 a.m. but the crowd was still thick at the bar. Atway Jackson reached for a glass of beer and pushed his way through the throng. He squeezed into a small booth, then fixed his eyes on Wiseman's drink. "What the hell is that?"

"It's called water, Atway. It falls from the sky, like tonight. As you know, my scooter has no roof, so that's why I look like a raisin and feel like a sponge. But I love pure water."

"I hope you've got all your vaccines," laughed Atway, "because the way you look you're headed for a serious case of pneumonia." Wiseman shook his damp hair like a wet dog.

"Very funny, my lawyer friend."

A waitress slid a plate of fries and a charcoal grilled burger in front of Wiseman. "I met Asst. Dist. Atty. Terry Mercer, tonight."

"Yeah? You did? She's one of the up-and-coming hotshots in the D.A.'s office . . . or she was gonna be a star until her old man cracked up."

Wiseman removed the hamburger from his face. "No, that's not correct," he said, trying not to choke. "Dr. Pritchitt's a man of integrity."

"Oh, shit, please. Bernie, he's a fruitcake." Atway leaned forward. "If these folks want to end it, then they should just do it, and keep the doctors out of it. Docs are supposed to help people." He tapped his finger on the table. "They take the Hippocratic oath. And you have, too. Pritchitt's gonna serve time." He chugged his beer. "Ahhh, that's good."

"So if I assisted a terminally ill person to end their pain, then you'd prosecute me?"

"I'd have to. The citizens pay my salary to enforce the law. In most states assisted suicide is a crime. This Pritchitt's got that carbon monoxide machine and he's knocking off people right and left." Atway squinted. "I hope you're not mixed up with that fucking nut."

Bernie smiled, "No, at least, not yet. Nothing yet to indict me for." They clinked glasses.

Atway Jackson was Bernie's best friend. An odd couple, they had known each other since childhood, attending the same high school and college. Atway could have been a basketball star. But he decided to study and become an attorney instead. Right now he was clerking at the D.A.'s office. "I'm a star in court and not on it," he liked to joke. Tall and good natured, Atway was a charmer.

They talked of the faxes Bernie had discovered and handed over to Terry Mercer. "Bernie, those fax messages are interesting, but I'm just a lowly clerk. Don't worry, the big guns will take a shot at figuring them out." His demeanor changed with a gulp of beer. "Really, keep out of it. This Justin Nash guy, the district attorney's top assistant, who's in charge, could make a case against you. You'll wind up as an accessory if you stick your normally nosey nose where it's not suppose to be. It could ruin your career."

"So you don't want to see me on *America's Most Wanted?*" Atway burst out laughing.

Bernie rose and wiped his mouth. "Good advice, counsel. I'm going home to dry off before I fall asleep on my feet and catch that pneumonia you mentioned."

Benjamin Pritchitt sat beneath harsh fluorescent lights at a long table. Tattooed muscular arms crossed the broad chest of the jailor as he stared at Pritchitt through a glass panel. A loud buzzer sounded. A metal door opened. A bearded man in a wrinkled suit was escorted into the room and stood across the table. The jailor pulled out a chair. The obviously tired man nodded and sat. He placed his black leather briefcase, battered and scratched, on the table. The guard left them alone.

"I'm sorry I had to get you out of bed in this weather at this time of night," Pritchitt apologized to his friend and attorney.

"It comes with the territory," yawned Todd Bohannon, a disappointing frown formed as he sat at the table. Through the glass panel the guard watched with a bored expression.

"Ben, what is it with you?" asked his lawyer. "You know that Jeremy Bates warned you not to be present at any suicides. You've disregarded the prosecutor's demand. Hell-fire, Ben, you defied a fucking court order. You've disregarded my advice and now you're in jail. You're just digging a deeper grave, so to speak. Do you understand? Jeremy Bates is an egotistical media hungry district attorney and no one to fuck with." Frustration showed in Bohannon's tired eyes. "Do you get my drift, Ben?"

"Yes, I understand you, Bates and everyone, Todd, while no one understands me."

"For the love of God, Ben, let me try. You're my client. My job is to defend you." The attorney's tone was now sharper, a simmering anger heating his words. "I understand your intent, to relieve the pain of your clients. But —" He slapped his briefcase, "but the law is quite clear. You're being prosecuted on a state charge. Do you understand?"

"Yes, I understand, Todd, I —"

"Ben! Shut up!" He removed papers from the briefcase. "Do you see these? These are indictments. You are fighting the People's lawyer. The D.A.'s office has a big budget. I have a retainer which will soon be gone, and I will ask you for more money." The attorney leaned forward. Each word was slow and deliberate. "You can either listen to my advice, Ben, or find another attorney. I'm too good a friend to stand by and watch you commit your own damn suicide." Todd Bohannon was a life-long friend and a mounting frustration grew on his wrinkled brow.

"Todd, I'm sorry. These people, my patients, they ask for nothing more than what we would do for our dog or cat. Why in the name of heaven are we forcing people to suffer?"

"I've heard all of this, Ben."

"Who are we, or for that matter the government, to tell patients that God wants them to suffer? The only thing making them legal victims is our blinded society."

"Ben, I'm down here to bail you out, not to debate euthanasia in this stinking jail at 3:00 a.m."

"If I handed you a gun, and you placed it to your head and pulled the trigger, am I guilty of murder? Is a liquor store owner guilty if he sells whiskey to a man dying of liver failure? These people I see are suffering horribly. Animals receive more humane care. Who is to say what is right or wrong?"

"The law decides! Do you understand? Not you, not me, but a jury will be asked have you violated a law!"

"This isn't killing. God knows the difference or at least I pray he does. Medicine is the art of healing. This is the easing of suffering. Whether by morphine drip or carbon monoxide, it's merciful to me. God understands."

"So now you converse directly with the Supreme Being? Have you ever heard of the Ten Commandments? Remember, it says 'thou shalt not kill.'"

"This isn't killing."

"Okay, Ben," sighed the attorney. "But we have to play this game according to the law. You'll get your soapbox and your day in court. And you may get lucky, but now Jeremy Bates is shotgunning for glory, trying to make you look like a monster."

"I didn't kill anyone."

"Ben, you personally created a machine that has a single purpose . . . to give the user carbon monoxide instead of oxygen. Are you an accessory? You know, my bull-headed friend, if a murder transpires during a holdup, the getaway driver, who doesn't pull the trigger, is an accessory to murder."

"This is a humane machine."

"Oh, yeah, right. Remember, Ben, humanity saw gas used to murder millions during World War II. There are hideous overtones here, which may or may not influence a jury."

Papers were pushed toward Ben. "Read these and sign them. It's too damn late for me to sit here and debate you. You're going to have to spend the night until I get bail set in the morning." Pritchitt hastily scribbled his name, then tossed the papers on the briefcase.

"You've already read them?"

"I trust you. Besides, I'm not going to skip bail."

"All right," Todd scolded. He grabbed his briefcase and extended his hand. "Let me get a few hours sleep. I'll see you in the morning."

The attorney rapped on the door. "Thanks for listening," said Pritchitt.

"I do understand," Bohannon said emphatically, as the jailor opened the door. "But I'm not the jury."

In the narrow cell Dr. Benjamin Pritchitt stretched out on the cot. Turning away from the grimy toilet next to his head, he closed his eyes. Shouts echoed through the hall, as a prisoner snored loudly, and others bitterly cursed him.

Pritchitt's body jerked as he drifted into a half sleep. In the darkness of a tired mind a roar trembled through his troubled thoughts, louder and louder. The sun was bright on a crisp afternoon in October. The quartet laughed and cheered their home team. The Tigers were far ahead. Henry was going for a beer at halftime. Benjamin stood and let him pass, playfully punching his friend on the shoulder. "You're buying dinner," said Ben. "All right, all right, my turn," yelled Henry. Ascending the steps he suddenly stopped. His arms shot out. Little circles became larger ones until Henry Taylor fell backwards on the steep stadium stairs. He was dead of a massive stroke. What a sweet death, Henry, how lucky you were, he dreamed.

The sun barely peeked over the horizon but already early morning activity was stirring at the hospital. Bernie Wiseman, bleary-eyed, parked his little yellow scooter. It was 6:25 a.m. when he dashed inside the building. The surgery department was still quiet. He nodded good morning to arriving staff. Walking over to where the coffee pot sat he began to brew his much needed black potion. The wonderful scent sharpened his senses. As he sipped his morning coffee, he approached the fax machine. Loose sheets were laying on the tray, awaiting review from various departments. He thumbed through the stack. His hand stopped. "Oh, oh, oh," he quietly muttered. There was another ranting message, with two new names conversing. He knew that could only mean the location of another dead body. His eyes carefully scanned the sheet reading the fax to himself.

"Mr. Anderson. Yes, Mr. Glenwood? I had a vision from God, Mr. Anderson. Another one? Yes, and another woman of sin found, to be taken out with the rest of life's garbage. Then Mr. Glenwood, Simon says it must be done."

A nauseous feeling swirled in the pit of Wiseman's stomach. He sat, palms sweaty, beads of perspiration on his forehead. Why are these coming here? Wiseman wondered. Removing his wallet, he emptied the contents on a table. He found a number. He dialed the phone. "Terry Mercer, please!" Wiseman gasped, catching his breath as his pulse raced.

"This is her desk, but she's not here. This is Asst. D.A. Justin Nash. Can I help you?"

Wiseman sucked in his breath. His tongue felt bigger than

his throat. He could either hang up or speak. If he told his story, he knew he would be a suspect and they wouldn't understand.

"Can I help you?" Nash asked a second time.

"I've got to talk to Terry Mercer now!"

"Well, it's like I said, she's not in yet. Call back."

There was silence. "Hold it, she's just walking in the office." Nash handed the phone to Terry. "It's for you." Terry pressed the phone to her ear.

"This is Bernie Wiseman," he said breathlessly. "I'm here at your father's office and there's another fax. I think we've got another dead body, ma'am."

"Wait a second, slow down. Dr. Wiseman, you're the guy from last night, right?"

"Of course I am. Did you hear what I said?" Wiseman repeated his find, then his voice lowered. "I'll meet you at the corner of Anderson and Glenwood Ave."

The line went dead before Terry could caution the excited Wiseman to stay away and leave this to the police. "He's crazy. This guy's gonna get himself in some shit," she fumed, slamming the phone down as she grabbed her purse and headed for the door.

It was an old neighborhood. The morning air was cool as Atway swivelled his long legs from the car. "I need my damn head examined, letting you pull me out of bed this early on a fucking Saturday." A pensive Wiseman examined the green street signs. Suddenly, his eyes fixed on a nearby alley.

"Bernie, you know I need my beauty sleep," grumbled Jackson. "This is my day to sleep in."

"I know, I know, Atway, but this is important. I need you with me as a witness."

"A witness? What the hell? A witness to what?" Atway shouted. Wiseman's stare was unyielding. He pointed for his irritated friend to pull the car to a stop at the approaching alley.

"This is it," Wiseman said opening the car door.

"This is what?" Atway asked following his guide into the alley.

"Remember what I told you about Anderson and Glenwood? The fax from Simon?" Impatience showed in Wiseman's face as he stared back at the trailing Jackson. "And you're my witness if I for some reason find myself in trouble with the police."

"What? That means that I'd be in trouble, too. I sure don't like the way this smells," Atway griped as they made their way into the alley.

"You worry too much, counsel. Just remember that I was with you late last night."

"Hey, pal, I'll let 'em know you were with me, at least until 1:00 a.m.?"

"No, it was 2:00 a.m., Atway."

"All right. So where's the stiff?"

"Stiff? What the hell kind of talk is that? They teach you that in law school?" scolded Bernie.

"I haven't even had a damn cup of coffee, yet," snapped Atway as his tall frame came to a stop next to his obsessed friend.

Garbage containers lined the long alley. "Open the lids, Atway."

"If you want those filthy lids opened, you open them. I'm just an innocent witness, remember? You're the crazy one here. I'm just the dumb ass for being out here with you. It's your idea. Therefore, you've got the honors."

"I just thought you wanted to help," chided Bernie.

"I am helping, Wiseman, but look, people around here are going to mistake us for a couple of crack heads or thieves messing around in this garbage. Let's call the police." Atway stepped backwards and turned to walk away.

"Please, just wait," pleaded Wiseman.

"All right, all right. You've got five minutes, then I'm out of here!"

Wiseman approached the first garbage container and with a deep breath flipped it open, jumping back as if expecting something to pop out. Atway struggled to keep from laughing. "Oh, man. Is that the way you do an autopsy? If this body is dead, like you say, it ain't gonna jump out at us, now is it?"

An elderly man watched from a kitchen window bordering the alley.

"Not a damn thing in there at all," said Atway. Then he noticed a curious face in the window. "Oh shit! We've been seen." Bernie opened the next lid, but stopped at the sound of screeching tires. A car slid to a stop on the graveled alley. Atway and Bernie jumped back, dodging the spray of dust and rocks.

"Goddamn it, Wiseman!" barked Terry Mercer, stepping from her car. "You are tampering with a possible crime scene!" Her eyes grew wide. "And what the hell are you doing here, Atway?"

"That's a damn good question. I do believe I've lost my mind. Either I'm too good a friend or a complete idiot," he explained.

"Wiseman, what's going on?" she asked.

He pointed to the last container. "In there is Simon's victim." He slowly raised the lid. Disappointment showed on his face. He kicked the container, then shrugged his shoulders. "I don't get it. It's what Simon said on the fax. I don't understand."

"No body? Good. In fact, very damn good. Simon says, can we go home now? How about that?" Atway blurted impatiently.

"Wiseman, not everything comes this damn easy," cautioned Terry Mercer. "You should know, being a doctor. When you're dealing with a psychotic mind, there is no predictable pattern."

"No, you're wrong," Wiseman half-shouted. He looked to the open garbage containers, then back at Mercer. "This bastard is a serial killer." He bit his lower lip. "There is a pattern."

"Old friend," said Atway, walking away, "you've been goosed by a wild goose. I've been robbed of sleep and a great dream. I remember a beautiful woman stroking my head . . . then you knocked at the door." Atway's voice faded as he walked toward his car.

"I've got to get back," Terry said, turning to her car, annoyance in her voice.

Wiseman mumbled, his dejection evident. Suddenly, a

faint sound alerted him. He swung around facing the far end of the alley. "Do you hear that?" Wiseman shouted standing alone in the alley.

"Hear what?" Terry asked, poking her head from the window of her car.

"For God's sake, that sound." Wiseman jumped into Mercer's car. "They're working these streets! The trucks. . . .it's damn pickup day." Wiseman's excitement grew. He leaned from his window directing Terry, down the shady alley.

"Atway, follow us!" shouted Bernie, waving wildly from the window. At the far end of the alley a monstrous garbage truck slowly passed by. "Let's go! Hurry!" shouted Wiseman.

The truck disappeared from sight. Terry hit the accelerator and sped down the alley, then turned toward the sound of the churning truck a block away. Atway followed Terry's speeding vehicle. Both cars rounded the corner and there before them was a huge howling garbage truck.

"They've emptied the garbage from the containers into that truck," Wiseman's voice cracked with anxiety.

The truck halted. Two collectors riding the back stepped to the street. They stared warily as Mercer pulled her car to a stop. "Did you just clear the alley on the next block?" Terry asked.

They nodded. A puzzled expression on both their faces.

Wiseman jumped out. "Did you find anything like a body?"

"A body? What the hell you talkin' about, man? We ain't paid enough to find no damn bodies. Do I look like some kind of undertaker, or something?" blurted one of the collectors, spitting to the ground.

"I'm Asst. D.A. Terry Mercer. We have reason to believe a body may have been in a garbage container in the alley at Anderson and Glenwood. It may have been dumped into your truck by mistake."

"What the hell you say?" the tallest collector snapped. A frightened look covered their faces. The shorter man ran. He returned with the driver.

"Open the back of the truck," Mercer ordered. The driver

and collectors stood and stared at one another, then back at her.

Atway walked up behind Mercer and Wiseman. "Man, it stinks!" he complained, then placed a handkerchief over his nose. A squealing grind sounded as the large rear door of the truck slowly opened, and hundreds of flies flew out. Within the back of the truck was the usual assortment of trash. A potent odor flooded the air. Atway backed up, waving his hand before his covered face.

The morning was still young and the cavernous interior wasn't yet filled.

"Do you have a probing stick?" asked Terry, grimacing at the stench.

"Jake, bring us the rod," said the driver. Jake handed Bernie a long steel pole with a hook shaped at its end.

"What's this for?" he asked.

"It ain't to eat with, that's for damn sure," the driver answered.

Bernie tried to return it. "Here you do it, I mean, you have the know how. I've never done this."

The taller worker stood with his arms folded. "That ain't in our job description. And I don't want to poke at nobody no how."

"That pole is for busting up clogged garbage, but it will work for this, too" said the driver, impatiently tapping his watch. "We got a schedule to meet."

Bernie looked at Atway, then Mercer as both shook their heads.

"Don't even ask," Atway said sharply. "This was all your idea, remember?"

Bernie placed a sure foot on the rear step, then hoisted himself into the back of the truck and into the pit. His distaste was visible. He swatted the flies which swarmed with each probe of the pole.

"Don't be playing around in there, Bernie," laughed Atway. "No telling what kind of diseases your gonna come out with," he shouted.

"Very funny, Atway," said Bernie sourly.

The driver slapped the end of the truck. "Come on, man, we

gotta get our truck moving on this route or we're gonna be in a mess of trouble." Swatting the flies around his head, Bernie lost his balance and plunged into the sea of reeking garbage. Laughter broke out. "Here, let me do it or you'll never get done," said the uniformed collector.

Bernie turned. "There's no need now," he said. He removed cans and cartons. A head with a gaping mouth emerged from beneath the garbage. He stood back. Grimacing, he turned toward the others. They gasped in shock knowing what he'd found. Terry approached the truck. She stared into the truck as did the others. Terry turned away.

"Dear God in heaven," the driver prayed, clasping his hands together. "Please take care of this poor woman." His companions chorused *amens*.

Terry rushed to her car. "I'll call the police," she yelled. Bernie stepped from the truck. The sanitation workers crowded together in shocked silence.

"You were right," said Atway apologetically.

Bernie looked at the grisly sight again. "What madman could kill like this?" he asked. Minutes passed and in the distance a police siren wailed, as it neared.

Benjamin paced nervously in his ten by eight foot cell. The shouts had long died and only a snoring prisoner continued loudly. Sunlight shone from the small window at the end of the vacant corridor. Steps in his direction made him rise. A large guard opened the cell door. "You made bail, Doc." Pritchitt walked swiftly down the hall. The large guard pushed open a steel door. As Pritchitt tried to pass, the guard blocked his way. "You gonna gas someone today?" he asked contemptuously. He gave a little push and Pritchitt stumbled into an outer room where Todd Bohannon puffed a cigarette. He grasped Todd's hand and squeezed it. "Rough night?" asked Bohannon.

"You have no idea. I hate this place. Thank you, Todd, for getting me out of here so quickly."

"Wait until you see the bill," remarked Bohannon, stroking his beard. The men walked to the security door and a buzzer released them into the bright sunlight. Bohannon turned. "You know somebody named Simon?"

"Simon?"

"I got the strangest message on my answering machine from someone named Simon, he asked if you enjoyed your jail stay." Pritchitt stopped his walk. His faced paled under an unshaven beard. Bohannon turned, looking toward his silent friend. "What is it, Ben?"

"Simon. Simon may be the name of the serial killer."

As they approached the car the television news team was arriving in the back parking lot. Pritchitt stared in a slow burning anger.

"Say nothing," advised Bohannon. "Damn, somebody must have tipped them off that I was here to get you." Both men stood quietly, studying the waiting camera crew.

Suddenly an elderly panhandler held an outstretched hand in Pritchitt's face. "Got a dollar?" the stubbled-faced man asked. The smell of alcohol permeated the air.

"Give me five bucks, Todd." The attorney handed him the money. "This is what I want you to do." Pritchitt slipped the money in the beggar's hand and whispered to him.

After a few cars passed the elderly man sauntered up to the news crew. He raised his hand, "Good morning, people."

A reporter's voice answered with an impatient, "Yes?"

"Just a quarter for a poor man who was mistakenly arrested for disturbing the peace."

The cameraman laughed. "You sure it wasn't for public drunkenness?"

"A quarter isn't going to buy you any booze, is it?" snapped the reporter.

"All I want is a cup of coffee, to clear my head, before I search for a good job."

"Bullshit, old man," the reporter sneered. "Now get out of here. We're waiting for something big to happen and you're going to just get in our way."

"It's funny that y'all are back here when all those other reporters are in the front of the building."

"What?" blurted the newsman.

"That doctor he's talking mighty big. Yeah, I was in the cell next to him all night."

"Let's go!" the reporter hurried off with the cameraman following close behind.

As they disappeared around the building Pritchitt and Bohannon darted from the door and hurriedly crossed the parking lot.

Bohannon passed a twenty dollar bill to the old man.

"And don't use it for food," he barked. The old man smiled a toothless grin and danced a little jig.

CHAPTER FIVE

The drive home was a restful blessing. It was another glorious fall morning with crisp air and a cloudless sky. The emotional fatigue of the last twenty-four hours had Benjamin drained. His eyelids were heavy from the lack of restful sleep. The drive seemed to end as quickly as it started, as if the car had been on automatic and found its way home without him.

Riley, their trusted gardener, waved from the riding mower as Pritchitt pulled into the long brick driveway. The Pritchitt's majestic house was a pillared residence, a stately vestige of the past century. Years earlier, Ruth had discovered it in ruins. It had seemed beyond resurrection. But together they had breathed life into the sagging timbers. After Ruth learned she was expecting, they pored over blueprints, redesigning the home wing by wing. In the spacious rear garage, which once housed carriages, Ben noticed Ruth's Cadillac was gone. She must be at the club. It was a bit early but he was glad she felt well enough to go. Maybe they'd seen the last of her drunken state. He walked past Ruth's flower garden and the glass sun parlor, punishing himself for causing her to drink. On the terrace he swept his hand in the cool water of the swimming pool, finding it refreshing and of perfect temperature. Beyond the terrace was a sloping hill which led to gardens of towering oaks and magnolias. He would have liked her at home to greet him with peace and serenity. Serenity. That's what they had planned. That's what he remembered. Cold winter evenings before a warm fire. He and Ruth stretched beside the hearth.

They had sunk piles of money into the home, keeping the architect happy; they adored their home. Downstairs was a broad hall, covered with shiny gray and white marble. Photographs of his family adorned the walls. His eyes scanned an antique table for messages. The table was a wedding gift, holding memories deep in its wood. He could still recall Ruth writing thank you cards at this table. Her beautiful shiny hair, the exposed, inviting white nape of her neck and the delicate scent of her perfume. He had kissed her neck, surprising her. The love in her eyes when she looked up into his penetrated his very being. Each time he passed the carved table he remembered.

The humiliation of his wife's drunken sarcasm echoed through his mind. In the den he rested his weary body in a recliner. He closed his eyes. His body surrendered to the exhaustion he felt.

Startled by the ringing telephone, he awakened. He rubbed his eyes and stretched his stiff, tired muscles, reaching for the phone.

"Dad, how are you?" asked Terry, her voice worried. "I tried to meet you at the jail, but Jeremy Bates gave orders to keep away. He is such an ass. I shouldn't have listened."

"Nonsense, Terry. I feel fine. I'm trying to rest but you know how that goes. Sleep is for everyone but us doctors." He forced a chuckle. Then he told her how he had out-foxed the reporters at the jail.

"I'm glad," she said. "But you're still going to make the news, they'll just have to use old footage. Ha! I bet they're mad as hornets." It was good to hear his daughter's familiar laugh.

"Terry, have you talked to your mother?"

"No, Dad, isn't she at home?"

"She's not here and it's going on noon."

"She's probably at the club."

"Oh, Dad, I've got to run now. There's a meeting about the serial murderer." Her voice dropped to a hushed tone. "Another body was discovered this morning."

"Oh, no."

"Bernie Wiseman, Atway Jackson and I discovered it. I'll see you later —"

"Wiseman? What about Wiseman? Terry?" But she was gone.

Pritchitt quickly dialed his office, reaching his secretary.

"I read they put you in jail last night, Dr. Pritchitt," she mournfully sighed, "I just hate this."

"This will all be over soon, and I'll be back, Patsy."

"I pray every night for it to end."

"Patsy, I need to speak to Dr. Wiseman. It's important."

"He just began an autopsy, and he's now on Dr. Peters' list of undesirables, if you know what I mean."

"What happened?"

"When Dr. Wiseman came in this morning he smelled to high heaven and was an hour late for a patient evaluation. In other words, he kept King Peters waiting. The entire department is in an uproar. He had to take three showers to get rid of the horrible smell. It was something about a garbage truck. I really didn't understand the young man. I think he was having some kind of manic event when he got to work. And of course Peters was Peters."

"Have him call me."

"I will, sir," she said in a concerned voice, "and we really do miss you around here."

Pritchitt glanced at his watch. He needed relaxation. He slipped on his bathing trunks and stepped outside.

The quiet beauty of his landscaped property was calming. He settled in an iron patio chair, wishing the experience of the previous night had been a bad dream. He glanced at the outdoor aquarium where exotic fish swam, and hoped someone had fed them. A dark blue butterfly darted beside him. What a lovely sight, thought Pritchitt. He trailed behind the flitting creature. It flew beyond the terrace into the garden, then disappeared in the shadows beneath the high trees. Pritchitt spotted it resting on the earth, its wings still. He slowly approached, then caught his breath. The butterfly had found nourishment on a dead robin. Maggots swarmed within the bird's body. Beauty feeding on death, observed Pritchitt. The gossamer thin blue wings slowly opened and closed. From behind, Pritchitt heard his name.

"Telephone, Doc," yelled the gardener from the terrace. Pritchitt waved him down.

"Bury that dead bird."

Riley squinted. "Must be that old tomcat. I've seen him around here." Riley handed over the telephone, then walked to the trellised garden shed.

"This is Sally Best, the board secretary," explained the caller. "Tomorrow there will be an emergency board meeting. The hospital board wants you here at 3:00 p.m. on the dot."

"I understand."

"Off the record, Dr. Pritchitt, a lot of us admire you. I just wish the public could understand. I watched my grandmother die a horrible death from cancer." Her voice grew tight. "I wish I could have done something. You are a saint."

"That means a lot to me."

"God bless you, sir."

Riley passed with a shovel on his shoulder. Sweat glistened on his gray temples and fell onto his muscular black arms. The shovel flashed in the sunlight and the blue butterfly sailed heavenward. The simple cycle of life, thought Pritchitt. Birth and beauty. Tragedy and death. Just as he stretched on the patio lounge chair, the telephone rang. It was the deep voice of Nathan Johns, manager of Central Gardens Country Club. "Dr. Pritchitt, this is Nathan at the club, sir."

"What can I do for you, Nathan?"

"It's the Missus, Dr. Pritchitt," he said hesitantly, "she's at the bar and had several drinks and is arguing with patrons. I think it would be good for you to come get her, sir. She needs someone to take her home and pretty quick."

"My God, Nathan. Don't let her drive. Keep her there."

"Doc, she's furious because I told the bartender to cut off her drinks. You know our rules."

"I know, I know," said Pritchitt with concern. "I'll be right there."

Pritchitt raced through the streets of midtown, screeching to a stop twenty feet from the main entrance of the club. At the entrance he was met by Nathan Johns. From the outer hall Benjamin recognized his wife's shrill voice, then the sound of smashing glass. He couldn't hurry fast enough as Johns trailed his anxious steps. Turning the corner and entering the grill he caught his breath.

Ruth was poised with a clenched fist. She cocked her arm, ready to hurl the glass at the bartender and two waiters stranded behind the chrome bar. Patrons scurried from the dining room.

"Well, bust my buttons," she cried out. "If it isn't Memphis' own answer to Jack the Ripper or maybe just plain old Bennie the Butcher!" She giggled drunkenly.

"Ruth," came her husband's calming voice, "put the glass down, please."

"Absolutely, sweetheart," she responded meekly, then sent the glass sailing, exploding the mirror behind the bar, and shards showering the huddled staff. Benjamin dashed toward her but she bolted behind a large round dining table in the middle of the grill.

"Come and get me, big boy," she laughed. "I might be drunk but at least I haven't killed anyone, yet!"

"Please, Ruth —"

"Look at 'em! I'm scaring them to death —" She reached for another glass. "We've more than paid for these with all the money we've spent here over the years."

"Ruth, you don't know what you're saying. Please, dear, let me drive you home," he pleaded, slowly edging around the table.

"Bullshit!" she spat. "I know exactly what I'm saying and doing. That's more than I can say for you." She threw the glass but it crashed short of the bar. Then she grabbed another. "Do *you* know what you're doing, Dr. Hotshot Pritchitt? I think not." She wagged a finger at him. "And don't you fucking patronize me," she slurred. The club manager quietly moved behind her. She swivelled and cocked her arm.

"I see you back there." Ruth was addressing the bartender. "You can't fool me. Let me ask you something, and you other guys behind the bar, too." She lowered her arm and banged the glass on the table. "Have you ever lived with someone for a long, long time and loved that person, and then one day you awake, and don't know who the hell he is? It's like being married to Dr. Fucking Jekyll and finding out he's really Dr. Fucking Hyde." She laughed hysterically, until her words garbled. Turning quickly to Nathan, she lost her balance and slid to the floor on one knee. Her husband ran and caught her wrist. From behind, he and Nathan Johns firmly grabbed her arms. "You bastards!" she screamed. "Get your hands off me!"

"Ruth, it's time to go home, sweetheart," pleaded Benjamin, ashamed of his wife's behavior.

Suddenly she grew limp.

"All right," she slurred. "But I'm sitting in the back seat."

Nathan Johns shrugged his shoulders, "Yes, Mrs. Pritchitt."

"Would you please be a gentleman and escort me to my car, Nathan?"

"I'd be happy to, ma'am."

Ruth staggered drunkenly, propped by Nathan and Ben. Suddenly, her head jerked back and she spewed vomit onto the thick white carpet, passing out. The stench was loathsome. A waiter brought wet towels, and Benjamin gently wiped the foul matter from his wife's face. Club members hovered, and Pritchitt heard voices of disgust and pity. He turned and met their eyes. He clenched his fists in anger, wishing he could smash the disdainful faces. His anger subsided knowing a scene would only humiliate Ruth even more.

Half asleep in the rear seat, his lovely wife of thirty-eight years cried. Looking into his rearview mirror he wiped a tearful eye. How he wished he could keep driving, leave the city and chaos of his life. Running would be cowardly and, in the end, Dr. Benjamin Pritchitt told himself he was not a coward.

Helping her from the car, he cradled Ruth in his arms. He ascended the steep staircase to their bedroom. Gently he placed her on the satin covers. He unbuttoned her soiled blouse, then washed her face with a wet cloth. Softly stroking her smooth cheek he felt ashamed, as if he himself had plunged a dagger through her heart. He had tried his best to explain.

Walk a mile in my shoes before criticizing me, went the old saying. Dearest Ruth, he thought, what if you were dying, then you would see things differently.

He returned downstairs and arranged for a nurse to stay with Ruth. Then he dialed Bohannon.

"Todd, they're going to nail me tomorrow," he stammered, then he listened as his lawyer spoke.

He heard his wife scream. He dropped the phone and dashed for the stairs.

The board room had the silence of a wake as Ben Pritchitt entered. Twelve drawn faces stared mercilessly. Distinguished members sat at the long table. This was the inner sanctum of the hospital. The outer world was locked away. The room was quite familiar to Pritchitt. Countless hours had he spent in this very room. For three decades his colleagues had valued his presence. Now he felt summoned to the scaffold for his own execution. The panel's animosity was tangible. Cold eyes stared as if he were a dishonorable stain. Todd Bohannon suddenly appeared, and a hushed murmur swelled to an anxious hum.

"Dr. Pritchitt, you were asked to come alone!" a voice shouted accusingly. Heads turned and Dr. James Peters stood.

"Can't you even follow simple instructions anymore?" he said with venom.

Pritchitt leaned across the polished table. "Incorrect, Dr. Peters, I was simply informed of the urgency of this meeting and my mandatory attendance. As usual, Dr. Peters, you're the one who is confused about the simplest of instructions."

Pritchitt glared at Dr. Peters. He paused. He saw many of his friends and colleagues in this room, but Dr. Peters had shown a rabid disdain for him. Pritchitt knew this meeting was called from the lips of a man whom, before he trusted him, he'd sooner swim naked in a pool of hungry sharks. Todd Bohannon had insisted that he accompany his client. Pritchitt was glad the attorney had come.

The meeting was quick and to the point. Dr. Peters and his contingent denounced the accused, hammering away at the less than desired notoriety heaped onto the department and the humiliation Memorial Hospital had suffered. Pritchitt stared straight ahead, listening but silent.

At one point he tried to speak but Bohannon stopped him. "Dr. Pritchitt has not been convicted of anything," Bohannon angrily scolded the board.

"It's just a matter of time," interjected Dr. Peters.

Bohannon dramatically waved a contract and issued a warning: "This stipulates dismissal must be based on just cause, so any unsubstantiated action against my client will be answered with great consequence if no conviction results."

Richard Minzer, chief financial officer, had the floor. "I recommend we adjourn the meeting, so the board may consult with legal counsel before taking action."

"There will be no action!" responded Bohannon.

Minzer removed his glasses. "Dr. Pritchitt, we urge you to refrain from bringing unwanted scorn on the hospital."

A tall woman with silver hair stood. She placed her hands inside of her immaculate white lab jacket. "Ben, I've known you for twenty-five years. You are the ideal physician which all of us here at Memorial admire. You are certainly one of the most brilliant practitioners I've had the pleasure of working with —"

"What's the point?" Dr. Peters interrupted.

"The point is this. I beg of you, Ben, don't destroy yourself. This battle can be fought and won in different ways without you having to be a martyr —" Her voice failed her and she walked from the room. The board rose.

"You'll be hearing from us," warned Dr. Peters, as he followed the others. "You're finished," he said acidly.

Pritchitt sat, pondering what had transpired.

"Be careful what you say around the hospital," Bohannon cautioned. "You're just barely hanging on. Now they're going to search for any legal way to boot you out." Pritchitt stood. Not a word was spoken as both men slowly walked from the now empty room.

As Pritchitt approached his office, Patsy's face brightened.

"I'm still alive," he smiled.

"Even after the board meeting?" she asked in an astonished voice.

"I haven't been convicted of anything . . . yet. They were ready for a burial," he laughed, "but the corpse walked."

"I'm so glad, Dr. Pritchitt."

"Thank you for your concern, Patsy." He entered the security of his office and telephoned home.

The nurse informed him that his wife slept, still sedated after a psychiatrist had examined her. "I'll be at my office, if you need me," he said dejectedly. Would she recover? he asked himself. Anguished thoughts filled his depressed mind.

By late Saturday afternoon the sky had grown overcast, staff workers in the District Attorney's Office glanced at their watches, hoping to leave before a cloudburst. Below their windows the river streamed along in muddiness, but beyond the river front, on the Arkansas horizon a dark rag of clouds flew against the blackening sky.

Deputy D.A. Nash entered with a scowl on his face,

ignoring the polite greetings of underlings. "Where's Jesse?" he asked sharply, then stormed into his office, slamming the door behind him. Heads turned with quiet apprehension, as Nash's secretary ran down the hall and entered his office. Jesse, his attractive young secretary, was obviously frightened.

"Mr. Nash, I typed the report like you asked, would you —"

"Get me Terry Mercer and get her now!" he blasted. The secretary, who had barely gotten through the door, stared in awe. "Who is the boss around here anyway?" he asked, kicking a wastebasket halfway across the office. The secretary rushed out.

Only a few minutes passed when a hesitant knock preceded the secretary's entrance. Behind her was Terry Mercer, briefcase in hand. "I know what this is about, Justin. And I can explain it to you," she implored.

"Oh, can you?" he asked, a sneer on his face, slamming his body into his chair. He propped his feet on his desk and retrieved a half-smoked cigar from an ashtray. "Start explaining, because this so-called head of the investigation doesn't know shit about what's going on. No, wait! Where's Bauers, the D.A. who is supposed to be assisting you with this case."

Nash inhaled deeply and stared at Terry. "Where is he?" he barked at the wide-eyed secretary, fidgeting near the door.

"Y-you didn't ask f-for him," she stammered.

"That's no damn excuse. Get him in here and get him now!" he shouted to his secretary.

Nash rocked back and forth in his chair, too angry to utter a word. Terry eased into a chair. An awkward silence filled the room. She sat, avoiding his fiery eyes. Tim Bauers appeared.

"Sit down, Tim. Don't be such a damn stranger," Nash growled, then his deep-set eyes darted from one to the other. "Tim, would you introduce yourself to Asst. D.A. Mercer."

Bauers cast a puzzled glance at Terry.

"I'm sorry, sir, but I don't understand."

Nash swung his feet from the desk and leaned forward.

"Just do it! You don't have to understand, son. Just do it!"

Bauers licked his lips nervously and removed his glasses. "Uh, Terry, I'm Tim," he said in a perplexed voice.

"Good, very good. Now it's my turn. Terry Mercer, I'm Justin Nash and I'm suppose to be the number two man in this department. I'm your damn boss." Nash rose and came to the front of the desk. "And as they would say on that old TV show, Terry Mercer, this is your life!" He sat on his desk and locked eyes with his young assistant. He removed the cigar. "And your life, Terry Mercer, is to work for *me*," he aimed his thumb at his chest with a blistering glare, "and *with him*." He jabbed the air pointing toward Bauers. Terry was unable to escape neither his penetrating gaze nor his condescending tone. "If there is something of importance in this case, please think of us, and just maybe let us in on it. Is that too damn much to ask?" His voice grew sharper with each word as the room filled with tension and the stench of a burning cigar.

"Justin, I can explain if you'll allow me," she retorted.

"You keep saying that but I haven't heard anything yet."

"That's because you're the only one doing any talking," she fired back.

Nash tossed the burning stub in an ashtray.

"I was on my way to tell you," she explained.

"What is going on?" asked Bauers.

"Our bright associate has stumbled upon a big breakthrough in the serial murders, and I dearly hope she'll share it with us," Nash said sarcastically. "It seems that she and our own Atway Jackson along with some young doctor who works at Memorial found another body this morning. And I had to learn about it from the police, where I just left, embarrassed as hell, because my own staff member left me in the dark."

"Is that right?" asked Bauers incredulously.

"They found the victim in a damn garbage truck of all places. A garbage truck just rolling around in midtown. I can hardly wait for an explanation from our esteemed colleague."

"Justin, if you'd just stop talking long enough I'll tell you everything I know," she said angrily.

"Speak," said Nash, silently admiring her spunk. "All I know is what the detectives told me."

"Dr. Bernie Wiseman, a doctor at Memorial, discovered that strange faxes sent to the hospital are cryptic messages concerning the murders. He concluded that names given in the faxes are streets. These streets give the location where the bodies can be found. All the messages begin with Simon Says and are signed Simon. That's it."

"Does your father know this, Terry?" asked Bauers.

"Yes," she said sheepishly, "the faxes were actually sent to him."

"Your father?" asked a suspicious Justin Nash.

"Yes, but he doesn't know anyone named Simon."

"Well, this Simon knows your father. This is just fucking great!" Nash moaned. "An indicted doctor who's helping people die getting cryptic messages from a person who's more than helping people die. Just great! Bates is gonna love this. Get me all those damn faxes," boomed Nash.

"That's what I was doing," said Terry, "checking out angles at the hospital."

"Let's get a dossier on this Wiseman guy, too," added Bauers. "He might have skeletons and some with meat on them."

"He's a good kid," said Terry defensively.

"Goddamn it, Mercer, I'll be the judge of that!" yelled Nash, a condemning tone spreading the smoke he exhaled.

"Well, as far as I know now, he seems to have a good reputation," she repeated.

Bauers sprang up from his seat. "Let's see the faxes."

"This is really great," Nash said acidly. "This is just really peachy cream. What a mess," he concluded.

"Let's see the faxes," pleaded Bauers.

"Sit down, Bauers," barked Nash. "Don't worry, we're gonna see *everything*. But this fax stuff can't get to the media under any circumstances." His fist hammered the desk. "No one gets any information unless it comes from me. And I want to know everything. Got it?"

"Well, just a moment," drawled Bauers. "If this goes public, someone might know something about these faxes."

"No, wrong!" shouted Nash. "There's already a circus atmosphere circling every move Benjamin Pritchitt makes. More publicity might run this nut off. If the killer is spooked, he'll stop communicating with Pritchitt and now, although I hate to admit it, Dr. Pritchitt looks to be our only link."

"Justin's right," said Terry.

Nash grinned in triumph. "Now you're learning, Terry." Nash jumped from his seat. "Let's see the evidence. We're gonna catch this son-of-a-bitch!"

Patsy cleared her desk and bid Dr. Pritchitt good night. Embattled and refusing to be defeated, he continued examining his patient's files. Patsy had left a list of medical appointments. As usual, there were new calls from the terminally ill, begging him to end their suffering. As much as he wished to help, he had to limit his care to his own patients first, then just maybe, once the legal storm died, he could go forward ending the pain of others. He made several calls to patients, those still loyal to him. But the heavy schedule of days past was gone, as many shunned him, seeking medical help elsewhere. There were heartbreaking letters in his desk, sent by longtime clients, who denounced him for what they regarded as murder. Losing track of time he easily slipped into his old habit of staying at the office late.

He called home about Ruth. The nurse gave him the same account each time.

"She's sleeping peacefully." Then he phoned Tyler. "I'm going to catchup down here. Even though I'm not actively working there's still much mail to go through. Check on your mother."

"Good idea, Dad."

But Pritchitt could not admit to his son he was in no hurry to get home. He hated seeing his wife disintegrate into the brawling boozer he did not want to know. He was hiding at the office, he knew; if he didn't, he too could crack up.

He stretched on the office sofa, drifting in and out of a fretful sleep until startled by the sound of the fax machine. Under the light of a small lamp, he stared at sheets sliding into the fax tray. He reached for his reading glasses. It was a letter for him and at the bottom it was signed, Simon. His heart pounded.

"Dear Friend, you don't know me, but I know you. You are killing to ease the pain and suffering in this world. I, too, am killing to punish the wicked. We both do what is right and just." The letter went on.

"In a parallel of minds and a parallel of death we share a divine purpose. I am destroying those who kill the innocence of the unborn life. Those murderers of the unborn, unborn who are living spirits, granted cellular formation by the living God.

"Yes, we are brothers in a most righteous quest. We perform good deeds in a sinful existence. Divine Will has brought you to me, brought us together for a purpose. It is you who will send me from this world, to join the only loves ever intended for me, but taken away by the sin of a corrupt life. Yes, Benjamin, you are to help me in my own death. It will be a joyous event. One shared by us and God. The time is near at hand. Please tell me you'll bond with me in this special brotherhood heaven itself has ordained. It was meant to be, I with you and you with me. It will happen at a place I choose. Your loving and admiring brother, Simon."

Pritchitt wiped beads of perspiration from his brow. He realized he held the thoughts of a murderer in his hands. He tossed the pages onto the desk. In the bathroom he examined his pallid face. He scrubbed his hands, trying to wash away the unclean madness. Fear engulfed him. Simon was a cunning executioner, a dismembered soul, insane, falsely believing he was orchestrated by God for a crusade of vengeance.

Pritchitt rushed to reread the message. Then he noticed the final page held a command. Reply Demanded. There was a fax number. Should he call the police? Simon's fax had to be connected to a telephone line. Perhaps it could be traced. But he decided to give Simon an answer to his depraved request.

At his computer he prepared a brief response. "We are not brothers. You are a madman created in hell rather than heaven. I want no part of such sickness. Call the police and turn yourself in. I will never participate in anything you do. We have nothing in common. For what I do, I do out of love. For what you do, you do out of hate. May God have mercy on your soul. "Yes," Pritchitt assured himself. "I would like to meet you, just to destroy you, for a quicker journey through the gates of hell would be my wish. But I am a healer not a killer." He sent the response.

An hour passed. Outside was blackness. Pritchitt tossed and turned unable to find comfort on the narrow sofa. The fax machine suddenly came alive. The message was short, begging for a change of mind, and a plea. *"You, and only you will send me from here. You will do as I say. If not, you will suffer a loss far greater than you could ever imagine."* Pritchitt's fear changed to anger.

"You truly are a madman," spoke Pritchitt. He crumpled the sheet and tossed it into the wastebasket. Grabbing his jacket he left the hospital and walked through the vacant parking lot, accompanied by the darkness of his thoughts. He used the drive home to unscramble his hate, anger, and worry. His thoughts were of his wife. Ruth's decline was horrid. Alcohol had crept into her life after Tyler's birth, precipitated by postpartum depression. Ruth had been the rock of her family's strength and still, despite her bouts with alcohol, she was the loving glue that had kept them a close family. Until his recent actions, she had been alcohol free for six years.

His thoughts were a living nightmare. He looked up and was home. He drove up to his well lit mansion. There was an emergency van in his driveway. He quickly pulled his car to a stop. Tyler stood quietly in the drive. Attendants pushed a stretcher. Pritchitt jumped from his car. "What's going on?" he anxiously asked his son. Ruth stared aimlessly, as the attendants loaded her in the van.

"It's not good, Dad." He placed a hand on his father's shoulder. "They're taking her to Memorial Psychiatric Clinic." Pritchitt nodded a reluctant acceptance. He stared through the van's rear window. Ruth's eyes were closed. The van backed from the drive and disappeared.

CHAPTER SIX

Beyond the window the moon was bright, but inside the bar the light was dim. Two men guzzled beer and cursed. At the bar a third person sat apart. A dark overcoat hung from the back of the chair. The loner had long hair. He was of moderate height with narrow sloping shoulders. He said nothing and looked up from his glass rarely.

The men called for more beer.

The solitary man waved his glass signaling a refill. The bartender nodded and brought him a drink. The strange patron said nothing, but snatched the drink from the tray. The jukebox began playing a Blues song.

The bartender frowned. "Shit, Simon, not again. Can't we hear something else? You've play the same song over and over."

The man remained silent, his head bowed, his eyes unmoved as the bartender spoke. Slowly looking up, the blurred face in the dim light stared beady eyes into the bartender's frown. The shadowed face, hidden by disheveled strands of matted long hair, was grave. The eyes cold.

The bartender stepped back, fearful of the dark scowl.

"You okay, buddy. You seem kind of lonely tonight. Kind of like you've lost your best friend."

From the darkness came a raspy reply. "I'm not your buddy. And I'm alone because I want it that way. You can't lose what is already dead and gone." The head dropped and again stared only at the glass in front of him. He took a long drink and abruptly rose from the stool. Money was tossed onto the bar. "Gotta go. Got things to do," came a raspy mumble. Placing the overcoat over his shoulders, the shadowy figure slipped into the black of night.

"Night, Simon," yelled the bartender. There was no reply.

The living room was cloaked in a mortuary-like silence. The once alive and happy house was strangely quiet. Benjamin sat at the grand piano but could play no more. He banged his fists against the keyboard with a dissonant crash.

Night settled and a bitter loneliness ensued. A gentle knock was followed by the ringing of the doorbell. Through the small glass pane Benjamin faced the Reverend Milton James, recently appointed associate pastor of his church. He opened the door.

"Reverend James, you surprised me."

"Pritchitt, may I come in?"

"Of course, come. Where are my manners," Pritchitt mumbled, his voice trailing off. His welcome was less than effusive, which the pastor noticed.

"Is this a bad time? Am I disturbing you?"

"I was just sitting with my thoughts."

The two walked into the living room and eased onto the long sofa. "We're all concerned about Ruth," the Reverend James began. "Word came to me about the incident at the club."

"She's suffered an emotional setback, that's for sure. Earlier tonight she was taken to a psychiatric clinic for admission."

"I am so sorry. Pastor Bivens mentioned there had been past troubles and I've been praying for the both of you. Pastor

Bivens wanted to visit but he's down with the gout, and you know how that is."

"Yes," said Pritchitt, rather formally, sensing what was coming.

Reverend James leaned forward, "Benjamin, you must think of what you're doing. You must think of the price your family must pay for your ill-considered actions."

"And what does that mean? I have considered the consequences," said Pritchitt evenly.

Reverend James pointed his hands skyward. "What you're doing is wrong and, perhaps this is God's way of telling you."

"You mean God's punishing my wife, a good Christian woman, for my actions?" Pritchitt snapped.

"You are very concerned for her, are you not?"

"Of course, she's my life. But who's to judge me? My patients seek my help and —" his voice took an angry hint, "they welcome and pray for my help."

Reverend James rubbed his chin. "I didn't come here to engage in a theological dispute." His voice flowed with irritation.

"Then why are you criticizing me?" asked Pritchitt.

"It is my duty to simply mention that suicide is not condoned in the eyes of Christianity. It is a sign of despair, a rejection of God's infinite mercy and help."

Pritchitt shook his head. "Reverend, I have done nothing but assist needy humans who are terminally ill, and in excruciating pain. I'm doing no more than what caring doctors did years ago."

"Oh, how?"

"Yes. There was a day when medicine was still an art and not a business controlled by government, with doctors squeezing fees by simply seeing how long they can keep someone alive."

"Only God can decide the moment of someone's death, Benjamin."

"That's your view, Reverend. But I can no longer watch people scream in pain. In the past doctors allowed their patients to fill themselves with morphine and depart this world without unnecessary pain."

"You mean the patients overdosed themselves?"

Pritchitt raised his hands in the air and shook his head.

"No, they simply overcame their pain."

"Dr. Pritchitt, I can see we are diametrically opposed."

"We even allow our pets a more dignified death —"

"We are humans, not pets, Doctor."

"Do you really believe that God has told us to make those in pain suffer more?"

"There is instruction in suffering. We learn humility and begin the journey to a righteous path. We must place ourselves in God's hands. You are in error, Dr. Pritchitt, both the law of man and divine law prohibit assisted suicide."

"Hogwash, Reverend James, I don't believe the God I worship wants anyone to suffer the horrible deaths I witness. And there we disagree." His argument vibrated in his voice. "I am an instrument of God's mercy."

Reverend James frowned. "And I see that my coming here has done nothing but upset you. I think I'll leave, but I'll keep praying for you and your family."

Pritchitt stood. "Reverend, if a tornado ploughs through a neighborhood and wipes out innocent families, is that God's will?"

"There are many inexplicable things on earth, to be answered in heaven," said the pastor weakly.

"Well, I seek answers here. I have answers. And don't bother to pray for me and my family. Pray for those in the world who have lost sight of what is merciful and humane."

Reverend James strode quickly to the door.

Pritchitt followed, blocking his exit for a final question. "Surely you don't believe that human suffering is preordained by God himself?"

"Doctor, you've no idea what God wants. But I do know that killing is wrong and I curse those who take lives."

"And you do know what God wants? Rev. James, I do believe I see fire in your eyes. You resent me, don't you?"

"I've got to go, Dr. Pritchitt." Reverend James tried to slip by but Pritchitt blocked his way.

"My belief is that a loving God would display mercy and provide peace for the tortured souls of the dying."

"I will pray for you. Remember, pride comes before a fall, and you are on the precipice. You must answer to God, and only His judgment will decide where your soul will spend eternity."

Reverend Milton James disappeared in the darkness and Pritchitt locked the door, his beliefs strengthened, but now he felt even more alone.

Beneath a full moon a car moved slowly. The clinic was always busy, but especially so late at night. Troubled women with unwanted pregnancies came to the midtown clinic for help. The car circled the block, passed the clinic for a third time, then parked down the street. A firm hand adjusted the rear view mirror. The dark silhouette revealed a man with long hair. The only sound heard was that of a light wind rustling leaves. "Simon says and Simon sees," came a whisper.

A young girl left the clinic. Her movements were painful and slow. In the rear view mirror she approached the car. She rubbed her lower abdomen. From the dark car, piercing eyes followed her closely. Strong hands gripped the steering wheel. Heavy breathing filled the car. Stalking eyes followed the unsuspecting prey. The door opened silently and a lone street light cast a sinister shadow. Panther like, Simon quietly followed the girl until he was near. The fragrance of her perfume brought a frightful moan from his lips. From across the street a woman called out. Her voice broke the silence as she ran toward the girl. They embraced.

"Why didn't you wait, sweetheart?"

"I'm sorry, Mom, I had to get it over with," the young girl cried. Both heard footsteps and turned. They stared as the stranger passed quickly. Frightened, they hurried into a car and sped away.

Long hair fell onto sloping shoulders as Simon dragged his

feet down a darkened hallway. He opened a door and his overcoat fell to the floor. Within the room were dozens of flickering candles. In the center of the room was a table. A firm hand lifted a framed picture. It was an ultrasound image of an unborn baby. Slowly raising it to his face, he stared at the image, then kissed it. "I love you." The voice was gravelly and breaking with emotion. The picture was lowered, then another picture was raised and kissed. "I miss you both and will be with you soon." In a far corner, atop a table was a small candlelit coffin. He bent and kissed the tiny casket. He clung to it and wept.

Like most mornings at the Mercer home, Terry was frantically busy, attempting five things at once, as she readied her two children for school. Near her bedside was a photograph of her deceased husband. It had been an idyllic union until the car wreck that had stolen her dream and taken away the father of her two children. Terry had been a lonely single mother until her hasty marriage to Professor Niles Mercer. Born of loneliness, the second marriage had become a disaster. She was now separated from him and in the middle of divorce procedures. Professor Mercer had drastically changed after their wedding. She had become frightened after discovering him asleep in bed with her children. He claimed he had been sleepwalking, but she felt there was a sinister reason which frightened her. It was then that she insisted upon the separation and started divorce proceedings. Everything on this particular morning went smooth. She shared a car pool with two other young mothers and didn't want to keep anyone waiting. Admiring her two young children, Benji and Claire, she knew the chaos of her life was worthwhile. Kissing each on the forehead, she watched as they ran to the waiting car.

Terry's morning drive downtown was a rare moment to collect her thoughts, but on this day even this was interrupted by radio news discussing her father's troubles and the upcoming trial. A second report criticized the D.A.'s office and police for their inability to catch the serial murderer. Women in Memphis were looking over their shoulders in fear, with no arrest in sight. She prayed for the case to end; if not, she was terrified her nerves would snap, and that she would be like her mother.

The department was buzzing with commotion as she entered. She realized she was late.

"Where in the hell have you been?" asked Tim Bauers in a stern voice.

"A whopping ten minutes!" she exclaimed with exasperation. "I've got children to get going in the morning, all you've got is an ugly cat."

"Right, Nash is having one of his early morning fits and he's not alone."

"Who else?"

"Nash has a very pompous and arrogant asshole with him, as we speak."

"Could it be Jeremy Bates, our illustrious boss?"

"You're right on the money with that."

"Shit!" Terry fretted following behind Bauers.

Approaching Nash's office, loud voices ricocheted into the outer hallway. Nash's secretary, Jesse, sat at her desk. As they paused before the open door, Jesse winced. "Boy, what language," she expressed in a shocked tone.

Terry smiled. "Pray for us, Jesse."

The door opened. "It's about damn time," bellowed Nash from within. "Get in here. Where have you been?" Before she could answer, Jeremy Bates was on his feet. "I've got the mayor's office hounding me daily to solve this thing. The public is terrified. What are you two doing about it?" he demanded, staring into blank faces.

"Wait a minute," cautioned Nash, "we're jumping on each other."

"I agree." Lt. Lori Bordeaux was standing at the rear. "It's no damn time to panic, Mr. Bates."

Bates sat and removed a stack of letters from his briefcase.

"These are very unhappy citizens. These are from voters. Got it?"

"You're the one hoping to be senator or governor," said Terry, to everyone's surprise.

Bates squinted. "You'd better believe it. I'm not going to let sloppy work by my staff wreck my plans. This maniac must be caught!"

"Don't worry, we're gonna catch the bastard," assured Bauers.

Bates had his eyes fixed on Terry. "You don't like me do you?"

"You could say that," she answered boldly.

"At least you're honest, but it really doesn't matter." Bates surveyed those present. "My political aspirations aren't why we're here. Nash, what I'm hearing is that your department is withholding vital evidence, keeping facts from the entire office and the homicide team. Tell me that's not true."

Nash searched for a cigar. "Well, we've got some things we're studying, so we're keeping them to ourselves, to keep the media out."

"So you are withholding evidence," exclaimed Lt. Bordeaux, "even from us."

"The police station is like a piece of Swiss cheese. You got too damn many holes over there."

Bates began pacing the room, visibly agitated. "My office better be informed of everything you guys have. And now, I hear Dr. Benjamin Pritchitt's receiving messages from the killer."

"Who told you?" asked Nash.

"I've got sources," Bates shot back.

Nash threw his hands in the air in disgust.

"I want a precise report by this afternoon detailing everything your staff has uncovered." He looked at Terry. "I hope to God nothing was withheld because Dr. Pritchitt's mixed up in this."

"Nothing," said Terry defensively, a smile betraying her real feelings.

Bates looked around the room. "One misstep here and all of you will be finished."

"Wait a minute, Jeremy," said Nash with a pleading voice, "I made the decision to sit on the stuff for a while. Trust me. You'll get everything. One favor though —" He glanced at Lt. Bordeaux. "Let's keep the police out for a time. Lori's all right, but no one else."

Bates straightened his tie. "I'm due in court. Send me the report and I'll decide what is to be done. Got it?"

"I've got it," assured Nash.

Bates turned on his heel, then paused at the door. "It's not the governorship. I'm aiming at senator." He smiled contemptuously.

Nash, miffed, ransacked desk drawers until he found a cigar. "The Department and the D.A.'s office are supposed to be working together," said Lt. Bordeaux. "You can ignore the future senator, but don't even think about not sharing with me everything you have," Bordeaux warned them.

The afternoon was spent analyzing the faxes, then the autopsy report of the recent victim was studied. Lt. Bordeaux walked to the window, observing the river below, snaking like a python between Arkansas and Tennessee. "Well, I have to agree with you, Nash. This is good material. There may be some strange connection between Pritchitt and this Simon character. Maybe we can use Dr. Pritchitt to lure this guy into a trap." She turned. "Keep Wiseman and Atway Jackson very quiet."

"Right," agreed Bauers.

"I don't want my father placed in any danger," Terry added. "He's already under enough stress, and now this." She collected her briefcase and purse.

"Sweetheart," said Bordeaux, "your father is already in more danger than you'd care to imagine. I mean, he's right in the middle of this fruitcake's thoughts. He's chosen your father to be his pen-pal." With a soft salute, Bordeaux turned and left. Terry followed.

Nash puffed his cigar and removed a folder from a file. It was labeled "serial killer." He called out to his secretary. "Jesse, I'm going to be gone the rest of the morning."

"Can I be of help?"

"No, I just need to pay a visit to someone."

"What about calls?"

"Tell them I've gone to Brazil."

"What?" she blurted. He patted her arm as he strode past her.

"It's just a joke. Just say I've gone to the law library. I'll be back after lunch. By the way, you might call maintenance and see if something can be done about the damn ventilation in my office. Its horrible. How can they expect me to smoke if the air doesn't circulate?" The puzzled secretary watched Nash disappear.

It was early morning and the water in the pool was cool but exactly what Pritchitt needed. He continued more laps, then rested, cocking his head, as if he heard a voice. But there was only silence. He climbed from the pool and toweled on the terrace. But he seemed to hear the voice again. Someone was calling his name. He scanned his property but saw no one; suddenly realizing the voice came from the side gate. He walked in the direction of the caller. Beyond the iron gate stood Bernie Wiseman. Ben removed a key from its hiding place and opened the iron gate.

"I rang the bell and knocked," said Wiseman excitedly. "I saw your car in the drive and knew you had to be here."

Pritchitt locked the gate behind them, and they crossed to the terrace.

"Some kind of place for sure," said Wiseman, turning in a circle, taking in the magnificent home. Pritchitt motioned toward a lounge chair.

"You've heard about the body we found?"

"Oh, yes," said Pritchitt, offering Wiseman a bowl of fresh fruit.

He reached for an apple. "I'm afraid our society has begun to self-destruct," sighed Wiseman.

"No, Bernie, murders have taken place since Cain and Abel."

"Yeah, but it's terrible to think someone standing next to you at the supermarket could be the psychotic killer."

"Welcome to the real world," said Pritchitt.

"Well, I noticed that you've got your gate locked."

"I have to, I've been threatened."

With the apple clenched in his teeth, Wiseman removed sheets of paper from his pocket. "This fax came this morning." As Pritchitt unfolded the message, Wiseman noticed the aquarium. He rushed to where colorful, beautiful fish swam in the salt water.

"Bernie, I can't see the small print without my glasses. Read it." Wiseman stepped away from the aquarium.

"I didn't know you liked fish?"

"The aquarium belongs to my wife."

Wiseman nodded and took the fax message. He wet his lips and began to read: "'Dear Brother, I write to you the most important letter of my life. You are a great doctor caring for those who are dying in needless pain. You will aid in my suicide when I've finished my task. We are angels sent by God.'"

Pritchitt shook his head. "There are deep religious connotations here and more than just a little sickness."

Wiseman agreed. "As I see it, Dr. Pritchitt, his death will give him his escape from a living hell. He hates life and the world he lives. He wants out. Maybe he wants to be with someone who's already dead. And you're a divine partner in his demented mind. Maybe, you just may be the only person left who he cares about."

"Sick, but sounds reasonable," agreed Pritchitt.

"I left without anyone's knowledge, and now risk castration at the hands of Dr. Peters if he finds out."

"Let me see that fax," Pritchitt said.

Bernie looked at his watch. "I've got to get back before I'm missed."

Pritchitt rose and Wiseman followed him into the main wing of the home, Wiseman admired the paintings and art objects. Pritchitt picked up his reading glasses from the table in the hall. "There's a number here for a return message," Pritchitt said.

Wiseman fumbled a porcelain statue he was handling.

"Bernie, please don't drop that piece. It's a gift I gave my wife."

"Then don't startle me like that," Bernie lamented, setting the tiny figure down.

"Bernie, these numbers —"

"I'm a step ahead of you, Dr. Pritchitt. All of the faxes have different return telephone numbers. I checked them out last night and this morning. Guess what?"

"Don't make me play a guessing game, I'm in no mood."

"The numbers correspond to different fax machines at branch libraries in Memphis. Some are tied to a portable fax which can't be traced. And others are from pay telephone booths."

"He's one clever bastard," said Pritchitt.

"This guy is crazy like a fox. He just bounces around from place to place."

Pritchitt reached for a pen and paper. "I want you to send this reply, Bernie."

"Sure, but there's one request."

"What's that?"

"Please get your trial over with and get back in time to save my career. Dr. Peters doesn't care for me at all."

Pritchitt smiled. "That makes two of us."

After Wiseman left, Pritchitt took a quick shower. He stared at his unshaven face in the misty bathroom mirror. He must look nice for Ruth. His eyes were dark and puffy, the result of another sleepless night. He dreaded going to the clinic.

He was nearly dressed when the doorbell rang. Could it be Wiseman with another fax? he wondered.

"Dr. Pritchitt, I'm Justin Nash, from the D.A.'s office."

Pritchitt was wary. "And?"

"May I come in, sir?"

Pritchitt studied the man. Nash was tall and elegantly dressed. He was well built and ruggedly handsome. But the cold eyes were penetrating, and they bored into Pritchitt's soul.

"No, I'd rather talk outside, so let's go to the pool area."

On the terrace Pritchitt faced Justin Nash. "Should I have my attorney present?" asked Pritchitt.

"That is up to you," said Nash. "This is an official visit. I am in charge of prosecuting the serial murderer. I've been informed that our suspect is now communicating with you."

"Yes, I've been receiving a few bizarre messages."

"We are trying to keep the media out of this revelation. Will you do the same?"

"Yes, of course," assured Pritchitt. "I want this madman apprehended as much as anyone else."

Nash tapped his fingertips together.

"So you'll answer a few questions?"

Pritchitt nodded.

"Do you have any idea why this Simon is contacting you?"

"It's obvious it has to do with my assistance in ending the pain of my patients."

Nash nodded. "Yes, well, I'm not here to talk about that. And I would recommend having an attorney present for that type of discussion since you are facing trial." Nash removed a cigar. "Mind if I smoke?"

"It's your life. Go ahead."

Nash grinned. "You're one of those anti-smoking proponents."

"I've operated on too many lung cancer patients to condone inhaling that carcinogen."

"Your daughter admires you tremendously. Even before all of this came up she has always praised your medical ability."

"Coming from the prosecutor's office I'll accept that as a compliment."

"Terry informed us that Mrs. Pritchitt is in the hospital."

"She's having a hard time. I just telephoned to ask about her."

"How is she?"

Pritchitt grew quiet. "That's a family matter I'd rather not discuss."

"Oh, excuse me. I didn't mean to intrude."

Pritchitt wondered if Nash was trying to obtain incriminating evidence.

"Well, I won't keep you, sir." Nash stood. "But I do feel the need to tell you something."

Pritchitt also rose. "What's that?"

"My parents suffered horrible deaths. Cancer. I just wanted to tell you that. But the law is clearly against assisted suicide."

Pritchitt said nothing, wary of Nash's intent. He escorted Nash to the side gate.

"Do you want police protection?" asked Nash.

"No, Simon hates young women, not an aging doctor. Threats do concern me, for my family's sake, but I don't want to be protected."

Nash extended his hand. "Jeremy Bates is out to nail you. He's going to use you to launch his political career but those of us who have witnessed the death of loved ones understand your motive. I wish the best for you and your wife," said Nash, starting up the drive. "As for these—" He raised his cigar. "I'm going to quit one day."

Benjamin packed his wife's personal effects into a bag, then hurriedly drove away.

Nash slumped in his car and watched Pritchitt's departure, scratching notes on a small yellow pad. He traced the license number of Pritchitt's automobile. Suddenly, a vehicle was beside him. It was Terry Mercer with her children. "What are you doing here?" she asked in a voice both astonished and accusing.

"Working," said Nash, stepping from the car.

Terry parked in the drive, and her children ran to play on the large green lawn. She walked to where Nash waited.

"Kids, go to the front door, and ring the bell for Papa.

"He's gone," said Nash. "To visit your mother."

Terry studied him curiously. "You think my father is involved in killing young girls?"

Nash loosened his tie and closed his legal pad. "I don't know who the killer is. Until the day we catch him, everyone is a suspect."

Terry's eyes flashed. "He's not a murderer!"

"Between you and me, Terry, I think you father has good intentions. I told him about my parents. They both had deaths I wouldn't wish on a stray dog. I think the medical community is going to eventually come around to your father's position. He's got guts. I hope he comes out all right."

"Justin, I'm surprised. I really appreciate your concern. You can certainly fool people with your toughness."

"I have to be tough sometimes. There was once a time—"

Terry turned toward the lawn where her children romped. "Benji, Claire, come here." She turned to Nash.

"A time when what?"

"Oh, nothing," he said with a nod.

The children jumped up and down on the sidewalk. "Mr. Nash, these are my wonderfully behaved kids. Did you both hear what your mother just said?"

"What's that, Mommy?" asked her son.

"I just told this nice man, who is Mommy's boss, that you kids are nice and well-behaved. Please don't make me a liar."

The little girl tugged at Terry's skirt. "Okay, Mommy, we'll be nice."

"Pleased to meet both of you," said Nash warmly. Benji shook his hand and Claire smiled. "Well, a true gentleman and a little lady. Terry, I can definitely see why they consume your life. "Nice kids," he added, then he walked to his car.

The psychiatric clinic held an eerie quiet compared to regular hospital floors. Patients roaming the hall had bewildered looks, a presence which disturbed Pritchitt. A glimpse into a room revealed a middle-aged man sitting in a chair clawing the air, crying out for his mother. Another open door brought the sight of an elderly woman who brushed her thin legs with a toothbrush, then offered it to Pritchitt. A sudden shriek from a room quickened his step as a pair of nurses ran to investigate. In the hall a teenage boy sang strangely, until led away by a nurse. Such sights unnerved Pritchitt, a man who valued clear thought as the foundation of human progress. He became upset, hoping his wife would not resemble the unfortunates he had seen. The unit had an excellent reputation as one of the best, and years earlier his wife's previous stay here had been successful. At the reception desk a heavy-set nurse looked up.

"I've come to see my wife, Ruth Pritchitt."

The woman scanned a directory. "She's in room 202."

"How is she doing?"

"She can receive visitors."

There was hesitancy in his step as he approached the room. Ruth sat in bed, clear-eyed and alert. "Ben, honey," came the soft voice he knew so well. She extended her arms. He hugged her, and kissed her cheek.

"Ben, you look tired and worried." He sat on the bed beside her.

She brushed his cheek. "I was bad, wasn't I? I did something crazy and foolish, didn't I?"

"Let's just put it this way, sweetheart, you pretty much trashed the bar at the club."

"I'm so ashamed," she said, her voice choking. "My dearest Benjamin. You're going through so much, then for me to —"

"No," he interrupted. "Forgive me, Ruth. I'm responsible for all of this," said Ben sadly.

Ruth grabbed his hands. "You seem to be carrying the guilt of the world on your shoulders. Don't. Even before you helped the first woman end her life, I had already begun sneaking drinks again. I haven't been a good wife."

Hearing this confession, Ben felt terrible. Ruth closed her eyes. A tear trickled along her cheek. Tan and slim, Ruth's loveliness remained. There was hardly a line in her face. Her one concession to age was that she colored her auburn hair, vowing never to have a single strand of gray. But Ruth was hardly the spoiled, rich wife. She was a true helpmate. Ben admired her sharp mind. She had acquired a solid knowledge of medicine in their years together. Ruth read voraciously and thrilled at every scientific advance and cure. She could make a fine speech at the many charitable conferences she directed. Pritchitt loved his wife dearly. She was near perfection. *Nearly.*

Ben searched for words. "I couldn't have a better wife, but . . . when you drink —"

She lifted her head and blue eyes opened wide.

"You're a caring man whose soul beckons you to help, that's all, Benjamin Pritchitt. A caring man trapped within his own soul's moral dilemma. Ben, I love and respect you, but my emotions can't stand the pressure of it all. I'm strong in many ways but so weak in others. Sarah Taylor telephoned me this morning."

"How is she doing?"

"She was so sweet. We had a long discussion about Helen. I was blind, too. I had no idea Helen was in such pain."

"She hid it a lot," said Benjamin, "and she asked me not to discuss her health with you. She tried to bear the pain, but it was just too much in the end."

"You were there for her, Ben, in a way that I wasn't. Sarah now understands what you did. She praised your courage."

"I love you, Ruth." He held her hand tightly and smiled.

"And I you, Benjamin Pritchitt." She began to cry. "I'm trying to fight this depression. I feel so terrible when I'm without a drink or a pill." Ben saw her anguish and his heart broke. "Ruth, I love you more than you'll ever know, my darling." They embraced. "And I know that you're going to be fine. I'm so very proud of you. I need to go and let you rest."

Leaning forward, Pritchitt kissed her lips. "Terry and Tyler will visit you later." Ben noticed an ornate basket of fruit and a box of chocolate candy. "Who sent these?" he asked.

"My bridge club sent the candy."

"When all of this is over, Ruth, we're going to Europe."

"I'd love that," she smiled.

At the nurse's station, Pritchitt asked about Dr. Blanche Tucker. "She's in room 400, but she's about to leave for the day."

Pritchitt raced to find his wife's psychiatrist. Dr. Tucker was far down the hall when he caught up with her.

"Dr. Pritchitt," she said, "I was going to call you this evening."

Blanche Tucker was a tall attractive woman in her mid-thirties. She had treated Ruth's previous breakdown and continued therapy sporadically. She ushered Pritchitt into a private conference room. Motioning to a chair, she sat across the table from Ben.

"I can't tell you how much of a disappointment this is to me, and I'm sure it is the same for you. However, she is improving rapidly. She has been very forthcoming about her setback. Her honesty and awareness of her problems are in her favor."

"When will she be released?"

"I'm not certain. I would like her to join various therapy sessions." She hesitated. "But constant worry has precipitated this setback."

"You mean . . . " Pritchitt's voice dropped off.

"Doctor, your actions have filled her with concern. She has been pushed to the edge. She escapes the pain by alcohol. For years, Mrs. Pritchitt has battled depression, beginning after your son's birth. Something you've probably never recognized is the guilt he carries for his mother's illness. But that's another story."

"Yes, her black moods began after his birth, but I've never seen anything in Tyler to suggest —"

"Because you aren't looking for it, Dr. Pritchitt, or subconsciously refused to recognize the problem because of the pain it would cause you.

"Getting back to Ruth, however, in her last few sessions I had noticed a significant change in her. The psychologist who works with me corroborates that Mrs. Pritchitt is showing signs of major depression associated with a bipolar condition, and a hormonal imbalance."

"Bipolar?"

"It is very treatable. It's the new term for manic-depressive disorder."

"Yes, I know, but what can we do to get her back home and well again?"

"This problem you're going through must end in her mind or she'll regress the moment she returns home. I believe that electroshock will definitely benefit her."

"I thought that treatment was outdated."

"To the contrary. There has been a revitalization of this approach in recent years."

"It sounds rather foreboding."

"Ruth is trapped in this depression and her subconscious is telling her to stay there. Medicine might not be the total answer this time where it has worked before."

"I trust you. Ruth and my family are my reasons for living."

"Very good, Dr. Pritchitt. For her entire adult life you've been her strength, now you're the instrument of her instability. If you fall, she will crumble. I'll need to keep her here in the hospital until treatment improves her condition, but you must resolve your problems as well. And, doctor, do so quickly for your sake and hers."

Her beeper sounded. Dr. Tucker looked to the flashing numbers, then stood and said good-bye.

CHAPTER SEVEN

A light drizzle fell as Terry drove to her parent's home. It was a dreary evening. After a busy day, the children were exhausted. "When will we be at Papa's?" asked Benji, his eyelids drooping.

"Any minute," said his mother. "Claire, how's my big girl feeling?"

"Tired, Mommy. Why couldn't we have stayed at home to sleep?"

"Here we are at Papa and Mama's home."

The house seemed brighter than usual. "Kids, I think your Papa has every light in the house on." Thunder boomed and a lightning bolt streaked the sky. Strong winds slanted the sheets of rain.

"Maybe he's scared to be alone without Mama," Benji said, with Claire nodding her head in agreement.

Terry grabbed an umbrella. "Let's get inside, kids."

A downpour struck, and the trio splashed their way up the front steps, running and laughing.

The doorbell rang. Pritchitt finished rearranging a

photograph of himself and his wife, then satisfied made his way through the entry hall. Opening the door he hugged both grandchildren. "Hey, you're wet!" he noted. "I was worried about you. Terry, didn't you hear the tornado warning?"

"No, and is that why you have every light in the house on?"

Her father looked around, "I guess I got carried away. This place is so lonely without your mother."

"Mom always did like it lit up when you got home from work."

"That's okay, Papa," said Benji, tugging his grandfather's pants, "it's okay to be scared in this big house, without Mama here to hold your hand."

"Benji, I'm scared, will you give your Papa another hug."

Pritchitt beamed.

"Okay, kids, Papa made some hot chocolate and bought some of your favorite chocolate chip cookies.

"Oh, boy!" Benji screamed, running for the kitchen, his tired eyes energized.

"Dad, you really know how to spoil them," Terry said, removing her jacket.

"I know," he sighed, "but it's so infrequent. I need their love so very much, especially now."

She placed her arms around her father's neck, frowning at the exhaustion in his face. "You look worn-out, Dad."

"I really am."

As the children amused themselves in the kitchen, happily devouring cookies and sipping hot chocolate, father and daughter spoke of Ruth, and the treatment Dr. Tucker suggested. Wiseman's discovery about the faxes was mentioned.

"I'll check out the fax machines in the libraries. He may be onto something," Terry whispered, then yawned.

"Your boss, Justin Nash asked me to keep silent about the faxes," Benjamin reminded his tired daughter.

"Right. I'll have Lt. Bordeaux assign a surveillance officer to each branch library. We'll make it seem as if obscene messages are being sent."

The lights flickered, sending the children scampering into their mother's lap. "Whoa!" she laughed.

"It's scary here," said a wide-eyed Claire.

"No way, Papa's house isn't scary," Pritchitt replied. "Come here, I'll show you some interesting books." In the library he removed a stack of books from the shelf. "This one belonged to your mother when she was a little girl," he said. Claire turned the pages, her eyes wide with wonder.

Terry removed a psychology book. "This is what *I* need to study."

Pritchitt shook his head. "As if we can ever understand human behavior," he said. Both children hurried into the next room with books in hand.

Terry talked openly about her problems with her estranged husband. Her marital difficulties were not new to her parents. Both had opposed the sudden marriage. Professor Niles Mercer was a quiet but brilliant college professor. Niles was known as a scholar until he befriended the Reverend Milton James. It was not until after their marriage that Terry had discovered Niles suffered from schizophrenia. The illness was hidden during their whirlwind courtship. Niles Mercer's noncompliance with medication was an overwhelming problem. His loss of sexual desire when taking the medicine had created strife. His condition was different from Terry's mother and his avoidance of medication was much more paralyzing. Wild emotional tirades exiled him to a world far from reality. In his psychotic relapses the handsome professor of mathematics belittled his wife, charging she was an idiot, incapable of simple addition or subtraction.

Terry pleaded with him to take his medication, but he'd refuse. One heated evening, he had taunted her viciously, yelling that he could satisfy her "all night long." What resulted was a night of bizarre eroticism, and Terry's submission to strange acts. His mounting emotional instability was the kiss of death for their marriage. Her father had heard everything during his years as a physician, so very little shocked him. But if Niles would not stay on his medicine and continue therapy, then he urged her to separate, for the sake of the children. Niles' severe mood swings had led to a forced leave of absence from the university. He had agreed to leave Terry's home, and see a psychiatrist. He had restarted his pills, and tearfully apologized for his behavior, begging her to take him back.

"So the marriage is over?" asked her father.

She shrugged. "Dad, when he's on his medicine he's the most charming guy I know. But when he's off, I don't know him at all, and that scares me."

Pritchitt approached his daughter. "And if he returns, there'll be no sexual fulfillment for you."

Terry lowered her eyes. "He says that maybe one day a new pill will come out, and he could be a man again," she whispered, embarrassment turning her face.

Pritchitt kissed his daughter. "You'll find someone else," he assured her. "You're young, beautiful and intelligent and have your whole life ahead." They embraced, then went in search of the children.

Tucking the grandchildren in bed was a delight. Benjamin and Terry kissed them, then all knelt to pray for Mama's return home.

"Don't close the door," said Benji sleepily, "the light will keep the boogie man away."

"Okay," Ben said, blowing a kiss.

In the den Benjamin opened an expensive bottle of wine. "Dad, you're not only a great father but one helluva grandfather." He smiled and handed Terry a glass of deep red wine. "Dad, I'm so worried about you. Your eyes, well they're so sad."

There was brief silence. "I believe in what I've done, Terry. I want you, your brother and mother to know that. My soul is comfortable with the decisions I've made for the good of my patients. What's gnawing me and tearing me to pieces is Mother and the repercussions to my family."

The telephone rang. "Let me get this call," Terry said.

Pritchitt walked to the large window where rain poured over the panes. The reflection cast Terry's face with a troubled expression. She hung up.

"What is it, baby?"

"It's Niles. He's going to ruin me if I don't get him out of my life." She pushed her glass over, spilling the wine.

"Okay, settle down, what's he done?"

"He's been arrested," she answered. "He's in jail. That was Lt. Bordeaux telling me to hurry down and make bail."

"What's the charge?"

"I should have listened to you and Mom. Tyler insisted I should get to know him better. But no, I had to run off and marry a man I barely knew, and an unstable man at that!"

"Why was he arrested?"

"For resisting arrest and picketing an abortion clinic — he's gone overboard on this abortion issue with his good friend, the Rev. Milton James." Terry reached for her raincoat.

"Terry, I'll go," Pritchitt pleaded, reaching for his coat.

"No, Dad. Unfortunately, he's still my husband and my headache."

"Has he always felt so strongly about abortion?"

"I don't know. But I do know he's over the edge, Daddy."

"Baby, I worry about you."

"And I you, Daddy."

Pritchitt saw only the five year old he taught to ride a bike. He wished they could go back to that day.

"It's really scary, Dad. Lt. Bordeaux informed me he violently resisted arrest. Oh, Daddy, if only Bob hadn't —" Terry began sobbing. "Oh, Dad, I've betrayed him."

"No, Terry, don't say that. Bob would understand your loneliness."

She rubbed her eyes. "Do you think he's watching from above?"

"I can't answer that. But if he is, he'll see what a great mother you are."

"I thank God the kids are too young to understand. I'm just adding to your problems."

"Nonsense, Terry. You're my baby girl. Never forget that." Their eyes met and tears swelled.

"Dad, I've got to get down there before the reporters." Thunder rumbled.

"Please be careful," he told his daughter. "And if there's anything —"

"I know, Dad, call you."

"Terry, I want you and the kids to come home and live here!" he yelled as she disappeared into the dark rain.

Pritchitt climbed the stairs to check on his grandchildren who slept through the ferocious thunderstorm. Downstairs in the den, he reached for a book, hoping it would provide momentary escape. A few moments passed, then the silence was broken by the intrusive ringing of the telephone.

"This is Elsie Lavender."

The surprise call jarred his thoughts. His tired body raised. "How did you get my private number, Mrs. Lavender?"

"I'm desperate and desperate people have their ways, Dr. Pritchitt."

He remembered the woman he'd diagnosed with lung cancer two years ago.

"How are the treatments going?"

"I hurt so bad," she cried. "I can't seem to get enough morphine to help. I wake up from a short nap to find myself soaked in urine and stool. My doctors tell my son that I can go on like this for maybe another year. They say it with a smile and my son seems to rejoice in the fact that I'll be here longer . . . longer in my living hell. Now I just moan in pain and my poor son doesn't know what to do, except to beg the doctors for more drugs. I'm all he has, but he doesn't understand."

"Mrs. Lavender, I wish I could help you, but —"

"Doctor, it's time, please help me end the pain."

"You know that I'm facing trial."

"Dr. Pritchitt, you are a saint. You have nearly ruined your life to help your patients. I pray every waking moment for God to take me. I was active in the church and a good person. I sang in the choir. Dr. Pritchitt, I'm so weak and have lost all self-respect. I'm so humiliated by the way I look and smell, my body has shrunk. You wouldn't recognize me. All I do is pray for death. I live on liquids, poured down my throat until I vomit. I suffer with a pain no human should endure." She grew quiet.

Pritchitt was speechless. Only her heavy breathing could be heard. "Mrs. Lavender, I will consider your situation."

The plea tugged at his heart. He wished that Ruth was beside him, so he could at least share his thoughts. Ruth was his strength and for now, he was on his own. His duty was to his wife, but what about Mrs. Lavender? he wondered.

Terry closed her dripping umbrella. Raucous voices echoed through the lobby. The police station knew no day or night, and each eight hour shift was as busy as the other. Terry hurried through the front door and walked quickly to the night sergeant who escorted her to Lt. Bordeaux's office. She opened the door and stopped with a surprised look. She had found not only Lt. Bordeaux but also Justin Nash and Atway Jackson.

"What are you two doing here?"

"I called your office," said Bordeaux, "and when I said it was an emergency, Justin came right down."

"Well, thanks, but I can take care of my own problems," embarrassment in her tone.

"He is your husband," said Nash. "I wanted to help."

"Yes, he is my husband, but . . . but I don't want him to disgrace me, my children or the D.A.'s office. We're separated."

Bordeaux looked down. "I was only trying to help, Terry."

"No, that's all right," assured Terry. "Where can I post bail?"

"It's already been handled," spoke Atway.

"By Mr. Nash." Terry glared. "That's just great," she said curtly, "now you're playing boy scout as well as boss."

"Terry, I just wanted to — You're going through so much. And the way I sunk my teeth into you yesterday . . . well."

"Thank you, Justin. I don't want to sound ungrateful, but

please allow me to be the judge of how much I can take."

The door opened and Niles Mercer was escorted inside. Lt. Bordeaux signed a release form and the guard left.

Niles seemed delighted by the attention, and beamed when he saw his wife. "Tonight we made a stand against murderers licensed to kill the innocent in this house of Sodom and Gomorrah we call society."

Nash and Jackson exchanged glances.

"Niles, how long have you been leading these protests?" Terry was asking.

"Not long enough, Terry, but tonight I made a difference."

He had a fanatical look as he spoke, triumphant in his righteousness. "Aren't you proud of me, Terry?"

"Let's go," she said, buttoning her raincoat.

The thunderstorm continued. Terry drove carefully, eager to reach Niles's apartment.

It was a dreary night. Downtown Memphis was deserted. The nightclubs along Beale Street were closed. Only the faint lights of the pair of bridges that spanned the river offered any color. Like most metropolitan cities, the affluent flocked to the suburbs. Terry was concerned.

"You're living down here now?"

"I'm broke. I'd still be in jail if —"

"You've got to get some help. Why did you stop therapy?"

"I don't need therapy!" he shouted. "I need help in stopping murders! Please, Terry, join me!"

"You're a brilliant instructor, don't wreck your career."

He became agitated, squirming in his seat.

"I'm finished with the ivory tower. They've booted me out!"

"Is this where you live?" she asked. The decrepit rooming house was gloomy. Beer bottles littered the lawn. On the porch a shadowy figure puffed a cigarette.

"Yes," he said. "Will you come in?"

"We're finished," she said. "It's time for a divorce."

He lifted her hand from the steering wheel and held it.

"I can be a man, Terry."

"I-I know, Niles."

He pulled her hand toward his groin. "See?"

Terry yanked her hand away in disgust. "Good-bye, Niles. Get out of my car, now!"

Opening the door the rain did little to cool his anger as the car pulled away.

The morning arrived sooner than Justin Nash desired. He turned from the uninvited morning sun and covered his head with a pillow. The alarm clock sputtered and he pulled another pillow to his head. He was awake. With an agitated groan he reached to turn off the alarm. He stared through the window into the bright morning light, then rolled over. The phone rang loudly and he raised himself. He fumbled briefly for control of the phone. It was Lt. Bordeaux.

"We brought a suspect in for questioning in the serial murder case."

Nash's tired eyes opened. "That's great!" He yawned and looked at the clock. "Lieutenant, it's not six a.m. What the hell time do you get up anyway?"

"Mr. Nash, you know my day never ends, just like yours. Right?"

"Yeah, we work for the people. I'll get dressed and be right down. Have you questioned him yet?"

"No, we're waiting for your team."

By the time he dressed, Justin Nash was ready for the day. He resided in a beautiful classic residence in midtown, built by his grandfather 70 years earlier. He had been born and raised in the house. The only family he knew was Emma, the elderly housekeeper. She had worked for his grandfather and been part of the family for over 50 years. She used a cane and sometimes a walker. Emma had no relatives, and had pleaded not to be dismissed, to end her days in a nursing home. Nash allowed her to stay.

Emma watched the master of the house descend the large staircase. "Slow down, Justin, for goodness sakes, you're going to do like me and break a hip some day. Do you have time for breakfast?"

"No, I'll save my appetite for tonight."

"Well, at least take this." She handed him a cup of steaming coffee. "I heard the telephone and your footsteps overhead and I knew you'd be in a hurry. Here — and don't spill it on that pretty tie."

"Dear and thoughtful Emma, thank you. What would I do without you?"

"For one thing you could get that upstairs cleaned for the first time in years," she laughed. "I'm ashamed I can't climb those stairs."

Nash playfully pinched her cheek. "Don't worry about me. I'm just an old bachelor anyway."

"Time to get you a wife," she scolded. Her left hand clung tightly to the staircase as she waved her cane aloft. "Come home hungry," she commanded.

Terry Mercer walked past the cluster of prostitutes, lined up in a row for bookings. The West Precinct station was chaotic, as usual. Atway Jackson surveyed the women attentively.

"Gee, he whispered to Terry, "one of them is a man."

"At least he's got nice taste in dresses," she remarked.

In a smoke filled room, they peered through a one-way mirror, observing a white male with long, dirty hair. He sat sullenly in the interrogation room, arms crossed, head down.

"That's him," said Lt. Bordeaux, puffing a cigarette and sipping a Coke.

"He doesn't look big enough to whip my grandmother," commented Asst. D.A. Bauers.

"Good point," said Terry, "the killer abducts women, kills them, then stuffs them in garbage containers. I would think he'd be a bit more muscular." There was a pause. "And our only possible description, furnished by two frightened women, was of observing a white male with long hair possibly stalking a patient leaving an abortion clinic. He was described as having a moderate frame." Silence followed as everyone stared through the glass at the less than convincing suspect.

"I'm not too damn sure about this guy," added Bordeaux, stretching her long legs onto a stool.

From behind them came a voice. "Looks can be damn deceiving," interrupted Nash, "and very misleading. Exactly what the hell do we have on him, Lt. Bordeaux?"

Bordeaux spread a police report on her lap. "He confessed."

"Wow!" exclaimed Atway.

The slight suspect began moving his lips wildly and pointing at the air. "Who's he talking to?" Terry asked, staring through the glass.

"Himself. He talks to himself," said Bordeaux, rising to her feet. "He's been doing that a lot, and making little sense, I might add."

Nash looked on with growing doubt and disgust. "Bordeaux, did you get me down here before the fucking rooster crows to observe a mental case? I mean, did he know any details about the killings that waved a yellow flag in that mind of yours?"

"Some of the locations," Bordeaux mumbled. Her voice faded with less than a persuasive tone.

"Anyone could know that just from the newspapers," said Terry.

Nash rubbed his temples. "Your opinion, Atway? For instance, do we know where this . . . this suspect has been lately?"

"Oh, we're in the process of checking on that as we speak. His name is Billy Robins."

"Well, sometimes that's his name," added Bordeaux.

"Do we, or do we not, know his name?" Nash fumed.

Bordeaux quickly walked to the door. "Need to get this show on the road," she said. She entered the interrogation room, and began a conversation with her long haired suspect. "Want an attorney?" she asked.

"Yes, I certainly do," he said, standing and slamming both hands to the table. Bordeaux returned to the viewing room and sat, as a request for an attorney from the Public Defender's Office went out.

"Wants an attorney?" Nash griped.

"Yes," Bordeaux grimaced.

"Damn. This should have already been done and the attorney here. We're wasting time, Bordeaux," he shouted.

"Yes, sir," she agreed. A frustrating nod shook her head as she reached for a cigarette. Minutes passed and between Bordeaux's cigarette and Nash's cigar, smoke built to a dense fog.

Atway blurted. "Hey, do you guys furnish gas masks with those things? I'll probably get lung cancer just by being in here."

"It's part of your job description to inhale," quipped Bauers.

"Take a real deep breath and you just may have a secondary smoke lawsuit," offered Terry, herself trying to avoid the smoke.

Amidst their banter a detective rushed through the door.

"He's Billy Robins all right. But he was just released a few days ago from the Tennessee Psychiatric Outreach in Jackson. He'd been there for six months."

"Goddamn it," shouted a disappointed Nash, tossing his cigar on the floor. "He's just some ordinary wacko looking for attention. Bordeaux, next time you call me, you better have something important to tell me. You hear me, Bordeaux?" Nash stormed from the room.

"Better luck next time," Terry said, patting Bordeaux's shoulder. The room emptied.

Bernie Wiseman had just completed his third operation of the day. He relaxed by reading yesterday's newspaper. The door opened and one of the doctor's peeked through. "Pritchitt's secretary has been calling you for the last thirty minutes."

Wiseman folded the newspaper.

"We told her you had cases, but now she knows you're finished, and guess what, she's crying out for you even louder. You'd better go see what Patsy wants before she has a stroke or something."

Patsy's short hair shook vigorously. She nervously jumped

up. "It's Mrs. Lavender. She's already called three more times this morning. That makes fifteen calls in three days. She won't stop. She sounds very upset. Please, Dr. Wiseman, you talk to her. She wants Dr. Pritchitt's . . . assistance."

"Patsy, you know I spoke to her yesterday," frowned Wiseman. "I feel sorry for her but enough is enough."

"She has lung cancer," offered Patsy.

"I know. But we're not oncologists in this department."

Patsy's eyes widened. "You do know what she wants."

"Yes, I do. But I cannot get involved in her death."

"Neither can Dr. Pritchitt," said Patsy.

"Correct. I am sympathetic to Dr. Pritchitt's predicament but hey, my career's just beginning."

"She desperately wants to talk to you. If she couldn't find Dr. Pritchitt, she wants you. I know you, Dr. Wiseman, I can see it in your face, and you couldn't sleep tonight if you refused to call her."

"Enough already. Now I see how Dr. Pritchitt stays organized if you're prodding him every day like this."

She laughed. "I've been with that wonderful man for over two decades."

"Give me her number and I'll call her, but this is it. For some reason she believes I can convince Dr. Pritchitt into aiding her own death."

"One additional favor, then I promise to leave you alone for the rest of the day —"

"For the rest of the day? How about for the rest of the month?"

"Mrs. Dot McCormick has also been calling —"

"Patsyyy," groaned Wiseman, "I said one call."

"Dr. Wiseman, you are a good and caring young doctor. You will call her." She handed him a slip of paper.

"This is not my area of practice."

"And why not?" came a familiar voice. Pritchitt walked through the door.

Thank God!" Wiseman gasped. He handed the note to Pritchitt and waved good-bye.

"Dr. Pritchitt, it's Elsie Lavender, the poor woman is calling here over and over."

"She called me at home last night," sighed Pritchitt.

"But she's not the only one," said Patsy. "Look at the pile of phone memos on your desk. I left them for you to sort through." She closed the door and Pritchitt thumbed through the messages. Outside, the overhead sun turned the river silver. A formation of Canadian geese streamed south. Pritchitt admired the beauty, but a sudden gloom clouded his head thinking of all the pain in the messages at hand. He dialed.

"Mrs. Caruso?"

"Who is this?" asked a deep male voice.

"I'm a doctor."

There was a long pause. Then came a hoarse voice: "This is Joan Caruso."

"May I speak with your mother?"

"She's dead."

"I'm Dr. Benjamin Pritchitt, your mother wrote me recently."

"She blew her head off, doctor."

"What?"

"About an hour ago," the voice weakened, "a neighbor heard a shot, and called me. Mom found my Dad's old hunting rifle, loaded it, stuck the barrel in her mouth and her pain was gone. It was horrible," she cried.

"I'm so sorry."

"I know who you are. You're the suicide doctor, aren't you?"

"I wanted to help your mother, but . . . "

"Doctor, she's out of pain now. I guess she just couldn't take it anymore. I'm happy," her voice cracked, "but so sad it came to this." Pritchitt was stunned. "The police have left and a cleaning crew is in her room. I can't talk anymore." The line went dead and Pritchitt sat alone; the phone dropped to his lap.

CHAPTER EIGHT

The interrogation room was quiet as Nash peered through the one way viewing window, standing between Terry and Atway. "This guy better be different than your earlier suspect," he growled walking past Bordeaux and into the room. The unkempt man squirmed nervously, playing with a pack of cigarettes and humming an irritating tune. Staring into the worn face, Nash snatched the cigarettes from his hands. "Did you kill anyone?" he asked.

"I don't know, did I?"

"You live on the street?" Bordeaux asked.

"Yeah, I'm homeless and a wino but I don't know about being a killer. That's against the Ten Commandments, if you haven't heard.

"Stealing and lying are too," Bordeaux added.

"Yeah, cop, but those are fucking small ones."

Bordeaux turned her back to the suspect. Another cigarette was lit. "He was living in an underpass, near the second body site," she told Nash. "He was bragging about the murders in his cell." She smiled at the man, who smiled back. A slight chuckle slipped from his chapped lips.

His hands trembled. "Can you get me a nip?" he asked Bordeaux. She shook her head.

Nash hovered menacingly over the suspect. "Are you someone special or just another bum jerk off the streets?" His voice was cold, his stare unflinching, following every move the man's eyes made.

"Man, I said I was a fucking wino, that's all." The suspect squirmed. Growing fear contorted his disheveled frown. "Lady cop," he yelled, looking to Bordeaux. "Give me a drink or I won't say another word."

Nash hovered menacingly a few inches away. "You scumbag. Not only are your teeth eroding from your bleeding gums and your breath that of a toilet, your vocabulary matches the filth I see under your nails and crawling your skin."

"I don't have to take this shit!" he shouted, looking around the room. He tried to stand, but Nash's firm hand dropped him back into his chair.

Bordeaux stood behind the suspect. Disbelief shook her as she nodded for Nash to back off.

"Justin, you've got him all riled up now."

"I can break the bastard," insisted Nash as Bordeaux pulled him aside.

"Give me a chance," Bordeaux pleaded.

Nash nodded, with a scowl.

"Hey, lady cop, I thought we was gonna have cameras and I was gonna be interviewed. What about TV? That's what one of your detectives promised me last night. You've double crossed me. I want a fucking lawyer."

"Well," said Bordeaux, "you've already waived your right to have an attorney present —"

"Goddamn it! I am changing my mind! That crazy ass guy over there," he glared, pointing to Nash, "wants a fucking confession mighty bad. I ain't even got a camera to talk to."

Nash rushed over. "You're crazy, man. Keep him away from me," he screamed as all looked at Nash's changing portrait.

"You like to kill girls, huh? Cameras? The only thing you're going to be interviewed for is a straight jacket," Nash threatened.

"I'm innocent, big shot. I was simply talking about the murders. I ain't never killed no one."

Nash grabbed the man's dirty shirt. "You will tell me everything you know because if you don't, you little pervert, I'll make sure you're put away for ten years on another charge."

"So now you're gonna frame me?" His voice quivered. "That's the way it always is, some poor drunk gets made the scapegoat, so you cops can get the glory."

Nash raised his fist, as if he were about to hammer the now fearful suspect. "We found traces of crack cocaine in your pockets," blurted Nash.

Terry Mercer bolted through the door. She pulled Nash to the side. "Justin, you'd better cool down. Maybe take a five minute break," Terry begged, her eyes concerned. Nash's face flushed, then he turned and left, as Atway walked to Mercer's side.

"Whew! I thought he was going to knock the shit out of that guy." Terry looked at Atway and Bordeaux with concern.

"Who in the hell is that guy?" shouted the suspect, fumbling with his cigarettes. "Are you gonna let him talk to me like that? He can't put me away, can he?"

"Say, what's your name, mister?" shouted Bordeaux, dragging a chair beside him.

"Peabody . . . Mr. Peabody."

"You want a cup of coffee?"

"Yeah."

She signaled for Atway to fetch a cup. "Weren't you going to tell me how you did the killings?" she asked pleadingly. "I'll get the cameras. You just tell me what you know."

The man bowed his head. "I . . . I was just trying to impress you. I haven't killed anyone. I . . . I . . . I'm a crack head. I went on a binge about two weeks ago. I was in rehab and slipped out of the program." He raised his head. "When most of them girls were killed I was in the city Rehab's House. Check it out, lady cop."

Atway handed Peabody a hot cup of coffee. Nash slipped back through the door. Lt. Bordeaux stood. "He's a phony." She pushed her chair away. "Atway, call the Rehab House and get the info on a man named —" She turned aside.

"What's your first name?"

"Homer."

"Homer Peabody?" she asked.

"What!" exclaimed Nash.

"Yeah," he acknowledged. "My name is Peabody but last week it was Graves. It depends on the circumstances." He leaned back in his chair, trying to find a comfortable position.

Nash pulled Lt. Bordeaux away. "We're wasting our damn time with him. He belongs in a nut house."

Nash called to Atway. "Let's go, this fellow is delusional."

"No, no, you'll be making a mistake if you leave," protested the seated man, recovering from a coughing fit. "Are you the top dog?" The man's eyes widened and he puffed anxiously between violent coughs and a raspy wheeze.

"Peabody," said Lt. Bordeaux, "please tell everyone what you told the detectives and me this morning."

Nash walked closer, staring coldly into his bloodshot eyes.

"Yeah, I killed 'em all," he said proudly. "I had sex with 'em, then dumped them in those garbage containers."

"You say you had relations with these victims?" interrupted Nash.

"Yes, sir."

"You didn't tell me that," said Lt. Bordeaux.

"I forgot," he answered apologetically.

The room quieted as eyes looked to one another.

Nash's face wrinkled with an impatient anger. "Go on, tell us more," said Nash, his fists gripped tightly as all watched.

Peabody grinned. "We men can talk about shit like this. Women don't like to talk about such stuff, do they?"

"Please, tell us more," said Terry.

Peabody's face beamed with sick excitement. "Lady, give me a light." Bordeaux lit a cigarette and placed it in his shaky hand.

"How long since your last drink, Peabody?" asked Nash.

"Too damn long."

"Tell us more and you'll get that drink," Nash assured the suspect.

"These women were killing babies, that's it. I had to knock 'em off. Gimme a drink, man."

Nash's face was tired. "I'm getting sick of this, Peabody. If you don't hurry, I'm leaving, and you're locked up — no smokes, no drinks, no nothing. I'll even tie your hands behind your back so you can't masturbate. You got me?"

"I sure do. I punished these girls, I put my juice in 'em, but no baby," he grinned, "'cause they was already dead."

Lt. Bordeaux lowered her eyes, shaking her head.

"Peabody, just how many women have you killed like this?" asked Nash.

"Maybe fifty. And you can throw in a gay guy or two, too."

Nash stood abruptly and motioned all to follow. The door of the interrogation room slammed shut.

"I've never heard such bullshit," Nash bellowed.

"It's all part of the process, Justin," Bordeaux defended.

"Wait a minute!" he shot back. "If you'd studied the autopsy reports of these victims you'd know that none were raped. This guy's a full-fledged nut. Hell, Bordeaux, he wants to be Memphis' answer to Jack the Ripper." There was a disappointing pause. "Especially you, Terry. You should know better. It was your brother's report. You should know it like the back of your hand, but you don't. Not one of the girls had a trace of semen. This Peabody guy, a serial killer? Give me a break."

"We know the report, Justin," responded Terry, indignant at his belittling attitude.

"That's the first we'd heard about having sex with the victims." added Lt. Bordeaux.

"Well, then you didn't talk to him long enough before dragging me down here on another wild goose chase. That's two, Bordeaux." He stared at both women. "Remember, the profile of a serial killer is that of a man whose intelligence is above average. They want to be found, but don't give themselves up.

End of interrogation. End of a wasted morning." Nash grabbed his briefcase and left.

"Whew!" exclaimed Atway. "That guy can sure get worked up. He's intense."

"You're right," agreed Terry. "But there's another, kinder side."

"Well, we didn't witness that this morning," said Lt. Bordeaux. Atway ran to catch up with Nash to ride back to the office. There was dead silence in the car. Atway fixed his gaze straight ahead. There was an anxious rolling of his thumbs as both hands rested nervously in his lap.

"Are you uptight about something, Atway?" Nash asked.

Atway cleared his throat. "No, sir, but I can tell when someone is in a bad mood or preoccupied may be a better description. Am I right, sir?"

"I am pissed off big time."

"Well . . . you made D.A. Mercer and Lt. Bordeaux feel about this big," Atway said. He held his thumb an inch from his index finger.

"Good."

"Mr. Nash, I think you went overboard. That guy changed stories in midstream." Realizing he had crossed a line, Atway continued, "but you also stripped that Peabody guy to his bones."

"He was scum, wasn't he?"

"Well . . . he's just nuts."

"Atway, when you've been doing this as long as I have, you can smell a fraud. Speaking of smell. Did you get a whiff of him? I mean he hasn't bathed since birth. His teeth were either gone or rotten. Ugh!" snorted Nash.

"It is a real shame to see a person disintegrate like that.

"He's crazy. He didn't disintegrate. He was cursed with insanity. Never forget that Atway. Some people are cursed, some blessed and the others, well . . . they just float along in life not really knowing." Nash turned off Union Avenue and onto a side street. "Atway, that's the classic interview technique. One person is sympathetic, the other's mean as hell. I guess I can be both," grinned Nash.

"That's for sure," agreed the young law clerk.

"I've got to run by my house for a quick clothes change. The smell of that scumbag has fouled my clothes and made me nauseous."

Atway sniffed his own shirt, then shrugged.

It was still early but Wiseman had already finished helping in his second operation of the morning. He welcomed a break as he hurried off for a cup of coffee. The fragrant aroma of freshly brewed coffee wafted down the hall. As Wiseman reached for the handle, the door exploded in his face. He stumbled backwards steadying himself against the wall. Dr. Pritchitt rushed through the doorway and down the hall. Wiseman called out without success. It must be a medical emergency, he thought and hoped it wasn't Pritchitt's wife. Wiseman walked to Patsy's desk. The secretary, unaware of his approach busily typed on her computer keyboard.

"Patsy—" She looked up. "Dr. Pritchitt passed me in the hall as if he'd seen a ghost or something. He crashed open the front door and blew by me. I'm lucky I didn't get a concussion."

Patsy lowered her head. "I'm not supposed to say anything but you'll hear about it anyway. Mrs. Caruso, a patient and precious lady, killed herself. Shot herself in the mouth."

"Oh, no," Said Wiseman, disbelief in his words.

"I saw Dr. Pritchitt pacing in his office," said Patsy. "When he's agitated he does that. Usually, he's in deep thought. That's when he told me. There's a Mrs. McCormick telephoning now. She wants to die."

"Terminally ill?" asked Wiseman.

"No," responded Patsy, "she's depressed because her husband walked out on her. It's her fourth or fifth marriage. Dr. Pritchitt advised her to seek a therapist. One of her husbands was a hospital board director, Richard Johnson."

"Wow! He's worth millions!"

"I know," said Patsy. "She was a beauty queen, years ago. My mother always said money couldn't buy happiness."

"No," mused Bernie, "but enough might rent it for the rest of your life." Patsy grinned.

"Poor Dr. Pritchitt," lamented Wiseman. "He's got everyone who wants to die calling him."

"So what would you do?" came a voice.

Standing nearby was a young woman in a crumpled suit. Her eyes were bloodshot and she smelled of alcohol.

"About what?" asked Wiseman.

"If your patient asks you to help them die, what do you do?"

"Nothing," said Dr. Wiseman. "It's illegal."

"And if the patient is your mother, what then? Is it still illegal," she asked.

"And you're —" Wiseman asked.

"Joan Caruso."

"Oh!" Patsy exclaimed.

"I'm so sorry. I understand now," said Wiseman with sympathy. "Patsy just told me of your mother's death."

"It wasn't a pretty sight." The young woman began to sob. "May I please see Dr. Pritchitt? I want to tell him what he's doing is right and God must love him for it. Please, may I talk to him?" she cried.

"He just left," said Patsy, placing her arm around Caruso. "Would you care for a cup of coffee? Why don't you come with me?" Patsy lead the woman away. Wiseman stood motionless, his thoughts confused but allegiance to Pritchitt never stronger.

At least thirty minutes had passed in the automobile, and Atway was bored by the country music station that was Nash's favorite. But he didn't dare change it. Not with the chief's unpredictable temper today, he thought. *I love my broken heart because it saved my broken life,"* crooned a singer in a nasal whine with a dozen steel guitars. Atway disliked the music, but sang along, mimicking the song just to kill time. Atway's attention shifted to the large residence. A stately home sitting in the heart of Memphis' Central Garden district. It had to be on the National Registry of Homes, he thought. It was just too elegant not to be. "He must have at least a dozen maids to clean that place," he said aloud, craning his head to see the third floor. "Born into money," he sang, "he's white and he's rich."

Justin Nash rushed down the wide front steps. "Sorry I was so long," he apologized.

"Hey, the music kept me company," smiled Atway.

"Do you like country music?"

"Uh, well, I'm trying to relate to it. Every song does tell a story, that's for sure."

"The lyrics teach us a lot about life. It's pain and depression."

"Yeah, I can relate to that."

Nash turned the music up and sped off.

"Nice home," acknowledged Atway. Ten rooms, I bet."

"No. Eighteen rooms. My grandfather built it. But it's just me and the housekeeper now."

"Yeah, I bet she's hot."

Nash smiled. "She's pushing eighty-four." They laughed.

The sky filled with gray, and from fast moving clouds a fine mist began to fall. Pritchett sped along the interstate with little concern for other drivers. The cars, nearly missed, blasted their horns as he dodged in and out of his own personal maze. He slowed, realizing his mind wasn't on the road before him. He drove for nearly forty minutes, then exited as the directions indicated. He was near Somerville when he saw the "Drive Safely" billboard, and took a sharp turn onto a crumbling road. Before him were rolling pastures filled with black and white dairy cows. A sheepdog shot out from behind a barn, barking. From the white frame house an elderly man in overalls whistled and the dog bolted for the doorstep and sat.

Dr. Pritchitt was surprised by the quiet of the countryside. There was a peace here that he'd longed for. Only the low mooing of the distant cows could be heard. The old man waved him to the home. "Maple Farm," read a hand painted sign.

Oscar Maple introduced himself, his voice hoarse and barely audible. "Doc, I can't thank you enough for coming. My wife, well . . . what can I say, she thanks God you've come, sir. Let me show you her medical file. It's in the parlor." Within was a quaint home, filled with antiques and lovely quilts. Pritchitt sat in a rocker, the sheepdog at his feet.

"That's Rusty," said the old man. "He's the smartest herd dog in Fayetteville County. A couple of years he won first prize at the fair. Something to drink, doc?" Pritchitt declined. As he petted the sheepdog, he grew easier.

"Mr. Maple —"

"Oscar," corrected the elderly man.

Pritchitt held a chart. "Says here the cancer has spread to all her bones," said Pritchitt.

Oscar sighed. Tears swelled his eyes. "Dr. Charles gives her . . . maybe six months, and that's if she's fed through a tube they want to put in her stomach.

"With the tube they'd give her enough dope to ease her pain to the point she won't know who I am. She's even got the cancer in her brain."

Pritchitt nodded. His eyes scanned the file.

"Yeah. Doc, her head hurts her so," said the elderly man, tears wetting his sun worn cheeks. He tried to speak, but for a moment, sadness choked his words and Pritchitt saw his pain. "I've been married to this old girl for some forty years and known her since she was six or seven. It's been tough, Doc. Too tough for words to say," he cried, his emotions finally caving in. Pritchitt stood and walked to his side. He placed a hand on his bent posture. The elderly man's head rose. His eyes filled with hope even in sadness. "I can't take her screaming anymore. It's back and forth to one hospital then another." His eyes begged of Pritchitt's. "You got her letter, didn't you, Doc?"

"I got it, Oscar. I need to get a few things from my car."

"Fine, Doc, and I'll go tell Martha you're here. She'll be so grateful. Her prayers will be answered."

Pritchitt returned with his suitcase in hand. "You do understand," Pritchitt cautioned. "This must never be known. I had nothing to do with this. I'm trying to help your wife, but I cannot hurt mine any more than I already have."

Oscar spoke. "God's in charge here."

He gripped the straps of his overalls and turned toward a back hall. Pritchitt lifted his suitcase and followed. "To tell you the truth, Doc, if you hadn't come soon, I was gonna take my shotgun and do what needed to be done," Oscar whispered, leading the way down a darkened hallway.

The room was dimly lit. Only a scant ray of sunshine pierced the closed shutters. An emaciated woman lay in the bed. Though only in her early sixties Martha could have passed for a hundred. Her skin was thin and bruised, barely thick enough to cover the protruding bones. "My dear Dr. Pritchitt," her voice spoke. She raised her hand a few inches from the sheet. He shook his head. Such a sweet voice coming from a cadaver, he thought. She gave him her fragile hand. "So nice to meet you. God has indeed answered my prayers," she said quietly. Her husband wet her crusted lips.

"It's my pleasure to meet you, Martha," Pritchitt sat at the side of the bed. "How are you —"

"I know you must ask but the truth is already known to you. You already know how I feel. That's why you're here. Exploding pain in every bone. The excruciating headaches that nothing, no nothing will ease. But you already know this, right? It's hard for me and harder for my beloved Oscar." She cried softly.

"Yes, I do know Martha. I really do know." She touched her withered fingers to her husbands cheeks and felt tears. Pritchitt stood and watched the last moments they'd have together.

"Oscar, you promised me that you wouldn't cry. Remember, this is the joyous occasion we've both prayed for. This is not the end but the beginning," she whispered. She moaned then grimaced in pain holding both hands to her stomach. She rolled to one side as Oscar looked to Pritchitt, then hurried a pill into her dry mouth.

"I'll step out and give you some private time," Pritchitt said, turning for the door.

"Dr. Pritchitt," she said, her voice stronger than before. "Oscar and I have already said our good-byes. It's time, Dr. Pritchitt. Time for me to go the rest of the way on my own."

Pritchitt positioned his equipment at the side of the bed. Oscar bent over, placing a soft kiss to Martha's forehead. "This shouldn't be painful in the least," Oscar reassured.

Pritchitt placed the mask to her face and adjusted the straps tightly. Oscar took her hand. The knob was turned and a humming sound filled the room. A peaceful smile was visible beneath the mask. "Thank you," she whispered.

"Peace be with you, Martha," Pritchitt said, as he turned closing the bedroom door behind them.

"Doc, she's at peace with Liza. God bless you, sir." Oscar turned and embraced Pritchitt. In a small fenced area under a large oak tree the men continued to shovel the earth. "Right next to our baby girl," Oscar lamented. Pritchitt glanced at the worn stone marker. Liza was only four years old. Martha has been waiting some thirty-five years to be with her."

"Time goes quickly, Oscar. Your day will come and they'll be waiting for you." Then, he added, "Remember, Oscar. Remember, what we agreed? Nobody must know."

The old man nodded. "Only God was here, Doc. You were never here. I'll call Dr. Charles. He'll fill out the death certificate. I told him when she went I would place her here."

Pritchitt pulled his coat over his sore shoulders. Oscar's sad face showed relief as both walked from beneath the old oak tree.

CHAPTER NINE

It had been a long day. Benjamin Pritchitt sat at his desk, reviewing cases. He made several telephone calls, conferring with patients, checking their recovery and offering referrals. Then his desk phone rang. It was Elsie Lavender.

"I'm begging you to help me," she cried.

Pritchitt paused. "My trial is a few weeks way, if you could wait?"

"No, I can't wait. I want help. Please, Dr. Pritchitt, I'm begging you." Her voice broke into tears. "Your machine, it's humane and painless. My agony is unbearable." Her pitiful voice touched Pritchitt's soul.

"Tomorrow morning . . . you'll be alone?"

"Yes."

"I have a plan. But you must help."

"I will. I'll do anything you ask, Dr. Pritchitt." He placed the phone down softly. He seemed at peace. Standing, he flipped off the desk lamp. There was a determined stride in his steps. Alone in the elevator he knew the decision was correct. I must help, he told himself.

He used the drive home to sort his many thoughts. On his arrival he was elated to find his daughter awaiting him, and the rich aroma of a savory roast.

"Come on, Dad. I've got dinner."

"Where are the children?"

"They just went to bed. Dad, you don't mind our camping here?"

"No, of course not, Terry, stay as long as you wish. I love having you here."

Terry wiped her hands on her apron. "I'm afraid of Niles. He's getting worse. He's becoming worse. The lease is up soon, so I want to get my divorce, start fresh, get a new house, everything."

Pritchitt kissed his daughter. "Great idea, sweetheart. I couldn't agree more."

"Oh, someone named Oscar telephoned. He was a very sweet old man. He said he just wanted to tell you thanks, again. He hung up before I could get a number."

"No need. He's very welcome," he answered with a nod as his eyes moistened looking away.

"What's that?" asked Terry, just noticing the folded quilt next to her father's medical bag.

"A gift from a patient." He held up the quilt which depicted colorful farm animals. "I'm going to take it to your mother."

It was nice to be home, thought Terry. After her father had dinner he retired to his bedroom, totally exhausted. He really needs someone to look after him, she told herself. He is such a giving person. But now her father was entangled in a steel web spun by the events threatening his life. She eased into the Jacuzzi, letting the churning hot water soothe her tired muscles. Her eyelids closed. Half-asleep, she stepped from the refreshing water, relaxed and calm. She reached for a towel. Seeing her reflection in the full-length mirror startled her. The turmoil of recent months had upset her to the point of avoiding heavy meals, and she had shed weight. She dried her long dark hair which she usually wore in a braid, carefully wrapped and stylish. Her hands gently tracked her breasts for any lumps.

Turning to the side, she admired her curvaceous figure, and caressed her pear-shaped hips. How horrible to be widowed, with a failed second marriage. She wanted so much to be with someone tonight, just to lay close in the darkness and feel the strength of a man who loved her. In her bedroom she stretched nude on the large bed. Nearby was a framed portrait of her late husband. She closed her eyes and he was with her, hungry for her loveliness. "Bob, I miss you so much," she cried. Slim hands cupped her breasts and her nipples became taut. Thoughts of past nights filled her mind and she recalled their lovemaking. But it was only the illusion of love. Bob was dead.

Slowing his car, Pritchitt scanned the mailboxes and numbers of the homes. His mind told him one thing, his heart another. It was a shabby neighborhood, made shabbier by the gray fall day. Comparing the number to that on the paper, he parked before the modest wood framed house. Opening the trunk, he removed the large suitcase. A note on the door instructed him to enter. Elsie Lavender lay on the sofa, carefully dressed, as if for a luncheon or church. Her makeup had been carefully applied. A Bible was in her lap. She smiled.

The living room was filled with tall shelves, stacked with hundreds of books. "You must like to read," said Pritchitt.

"Indeed I do. I was a librarian. Take a book, if you wish." The kindly face expressed admiration for him. "I'm ready, my good doctor."

She pointed to a folder on the coffee table. Pritchitt read the medical reports and was satisfied.

He knelt and removed the mask. "Thank heaven for you, Dr. Benjamin Pritchitt. Only God knows my suffering, but he has opened your heart. My bedroom smells worse than any public bathroom. I —"

Pritchitt raised his hand. "I understand. I truly understand."

"Yes, of course you do. The law has forgotten about mercy. I can tell there's a glowing warmth about your soul. I have read the Bible through and through and nowhere do I find where it says God wants us to suffer. Someone has already suffered for us on that cross." A smile brightened a pain-riddled face shrunken by her spreading cancer. She pointed to an envelope on the coffee table. "I have written this letter to the newspaper. My son mailed it this morning.

"What does it say, Mrs. Lavender?"

"It explains what you've done for people like me. It explains what I've experienced in my living hell. It exonerates you, both directly and indirectly."

"Mrs. Lavender, remember what I told you on the phone, that I cannot be present when this happens. I've been ordered not to assist nor be present at any aided deaths." He placed the large suitcase on the coffee table next to her.

"But you are assisting me."

"Yes, but that risk I will take, but I don't want to directly defy the court."

"I understand." She grimaced holding her stomach. The sweet face contorted. "Oh," she moaned. "I was up all night getting ready," she said through clenched teeth. "Please, now. The pain is unbearable." Pritchitt found the telephone. "Don't be troubled as I know you are, Dr. Pritchitt. God will take care of you and your family."

Pritchitt slipped on his latex gloves and handed her the telephone. She dialed 911, gave the address and said, "It's an emergency. This is Elsie Lavender, please send an ambulance."

Pritchitt lifted her hand, placed it on the valve and turned. She groaned in pain. Her lipstick smeared the mask, and her mouth gaped widely. The machine began to whir and hum. Pritchitt waved a good-bye and slipped the copy of the letter in his pocket.

A cascade of leaves rained, as the wind blew. Pritchitt glanced at his watch. Six minutes had passed. Then he could see the flashing lights of an ambulance coming toward him. The van slowed and sped, as the driver looked for the address.

The paramedics rushed from the ambulance and through the open front door. Mrs. Lavender was in the middle of the room. Her slumped body threatened to fall from the chair.

A neighbor ran from her home. "Did the poor thing die?" asked the woman, tabloid in hand.

"I don't know, " answered Pritchitt. The neighbor came closer, squinting to see inside the home. "She has lung cancer, you know."

"That I do know," responded Pritchitt. The woman eyed him curiously, then looked over the large automobile, with hospital stickers on the window.

"Are you a doctor," she asked.

"Yes."

"Why ain't you helping her?"

Pritchitt was silent. He looked away, toward the front door and the activity inside the house.

The woman's eyes widened. She pointed the rolled tabloid at him. "You're the suicide doctor," she gasped, recognizing his picture on the front page. She then ran inside her home.

The sound of a sputtering scooter became louder. Bernie Wiseman removed his helmet. "Doc, what the hell are you doing here? What have you done?"

"I'm attending my patient, Wiseman. What are you doing here?"

"No, don't tell me, you couldn't have, Dr. Pritchitt, you didn't? I saw the last letter you were reading before you rushed out. I was right." Wiseman glared into Pritchitt's silence. "You gave into her pleas."

"I wasn't present when it happened."

"Oh no, you were just standing in the driveway waiting for the mail. Why? Why destroy yourself? There's got to be a better way? Legislation? Divine intervention?"

"And when will that happen? If it does, won't it be too late for the likes of Mrs. Lavender and others."

The woman stared from the window, telephone in hand. Neighbors emerged from their homes, curious about the flashing lights. They began huddling on the sidewalk before the residence. Pritchitt was content.

A motorcycle roared down the street. The biker eyed Pritchitt and Wiseman, then careened his cycle toward them.

They jumped as his cycle slid into the bushes of the front yard. Bearded, with long hair, the heavy-set man staggered to his feet. He ran into the house only to hurry out the front door within seconds. On the front lawn he faced Pritchitt. A heavy link chain was in his hand. He tossed his helmet, and pointed at Pritchitt. "Did you kill my mother! I told her to stay away from you," he screamed at the top of his lungs.

"Oh shit!" Bernie blurted.

"Your mother was a patient. I was there for her, that's all," Pritchitt answered.

"You bastard!" the man screamed. He pushed past Wiseman and tackled Pritchitt onto the driveway.

The bodies rolled onto the lawn as people screamed. Wiseman momentarily froze, then reacted. He managed to snatch the chain from the biker's hand before being pushed away.

Neighbors stood in shock as the biker hammered Pritchitt's face and blood oozed from his mouth and nose. Wiseman yanked the shoulder-length hair and the man screamed. He turned to hit Wiseman. From behind Pritchitt grabbed his legs and the man toppled. Two husky paramedics rushed from the house, restraining the brawling biker. Pritchitt struggled to his feet as the wail of a police siren grew louder.

"I'll kill you," spat the man.

"You're not going to kill anyone, mister," said a paramedic.

"Now, please, just settle down," said Pritchitt, wiping his mouth with a handkerchief.

"It's just superficial," said Wiseman, examining the wound. Pritchitt nearly fell backwards. "Oh, my neck hurts like hell."

The police rushed up. "What's going on?" asked one.

"He killed my mother," shouted the man trying to free himself.

"Calm down," said the cop. "How do you know he killed your mother?"

"My neighbor, Mrs. Hill, called me at my mechanic shop. She said the suicide doctor was here."

"Is there anybody dead here?" asked another officer.

"A woman in the house," said a paramedic. "Looks like an aided suicide, all right."

"No shit," said an officer turning toward the house.

"Okay, who hit who?" asked the second officer, staring at Pritchitt.

"I did!" screamed the man. His tattooed arms struggling to free himself from the paramedics tight hold.

"Charlie, put him in the squad car and get his story. I'll talk to this other guy. And Charlie, call homicide. Tell them we've got another suicide, and I assume," he muttered, turning to Pritchitt, "the participation of Dr. Benjamin Pritchitt."

"My God," exclaimed a paramedic, that accounts for that humming machine inside."

"How'd she die?" asked the policeman.

"It looks like carbon monoxide. She had a mask on."

"Is that your machine in there? You are Dr. Benjamin Pritchitt, aren't you?"

Pritchitt identified himself.

"He wasn't present," piped in Wiseman.

"And who the hell are you?"

"Dr. Bernie Wiseman. I work with Dr. Pritchitt. I saw him outside the house when I drove up.

"Hope you didn't work with him today."

"He had nothing to do with this, officer," Pritchitt interrupted.

"I saw him standing outside," the neighbor added. "He wasn't in the house. I had just tuned in on *Tomorrow's Lives* when I heard the ambulance coming."

Chaos reigned. The street was now jumping with television vans. Reporters ran about searching for interviews.

Lt. Bordeaux was on the scene. She listened as police questioned Lavender's son. Approaching her was Justin Nash and Atway Jackson.

"Pritchitt must be insane," said Nash to Bordeaux. "The

entire D.A.'s office is in an uproar over this stunt."

"He's on a mission, that's for sure," remarked Bordeaux.

Atway was surprised to see Bernie Wiseman. He waved him over.

"What are doing here?" asked Bordeaux.

"I tried to —" Wiseman's eyes met the fierce glare of Justin Nash, he paused. "Is this an official interrogation?"

Nash jabbed Wiseman's chest. "Your boss, Pritchitt, is in trouble."

"No, you mean that guy," said Wiseman, pointing. "That long-haired, tattooed monster attacked Dr. Pritchitt. Hell, he tried to kill him."

"That's Danny Lavender," said Bordeaux. "In his mind he had cause, seeing that Pritchitt just helped kill his mother." The man's long hair shook and his tattooed arms flailed wildly. Camera lights shone on the enraged son. Curious reporters rushed to get closer as police pushed Lavender into a squad car.

Nash's face was angry. His brow wrinkled with irritation and stress looking at the media frenzy surrounding him. "What's your name? Wiseman?" Bernie nodded. "Don't mess with me, young man! You keep your naive butt out of something that can swallow it whole like this shit Pritchitt's into. Do you hear me?" Nash shouted. He turned toward Bordeaux. "Jeremy Bates is going to have him for lunch after this blatant violation of a court order."

"I know," Bordeaux agreed. "It's a damn circus. An atmosphere, as we all know, which Mr. Bates thrives in. The more cameras the better. The more witnesses to Pritchitt's funeral the greater climax for his ego-fed mind."

A voice blurted from behind. "He didn't go against the court order. It wasn't the same this time," said Wiseman.

"Oh, he didn't?" Nash asked. "That's funny, because from what I'm hearing he just killed another person and had a near death experience at the hands of that warmed over hippy."

"Bernie, I'd shut the fuck up, if I were you," Atway said.

Wiseman shook his head side to side. "The court order was for Pritchitt not to be present at the time of an aided death, and he wasn't. I'll dare say the emergency call was placed by the lady and she turned the valve herself. Pritchitt wasn't even in the house. I was standing here in the driveway with him."

Nash seemed stunned. "Bordeaux, get an official statement from him." He huffed away.

Atway's face was serious. "Bernie, you're getting in too deep in this mess."

"And what law has Pritchitt broken now, Atway?" fumed Bernie

"Question Wise-ass!" ordered Nash.

Bernie's face reddened. "Hey, my name is —"

"Calm down," said Bordeaux, grabbing Wiseman's shoulder. "I want an official statement from you."

Atway watched as Bernie Wiseman was taken to a squad car.

The sun cast long shadows as the afternoon faded. Nash was unable to concentrate as a feeling of restlessness kept gnawing at him. He ran his nervous palms through his hair and puffed a cigar. Office workers crossed the mall below, heading for home. Without notice, the office door swung open and in stormed his boss, District Attorney Jeremy Bates. Or *the little rooster*, as Nash described the balding, pot bellied Bates.

"I didn't hear you knock."

"Cut the crap, Nash. You're about to get yourself into some awfully deep trouble interfering with my case."

"Would you like a cigar?"

"You think this is real funny, don't you? Just who do you think you're dealing with, some kind of dick-head?"

Nash's secretary Jesse entered.

"Out!" ordered Bates, slamming the door in her face.

"What the hell were you doing at the scene of a suicide, and driving around with an indicted suspect?"

"Pritchitt was assaulted by Danny Lavender. I just gave him a ride home. His face was swollen and he couldn't drive —"

"Don't get friendly with that bastard."

"Jeremy," explained Nash in a tense voice, "Dr. Pritchitt is my only link to the serial killer. I don't want anything to happen to him."

"I want to know what's going on."

"I think the serial murder case is more serious than an assisted suicide conviction, don't you?"

"I know what's more important," shot back Bates.

"Important for you, but remember, Jeremy, there's no election going on right now. Am I correct, Mr. Candidate?"

"I have my duty, and I'm in charge, Nash. That's something I pray, for your sake, you never do forget." Bates walked to the door. "You remember this, I'm top dog and I'll chew a little puppy like you to pieces if you botch my case. Got it?"

"Yeah, I got it Mr. Bates."

"Then give me a report on exactly what happened today." Bates glared at Nash, a hateful look covered his face. He left the office.

Jesse poked her head inside. "The man has no manners," she said.

Nash scoffed. "Jesse, make a note for me to get a book on etiquette as a Christmas gift for good old Bates. Hell, if he wants to be a politician he better brush up on how to get along with people and influence friends."

"Yes sir," she nodded. "This fax just came in. It's addressed to you but I don't understand it." Nash looked it over.

Without lifting his eyes, he spoke with deep concern, "Get Bauers and Mercer in here, right away."

Pritchitt sat in his den, cuddling his two grandchildren.

"Papa, when is Granny Ruth coming home?" asked Benji, turning his blue eyes upward. "Soon," he smiled. The small freckled face frowned, "What happened to you, Papa?"

"Oh, it's just a few scratches from . . . trying to help someone."

"It was an accident," said Claire.

Pritchitt laughed, "It's not so bad an accident, honey. Believe me, it could have been much worse."

"The next time you wear your seat belt," said Benji.

"Right!" laughed Pritchitt.

Claire made a pouty face and sat on the floor. "I miss Granny Ruth. When is she coming home? My birthday is soon."

"Sweetheart, I miss her, too. I talked to her today. She said to give you two a big hug. She'll be home soon. She wouldn't miss your ninth birthday party, Claire."

"Then we'll be a big happy family," smiled Benji.

The words seared Pritchitt's already wounded heart. He gave them both a gentle kiss and a hug.

"Why did Mommy have to leave tonight?" asked Claire. "I'm hungry."

"Boy, you two are certainly filled with questions."

"Mommy wanted to stay and eat with us but she had a big meeting downtown."

"You know how busy a lawyer your mother is," Pritchitt smiled.

"And a busy Mommy, too," added Benji.

"Yes, but she did bring us some food to eat."

Claire pranced toward the kitchen.

"Are you in trouble, Papa? asked Benji. "Lawyers help people."

"Who told you I was in trouble?"

"I saw the television."

"Oh," sighed Pritchitt, at a loss for words. "Well, Benji, it's a-a misunderstanding. And you know what?"

"What Papa?"

"It's all going to be straightened out soon. Now let's eat."

"I'm happy now, Papa," beamed Benji.

"Well, good."

"Because," said Benji, "you won't be leaving us like Granny Ruth, Daddy, and Niles."

Pritchitt's heart sunk, realizing the deep fear of his seven-year-old grandson. He bent down. "Well, I'm right here, aren't I?"

In the kitchen Claire was standing on a stool, searching through grocery sacks on the table. The telephone rang. Pritchitt picked up the phone. It was his wife.

"Ruth, how are you feeling, dear?"

"Like anyone else who has been drugged with medicines and drained by group sessions."

"You sound so wonderful to these lonely ears. You sound like your old self again."

"I'm trying to be someone besides that terrible alcoholic." She began crying.

"You will, Ruth. I know you will."

"I still have a lot of work to do before I can come home."

"Of course, but we all miss you so much."

She was silent, as if searching her thoughts. "I saw you on TV, Ben. You're a little too old to be fighting in the streets."

"Don't worry, I'm fine, a little bruised and battered but fine."

"You were always such a good and decent man, Ben, now to hear you described as being in a street brawl. I-I-Ben, you've always been my rock."

"I will face my Maker with a clear conscience."

"I'm glad for your sake, Ben."

He carried the phone from the kitchen.

"But you do know I feel a tremendous guilt over what my family has gone through." His voice broke with emotion. "I adore you, Ruth, and want you home."

"My doctor says my depression is deepened by fear of losing you, so I drink to deaden the pain and fear."

"Ruth, I promise you won't lose me."

"Sometimes I only see darkness. I'm terrified of ending up like some of the people up here. They've lost their minds forever." She began sobbing.

"Ruth, guess who is here, missing you very much?"

He handed the telephone to Benji. "We're living here now," he said excitedly. Then came Claire. "I miss you, Granny Ruth, but I got to go because I'm hungry." Pritchitt took the telephone.

"The cook's got to go to work, Ruth."

"Please tell everyone I'm trying so hard, Ben."

"I will."

"And thank your friend, Benjamin. I think his name is

Steve, but I'm not sure. He's so very nice and his voice is so calm and reassuring on the phone."

"Steve who?"

"The same one who sent me that big fruit basket you were raving over. Remember, the big pretty basket?"

"Oh, yes. Is it Dr. Steve Crane?"

"No, that's not the name. I forget now, with all these drugs. It was scribbled on the card. He sounds like a special friend who's really concerned about you and our family. I can't remember his name. It makes me so mad. They say it's not unusual for the tranquillizers to blur my memory."

"That's right, honey. Don't worry." Delivering a gentle kiss to the receiver he lowered it slowly from his ear.

Pritchitt began sorting through the grocery sacks on the kitchen counter and what he saw raced his heart. It was the identical ornate fruit basket Ruth had in her hospital room.

"Did your Mommy buy this?" stammered Pritchitt.

"No," answered Benji. "It was on the front porch and Mommy brought it inside."

"Are you sure?"

"I saw it outside, too," offered Claire.

Pritchitt rummaged through the large basket. He had a chilling suspicion something wasn't right. Toward the bottom was an envelope. "Now we'll find out who this gracious friend is," he said to his curious grandchildren.

"Let me open it, Papa, please," implored Claire, clapping her hands.

"All right, but don't tear it." Claire proudly broke the seal, then Benji snatched it and lifted out the card. He licked his lips, then read slowly, "Best Wishes. Your Friend . . . S-S-Simon." Benji smiled broadly.

Pritchitt snatched the card. His expression was one of shock. He slowly looked up. "Did you kids eat anything from here?" They shook their heads innocently.

"What's wrong, Papa?" asked Benji. Pritchitt dropped the card on the table. The children stared, frightened frowns replacing their happy smiles.

"What's wrong, Papa?" asked Claire.

Pritchitt knelt. "Everything's fine," he assured them. "I want both of you to go in the den and watch television for a little while."

Claire reached for an apple on the table.

"No!" yelled her grandfather, taking it from her.

The little girl pouted.

"The apple is bad," he said. "Now please, kids," he pleaded, "go into the den."

Pritchitt's face paled and the confused faces of the children stared back. "I need to make a telephone call, then we'll eat," he said, calming himself.

Claire took her little brother by the hand and led him from the kitchen.

Pritchitt hurried to the telephone and dialed his wife's room. But there was no answer. His breathing raced. He searched a directory for the clinic number.

"Memorial Psychiatric Clinic," droned a woman's voice.

"This is Dr. Benjamin Pritchitt. Ruth, my wife, I-I must talk to her."

"Is she a patient, sir?"

"Of course, she's a patient, for God's sakes. I can't get her on the phone. Please get her for me."

"Her name again?"

"Pritchitt. Ruth Pritchitt. Please hurry. It's room 202."

"Sir, after 8:00 the patient phones block, so they can sleep. It is now 8:02."

"For God's sake, this is a damn emergency!" he shouted into the receiver. I'm Dr. Benjamin Pritchitt."

"Sir, you'll have to control yourself. Let me connect you with the second floor nurse's station."

Pritchitt's stomach was in knots as the phone rang and rang. Finally, there was a voice. "Second floor, Nurse Jacobs."

"This is Dr. Benjamin Pritchitt, please, please I must locate my wife. She's not in her room. I need to talk to her. It's very important, please hurry."

"Mrs. Pritchitt just left the floor with a visitor."

"What? What visitor?"

"A gentleman. Mrs. Pritchitt seemed to know him. He brought her a gift earlier and she was happy."

"A gift? Was it a basket? Who was he?"

"Sir, I don't know. They came to the desk and said they were going for a walk. He said he was going to get her some fresh air."

"You mean you just let my wife walk out of the clinic with a stranger?"

"Sir, he hardly seemed a stranger. And as of today she is allowed to see visitors."

"Please find her and call me!" shouted Pritchitt, slamming the receiver down. Perspiration formed on his forehead. He telephoned his daughter at her office. The telephone rang and rang. Frustration grew. A voice finally answered.

"This is Asst. D.A. Tim Bauers."

"Tim, this is Benjamin Pritchitt. I need to speak to my daughter. It's an emergency."

"She's in a meeting, but I'll get her."

"Please, for the love of God, hurry." The concern in Pritchitt's voice sent Bauers scurrying. The wait was interminable. Pritchitt could hear his grandchildren playing in the den as his heart pounded.

"Dad? Dad, are you there?"

"Terry, thank God. Listen, baby. I think your mother could be in great danger. You're close to the clinic. Call the police."

"What are you saying, Dad?"

"I got a card from Simon. I think your mother got the same thing. I think he's been calling her at the hospital. She left the floor with a man. God, I'm afraid."

"Dad, are you sure?"

"Yes!" he shouted. "I found a card signed Simon at the bottom of the fruit basket you brought inside. Your mother received an identical basket. The operator said she was taking a walk with a man who brought her a gift. Terry, call the police!"

With that, Terry hung up and called the police. She ran

back into Nash's office. Heads turned in a sudden hushed silence.

"What the hell is going on?" asked Nash.

"It's my mother. My father believes she's in danger. Simon sent a fruit basket to Dad, and my mother, too. For God's sake, Dad thinks Simon has taken her out of her room at the hospital."

"Call the police," blurted Nash, rising to his feet, cigar ashes falling to the floor.

"I already have," said Terry. "I've got to hurry," she mumbled grabbing for her purse.

"Wait, Terry, I'll go with you," said Bauers.

"Go on," said Nash. "I'm expecting a call but I'll get there as soon as I can."

CHAPTER TEN

An orderly passed the abandoned nurse's station. A door burst open and a rotund nurse frantically waved her hand. "Frank, check room 202 and see if Mrs. Pritchitt has returned."

"What's up?" asked the puzzled orderly.

"We can't find her."

He shrugged and strode down the hall just as two elderly and overweight security guards emerged from the elevator. Both panted as they approached the frantic nurse in the hall. One bent to catch his breath. The other ran to the nurse. "We looked in the flower garden. There ain't nobody there."

"You think somebody kidnapped her?" asked the second guard, raising his head, still gasping for a deep breath.

"Kidnapped? Holy shit!" exclaimed his partner.

"One of you watch the lobby and wait for the police," said the nurse. "They called and they're on their way."

"I need backup at Memorial Psychiatric," radioed Lt. Bordeaux, arriving at the entrance.

Terry Mercer's car raced up the circular drive. Bauers spotted the police cruiser and Terry screeched to a stop.

"Have you found her?" asked Terry breathlessly.

"I just got here," said Bordeaux, flipping a cigarette to the ground. A security guard ran outside.

"You're parked in the handicapped zone, lady," he shouted. Terry cast a disbelieving look at Bordeaux.

"Want it moved? Then, you move it," she said, throwing him the keys, as she hurried toward the front door.

"Have you found Mrs. Pritchitt?" yelled Bordeaux.

"Who's Mrs. Pritchitt?" the guard asked with a blank stare.

"That's just great!" Bauers shouted hurrying to keep up with the fast moving Bordeaux.

On the second floor nurses huddled together, then stared apprehensively at the approaching group.

The rotund head nurse stepped forward. The woman was afraid.

"We don't know where she is. Is there some kind of killer after her?"

"Killer?" queried an elderly security guard.

The nurses looked at each other. The receptionist came up. "She told me she was going for a walk with this man."

"What did he look like?" Terry begged, a frenzied look sweeping the vacant halls.

"He was a normal looking fellow. Nice looking, I'd say. He had a suit on, if that helps. He was smiling and seemed pleasant. Mrs. Pritchitt seemed very happy. At least, she looked happy."

Pritchitt recognized his daughter's parked car at the hospital entrance. In the rearview mirror he observed his grandchildren's sleepy eyes. A police cruiser with flashing lights rolled past the entrance, shining a light into the foliage beside the building. It continued down the drive with it's white light penetrating the darkness.

"Is there a fire, Papa?" asked Claire with a long yawn.

"No, but let's go inside, kids."

He seated them in the spacious marble lobby, then asked

the lobby security guard to keep an eye on them. "I'm going to find Granny Ruth. I'll be back soon, then we'll get an ice cream. All right?"

They nodded, barely lifting their tired eyes.

After he disappeared, a white haired woman escorted by a male attendant passed them. She smiled and waved. The children waved back. The woman began to skip and sing in an odd voice. She suddenly began screaming, and was led away. "I don't like it here," said Claire, near tears. "Me either," agreed her tired little brother. "Let's go back to the car, Claire." They started for the door.

"Whoa," said the security guard. "Your Dad said to wait right here and that's what you're gonna do."

"He's my grandpa," said Benji, "and we're going to his car right there." Benji pointed outside.

"Please, mister. It's spooky in here," pleaded Claire.

"All right," agreed the guard who escorted them to the car. "But you stay in the car, okay. I'll be watching you. And keep the doors locked."

"Yes, sir," Claire promised as the car door slammed.

On the second floor Pritchitt emerged from the elevator. All heads turned his way. "Terry, where's your mother?" he asked.

"We don't know, Dad. Lt. Bordeaux is leading a search inside. There are police cars outside. Hospital security is looking." She wrapped her arms around his shoulders. He clenched his fists.

"I just can't stand here. There's a madman stalking me and my family now." Terry had never seen her father so upset. His hands trembled.

Suddenly, Terry asked, "Dad, where are the kids?"

"In the lobby. There's a security guard watching them."

A full moon peeked through black clouds. The guard watched the car from the front door. His pager beeped. Glancing down he read the flashing numbers.

He ran to the car and tapped on the window.

Benji rubbed the frosted glass. "Stay right here. Don't get out of the car," he ordered looking through the fogged windows.

"I want to go home," said Claire.

"Me too," added Benji.

His beeper sounded and the guard turned. He hurried back through the front door. In the lobby he picked up a red telephone. "No. I haven't seen Mrs. Pritchitt, Joe." He cradled the telephone, casting a quick glance toward the car. "No! No stranger has passed through the lobby," he repeated.

A shadowy figure stepped from the tall bushes lining the circular drive. The dark figure wore an overcoat. Shoulders hunched, he pushed long stringy hair from his face. He wiped the moisture from the side window, and crouched. The two children inside were half asleep. He removed an envelope from a pocket of the overcoat and rapped his knuckles against the window. The children sat up and looked to the window. The figure motioned for the window to be lowered. Benji pushed the button bringing the window down a few inches.

"Don't, Benji," Claire shouted.

"Just that much," Benji said, looking to the two inch opening.

"Open the door," a raspy voice whispered.

"No way!" said Benji.

"Then come closer. I want to talk to you, Benji."

Both children edged toward the window. Their warm breath fogged the glass. They stared into the shadowed face.

"I'm a very special friend of your Papa's." He slipped the envelope through the narrow opening. "Give this to him, but wait until you get home. It's a surprise, okay?"

Claire hid her face behind her brother's shoulder. "Promise, Benji?" asked the stranger.

"How do you know my name?" asked the boy.

"I know everything," came the whispered reply.

"Bye, Claire," he said sweetly, then turned.

The guard glanced up from the telephone, observing someone at the car. He squinted. "Something strange outside. Joe, I gotta go." The guard hurried toward the car but the person was gone. He banged the window and the kids jumped.

"Are you kids all right?" asked the guard.

The door opened. "Yeah, but we want to come inside," said Benji.

"Did you talk to someone?"

"Yes, he's a friend of Papa's," smiled Claire.

"Oh," said the guard. The beeper sounded again. "Dammit!" He ran toward the front door the children at his heels.

"Gee, he was kind of scary," said Benji, dashing up the steps beside Claire.

"That man?" asked Claire.

"Yes, Papa's friend. He looked like the boogie man."

"Don't be a fraidy cat, Benji."

They ran into the lobby, relieved to be out of night's dreary darkness.

"I can't believe she could just vanish like this!" complained Pritchitt, his frustration obvious.

"Dad," said Terry calmly, "it's getting late and it might rain. I think you should take the kids home. Mom will turn up." She looked down at the floor. "Maybe she had to have a drink." Pain pierced Terry's face.

"It's possible," he agreed. "Addictions are hard to fight, especially in the loneliness of night. No. She wouldn't do that. She's with this man and I pray it's not Simon."

"I'm going to sit with the children, Dad. Please come down to the lobby and tell me if —"

"I will, Terry, I promise." Pritchitt walked to his wife's room. It was empty. He found the near-empty fruit basket. He slipped the card from the envelope. There on the card in blue ink was the signature, Simon. The rotten bastard, thought Pritchitt. Poor sweet Ruth, and she thought it said Steve. She must have been confused from those damn drugs. Why my wife? What does he want? He stepped into the hall. Far down the long corridor a woman in a white robe approached. His heart leaped.

"Ruth!" shouted Pritchitt, and he ran toward her. He held her tightly. She kissed his cheek. She was strangely calm, thought her husband. "Ruth, are you okay?" The nurses came running up.

"Of course, I'm fine, Benjamin. What's all the commotion about?

"The man you were with, Simon. Do the police have him?"

"Simon? I —"

A voice from down the hall interrupted Pritchitt's confused excitement. "Dr. Pritchitt, we have your Simon!" shouted Lt. Bordeaux. He turned and stared at Bordeaux and her prisoner.

He faced his son, Tyler Pritchitt.

"Tyler, what the —"

"Not him," said Bordeaux. A smirk lit her face. "How about this guy," she pointed. Behind Tyler stood Reverend Milton James, flustered and confused.

"Benjamin, what's this all about?" Ruth asked.

"We found both these suspects talking to your grandkids in the lobby," Bordeaux offered.

"Reverend James visited me this evening," said Ruth. And Tyler came just as we started to walk." Pritchitt shook his head.

"I'm sorry. I'm so very sorry," Pritchitt apologized.

"You didn't answer me, Benjamin. What's all this about?"

"Yeah, that's something we'd all like to know," voiced Bordeaux.

"Ruth, I received a fruit basket, just as you did from Simon. That's the name of the man who has contacted me, claiming to be this serial killer. My fruit basket came to the house today. It was just like the one you have. I called to check on you and . . . Oh, what the hell it was a big mistake and I'm terribly sorry," he mumbled lowering his eyes, obviously embarrassed. "They couldn't find you, and —"

"Benjamin, didn't I tell you that Reverend James was coming to visit me?

He shook his head.

"Oh, my dear sweet husband," she held him tightly and kissed his cheek.

The fat head nurse placed her hands on her hips. "Just where were you?" Ruth turned to answer.

"We took a short walk in the garden," answered Reverend James, "then we ran into Tyler and went to the little chapel to talk and pray."

Lt. Bordeaux frowned. "It looks like we owe you an apology, Reverend."

"No harm done. I was here to counsel and pray for both Mrs. Pritchitt and Dr. Pritchitt. I am just glad everything is all right."

"Good night everyone. I think it's time for the police to go," said Bordeaux.

"I'm sorry for the misunderstanding," said Pritchitt sheepishly.

"You should be, it upset the whole damn hospital," shot back the rotund charge nurse. The security guards pushed through.

"Did you catch 'em?"

"Did you two search the chapel?" asked Bordeaux, grabbing her cigarette away from the nurse.

"Well, he did," said one.

"Naw, I thought you did," said the other.

"Well," said the head nurse with venom, "I almost had a heart attack just thinking that one of our patients had been kidnapped or murdered. And while my nerves are breaking, she's in the chapel praying," she growled at the guards.

"We prayed for the staff," said Reverend James. He clasped his hands together. "All's well that end's well. Praise the Lord."

"Why didn't you use the elevator?" asked the nurse, glowering at Ruth.

"I hate to be seen in public in a housecoat, without makeup, without my hair styled."

The group dissolved but not before Pritchitt overheard a

comment from a nurse, "Well, what do you expect from a suicide doctor?"

Terry rushed toward Ruth, clutching the hands of her children. "Granny Ruth! Granny Ruth!" they shouted and hugged their grandmother. "

"My goodness, what are the kids doing up so late? And here of all places?"

"It's a long story, Mom. Right, Dad?"

"She was with Reverend —"

"I know, Dad."

Bordeaux looked at Pritchitt and slipped a cigarette between her lips. "I'm not going to smoke it," she fussed, pushing the nurse's hand away. "Remember, I'm a cop. Not every lead pays off."

"Thanks," said Pritchitt.

"Let me have that card from Simon." She held out her hand.

Pritchitt rushed in the room, and soon returned, carefully holding the card in a handkerchief.

Tyler leaned against the wall, his arms folded. "Better a fingerprint than an autopsy. Right, Lieutenant?

"I agree," smiled Bordeaux.

"Tyler, are you married to your work like most doctors?" asked Bordeaux.

"I'm not married to anything else, at least not yet."

"I've always wanted to see a complete autopsy," said Bordeaux mischievously.

"Well, I'd be glad to show you one sometime, Lieutenant."

"Can't think of anything more romantic, can you, Terry? Your sister has my home number," she said seriously, then waved good-bye.

Tyler admired her shapely hips, and slim physique. "She must jog a lot."

"So give her a call," smiled Terry.

"Something positive may yet come out of this nightmare after all," Terry said.

"Yeah, Dad, quite a family reunion you arranged here," laughed his son.

"I'm getting woozy, and my mouth is dry," said Ruth. "I need to take my medicine and lie down."

"We all need to go home," said Terry, who helped her mother into the room and help her prepare for bed.

"Ben. I understand now," said Ruth tearfully. "Thank you for your concern."

After the family left, Ruth lay in her bed. She stared at the window. The night's unsettling darkness brought a fearful chill to her. There is horrible evil is in this world, she thought, and closing in on her family. Simon, leave us alone! she begged. She pulled the cover under her chin. "Protect us, God," she prayed, then slipped into a troubled sleep.

The drive home was quiet with both children fast asleep in the back seat. Pritchitt could do little to rid his mind of Simon and the trouble he had created for his family. His strength was showing cracks, he thought. He wasn't as tough as he imagined. What if Simon had murdered his wife? Or poisoned his grandchildren with the fruit basket?

Terry ran ahead to open the front door of the home and Ben and Tyler each carried a sleeping child to bed. It took but a few moments for the children to be tucked in and kisses planted on each forehead. Pritchitt turned on a night light and began to gently close the door.

"Papa, don't close it all the way," said Claire.

"I thought you were asleep, my little princess."

She raised herself up in the bed.

"Leave it open so the boogie man won't get me. The boogie man is scared of the light. Did you know that, Papa?"

"You know, sweetheart. I do remember that from when I was about your age. How about this?" he asked, leaving the door open about a foot.

Benji stirred. "Papa, I almost forgot," his voice suddenly strong with emotion. With a surge of energy he sat up in bed.

"What is it?" What did you almost forget?" Benjamin asked, opening the door and switching on a small bedside lamp.

Benji jumped from the bed. "Where's my coat, Papa?" Benji's wide eyes searched the room.

"It's on the chair, Benji. I took it off before tucking you in."

"Your friend, Papa. Your friend at the hospital. He did look like the boogie man."

"What friend? What are you talking about? I think you're so tired you're confused. Now I want you to lay down and go to sleep."

"No, Papa. I heard Claire talk about the boogie man. I thought your friend looked just like him."

"Come on now, it's time to go to bed. I think you're dreaming."

"Give me my coat, Papa, please," he whined.

Pritchitt handed him the coat.

Benji yawned.

"You can barely keep your eyes open, Benji."

"Here it is, Papa." The boy removed a white envelope from the coat pocket.

Pritchitt examined the envelope under the night lamp. Horror filled him. His voice trembled.

"Who . . . who gave you this, Benji?"

"I told you, Papa. Your friend who looks like the boogie man."

"I don't have a friend like that," said Pritchitt.

"We were in the car, Papa, and your friend with long hair came to talk to us. His voice was funny, but he was nice. He knew my name, Papa, and said you were like his brother. But I only opened the window a little bit because he was scary."

Pritchitt's heart raced.

Benji returned to his bed. "He said it was a surprise," Benji yawned, laying his head against the pillow. Benji looked into his Papa's face. "Don't be mad."

"No, I'm not mad. I . . . I just thank God you're okay. Now go to bed. And Benji, thank you."

"Night, Papa."

Walking down the long hall Pritchitt held the envelope tightly in his sweaty palms. His mind sped with the terrifying thought of Simon being so close to his grandchildren.

"Dad, can I fix you a drink?" asked Tyler from the den.

Deep in thought, Pritchitt sat in his favorite chair before the fireplace.

"Dad, you look exhausted," said Terry.

"Terry, would you bring me my medical bag?"

"What?"

"It's in my bedroom."

"I'll get it," said Tyler, glancing nervously at his sister.

Benjamin placed the letter on the table beside him, then polished his reading glasses.

"It's kind of late for patient work, isn't it?" remarked Terry, perplexed by his odd request. Tyler arrived with the medical bag.

"Hand me a pair of examination gloves."

"Dad, what the hell?"

"Please, Tyler."

Pritchitt donned his glasses, then the latex gloves.

"Tyler, what happened to my drink?" Pritchitt's head remained bowed, his eyes not moving from the letter he held.

Tyler sat on a small footstool, speaking to his father, waving the drink, vainly trying to get his attention. Finally, he placed the drink on the table next to his father.

Benjamin finally looked up. His eyes were filled with fear.

"You are scaring the hell out of us. What is it?" cried Terry.

He drained the glass. "It's . . . it's from him," Pritchitt stammered.

"Who?" Tyler asked.

"Simon," answered his father.

Pritchitt picked up the letter and placed it on the table. He stripped off his gloves and wiped his wet brow. Terry fell on her knees and scanned the letter.

"That's from the serial killer, you say?" asked Tyler.

"Yes," nodded Pritchitt, "he goes by the name of . . . Simon."

"The rotten scumbag," Terry angrily cursed.

"My exact sentiments, and much more," said Pritchitt.

Tyler stepped to the bar for another drink. "Remember, I'm practicing medicine, not playing detective like the two of you. So, if the two of you wouldn't mind, fill me in."

"Refill, please, sir," Benjamin growled. "Tyler, this monster, Simon, is a . . . a . . . fiend. He is the person we believe is killing these young girls whose autopsies you're performing." Pritchitt downed his drink.

Pritchitt stared into his glass. "The faxes are crazy, but I can deal with that." He took a drink. "But what I can't deal with is tonight. Simon hand-delivered this letter to Benji in the parking lot of the hospital."

Terry's face showed shock. Her mind was suddenly a prisoner of Simon's madness. "Tonight? You mean this maniac killer just walked up to Benji and handed him this letter?"

"My God, what are you saying?" asked a shocked Tyler.

Pritchitt raised his hands. "I left them in the lobby with a security guard, but they went to the car, and that's when Simon came."

"For the love of all that's holy, Dad, my children!" Terry broke her silence.

"Terry, I'm so sorry. I thought they'd be safe —"

"I want to see this guy burn," she said bitterly.

Tyler reached for the phone. "Let's call the police."

"Put the phone down, son."

"Why? This madman is watching our family. Something bad is going to happen if we don't do something and do it now."

"I knew in my bones that Simon was at that hospital tonight," said their father.

"The police will want to question the children," added Terry. "That low life son of a bitch getting that close to my kids. That madman is a dead man!" she raged. "I may have to kill him myself!"

Tyler paced the room, his hands in his pockets. "Why you, Dad? Why is he communicating with you?"

"Because for some insane reason he thinks we're bonded by fate. Parallel lives, parallel deaths, something like that. He says we're both killing. We're bonded by God."

Tyler listened in disbelief. "Fate? God? How bizarre."

"He believes his killings are preventing these girls from murdering more of God's unborn. In his demented mind he sees me as some kind of angel of death. He believes I've been predestined to aid in his suicide when his mission is finished."

"That's the craziest damn thing I've ever heard," expressed Tyler.

Pritchitt rested his empty glass on the bar and turned. "And who said it wasn't. What he wants is an answer by morning." Pritchitt poured another shot. "The letter speaks of insurance, for assurance that I'll cooperate."

"What the hell does that mean?"

"That, my dear daughter, I have no idea," mumbled Pritchitt. "And something tells me I really don't want to know."

There was a pause as each stood quietly. A silence that seem to beckon for one of them to say this was all a bad dream and they'd wake up soon.

Pritchitt looked to Terry. "How are you doing with your problems?"

"I can't believe you're asking me this, Dad. I mean with everything else crumbling down around us and you're asking me about a man I'm divorcing." Frustration blended Terry's astonished frown. "Niles is crazy. He's mixed up with that Rev. Milton James. They're protesting every day. Anything else?"

"I'm sorry if I upset you," said Pritchitt.

"Dad, it's late. You have to surrender yourself at the police station by 9:00 a.m. tomorrow," reminded Terry.

"For Mrs. Lavender's death?" asked Tyler.

"Yes," said Terry, "I'm afraid Dad's going to be Jeremy Bates' ticket to Washington. He's going to milk this for all the publicity he can."

The hour was growing late but the ballroom of the Peabody Hotel was packed with an attentive audience. Justin Nash concluded his speech. Nash took his seat behind the podium. The speaker cleared his throat, and gripped the microphone. "All of you have truly made our Unity Charity banquet a tremendous success." The audience stood and clapped enthusiastically.

Nash hurried from the stage. He edged his way through the throng of well-wishers. He was intent on a quick escape. He excused himself from an elegantly dressed couple and pushed open a side exit door. He breathed the crisp air of autumn and searched for his keys.

"Justin Nash," called a voice from behind.

He turned reluctantly.

"Justin, how are you? It's been what — seven years?" An attractive woman in her mid-thirties extended her hand. He grasped the hand hesitantly. "It's Blanche Tucker," she reminded.

"Blanche! Yes, it's been that long," he stammered.

"I'm Dr. Blanche Tucker now. I finished medical school and here I am, a practicing psychiatrist."

"Well, congratulations." Nash pulled his hand from her tight clasp. "Listen, Blanche," he said, glancing at his watch, "I'd like to talk, but I'm really in a big hurry."

She smiled coyly. "A hot date, I bet."

"You know attorneys. We always have to prepare for the next day in court. Let's make it another time. It's good to see you're doing well. Gotta go. Bye."

"All right, I'll call you," she shouted, as he hurried off.

A reporter approached Nash in the parking lot. "Making any progress with the serial murders?"

Nash paused. He carefully chose his words. "I won't rest until Simon is resting for good. I promise that."

The room was dark. Dim light from the outer hall trickled inside as the long shadow of Simon spread against the wall. The dragging sound of a chair being pulled over a wooden floor trailed him across the room. The long hair was unkempt and rested upon sloped shoulders covered by a long overcoat.

He tapped the typewriter keys and hummed a strange song. Then the typing was complete and he stood.

He walked down a dark passage to another door.

Hundreds of candles flickered within. He lowered his head onto a small casket and placed his lips against the cool metal. On a small table, lit by candles, were two framed pictures. "I love you both," cried a soft voice. Each picture was kissed, then returned to the table with care. He stood before the small casket. Bowing his head, a prayer was said. The casket was opened. From within he took a doll which resembled a newborn baby. He cradled the doll, gently rocking back and forth.

"I'll be with you soon, my sweet child. I love you so." The doll's face was kissed, then returned to the small casket. The lid was closed. Like an animal in the wild Simon howled. A blood-curdling scream followed. The flickering candles cast a long shadow as Simon departed.

CHAPTER ELEVEN

A full moon brightened the cloudless sky of the late night. The Women's Clinic was busy as usual. It was one of two clinics open twenty-four hours. Both provided prenatal care, as well as abortions, performed late at night. The air was frosty. Leaves flirting with the wind were the only movement on the street. A security guard stood at the steps of the front entrance of the clinic.

A young woman emerged and was escorted to the parking lot by the guard. She drove along Hudson Street, until she stopped at a traffic signal, then a strange moan caught the woman's ear. She glanced in her rear view mirror and saw the predatory eyes. Before she could utter a word a plastic bag covered her head. She slumped down into the seat. Her struggle to free herself was without success. Her strength was sapped against her stronger attacker. Screams were blunted by the plastic and her breath was without air. Only plastic made its way deeper with each gasping effort. The swallowed plastic worked its way down her spasming throat. Seconds passed. Her effort stopped. Her body went limp and with a final retch vomit filled the plastic bag. The long haired figure was still in the back seat. Strong hands released their consuming grip of the plastic bag. The lifeless body was pushed to the side. The man with the long hair sat behind the wheel, breathing heavily. Simon had another victim.

It was a typical day at the West Precinct. Burglars, dope pushers, carjackers, prostitutes, gang thugs and wife beaters were processed in an endless stream. It was a human zoo, with free admission for the right crime. Lt. Bordeaux poured her third cup of coffee and lit a cigarette.

Nicotine and caffeine were her only true vices. Bordeaux had been married for two years to the day, when her husband, who was a damn good cop, died in a freak accident. They were on vacation in Colorado, riding their bikes on a country road, when a truck spun out of control. It missed her but Mike, her husband, went over a cliff. He died of a broken neck. She became a cop after Mike's death, it was her way of staying close to him.

Terry and fellow Assistant District Attorney Tim Bauers arrived at the same time. Terry took off her coat, filled a mug with coffee for herself, offered another to Bauers. Her mind drifted to the events of the previous night.

The door blasted open and Justin Nash stormed inside.

"I'd have been here about twenty damn minutes ago if you had better parking around this old building." He threw his coat on a chair. Nash's jarring presence broke the tranquillity of the office. The day has officially begun, Terry told herself.

Nash's disgruntled voice barked. "Now Lt. Bordeaux, if I could have a cup of what you're drinking. Maybe it will take a pot for me to be happy about this emergency meeting."

Bordeaux handed him a cup of coffee.

"I realize this cuts into your breakfast time but I thought it best to get it over with."

"The meeting I don't mind, it's the timing of it. Can't you be normal and jog through the streets like every other health freak out there this time of day," he grumbled. Nash sipped his coffee, then wiped his lips with distaste. "Damn, who made this crap?"

"Justin, it's early for everyone and we're all cranky," said Lori, "but let's remember we've got a long day ahead of us."

He shot her a haughty stare, then sat down. "All right, start the meeting," he said.

"We've been tracking some fringe groups," explained Bordeaux.

"And?" asked Nash.

"We've got a profile of fanatics and will start surveillance soon. And, we do know this, Simon's not using the library fax machines anymore, because our plants are watching very closely."

"Or, lieutenant," suggested Bauers, "your people have just missed him."

"No, we've determined he's using a portable fax and tapping into telephone lines."

"Now that's something new," said Terry.

"This guy is smart," offered Bauers. "He knows we can't watch every phone in Memphis."

The door opened. A beefy detective charged through. "He got another one. Here's the report."

Bordeaux grabbed the sheet.

"They found her down at Morris Park."

"Just up this street?" asked Bauers' incredulous voice.

"Early this morning. Some winos looking for cans found the body. A young girl, a plastic bag was used."

"Oh, my God," said Terry.

"It's pretty gruesome." The detective's voice was grave. "She was stuffed in a garbage container like the rest, but this time there was something different." He paused and looked down.

"Spit it out," Bordeaux prompted impatiently.

"Her female organs were ripped out."

Disbelief swept the room. "It's Simon," said Bordeaux. "Now he's performing abortions himself," she sickly mumbled in the quiet of hushed silence.

In the courthouse lobby Terry paced near the entrance,

occasionally glancing outside. The media was beginning to gather. Bates' underlings had whipped the media into a frenzy. This story was big news regionally and Jeremy Bates was trying to make it big news nationally.

Outside the building swarming television crews had attracted more than a gallery of curious onlookers.

Local stations had been fed information. Jeremy Bates had arranged a press conference earlier that day, stressing points he thought would endear him in the public eye.

Jeremy Bates strode up the court steps, surrounded by cameras and reporters. "I cannot comment," Bates kept repeating. At the top of the stairs, he suddenly stopped and lifted a file. "I will say this. I work for the state of Tennessee and the people of Memphis. I am sworn to uphold the law. My team has prepared a case that will show every citizen that no one is above the law. And absolutely no one can play God."

"Who will represent the people's case in court," yelled out a reporter. "That sacred duty falls squarely on my shoulders," answered Bates. "It is an obligation I accept." Other questions came fast but Bates slipped through the large doors and the media dispersed to the street below.

The crowd's murmur grew into strong excitement. The crowd surged as the media teams ran to a near parking lot. A swarm of cameras circled Pritchitt and his attorney Todd Bohannon, as well as hundreds of gawkers, as they got out of the car. Placards suddenly shot in the air and cameras turned. "Suicide is against God's law," read one. "Dr. Pritchitt understands," read another.

A chant of recited prayers emerged from a knot of protesters. Reverend Jenkins, a well-known fundamentalist preacher, spoke into a mike. "We must suffer in this world, to prepare for the next life," he preached in a deep solemn voice.

"Through pain comes understanding. Understanding of Jesus' sacrifice." His voice rose to an oratorical pitch. "On the cross Christ suffered for us to open the gates of heaven. Gates open to the chariots of all Christians." His finger tapped his chest. "We are sinners, we must purge ourselves of evil." He turned to the camera with a look of satisfaction. "Those who die by their own hand will be cast into hell, for they have destroyed the temple which God on high created."

Pritchitt pushed through the crowd and toward the preacher. "I disagree, Reverend."

Todd Bohannon grabbed his client's arm. "Benjamin, don't do this," Bohannon implored as the crowd pushed and shouted. But Pritchitt shook loose and confronted Reverend Jenkins as the cameras pushed closer.

"You must repent," Dr. Pritchitt. "Satan has captured your mind."

"No, you are wrong. Compassion for those in pain has captured my heart."

Jenkins shook his head. "Thou shalt not kill!" boomed Jenkins.

"Are there exceptions, Rev. Jenkins?"

"No! There are no exceptions, Dr. Pritchitt." The throng of people grew around Pritchitt as Bohannon continued to plead with his stubborn client. The aggressiveness of the crowd mushroomed as police fought hard to keep them back from Pritchitt. Momentarily confounded, Rev. Jenkins grew silent. "Don't try to muddy the issue, Dr. Pritchitt, what you are doing is assisted suicide. It is immoral and illegal. You are killing those who are confused, who have abandoned God's comfort."

"I don't kill anyone," said Pritchitt. "I end their pain."

Applause erupted. "You're a good man, doctor," shouted a white-haired woman, Bible in hand.

The crowd closed in upon Pritchitt and Bohannon. The pair pushed their way toward the steep court steps as a heated debate sparked behind them. The crowd grew angry.

Terry Mercer elbowed through the frenzied crowd toward her father.

"Nice reception, Dad?" she shouted pushing a hand away from her face.

"Nice of you to meet me, baby," he shouted over the continued prodding of Bohannon to keep moving. The assault of swarming cameras and microphones focused on her.

"Mrs. Mercer, do you have a comment?" shouted a familiar voice. Terry stared into the face of reporter Dorothy Cohen. She shook her head and lowered her eyes.

"You're his daughter and an assistant D.A. What's your opinion?" shouted Cohen.

"Dr. Bastard! Dr. Murderer!" yelled an angry voice. A voice whose tone stood apart from the hundreds of others heard.

"Everybody move back!" a policeman ordered. With a long baton he pushed the crowd away from Pritchitt. A narrow path was made as Pritchitt climbed the steps. An enormous stone figure of justice, depicted as a blindfolded woman, towered at the end.

"We're almost there, Benjamin," assured a relieved Todd Bohannon with an exhausted sigh. Police held the pressing throng away from them. From behind the large statue a burly man emerged. He screamed and it was his voice that stood out and above all others.

"You bastard, do you remember me, Dr. Pritchitt. Or should I call you Dr. Death?" came the angry voice of Danny Lavender, his scowl framed by long and unkept hair. Tattooed biceps crossed his chain laden chest. Terry held tightly to her fathers arm. Pritchitt stared into a face filled with hate. Urgency swept Pritchitt's thoughts as he moved quickly toward his daughter. Comforted by her smile, he ignored the menacing tattooed figure.

"Get out of the way!" shouted Bohannon.

Pritchitt heard a smack, then a groan of pain. As he turned he saw Bohannon careening through the air, rolling down the steps. Then a large hand slapped against his face. A stranglehold to his neck left him gasping for air.

"No!" screamed Terry, gripping Lavender's powerful hands. Terry screamed for the police but all were battling the encroaching mob. Pritchitt's vision blurred as muscular hands squeezed his throat tightly. Lavender smiled fiendishly and squeezed tighter. Pritchitt felt a gun muzzle placed against his temple.

"Lie down!" Lavender shouted at Terry. She backed away and down the steps.

Lt. Bordeaux pushed her way through. She stopped cold, seeing the gun.

"Get back down those steps!" screamed Lavender. Bordeaux motioned the police to retreat and she did the same. Lavender raised his gun over his head. One shot dispersed the crowd. Panic reigned. People were knocked to the ground and others run over to escape danger.

"Now you know who the fuck I am, don't you? You murdering bastard!" Another shot forced Pritchitt's head back. The bullet ricocheted against the precinct building and echoed throughout a nearby plaza. People ran and screamed as hysteria grew. "You killed the only person who ever loved me," cried out Lavender. Quiet prevailed as the retreat was complete and all froze with anxious anticipation. Terry slowly advanced up the steps. He swivelled the gun toward her head a few feet away. "You want some of me, lady? Is that why you're trying to get close to me?" he screamed, wiggling his protruding tongue back and forth through an open mouth. "I'll give you everything you want and then some, baby, but I need to finish my business here, if you know what I mean," he shouted. He pressed the barrel of the gun tightly to Pritchitt's cheek.

Her advance halted; Terry backed down the steps. Lavender's fierce glare scanned the distant crowd of police who held drawn guns. "Now you'll see what it's like to die, Dr. Death."

"Please, don't —" pleaded Pritchitt.

Lavender's face was depraved. His eyes were aflame. He pointed the barrel at Pritchitt's temple. "You scared now, Dr. Benjamin Pritchitt? I know that's your good looking daughter, Doc, maybe I should shoot her instead of you," Lavender shouted, pointing the gun at Terry. He clicked the chamber at Pritchitt's ear.

"Please, don't hurt her," begged Pritchitt.

Lavender snorted. "If I kill her, then you'll know what it's like to lose a loved one."

"Please, do anything with me, but leave her alone."

"I'm not gonna hurt her, Doc. I just feel sorry for her because she's gonna know what's it's like to lose a parent. I only had one." He began sobbing.

"Please, your mother wanted me to help," said Pritchitt.

"Bring me the TV people!" shouted Lavender. "Or I'll kill them both!"

Lt. Bordeaux walked forward taking each step slowly.

"Stop!" shouted Lavender.

Bordeaux froze. "Let them go before this goes much farther than you want it to."

"Oh, and how far is that, lady cop? I told you what to do!" he screamed. "Get me some damn reporters. I want TV and radio coverage and I want it now!"

Lt. Bordeaux backed off. She waved to the surrounding officers to get what he wanted. Frightened cameramen and reporters were summoned and hovered close to accompanying police officers.

"All right! Good!" shouted Lavender. "Now I'm gonna show the world what true justice is."

Pritchitt turned his head toward Lavender. The gun pressing hard against his jaw. "About your mother. I don't think you really knew how sick she was."

"Shut the fuck up."

"She wrote to me, explaining that her only son loved her but that you didn't understand the deep pain she felt. She prayed for me to help her."

"You just shut the fuck up, you hear me! I'm tired of your bullshit," he screamed, banging the gun against Pritchitt's head. "Get those cameramen up here or I'm gonna spill his brains on the sidewalk, now!"

The few bold reporters who braved the first shot had run for cover with the second round. Lt. Bordeaux waved them to the bottom of the steps. Behind them was a line of flashing blue lights from cruisers with police crouched and weapons drawn.

Lavender's gun again pointed skyward and there was another booming shot. "Everybody listen! Pritchitt killed my mother and he will pay right now. If the cameramen ain't up here closer in ten seconds, he dies now."

One man lugged a huge camera up the stairs. It was Justin Nash. He lowered the camera. "Son, why don't you put that gun down and let the doctor go?" he said in a calming voice.

Terry stood as Nash took a few more steps. Step by step he closed in on the rage holding Pritchitt at the brink of death.

"You better stop right there, mister," Lavender said angrily. "Get that camera rolling or I'll kill you, too."

"And why is that?" Nash asked calmly, stopping on the steps below.

"Because I got the damn gun, butthole," shot back Lavender, growing furious. "And because my mother was all I had in this shit-eating world, and I want Pritchitt to die right now!"

Nash raised the video camera to his shoulder. "You've had a horrible experience. You need to think of what you're doing," he said, with no trace of panic in his voice.

"No, no, no," Lavender moaned, his eyes wet and red. A frightening scream filled the air. "Mamma!"

"Son," yelled Nash, "at least your mother had a chance to make her own choice, that's more than you're giving Dr. Pritchitt."

"I want to speak to the man in charge, you know that Bates guy, who's always on TV, always talking about how he's gonna put this man away! And now my mother's dead! Where is he?"

"Somebody get Bates," shouted Nash, turning his head toward the street.

"I'm here," came a voice from behind the long line of police cars. Bates walked slowly between the armed officers. Even more slowly he approached the steps.

"Start filming!" screamed Lavender. Nash raised the video camera.

Bates nervously swallowed, then lifted his palms upwards. "Let's end this peacefully," he pleaded. Fear struck Bates' face and his fractured sentences showed anything but calm. Lavender shook his head in disgust.

"Tell me, tell me, Mr. Big Shot Bates, is it true this man will get the death penalty for what he done to my mamma?"

There was a longer than desired pause as all heads turned to Bates, then back at Lavender and Pritchitt's hollow face. "I don't want to mislead you, sir," Bates began.

"Cut that lawyer shit," spat Lavender. "And I ain't no 'sir.' Just tell me what your justice is gonna do to this man."

"N-No, he won't die," stuttered Bates, finding it more difficult to hold his composure. "He will serve jail time."

"That's bullshit!" screamed Lavender. He pushed Pritchitt to his knees. The gun barrel now resting firmly at the base of his skull.

"You really don't want to do this," said Bates. "You've had a horrible experience."

"Let the doctor go," Nash pleaded. The quiet was deafening. Stunned silence swept the more than 100 people crowded within a 200-foot radius. No wind. No background of busy traffic heard. Even the air seemed absent as Nash took a deep breath and stepped closer, still aiming the camera.

"Fuck you man! Fuck all of you!" Lavender cried out. He flashed a strange smile and his head began to sway back and forth. He began to hum a gospel tune. He pulled Pritchitt to his feet.

"Killing me isn't going to do anything but ruin your life. Your mother wouldn't want this. She loved you," Pritchitt gasped, choking for breath beneath the strangling grip around his throat.

"That fucking did it. I didn't ask you to talk." Lavender turned Pritchitt's head forcing the barrel of the gun into his mouth. Pritchitt gagged, the end of the barrel pressing the back of his throat. Nash took hurried steps toward Lavender. Terry turned her head in fear. "Stop right there or I'll pull this little trigger and make a big fucking hole in the back of his head." Lavender laughed. Nash stood paralyzed by the insanity of Lavenders eyes. "I want you to get this on camera," Lavender screamed madly, "closer, closer!"

"Tell us about your mother," Nash said, advancing slowly, camera in hand.

"I loved her," said Lavender. "She was a librarian who tried to help people." He removed the gun from Pritchitt's mouth and stepped toward the camera. He pointed to his forearm. "See?" There was a tattoo of a heart encircling *Mom.*

"Nice!" said Nash. "What else have you got?"

He began unbuttoning his shirt. "Look what's on my back" he said proudly. He threw his shirt down and smiled at Terry who crouched onto the ground in a terror stricken pose. Lavender turned, about to remove his undershirt when his head jolted upwards. He cocked the pistol aiming it at Pritchitt's left ear. A foul grin spread across his face. He looked to the sky and nodded spastically. "It's time, Doc. Say good-bye." Pritchitt's eyes closed in painful squints. Two deafening blasts roared through the crowd. Lavender's head exploded. Blood sprayed onto Nash's camera and the side of Pritchitt's face. Shocked silence followed the echoing shots.

Lt. Bordeaux stood steadfast, crouched beside the statue of Justice. Steady hands clung tightly to her gun. White smoke covered a vacant stare — powder burns on her sweaty hands.

Lavender's body slumped, then tumbled down the steps. His head now framed by a pool of blood. His long hair now dark red. Pritchitt dropped to his knees gasping for air. Policemen swarmed the steps. Cameras zoomed in for close-ups and reporters, now struck with a sense of bravery, talked with excitement into microphones. Panic swept the crowd. People moved about in a frantic state. Screams were heard.

Pritchitt rose with an unsteady gait. Terry was retched in agony. Hysterical and too weak to stand, her knees pressing tightly against the steps. Her crying drowned by the growing cries of the frenzied mob. Pritchitt knelt over her, both spattered in blood. "It's all over, baby." He caressed his weeping daughter and helped her to an unsteady stance.

"I'm all right," she cried, as Todd Bohannon grabbed her arm.

"Let's get the hell inside!" shouted Bohannon.

"This is a madhouse," said a reporter for Channel 8 as he snatched the camera from Nash. "Great job!" he said excitedly, wiping the lens and camera clean of blood. "We're already on cable."

"You mean you broadcast this live?" asked Nash with surprise.

"Sure," nodded the cameraman. "And I thought we were finished when one of our reporters got hit. One of his shots ricocheted off a building and hit Dorothy in the arm. They rushed her to the hospital. Boy, is she gonna be pissed she missed this. I mean, live on Cable News!"

Jeremy Bates removed his blood-stained suit jacket, then stepped to the body of Danny Lavender. He pulled up the undershirt which revealed an elaborate tattoo of a home. Within the house was a woman, child and dog. It read: *Mommy, Danny, Skippy.*

Lt. Bordeaux stood near the line of squad cars, as colleagues looked on. Flashing lights cast a blue haze over the depressing scene. There were supportive pats and quiet words of admiration. "This is her first kill," said a police sergeant. The sergeant walked over and, as policy demanded, Bordeaux handed over her gun.

"You did a fine job, Lt. Bordeaux," said the sergeant. Bordeaux dropped her head. She felt an emptiness in her soul. But she had done her duty.

The after shock of the courthouse scene was chaotic. A helicopter circled above and the media scurried in search of Pritchitt who had disappeared. In the courthouse lobby a throng of city clerks, secretaries, dismissed jurors and plain gawkers stared in awe. The near victim followed his lawyer, with Terry in his grasp into an empty office. Bohannon closed the door. No words were needed. Anguish and relief were Pritchitt's twin emotions.

A small television broke the silence. It was a live news report from the front of the courthouse building. Jeremy Bates stood next to a reporter.

"This is Cathy Williams, speaking live from the steps of the courthouse where this horrible tragedy has occurred. A tragedy that, if only for a moment, sped the hearts of all who watched. With me is Dist. Atty. Jeremy Bates. Sir, I know you've been through an unbelievable nightmare, but would you please comment?" asked the reporter.

"Yes. This is something no one should ever have to endure. A tragedy that brings no happiness to the people of Memphis and the fine state of Tennessee. This is what happens when a horrible chain of events is triggered by those who ignore the law."

Pritchitt stared at the portable television, his drained emotions now simmering in anger. "This poor boy's mother was dying, true. But suicide is not the answer. Nor is it legal for anyone to aid in a suicide. Danny Lavender just snapped. And now he's dead. Now a whole family is dead, mother and son."

"It could have been me and my daughter!" shouted Pritchitt. "So Bates is trying to make Lavender the victim? Is this what I'm hearing? This man's response to his mother's suicide was to kill me. I've had family members praise me for understanding, for easing their burden —"

"Ben, Ben, calm down," urged Bohannon. "Please sit down. We're not in court yet."

"Surely, your court hearing is canceled," said Terry.

"Well, my day is over," came a loud voice from outside the room. The door opened and a judge robed in black entered. He stood looking at his three visitors. "Well, well," he said, unbuttoning his robe.

"Judge Davis," said Bohannon, standing.

"Yes, Mr. Bohannon. Quite a morning, wouldn't you say? And Dr. Pritchitt and Asst. Dist. Atty. Mercer? You both look like hell. You don't look much better, Bohannon," said Davis, hanging his robe on the door. "Everything came to a stop when the hostage situation unfolded outside. I'm so sorry you had to suffer that experience."

"This is a private exit," offered the judge, pointing to a side door. "You may be able to avoid some cameras that way."

"Thank you, Judge Davis. Thank you very much, sir," Pritchitt smiled and extended his hand.

"No. Thank you, Dr. Pritchitt. Thank you for understanding the pain my wife and others like her have had to endure before dying. God bless you. And, Dr. Pritchitt, good luck."

The television screen came alive with a rebroadcast of the hostage crisis. Pritchitt and Terry watched in horror, reliving their terrifying experience with Danny Lavender.

"He looks even crazier than he did standing next to him," Terry mumbled, staring at the tape of Lavender holding a gun to her father's head.

Bohannon led Pritchitt and Terry out the side door, down a private stairway where they entered the marble lobby. Justin Nash spotted them.

"Thanks for helping," said Terry.

"Yes, thank you," added her father.

Nash gripped Pritchitt's hand. "You've got an admirer in me, sir. I can't support you publicly, but eventually minds will change."

"Nash! Asst. D. A. Mercer, just where are you two going? came the obtrusive voice of Dist. Atty. Jeremy Bates as he raced across the lobby toward them. "May I be so bold as to ask just where you are going with the accused?" Bates demanded, walking into Nash's face.

Bohannon stepped between them. "Surely, you'll allow rescheduling of the hearing?"

"Nope," said Bates cockily, "we're all expected right now in Judge Winston's courtroom."

Bohannon squinted. "My client has just undergone a terrible ordeal."

"Todd, please," interrupted Pritchitt, "let's just get this over with. I've already been to hell and back."

The sparsely occupied courtroom rose as Judge Winston entered. Pritchitt removed his blood-flecked coat and eased into the wooden chair next to his attorney. Jeremy Bates straightened his tie and stood. "In direct violation of your court order not to participate or be present at any aided suicides, Dr. Benjamin Pritchitt purposely and willfully ignored the court's instructions and assisted in the death of Elsie Lavender." Bates turned and pointed. "Bail should be revoked and Dr. Pritchitt should be immediately incarcerated."

Todd Bohannon stood. "Mrs. Lavender took her own life," asserted Bohannon, stroking his beard.

"How did she die?" asked Judge Winston.

"Carbon monoxide poisoning," answered Bohannon. "It's in the death report, your honor."

"Counsel, I've read the report. It seems your client operated the machine?"

"That's absolutely true," gloated Bates.

"That is incorrect, your honor."

"What?" shot back Bates.

Bohannon opened his briefcase. "This is a canceled check, sent to Dr. Pritchitt by Elsie Lavender." Bohannon waved the check. "Mrs. Lavender bought the machine in question."

"Approach the bench," frowned Judge Winston. He motioned for Bates to also come forward. Bohannon dramatically presented the document to the judge, as Bates glared. A murmur swept the courtroom. "Silence!" gavelled the judge.

The attorneys returned to their tables. Bates rose.

"Your honor, the people acknowledge Mrs. Lavender bought the machine, but its design is for one purpose, to poison the lungs with a lethal gas."

Bohannon spoke. "That is quite true. However, it was the legal property of Mrs. Lavender. An automobile may be used in a suicide or a knife or a gun. My client did construct the machine, to end pain, but he sold it."

Bates sprang to his feet. "What we hear is clever equivocating. Dr. Pritchitt was present when Mrs. Lavender died."

"Incorrect," responded Bohannon. "Mrs. Lavender called Dr. Pritchitt as a prospective patient. He conferred with her in a sympathetic manner. But she committed suicide. Her fingerprints alone are on the mask, valve and telephone. Dr. Pritchitt was outside, on the sidewalk, as witnessed by a neighbor. To construct a machine to end pain is not illegal nor is it illegal to counsel those considering suicide. There was no direct participation by Dr. Pritchitt whatsoever."

Judge Winston was silent for a long time, then he spoke. "The request to revoke bail is denied." He removed his glasses. "Dr. Pritchitt, you came close to violating the order of the court, which still remains. Do you understand?"

Pritchitt nodded.

Judge Winston rubbed his eyes. "Court dismissed."

Jeremy Bates glared and tapped his fist on the table. He stared coldly at Bohannon and stuffed his papers into a briefcase. He walked to the defendant's table. "Todd, I'll see you in court in two weeks. It'll be different then," he sneered. "That is, if Dr. Pritchitt's doesn't meet any more angry children of his victims." Accompanied by his two assistants, he stormed away.

"We whipped that ego-filled jackass today," smiled Bohannon.

"Yes," replied Pritchitt wistfully, "but a battle is not a war."

CHAPTER TWELVE

The Department of Surgery was abuzz. Whispers of Pritchitt filled the air. The death of Danny Lavender had propelled Dr. Pritchitt into the national spotlight. Covered live coast to coast, it was broadcast by all major networks. Calls from media outlets around the country, as well as suffering patients, and those condemning aided suicide inundated the telephone lines.

Dr. Peter's face was anything but friendly as he paced his office. The telephone rang. "I have no comment on Dr. Pritchitt," he said sharply, then slammed the receiver down for the tenth time in less than an hour. There was a knock at his door.

"Please sit down, Dr. Wiseman," instructed Peters brusquely.

"I'm fine standing, sir, if you don't mind."

"I do mind," answered Peters. Wiseman sat. Dr. Peters did the same. "You do enjoy your residency here at Memorial Hospital?"

"Very much so, Dr. Peters. I love it."

"Good. I'm delighted. Like you, I have aspirations. I hope to be more than the acting head of the department. I want to be appointed chairman."

Wiseman smiled pleasantly. "We all have dreams."

"If you value your position here, Dr. Wiseman, then I suggest you do a better job of learning your chosen profession and less —" He paused and stared straight into Wiseman's apprehensive face. "And spend less time associating with the criminally indicted and disgraced Benjamin Pritchitt." Wiseman's forced smile vanished.

Peters went on, "In case you haven't heard yet, Dr. Pritchitt most likely will soon be occupying a prison cell." His lips curled into a snarl. "He won't even rank as jailhouse physician."

Wiseman cleared his throat. "I've learned a great deal from Dr. Pritchitt."

Peters shook his head and a look of disgust wrapped his face. "Nonsense, Wiseman. He is participating in criminal acts that not only bring shame to this great hospital but to the art of medicine as well."

Wiseman swallowed and took a deep breath. "I disagree," he answered.

Peters glared. "Wiseman. You listen carefully. If you want to keep your position at this hospital, then you had better separate yourself from the disease gnawing at its reputation."

"Sir, you have already tried Dr. Pritchitt in your own mind and found him to be guilty. And now you're threatening me for guilt by association."

"This is not a threat. This is merely a warning, Wiseman. Every resident makes mistakes, some are overlooked, if a sympathetic director sees fit to do so. If not, you'll be practicing medicine in Tijuana."

Wiseman arched his back looking straight into Peters condemning eyes, "You are prejudiced against Dr. Pritchitt."

"I detest anyone who sullies the profession I revere. This position should have been mine years ago, but like a good soldier I followed orders and waited my time. My time has come, and I will not permit the good name of Memorial Hospital to be tarnished by a crackpot."

"He's an idealist."

"Oh, I stand corrected. Pritchitt is an idealistic crackpot. Even though you are a brilliant young doctor, you too are replaceable, and don't you ever forget it."

"Is that all, Dr. Peters?"

"That's all . . . for now."

In the corridor Wiseman's anger grew. He had been treated as if he were vermin. But he did have a career ahead of him. He would have to be very careful.

Patsy's voice called from behind. "There are two more calls from Dot McCormick."

Wiseman turned away. "Maybe you should let Dr. Pritchitt talk to her."

Patsy waved the telephone memos. "Mrs. Lavender wasn't unstable like this one, she was physically ill, but this one —"

Wiseman pushed her hand away. "I really don't have time for all of this," he said apologetically, "I'm about to get my ass kicked out of here."

"It's Dr. Peters, isn't it?" asked Patsy.

"He hates Pritchitt and anyone friendly to him. Patsy, I'm sorry. Tell all of these crazy callers that Pritchitt's out of town and won't return until next year. In other words, I'm not his messenger boy." Wiseman closed the office door quietly.

An hour had passed before Patsy had regained her composure. She was startled by the harassing telephone as it cut into the silent calm, she jumped. Angry, she was ready to bark at the receptionist, and remind her that all calls from reporters be directed to the public relations office.

"It's Dot McCormick," said the receptionist.

Patsy's anger took on a sudden surge. Impatience was evident in her voice. "Mrs. McCormick, I've told you that Dr. Pritchitt is not here."

"Yes, but I need him."

"I have no idea where he is or when I'll see him again."

"If he'd just hear me out, I know he'd help me."

Taking a deep breath, Patsy once again patiently explained. "Your illness is not physical but emotional, as you yourself have told me. Dr. Pritchitt will not, and he told me this himself, confer with non-terminally ill callers. Why not try Dr. Sonia Samford, she's quite well known as a prominent psychologist." The caller began to sob.

"What about his associate, Dr. Wiseman?" begged McCormick.

"He's a resident physician, not yet even in private practice. There's no way he can help you with what you ask."

Bitterness laced the callers words. "And who the hell are you to tell me who can and who can't help me?"

"Please, ma'am."

"Who are you to make such decisions? In my mind my suffering is more painful than death itself. Death will be my final celebration and I welcome it." The tone of finality aroused deep concern in Patsy.

"Mrs. McCormick, are you at home now? I'll have someone call."

"If I tell you, I'll have a policeman banging on my door with a straight jacket. I admit I hear voices and even see strange things. You'll be sorry someday."

Suddenly, the line went dead. Patsy had heard the same conversation from other callers but always Dr. Pritchitt returned their desperate calls, and suggested help. An empty chill swept Patsy. Guilt tugged at her concern for a desperate woman. She leafed through the telephone book. There was no listing for a Dot McCormick. What would Pritchitt do, she wondered.

Wiseman walked down the long corridor into the anteroom of the chairman's office. Patsy sat with a forlorn expression. "I just saw the afternoon news." Wiseman held up his thumb and forefinger. "That maniac came this close to killing Dr. Pritchitt."

"It's horrible," said Patsy, visibly upset and paying little attention.

Wiseman waved a single sheet of paper. "And this fax

just came." He handed it to her, and she read it aloud.

"My dear Benjamin, I'm so very glad you're safe from the madness of the tormented soul we confronted today. I say *we* because I was there as well. Benjamin, I'll always be with you, like a twin brother. Our bond is unique. And when my time comes to leave this world, you will aid me. We work as twin angels of death." Patsy lowered the sheet of paper, fear in her eyes.

"I think Dr. Pritchitt should ask the police for protection."

"I agree," said Wiseman.

Atway Jackson and Tim Bauers sat inside the dim surveillance room. As a bank of television monitors scanned the hospital premises a security guard sat with a dull expression. They watched the black and white screen.

"Let's see it one more time," said Bauers.

Atway frowned. "We seen it thirty times already."

"Jack, just once more," assured Bauers.

The technician rewound the tape. Benji and Claire emerged from the lobby into the front entrance and entered the car, barely visible on the screen. "Here comes Simon," said Bauers.

Atway yawned. "You mean here comes the shadow."

The blurry image of a man appeared on the screen. He then crossed the entrance drive, crouching behind the car.

"Stop it right there," said Bauers, scribbling notes in a yellow legal pad. "There's Simon."

"Point one," said Atway, "we're certain that this image is not Danny Lavender."

"Correct," answered Bauers. "He's way too trim."

"Point two, he has long hair, but longer than Lavender's."

"Yes."

"Point three, he's wearing a winter overcoat on a rather mild autumn night."

"Right."

"Point four, that's all we know."

"Maybe a lab can enhance this," replied Bauers, closing his

legal pad. "Take it to a video studio, make a dupe for work purposes, then bring the original up to Nash's office."

"Will do," said Atway, fidgeting.

"All right," said Bauers, "you can go."

Atway placed the videotape in a metal box. "Thank God," he said with relief. "I hate being in a hospital."

It was late afternoon before Pritchitt and Terry could leave the West Precinct Station. As Todd Bohannon supervised, they gave several statements to the police interrogators. "Lt. Bordeaux saved my life," Pritchitt stated over and again. "I was sure he was going to kill me."

"The reporters know you're here. Do you want to make a statement?" asked a captain.

"There will be no statement," said Bohannon.

Pritchitt protested. "Ben, let it cool for a few days. You don't want some copycat finishing what Danny Lavender attempted."

"I just want to thank Bordeaux publicly."

"That's not necessary," came a voice behind him.

Pritchitt turned to see Lori Bordeaux enter the room. He gripped her hand. "From my heart. I can never repay you."

She shrugged. "Maybe you can do me a favor one day."

"Anything," answered Pritchitt.

"Dad, do you want police protection?" asked Terry.

"Absolutely not."

"There are a lot of screwballs out there, Ben," said Bohannon.

Pritchitt shook his head. "No, I don't want to make myself a prisoner of paranoia. My life's already miserable enough without my being scared of my own shadow."

"It's not your shadow I'm worried about," argued Bohannon.

Terry took her father's hand.

"Dad, I'm taking the children to a house I just rented."

"Nonsense, Terry. I've thought this out. You and the children will stay with me until this is over."

"But, Dad."

"No butting about it, sweetheart. This is a done deal."

"But I've rented the apartment and already moved my furniture."

"That's perfect."

"What?"

"Yeah, that's where you'll store all your stuff until we wake up from this nightmare," smiled Pritchitt. A soft wink preceded Terry's reluctant nod. "Have you explained everything to your mother?"

"The best I could, Dad."

"I think the less she knows the better," instructed Pritchitt.

Attorneys sat around the room. Justin Nash surveyed the faces before him. He opened a folder. "Okay, what do we have? Do we have anything?"

Tim Bauers spoke. "We have Professor Niles Mercer and the Rev. Milton James." A pause of intense silence followed. Bauers deep sigh broke the smothering air. "They are two pretty strange guys," he said.

Nash's stare vibrated the tense room. "Evidently they are, Mr. Bauers, and many more people in this report are, as well. But I need more than your tenth grade summation, sir. Do you get my drift?" Nash scowled.

"I understand, sir."

"I hope you do, Bauers. Now, let's find this maniac before he kills again."

The door flew open and Jeremy Bates entered. He stood in a menacing pose. Nash flicked cigar ashes onto his desk.

"I didn't hear you knock, Jeremy."

"That's because I didn't, Justin," Bates barked as he held a sheet of paper before Nash. "I just received this."

"And what is this, I pray?"

"It's a damn fax. A fax from this Simon character. What a twisted bastard. He's threatening to kill me."

"Not good, Jeremy. Not good, at all," said Nash, viewing the fax.

"Solve this damn case, Justin."

"I don't have a magic wand, Jeremy."

"Then get one," shouted Bates, who turned and stomped from the room. The slamming door shook the walls.

Nash leaned back, his feet on the desk, puffing his cigar. "Now Bauers, what about Niles Mercer and Milton James?"

The church parking lot was vacant. Benjamin Pritchitt climbed the front steps and pulled open the heavy oak doors. A spiritual silence cradled the sanctuary. He felt peace. Stain glass windows muted the light. Benjamin knelt in a pew, bowed his head and prayed. With his face buried in the security of his arms he softly wept. A sense of relief and new found strength swept him. A soft voice spoke. A gentle hand touched at his sense of loneliness.

"Pastor Bivens," spoke Benjamin. He cleared his throat and started to stand, only to be held down by a calming hand.

"Ben, don't get up. It's good to see you." The portly bald reverend sat in the pew.

"How's the gout, Pastor?"

"Fine, Benjamin. How are you? And Ruth, how is she?"

"She's better. Everyone's doing quite well, in spite of me. "

"Feeling a little guilty? Remember, there was a carpenter years ago who knelt in a garden and pleaded with his father to find another way to complete his mission. There was no other way. Sometimes there are no easy ways out of our predicaments."

"I just don't know."

"Oh, but I do. I know that what is bad will not conquer the man sitting next to me. I know your heart, Benjamin, and God created it."

Ben stood and walked from the protective sanctuary. A rekindled spirit warmed him.

CHAPTER THIRTEEN

It was late afternoon by the time Nash's secretary, Jesse Matthews, handed her overdue report to him. She donned her jacket, and turned to leave. Nash caught her attention.

"What is it, the flu?"

"No, but . . . I'm not well."

"Well, take tomorrow off. I'll get Sally to cover for you."

She raised her eyes. "I can't tell you how much this job means to me, Mr. Nash. I just hate letting you down in any way."

"Nonsense, Jesse. We all get sick. You're the best damn secretary this man has ever had."

She spoke reluctantly. "I'm . . . I'm not really sick."

Nash saw her troubled face. He took her by the arm and sat her in a chair. "I'm so very ashamed, Mr. Nash. It's hard for me to talk."

"Please, the work day is over. Take a deep breath and remember I'm not your boss now, just a friend."

Her eyes glistened through an ashen complexion. She cleared her throat. "I think I'm pregnant."

"Oh, now I understand."

"I'm not sure. I'm going to see my doctor to make certain. My boyfriend, my fiance, will be there, too."

Nash patted her shoulder. "These things happen every day, Jesse. Don't worry about it." He lit his cigar.

"Please, Mr. Nash, the smoke," she pleaded.

"Of course, how stupid of me," he said quickly, putting the cigar out.

"I am worried because Bob, my boyfriend —"

"You mean the father."

"Yes, I mean the father. Well, he's not so eager to be a daddy now. He just started law school." Nash turned to the window, watching clouds swallow the sinking sun. Jesse, ashamed and embarrassed, began weeping. "I'm so confused. And I hate to miss work. I know it puts you in a bind."

"Don't worry, that's months from now. I'll get a temporary replacement."

"No, you don't understand. Bob wants me to . . . to . . . terminate the pregnancy."

Nash took a long hard look at the vanishing sun, then turned to his young secretary. "This is a bigger problem than I imagined. I think you should consult your parents."

"No," she responded meekly. "My father's gone. I think he would've understood but my mother. . . no way. I've sinned."

"Jesse, don't you know there are many couples who would adopt your baby in a heartbeat." Her red hair shook in disagreement.

"It's not a baby, yet. It's just a few weeks formed." She stood. "I'm sorry I've burdened you. This is my problem, Mr. Nash. And I'll solve it."

"Don't be too impulsive, Jesse. This is your decision more than the father's. He can't make you do anything you don't want to."

"But I love him —" She searched for words. "And, well, I'm not ready to be a mother. I must decide what to do."

"I know a good family. The wife wants another child but she's unable —"

She shook her head. "I knew you'd think poorly of me. Now I have to leave."

In his office Nash sat dejectedly, smoking his cigar. He had learned more than he had wanted to know from his young secretary. The meeting he wished he hadn't called was about to begin. His associates were sitting in wait but his mind was far away. He took a long draw from his cigar, then spoke in a wistful tone. "The disintegration of the family is what's ruining America today."

"I agree," said Terry.

"And you're getting a divorce?" asked Bauers.

"Well, excuse me, Mr. Perfect," she asserted. "My marriage was a mistake from the start but I guess you wouldn't know about mistakes, would you?"

Nash leaned back. "And how was it a mistake?" he asked. A serious face matched his voice.

"Well, aren't you the nosey one, too. Married too fast, never really got a chance to know him. Any other questions?"

"You never had children with him?" asked Justin, darting a glance at Bauers.

"No, not at all. Plus —"

Anticipating silence quieted the room. "Plus what?" Nash asked.

"There were problems," answered Terry.

"What kind of problems?" asked Bauers.

"I think we need stop talking about this, now!" Nash interrupted.

"No," Terry said, "it's okay. It helps. It was his medication, to correct his mood swings. When he was on it, he felt less than a man. When he was off it, he was anything but human."

"You couldn't see this before you married him?" asked Bauers.

Terry's glare was chilling. "Hey, we're not here to discuss my stupidity, are we? I mean, give me a break, I made a mistake, okay?"

Nash's voice took on a fatherly tone. "Terry, no one is blaming you."

"How nice," she sniffed. "Enough of this, we have something to show you."

Terry tossed a fax sheet onto Nash's desk.

"What do we have here?" he asked, lifting the paper to read it. Bauers leaned forward as Terry quietly waited.

"He's faxed a message to you," she said.

"Who?" asked Nash, raising his eyes. Nash read the message. He glanced up. "Simon's thanking me for helping your father this morning. I really didn't do anything."

"Well, hell, you walked into the line of fire," reminded Bauers.

"You weren't afraid. I'll always be thankful," added Terry.

"Oh, come on, accept a compliment. I agree with Terry," said Bauers, "it was pretty daring . . . and stupid, too."

Nash exhaled smoke, stood, and walked to the front of his desk. "Simon is now contacting me. Why?"

"It's obvious," answered Terry. "Simon wants my father to put him to death, and wants him alive and healthy until then."

Nash nodded. "That makes sense," he agreed. "What a paradox, me getting a love letter from Simon and Jeremy Bates a death threat."

"Is that so hard to understand?" said Bauers. "It's obvious who's the most likeable between the two of you."

Terry looked at Nash, then at Bauers. "Talk about a twisted bastard. A sick wacko, that's what Bates is," she said.

The study was elegantly trimmed in cherry paneling. A small lamp atop a marble table cast its glow as late afternoon darkness descended. Surrounded by leather bound books and paintings of religious leaders, Pastor Bivens of the First Avenue Church sat quietly. His face was troubled. His fingers fidgeted with a broken pencil. He glanced up at the ornate clock on the mantel. Pastor Bivens turned a page of scripture, but his mind was on the meeting, now fifteen minutes overdue, still the knock startled him.

"The door is unlocked," he announced. The door opened cautiously. Reverend Milton James peered into the shadowy study. Bivens motioned toward a carved oak chair. An awkward tension permeated the room. "Milton, I'm sorry to have to do this."

"You don't have to play the role of aggrieved judge with me," Reverend James said sharply.

"Milton, perhaps you don't understand."

The small eyes squinted. "All too well do I understand. You're doing what all the others have done." Bivens was visibly upset, rubbing his forehead. He sat back and observed his associate pastor.

"You sit here to judge me, " continued Milton James, "because you've been in charge here for a long time, and you know how to convey a self-proclaimed piety just like the rest of the city's pious preachers." James thumped an open bible. "Like the Pharisees you're all smug in the belief that only you know right from wrong."

Bivens lowered his eyes in disappointment, knowing all too well that he had made a poor selection. He alone was to blame. James' voice now had a surly tone. "I know plenty about you high and mighty pillars of Memphis. Adultery and other sins are no strangers to you hypocrites."

"We are made of flesh, just as you, Reverend James."

"How humble of you to admit your humanity." He sneered, continuing his attack on the city clergy, preventing Bivens from speaking.

Finally, Pastor Bivens broke through the rambling diatribe. "Your being arrested with Niles Mercer and that group of extremists —"

"Extremists!" James broke in.

Bivens stood and quickly and forcefully raised his large hand to silence the angry words.

"Milton, you've been arrested and jailed for an anti-abortion demonstration."

The young pastor stood, eyes blazing. "Abortion is immoral and sinful in the eyes of God!"

"I agree. But we are a nation of laws. Change will come."

"If there were more like me in Germany, the Nazis would not have murdered the defenseless. My activities may alarm sedate parishioners. But I am a leader, Reverend Bivens, not a follower."

"You are associating with fanatics. There is talk about threatening doctors' lives and bombings against clinics. Christ never condoned violence."

"Self-defense is permitted by Christian morality. And who defends the innocent and helpless?"

Bivens stared at Reverend James. "The activist rhetoric you spread at this old church must stop and it will. After listening to you just now, you frighten me."

Milton James cocked his chin upward and narrowed his eyes. "I resign. I will not be threatened or bullied by those who believe themselves to be morally superior than the common man. I have strong feelings about abortion and other sins against God. I am indeed more of an Old Testament believer than a New Testament adherent." He rose and his face reddened. "An eye for an eye and a tooth for a tooth is more virtuous to me than turning the other cheek." He turned and walked to the door. "I will be gone by next week."

In the shadowy gloom Reverend Bivens folded his hands and bowed his head.

The fresh flowers gave off a sweet aroma. Ruth placed them on the small table. She stood before the mirror and traced the thin lines at the corner of her mouth. Though a few years younger than her husband, she felt her beauty was fading.

"Mrs. Pritchitt, are you ready?" called a voice from the door. Ruth turned from the mirror startled but relieved to see her doctor.

"I've been noticing my faded youth."

Tucker smiled. "Do you still hear the disapproving voices we were discussing the other day?"

"Those inner voices? The negative thoughts? Oh, no, they're gone or at least I can now express my doubts." Ruth reached for her lipstick.

"That's excellent to hear. And what of this person who was calling you. Has he stopped?"

Ruth looked up with a queried gaze. "Who was that?" she asked, painting her lips.

Tucker's gaze was serious. "The person who sent the basket of fruit, the one whose name you could not remember."

"Oh," laughed Ruth. "The one they call Simon. He is friendly, asking about my progress. Maybe he really is a secret admirer," laughed Ruth nervously. Ruth's hand began to tremble and the laughing ceased. "This treatment . . . electroshock. It will help me?"

"Yes, Ruth. ECT will give you a new outlook. Your depression will vanish just as we discussed. Although your family has been told it will start tomorrow, an opening came up today, so we're going for it."

Ruth was wide-eyed, listening to the risks and side effects, but also the benefits. After a long discussion, they walked along the corridor. "I'll be right with you, Ruth." A nurse escorted her to a seat. "Aren't you coming?"

Dr. Tucker took Ruth's hands. "I'll be there with you, but I must call my office."

The nurse disappeared and Ruth began pacing. "I'm nervous," said Ruth, a tremble in her voice. "I'm waiting to get my brain roasted and I need a martini or cigarette."

"I'll get you something," assured the nurse, punching the intercom. Two male assistants came hurriedly to the desk. A second nurse arrived with a sedative. The injection took effect immediately, and Ruth's mood grew calmer. Her limbs grew weak and she collapsed into the arms of one attendant.

Benjamin Pritchitt turned to park in an emergency parking spot. But just as he turned off the ignition, he saw his old friend Dr. Herskovitz walk toward a car.

"Mickey!" shouted Pritchitt. "How about a space?"

The doctor smiled. "All right but it'll cost you lunch one day, Ben!"

"You got it, pal."

It's a good omen, thought Pritchitt, jumping from the driver's seat.

At the flower shop in the lobby of the clinic Pritchitt asked for a dozen red roses. "We just sold the last we had, and they were gorgeous," said the elderly woman. "You look familiar." She adjusted her glasses.

"I'm Dr. Benjamin Pritchitt, I'm sure you've seen me around the hospital. And in the news."

A girl peered from a mound of flowers. "You're Ruth Pritchitt's husband?"

The elderly woman grinned. "Oh, doctor, then it's you whose been sending all of those flowers?"

"No," came the puzzled response.

The young clerk came to the counter. "There were several bouquets, with very romantic messages," she explained innocently.

"Maybe it's my son," offered Pritchitt.

"It wasn't a son's message," interjected the young clerk.

"Janie, that's enough," reprimanded the woman.

Standing at the door he could think of nothing more to say or do, but to turn and run to Ruth's room. The name of Simon pounded in his head.

Pritchitt whisked past the nurse's station, alarming the chatting knot of women. Room 202 was empty. Perched atop the bed were four baskets of red roses. He yanked the card. "You give love. You give life. Your children love you. You are always in my thoughts. Your Guardian Angel."

"Can I help you, Dr. Pritchitt?" asked a curious nurse from behind.

"Where's my wife?" he asked.

"She's having an ECT treatment down the hall," she answered. Pritchitt sat. An icy sweat was upon him.

"Another jolt, with increased voltage," ordered Blanche Tucker. An attendant hit a switch sending Ruth's body into a convulsive arc. Her arms shook with a distinctive tremor and her head jerked. Ruth's eyes rolled back and a seizure began.

Arms and legs flailed wildly and her mouth frothed. Her teeth
clenched on a plastic mouthpiece, to prevent biting through her
tongue. Dr. Tucker administered an injection. Dr. Tucker's
voice continued, shouting orders, then the room was quiet.
When Dr. Tucker emerged, Ruth, unconscious, resting on a
gurney, followed close behind.

CHAPTER FOURTEEN

"How are you feeling?" Dr. Tucker asked, wiping the moisture from Ruth Pritchitt's brow.

She moaned and her eyes fluttered. "I hurt," she sighed. Ruth surveyed the room, only recognizing the face of Dr. Tucker. "I feel as if I've been hit by a runaway train."

"Ruth, sweetheart, you had a seizure. You're going to be just fine," explained Tucker.

Benjamin sat in his wife's room staring at the roses, the small accompanying card in his hand.

Dr. Tucker stood in the doorway, arms folded. "Dr. Pritchitt, I tried to reach you to let you know of the change in her ECT schedule."

Pritchitt raised his eyes but said nothing. His hands trembled. Tucker seated herself. He handed her the small card.

Tucker read the card. "This Simon, is he a friend?" Her expression was puzzled staring at Pritchitt's lost gaze.

Pritchitt stood and walked to a small dresser. Anxiety paced his movements as he straightened his tie and ran his hands through his hair. "It's a long story. But I believe this

Simon is the murderer of the young women you've no doubt heard and read about."

"My God!" said Tucker.

"My God is right. And for some very unfortunate reason he has a perverse fascination with me and my family."

"Ruth has mentioned a Simon to me."

Pritchitt turned abruptly. "What did she tell you?"

"I thought she was having some kind of delusions, which are common with extreme bipolar fluctuations, but now I know. The roses, they are from him."

Pritchitt's eyes scanned the room. "The fruit basket, flowers, candy, everything here is from that madman." His tone was of anger and hate.

"So that's why the unsettling commotion the other night. He's the one you thought was here with Ruth?"

"Yes," answered Pritchitt. "Curse him and his sick love," Pritchitt said aloud, turning to the window and bracing both hands upon the chilled glass.

Night descended and Pritchitt's visit with Ruth had passed hours ago. He sat peacefully in the lobby, simply watching the front door. "Are you okay, Dr. Pritchitt?" asked a security guard.

"Oh, I'm fine, Henry. Thanks for asking."

"Well, if you need anything, Doc, I'll be right over there," Henry motioned toward the information desk.

"Thanks."

Pritchitt liked to sit in the hospital lobby, especially after a difficult night when a patient had died.

Near the entrance expectant mothers came and went. Both the sick and the healthy passed through the doors of what had been his home for years. He often recalled what his elderly mother had told him years before, that old folks of the world had to make room for the young folks, that death was a natural cycle of existence.

It was almost eight and visitors were leaving. He buttoned his overcoat as an excited couple came into sight. The woman clutched her round tummy, and waddled down the corridor. A new life was about to begin. He smiled, always amazed by the dramas unfolding in the hallways of Memorial Hospital.

Now he was more than a small actor in a life and death drama and he was uncomfortable. He was a medical doctor who was challenging the law of both state and man; a man both hated and loved. What would his own parents think of his actions, he wondered. He detested returning to an empty home. How he wished his wife would soon come back to him. It was time to go. Fumbling for his keys, he experienced a strange sensation as if someone was watching him. He quickly turned. But there was nothing unusual. He walked toward the exit but stopped, then turned once again. He slipped his keys into his pocket and peered down the long corridors which branched out from the lobby. After a third corridor was examined he relaxed. But on the fourth his eyes widened and his heart raced.

Far away a long-haired man in an overcoat stood motionless, staring at Pritchitt. Then he turned and strode away.

Pritchitt hurriedly followed. His gait reaching a slow trot.

The security guard called out, "Dr. Pritchitt, are you okay?" But the man had disappeared.

In the corridor Pritchitt stood with vacant thoughts. His mind flooded with unanswered questions. Had he really seen Simon or was this his imagination? What was happening? Was he no longer the man he'd thought he was? Was he hallucinating? His head dropped and he turned back toward the lobby. His walk was slow and alone.

On the drive home, his jaws tightened and his hands choked the steering wheel. He had never felt such anger. He had never felt so abandoned.

Hundreds of candles cast a mournful shadow against the wall. Amidst the blackened room, a fluttering glimmer of light was the candle's chore. From a large plastic bag a doll was removed. A harsh cry and a raspy mumbling of words came before an utterance of amen. The doll was cradled and rocked back and forth, then placed atop a small casket. A photograph of a lovely woman was kissed. "I detest your sin, but I miss you so," cried a sad voice. "Three lives shattered. An unholy love it was." Surging anger sounded a ferocious wail.

A long overcoat was donned. A whimpering cry was heard. "Simon says . . . and Simon does."

Terry had tucked her children in bed for the night. After baths, prayers and bedtime stories, they were left with a mother's kiss.

From the refrigerator Terry removed an expensive bottle of vodka. She poured a drink in a glass and sat at the kitchen table. The chilled nectar relaxed her tense body, relieving the stress of the day. It was merely a panacea, she understood, just a way to rid herself of the deep problems filling her life. As she was about to pour another, the doorbell rang. Niles Mercer was at the doorstep. His eyes half-closed as he tottered unsteadily. "Terry, let me in. I must talk to you." His words were slurred.

"Niles, go home," she spoke loudly. "This is not a place where you are welcome." Niles leaned toward the peephole, steadying himself against the door with his forehead. "If you don't let me inside I'm going to knock on the kid's windows and they'll let me in."

"Niles, you're drunk. Go home."

The face flashed a twisted smile. "You are, too. I know about your vodka. And you've just had a few nips."

Terry was speechless. Her anger grew with his intrusion. She knew he just wouldn't go away. She felt his sickening presence. His spying raped her of any privacy even in her father's house.

The door flew open. He'd been spying on her. "You bastard!" she shouted.

He responded swaying in the doorway. His sick mind bled through a sheepish grin. "I'm just trying to make certain nothing bad happens to my wife, that's all."

He grabbed at her arm. Terry's anger turned to fear. "Get your hands off me."

Niles pushed himself inside along with the odor of a case of stale beer. He collapsed in a chair.

Terry hovered above him. "Say, what you must, then get your pathetic self up from that chair and get out!" she yelled.

"It's wrong to be angry with your husband, Terry."

"Niles, I'm divorcing you. I don't want you for a husband anymore. Are you a complete idiot?"

"I'm not here to argue. I just want to win you back, darling."

"Impossible," shot back Terry. She leveled her voice. "Look, you have your causes and protests to occupy you. You'll find someone who has the same interests."

"They fired Milton James. Reverend Bivens was scared all the fatcat money would dry up, so he booted out a true man of the gospel. Milton is my greatest friend. Milton and I are starting a national group. He's going to be a famous leader."

"It's time for you to leave. Do you want me to call the police?"

Niles stood. "Can I just kiss the kids good night?"

"Absolutely not." Her eyes narrowed. "You're not their father."

"I know," he nodded. "But we can have our own child."

"Niles, our time is over. I served divorce papers on you last week."

"Yes, but I . . . I want to try again."

Bitterness swept his face. "Terry, you really shouldn't treat me like a piece of dirt. Biblical teaching makes it clear that what God has joined, let no man place asunder. I think you'll live to regret the day you treated me like this."

Terry took a few paces and grabbed a telephone. "If you don't leave now, I'm calling the police." She cast a hateful stare into the mounting anger of his eyes.

"I'm going. I'm going, you fucking misguided bitch. All of you will be sorry for this. You just wait and see."

Terry stood beside the open door. "I'm going to have my attorney obtain a restraining order. I don't want you to come here again." She slammed the door behind, then sank to the floor, huddling against the door, sobbing deeply, regretting her marriage to this virtual stranger.

CHAPTER FIFTEEN

It was early Sunday morning, the hospital draped in a morgue-like silence. There were no surgeries scheduled or any other elective procedures. It was a day of rest for everyone. A day when only emergencies would be dealt with. Refreshed, Pritchitt entered his office, now a safe haven from staff and patients alike. He spread the Sunday newspaper on his desk and savored the peace and quiet as the morning sun cast its golden glow.

He paused, on the editorial page there were articles for and against a proposed assisted-suicide law. It posed the question: Should doctors be able to help their terminally ill patients die? Thirty-five states had strong laws prohibiting such acts. But there was a strong national movement in support of compassion, acknowledged in the article in favor of the state bill. Doctors would be able to prescribe lethal medication but not injections for those who were thought to have less than six months left to live. The article opposed any law permitting assisted-suicide, and denounced society's willingness to euthanize the elderly and helpless.

Next to Pritchitt's desk were boxes of mail. He stacked several envelopes on his desk. From a drawer he removed a pocket knife which he used as a letter-opener. He stared at the cherished possession. It was a gift from his grandfather who had tried to interest him in hunting as a boy. He remembered trudging through the backwoods of Arkansas on a freezing morning with his grandfather, when they had come across a small doe, limping pitifully. An arrow pierced its leg, preventing flight. Grandfather Pritchitt raised his gun, whispering that it was only humane to end the life of the suffering creature. Etched deeply in his thoughts was the sight of his grandfather slowly raising the long rifle barrel. But a creature so lovely and helpless could not be destroyed.

Ben had begged his grandfather to help him remove the arrow. The old man had held the frightened deer as Ben snapped the arrow and extracted the shaft, only to discover a second wound where a razor-sharp arrowhead was embedded. His grandfather handed him his pocket knife and Ben had carefully slit the metal triangle from the doe's flank. A small silver flask was handed to the boy and alcohol was poured in the incision. Thereafter, he was "Dr. Ben" to his grandparents who made certain he was bequeathed funds for medical school. How strange, he pondered. Was he now a healer or destroyer?

Pritchitt opened the long blade and slit open the first envelope. He grimaced looking at the message as he read it to himself. "Too bad you've escaped justice. The next time the victim's family will get you. You are a very evil man." The next envelope was opened. "How I wish you could have helped my sister who died of ovarian cancer. She screamed for pain killers but was barely given enough for 'fear of addiction.' Her doctor had said he could lose his license for over prescribing narcotics. What a horrible irony. She was dying and they still wouldn't give her relief. We all have a rendezvous with death. The public must understand there is nothing noble in suffering. Thank you, Dr. Pritchitt, for truly caring for your patients. My sister was only thirty."

He had read enough. Turning his chair toward the window

he felt the warming sun soothe a bitter chill. A chill his body had felt too often. Beyond the river in the distance he imagined the offspring of that little doe prancing through the forest. And he heard the echo of his grandfather's praise. "Why, Ben, you're gonna make a fine doctor. Now let's don't tell your grandmother about this." He winked. "We might have to operate again."

But his terminally ill patients could not be saved. He had no magical pocket knife. Diseases ravaged their bodies. His grandfather's words returned. *It's only humane to end the life of a suffering creature.* How right, Granddad. Ben closed the pocket knife and slipped it inside his trouser pocket.

It was late morning at Memorial Psychiatric and Pritchitt, immaculately dressed in a blue suit, pressed shirt and bright tie, stood at the receptionist's desk. The nurse on duty was deep in thought, a crossword puzzle before her.

"Ruth Pritchitt." he said.

"She's in room 202."

With a startled jerk of the head, she looked up. "Oh, excuse me," she said with embarrassment. "Why, Dr. Pritchitt, you served on the Scout council with my husband. Remember? Ellsworth Galliger. Do you remember him?"

"Sure. Lieutenant with the fire department."

"Oh, I'm so pleased you remember." She smiled. "He's gone now. When we buried him he had his old metal fire hat right on his chest. He liked to joke, 'You never know where I'm gonna end up, so I might need my helmet.'"

Pritchitt forced a laugh. "That was Ellie all right. He was always making everybody laugh." Pritchitt glanced at his watch. "Please let my wife know I'm here."

"I certainly will." She conveyed the message. "She'll be out in a minute." Pritchitt straightened his tie. The nurse looked up.

"Doctor, by any chance, would you know a seven letter word for fat?"

"Adipose. A-d-i-p-o-s-e."

"Bless you, Dr. Pritchitt."

From down the hall, he was surprised by the vision before him. Ruth, carefully coiffed and dressed, approached. "Hey, sweetheart," said Pritchitt with admiration. He gave her a kiss on the cheek. "You look lovely."

"Do I really?" beamed Ruth.

"Absolutely."

She smoothed the new dress Terry had bought her. Pritchitt took his wife's arm and they strode past the reception desk.

"You two have a wonderful day," said a nurse.

"Yes, do," came a familiar voice from behind them; Dr. Tucker smiled broadly.

"We will indeed," Pritchitt responded.

Suddenly, Ruth looked perplexed. "Did I have my birthday, Ben?"

"Why of course, Ruth," he replied. "Don't you remember, the children and I brought you dinner, but you were too tired."

Ruth looked down, her face confused. No, I don't remember."

"Short term memory loss is perfectly normal with ECT," he explained. You do remember your wedding anniversary?"

"March 5," answered Ruth with relief.

"Oh, it is such a beautiful day," she said, leaning strongly on her husband.

Pritchitt noticed the many startled glances of fellow parishioners. Approaching was Pete Michaels and his wife. They exchanged pleasantries and continued in the church together. Inside the vestibule shocked stares came their way. Benjamin felt the invading glares as Ruth proceeded untainted. As she led the way toward the Pritchitt's regular pew a hand gripped Benjamin's.

"You've got a lot of nerve coming here," a voice hissed. "This is the temple of God, not a den of murderers. This is where we worship God, not come to play God. And if you kill people, then you are a murderer."

Pritchitt contained his dignity, exercising self-control at the anger of the self righteousness.

The organ played and the church service began. Ben and Ruth took their seats. A growing murmur in the crowd grew until heads turned and a buzz spread through the large church. Voices rang out.

"Dr. Pritchitt is a man of conscience!"

"Get him out. He's shamed our church!"

From the altar Reverend Bivens' voice boomed at the lectern. "Please. Quiet!" he commanded visibly upset. "We are here to worship and find solace. If there are any who are without sin in this congregation, then let them go now."

The church grew silent. "I am a sinner, as we have all sinned," spoke Bivens. "Now is not the time to debate social or moral issues. This is where we turn our troubles over to the Lord and do not judge those among us, for it is God who will be the final judge and none seated here."

"What has become of Milton James?" a voice rang out. A hush swept the congregation.

"He has been dismissed from our parish," answered Reverend Bivens. "This is not the time or place to discuss that issue. But clergy need be without controversy."

"Well, wasn't Jesus controversial?" someone shouted.

"The Bible says thou shalt not kill!" cried another. Sentiments of support and damnation rang out as Ruth held tightly to her husband. Pritchitt's anger was tempered with shame holding his fragile wife. Bivens signaled the organist and a deep roar swelled until it drowned the rancor. From the balcony above the choir's beautiful voices filled the church.

Ruth gripped her husband's hand.

The service continued unmarred by further outbursts. Reverend Bivens' sermon held a simple message. "Blessed are the peacemakers . . . "

Fearful of more disputes, Pritchitt whispered to his wife to meet him at the side door when the service ended. All eyes were cast his way as he walked down the side aisle, his head held high.

On the windshield of his car was a page torn from a hymnal. Hastily scribbled was a message. "You're not welcome here. Don't return. To worship God is not to play him." He ripped the sheet from the car and slipped it in his pocket.

At the side door Ruth stood alone. She waved assuring her husband she was all right.

As she started for the car Reverend Bivens came through the side exit. "Ruth, I'm sorry for the scene."

"No apologies are necessary," she answered. "People have strong opinions and convictions, as do we all."

"Please return," pleaded Bivens. "Everyone is welcome. You know that. Be sure to tell Benjamin. You've both meant so much to the church over these years. Don't let a misguided handful tarnish the love we have for you and your family."

"We are resigning our membership." An angry parishioner circled Bivens, his wife and children in tow. "And it's not just us," he yelled, pointing to the front of the church. Parishioners poured from the church. Heated arguments could be heard as Bivens' head dropped, feeling helpless and beaten.

Pritchitt eased his car toward the side entrance where Ruth got in beside him.

There was silence as they drove downtown. "I'm sorry for what happened in church, Ruth," he said, worried that all this would send her back into her depression.

She turned. "Don't be sorry for me, Ben. Be sorry for those narrow minded Sunday Christians. I'm so proud of you. I know why you've done what you've done. You nearly paid for your beliefs with your own life this week," she smiled, then stretched to place a loving kiss on his cheek. "I have had long discussions with Blanche Tucker. She showed me newspaper clippings. Mercy is a Christian virtue."

"I love you, Ruth Pritchitt."

"I know that, Benjamin. That, I do know." He looked to her eyes and, for the moment, saw her depression gone. Rested from her troubled emotions by love. Suddenly, he swerved to avoid a stray dog crossing their path.

"Oh, Ben!" she exclaimed. "We almost had another Rebel."
Pritchitt glanced in the rear view mirror.

"He made it across the street. And there will never be another Rebel."

Ruth's voice filled with the memory. "We hadn't been dating long."

"No, I had just met you."

"Well, the Benjamin Pritchitt I met was a young intern who found that injured dog on the side of the road. You took that beat up old hound into the outpatient clinic and cleared a table. You worked on that dog for the better part of three hours to save its life. That was the best pet we ever had and the Benjamin Pritchitt that I've grown to adore."

Pritchitt laughed. "He only bit me once in twelve years."

Ruth slid closer to her husband and repeated a kiss. "The Benjamin Pritchitt I love cares about people who are suffering, maybe too damn much for his own good. But, partner, I'm with you, no matter what."

The Peabody lobby was crowded with hotel guests. Beneath the ornate chandelier, couples drank seated at tables or in the clusters of plush sofas and leather chairs. Others pressed for drinks at the bar. They stood at the marble fountain where the hotel's famous ducks swam.

Ruth knelt and spoke with children fascinated by the playful ducks. Ben knelt, too, explaining to the children the ducks were the descendants of those captured by hunters years before. Ruth motioned to a red carpet which led to an elevator and the roof penthouse where the ducks resided.

"Oh, it is so wonderful to be out." She grabbed Ben's hand and led him to a sofa where they sat.

Pritchitt frowned, noting the cocktail waiters moving about. "Maybe we should sit in the outer lobby."

Ruth shook her head. "There will always be temptation for me." When the waiter came to them, Ruth simply said, "Ginger ale."

"I can't tell you how proud of you I am, my love." Ben gave her a warm kiss.

"Hello, doctor," came a friendly voice. "Jenkins is my name," the elderly man smiled. He held up his camera. "Can I take your picture, sir? It's for you, not the papers," he assured them.

"Sure," said Pritchitt slipping his hand in his pocket searching for a twenty dollar bill.

The elderly man raised his hand. "No way you're gonna pay, doctor. Cause I still owe you for what you did for my wife."

"Well, it's hard for me to remember."

"She's just fine. She's using a cane. But you know how that is, when old age comes upon you —"

Pritchitt embraced Ruth.

Flashbulbs popped and so did Pritchitt's memory as the old man fiddled with his camera. Pritchitt snapped his fingers as the waiter brought their order and placed it on the coffee table. "Robert Jenkins, that's your name."

He nodded.

"I remember now. Your wife was struck by a car."

"Well, I know one thing, sir. You're a damn good doctor. You saved her life." He placed the photograph he had just taken on the table. "A lot of doctors would have kept right on driving," said Jenkins. "I guess they're afraid. But from the likes of you, Doc, you ain't much scared of nothing. That's because you're a good doctor." The old man turned and walked away, but left good thoughts for a troubled mind to dwell on. Ruth glowed.

"So?" Benjamin said coyly, when they had finished their drinks. He took Ruth's hand and escorted her toward the elevator. Now it was her turn to be coy. On the eighth floor they exited. Ben slipped a card in a slot and pushed the door open.

"It's all ours," said Ben, taking his wife in his arms. "And this is *our* room." And he kissed her passionately. His fingers gently caressed his wife's back, then circled her full breasts. He led her to the bedroom where a bouquet of flowers was on the pillow.

He drew in her familiar perfumed scent. Their lips met again and Pritchitt's hands roved over her hips and along her thighs. She sighed. "Do you remember the first time, Ben?" He grinned broadly. "How could I forget? I was so damned scared." Ruth laughed.

He slipped his wife's dress over her head. "And your parents were sleeping right below us."

Ruth loosened his tie. She gave her husband a loving embrace which was followed by a passionate kiss.

Their lovemaking lasted all afternoon. Both were surprised by the physical depth of their emotion. A powerful surge of passion infused their hearts and bodies. When the fire was spent, Benjamin curled next to his wife, experiencing a relaxation not felt since his indictment. A blanket of security wrapped him in her arms. Sleep came easy.

It was almost 6:00 when they arrived at the hospital. Nurse Galliger was gone. A pair of beady eyes squinted from the fat face sitting at the nurses station. "Hmmph, you were almost late," said the rotund nurse. "I was gonna call the police. Don't want nothing to happen to you on my shift," said the nurse, staring.

"It was such a wonderful afternoon," Ruth smiled. "An afternoon I wish could last forever."

"You are feeling better, aren't you?" said the nurse.

"I still have more than my share of moments, but, yes, I'm better."

Pritchitt escorted his wife to her room. On a table next to the window were two dozen roses. The sweet fragrance was overwhelming. "Those are the most beautiful flowers I've ever seen. Benjamin Pritchitt, you shouldn't have." She hurried to the roses, then turned wide-eyed.

"I didn't, Ruth. Wish I could say I did, but they're not from me."

"Oh! Maybe they came yesterday," said Ruth, trying to straighten her thoughts. She opened a drawer and removed four cards. She looked at each and read aloud. "From your loving Guardian Angel." She paused and looked up. Benjamin waited with more concern. "Each one says that, Ben. These aren't from you, Ben?"

"No, sweetheart," he answered.

Confusion set on Ruth's face.

"Ruth, is there any mention of a Simon, like there was on a card the other day?"

"Simon? Who's Simon?" she asked with a puzzled stare.

"You don't recall the fruit basket and flowers and the cards that came with them?"

She dropped her head, rubbing her temples. "No, I can't remember, but I can't remember a lot of things about the last week," she cried softly, obviously alarmed, as her face reflected fear and confusion. Ruth threw herself on the bed and wept.

There was a knock on the door. Dr. Blanche Tucker entered. "Time for my evening rounds. I . . . what's wrong Mrs. Pritchitt?"

Ruth said nothing.

"She couldn't remember something," answered Benjamin, reaching for the cards. He stood quietly looking at the roses, then the cards Ruth had dropped on the bed.

Dr. Tucker rubbed Ruth's shoulder. "Please don't worry," she said soothingly. "It does happen."

Ruth sat up in bed and wiped her cheeks.

Pritchitt offered his hand to Dr. Tucker. "The family wants to thank you for all the concern and care you've shown Ruth."

"You are quite welcome," she responded. "I'll be at the nurses's station for a while. Dr. Pritchitt," she said walking to the door. "I'd like a word with you before you leave."

"I won't be very much longer. I know Ruth needs to rest."

Dr. Tucker left. Ruth undressed and stepped inside the shower.

Pritchitt searched the first three baskets but discovered nothing. But the fourth basket of roses held a note. He knew who the author would be. Unfolding the note he stood at the window and read: "To the soul-mate of my soul-mate. The roses are a gift from the heart and a symbol of love. If not for you there'd be no Terry, Tyler, Benji or Claire. Four beautiful lives, four baskets of roses. The script is written. The curtain ascends. Those who attack the innocent unborn are Satan's minions. I will punish the wicked until my time arrives. Then I shall be with my own. Forever yours. His Guardian Angel, your admirer. Simon."

Benjamin stared out the window into the black of night. A too common chill passed through his spine. He was quiet with the loneliness of his thoughts. In night's darkness he saw nothing, not even hope. Depression gripped him. He knew the black of night would pass and daylight would come, but Simon reigned. Was he invincible? Dear God, prayed Benjamin. His mind dwelled on everything yet nothing.

Ruth emerged in a light pink hospital gown. Pritchitt slipped the note in his pocket as she pulled the covers over her. He knelt by the side of the bed and gently kissed her lips. "I love you, my precious wife. We will see the light of day together. I promise you we will."

"And I love you, Benjamin. And thanks for the afternoon." She caressed his cheek. Their eyes met. "Benjamin, who is this Simon?"

"A bad person. That's all you need to know."

He gently tucked the covers beneath her chin. She smiled and closed her eyes. Quietly he walked from the room.

CHAPTER SIXTEEN

Dr. Blanche Tucker sat in a small charting room near the nurse's station. It was hard to mask the concern in Pritchitt's face. He paced the room. "I can see you're worried," she remarked, placing her pen on the table. "She's tough. The ECT has brought on this memory loss and confusion. It will pass. She's still in a healing process, doctor. Give it time." Pritchitt's pace quickened. "But I can see you're having a hard time. This must be the toughest time in your life," said Dr. Tucker. "Would you like me to prescribe something for you?"

"No," responded Pritchitt sternly. "I don't need anything."

"You're not made of steel."

His steps halted. "This is what's killing me more than anything." He reached for a note from his pocket, his face grew red with anger.

Tucker uncrossed her long legs and reached for the note. "And what is this?"

"A note from Simon, to my wife." Vile disgust stirred his mind and Pritchitt paced.

"Public figures attract twisted minds," explained Tucker,

handing back the note. "Are you certain you do not wish to confer with a therapist?"

"Therapist? I want to buy a shotgun and blow this bastard's head off. If I didn't have enough problems pulling at my family's very existence. Now I get this maniac."

"You are displaying a lot of pent-up rage."

Pritchitt waved a fist. "Justifiable rage. He's the maniac killing these young girls. Simon is the serial killer. A serial killer in love with me and my family. What luck, right?"

Dr. Tucker straightened herself. "You must have something this Simon wants. I suspected Ruth had delusions and hallucinations the first days she was here. Now I understand. The first week she talked of a caller on the telephone and seemed to indicate his actual presence in the room. I assumed it to be a psychoses related to her acute withdrawal."

"Oh, he was there all right. He was in her room and on the phone," said Pritchitt nervously. "He was as close as a breath to my grandchildren's cheeks. I've had the strangest feeling he was here, right here in the hospital with Ruth."

"Fascinating," said Dr. Tucker.

"No. Not fascinating at all," he blurted with eyes raised. "A psychotic murderer is anything but fascinating." There was a pause. Pritchitt glared at Tucker's watchful stare. "And this Simon is weak. He's a person carrying tremendous guilt who can't face the life dealt him. Yes, a coward who wants to die, that's the only fascination of Simon. A spineless murderer of troubled defenseless women."

"How do you feel about abortion?" asked Dr. Tucker.

Pritchitt rubbed his tired eyes. "What does that have to do with any of this? Besides, it's a decision a man will never make alone, so I can only surmise what a young woman experiences when deciding to terminate a pregnancy."

"It is a very difficult decision, Dr. Pritchitt."

He turned and stared directly into her eyes. "Have you ever had an abortion?"

"Me? Heavens, no," she blurted defensively. "These days

wise people are very careful in their sexual relationships. Safe sex prevents both pregnancy and AIDS."

Pritchitt nodded. "Smart lady." He crossed his arms, his thoughts deep. "You're a woman, would you have an abortion?"

"Like you said, what does this have to do with anything?" replied Tucker. An awkward silence chilled the room. Tucker shifted in her seat, ill at ease. "Dr. Pritchitt, I didn't mean to pry into your beliefs. We psychiatrists have a nasty habit of asking too many questions." Pritchitt shrugged. "Do you really believe that you or Ruth have anything to fear from this Simon?"

"He says he won't harm us, but then how can you trust the word of a madman? He should be on death row."

Dr. Tucker raised her hand in protest. "I'm a psychiatrist, not a district attorney. I work with the mind and not the legal system. Truth be, I find the minds I deal with less complex than the law." Her voice was blunt but professional.

Pritchitt had said more than he had wished. He felt interrogated, as if he were her patient.

"Dr. Pritchitt, it does one good to talk their troubles out. Don't keep your demons to yourself."

Pritchitt regained his brief loss of composure. "I feel something has upset you in my comments. I want to know what it is." His harsh tone stirred concern in Dr. Tucker.

"No, absolutely not," she answered with an even voice. "Nothing you said has upset me. I've just had a long day, as have you."

His eyes locked onto hers. His intensity alarmed her.

"Please, doctor, sit down. You're making me nervous."

Pritchitt sat. "Tell me, this Simon could not possibly be a patient of yours, could he?"

"Absolutely not." Tucker placed her hand to his shoulder. "You have indeed been through much." Her eyes never left his challenging glare. Tucker stood and walked to the door. "I have patients to check." Tucker turned and vanished, seemingly distraught. A deep sigh stirred the still room as Pritchitt stood and slowly followed.

Bernie Wiseman squinted at the clock. It was half past midnight. His short nap had been interrupted by his beeper summoning him to begin late rounds. He readied himself in the on-call room, smoothing his hair and splashing water on his face. Nearing Pritchitt's office Wiseman's keen hearing made him halt. He tapped lightly but there was no response. The office was empty but the fax machine was off and running. "That's peculiar at this late hour." He yawned. Entering the office, he looked to the printing sheet and his exhaustion vanished. "Holy shit, another one," he gasped, waiting for the message to complete.

Taking the sheet he hurried to Pritchitt's desk. He studied the message. "What the hell does this mean?" he wondered. He read it aloud, as his concentration sharpened. "Dr. Overton and Dr. Park? Of course, Overton Park. What the hell . . . an ostrich hiding its head in the sand and the three wise men? This guy is a nut, and a certified cashew at that. A quiz show wouldn't have clues this vague," he whispered, his voice trailing off in frustration.

Bernie sat in Pritchitt's chair, determined to decipher this fax, as he had the others. But this one was different and he knew it. It was more than ambiguous. Under a small lamp he read and re-read the message. He was startled as his beeper erupted and a string of six continuous blips displaying the number of the emergency room followed by 911. "I'd better get my ass down to ER or Peters will have my head on a platter." He stood and folded the fax, placing it in his shirt pocket, and hurried from the room.

The alarm hit a high octave and with it the peace of night surrendered to the morning sun. Pritchitt stretched and performed several deep knee bends, loosening his stiff muscles.

He stepped into the shower and allowed the warm water to relax his tension. He poked his head from the shower and recognized Wiseman's voice on the answering machine. As he stopped the flow of water the name of Simon was clear in Wiseman's anxious plea.

Pritchitt jumped from the shower, grabbing a towel. In his haste he lost his balance and fell to the floor.

Pritchitt stretched on the long sofa in his living room, sipping coffee. His ankle swollen and aching from his clumsy trip. The putt-putt of a motor scooter was audible as it pulled to the front of the house. Loretta, the housekeeper, opened the front door and Wiseman breezed his way through the entry hall. He halted and peered at Pritchitt's naked ankle, an ice pack resting on it. "What happened?"

"Do you have to know? Let's just say, haste makes waste . . . and bad accidents, too."

"I don't get it."

"I was rushing to answer your call earlier."

"Oh, I see," Wiseman said, pulling a chair close to the couch. He removed fax sheets from his helmet.

"Loretta!" called Pritchitt, "coffee for Dr. Wiseman, please."

Wiseman grinned. "Hey, this is classy. Thank you very much," he said, taking a cup from the tray. "If hard work is the precursor to having a place like this," he said, "then let the hard work begin." Raising his cup in toast, he sipped the steaming brew.

"Let's try to logically dissect the writings of an illogical mind before my daughter comes back with the police."

"The police?"

"Absolutely," scolded Pritchitt sharply. "I don't want to make a mistake. I'm no damn detective and you aren't either." Pritchitt's mind shook with concern as Wiseman viewed the surrounding decor.

"It is someone close to you," said Wiseman.

"Why do you say that?"

"Simon knows too much about you. And he's damn sure you're going to be there for him at the end, to finalize this bizarre chapter of insanity he's begun." Wiseman drained his cup of coffee.

"And I am worried. He just may do something horrible

enough to you or your family . . . well, that may force you to cross the line —"

"There'll be no damn line crossing from this man," Pritchitt snapped. Pritchitt stood and paced with a slight limp.

"Yes, a line that separates insanity from what is temporary insanity. It would be easy for you then, Dr. Pritchitt. Easy for you to kill Simon," Wiseman lowered his voice to a whisper, "just so you do kill him."

Pritchitt lifted the sheet and read aloud. "Simon says: 'Dr. Overton, this is Dr. Park. Sins must not escape punishment. I'm not an ostrich to life's sinful ways. Three wise men sought the world's first innocence and found one who forgave sin. The Father, Son and Holy Ghost are seekers of the faithful. Life's love is nothing but a triangle of searching souls. Souls searching for love. And soon, Dr. Pritchitt, you will send me where I will complete my triangle. If one is up to par, sin will be exposed; if not found and destroyed, then love could be lost forever. With life's triangle never complete, sin could hide forever where the ostrich hides it's head.'"

"What a bizarre message," Pritchitt sighed. He removed his glasses. Both stood in deep thought. "Overton Park has a zoo," said Wiseman. "So where do we start?"

"The Ostrich Pit?"

"That's right, Dr. Pritchitt."

"And what does an ostrich do?"

"Hides it's head in the sand, of course," answered Wiseman. "Damn, we need to be going," he fussed. Both were anxious.

Pritchitt glanced at his watch. "I wonder what's keeping them?" Pritchitt asked, rubbing his sore ankle anxiously. "We can't wait any longer." He struggled into his shoe. "Loretta!" he shouted.

Her face peeked from the kitchen.

"Tell Terry I've gone to the Overton Park Zoo. She should bring the police with her and hurry."

"The zoo?" she repeated in a babbled voice.

CHAPTER SEVENTEEN

Poplar Avenue led from the suburbs to mid-town Memphis, the older section of the city where stately homes were surrounded by enormous oaks and elms.

The Cadillac roared past a row of mansions.

Motorists were oblivious to the frantic sense of urgency in the speeding automobile. Bernie had dissected the most recent message over and over as they roared through the heavily trafficked main thoroughfare of Memphis. He'd prepared for the worst.

Turning off Poplar, Pritchitt shot through Overton Park's narrow wooded lanes. Beyond the tree lined lanes, golfers swung gracefully on the beautiful fairways. Pritchitt honked at bikers foolish enough to challenge his speeding car as he sped toward the park's zoo. Suddenly, they hit a snail's pace, as Pritchitt found himself in a waiting line of cars. "Son-of-a-bitch," Pritchitt uttered with a frantic glimpse toward his strapped in passenger. "We can't have this," he shouted. With a quick jerk of the steering wheel the car careened onto a fairway of the adjacent golf course.

"Oh, hell!" Wiseman gasped, tightening his already fastened seatbelt. Racing through open fields, shocked picnickers fled for safety from the honking car, dodging in and out between clusters of trees. "I'm gonna die," Wiseman mumbled, shifting his eyes upward. "Holy shit!" he shouted with tree limbs brushing his window. "I hope you know your way through these fucking woods and to grandma's house!" He braced his hands against the dashboard as the tires pounded the rugged terrain below and his head bumped against the roof. Dodging trees and golfers, they sped through the park, until the zoo's parking lot appeared in a clearing ahead. The car suddenly nosed, then bounced high in the air. Briefly airborne it landed with a thud, maneuvering quickly as it brushed a large oak. "You're set on killing us, aren't you?" Wiseman screamed. "Remember, it's Simon you need to kill, not me, for God's sake," Pritchitt slowed his speed and drove his nervous passenger into the crowded parking lot where the car stopped.

"We're here. Wasn't too bad, was it, Wiseman?" he said getting out.

"You've got to be kidding," gasped Wiseman, who before he could catch his breath, saw Pritchitt hobbling toward the main entrance. At the ticket booth Pritchitt tossed down a crisp twenty leaving Wiseman to collect the change. Pritchitt headed to the mapped directory of the zoo just inside the entrance.

Pritchitt moved past excited children and women pushing strollers with Wiseman close behind.

The Ostrich Pit was far removed from the zoo's most popular exhibits. Two languid ostriches stood near the stone fence. A woman with a camera posed her small child nearby.

"Geez, they're ugly!" gasped Wiseman, doubled over, panting for breath. Pritchitt rubbed at his sore ankle, numbed by an adrenaline rush. He limped toward the stone fence.

"Shouldn't we call the zookeeper or something?"

Suddenly Pritchitt climbed atop a stone barrier. A young mother turned, wide-eyed.

"Look, Mommy," a small boy yelled, pointing to Pritchitt's stance atop the stone fence.

"Nothing to be alarmed about, ma'am. We just think there may be a dead body in there," explained Wiseman in a matter of fact manner.

The woman grabbed her child's hand and pulled him back as Pritchitt leaped into the pit. Others crowded around.

Bernie straddled the fence, catching his pants on a protruding edge. "Shit!" He looked up. "Watch out!" he cautioned Pritchitt. "Those ugly overgrown chickens have powerful kicks if they get nasty." He pulled free from the captive snag, ripping his pants. Freed but frustrated he jumped and toppled over into the sandy dirt. Bernie followed. They eased toward a large rock and a mound of fresh sand heaped in the rear of the pit, near a cavernous shaped structure. Cautiously they moved not to disturb their anxious and seemingly unhappy hosts. They searched the rocks, then began to dig through the sand, but without success. An ostrich began scratching at the dirt, like a bull targeting a red cape. It was nearly eight feet high, weighing three hundred pounds.

Wiseman looked up. "I don't like the way he's looking at us, sir." Agitation showed in the bird's loud chirping. The huge black wings flapped and the legs turned a bright pink. The sharp toes scratched the earth.

Pritchitt stepped slowly toward the back of the pit and peered into its dark cavern. Looking back, he gave a thumbs up to Wiseman then turned, disappearing into the darkness of the cave.

"What the hell's going on here?" shouted a loud and angry voice from the fence.

Wiseman turned to see curious gawkers and a fuming attendant leaning over the fence.

Pritchitt suddenly emerged. "It's too dark in there, Wiseman. Can't see anything." His thumb pointed toward the dark cave. A charging ostrich bolted from the cavern knocking Pritchitt to the sand. The attendant jumped the fence. A large clawed toe reached out at Pritchitt, ripping his jacket. Wiseman scooped up sand and threw it toward the furious creature as the attendant chased it back with a long pole. The bird flapped its wings, then turned and ran to the rear of the pit. Pritchitt pulled himself up and suddenly both men were encircled by a trio of hostile ostriches, their feathers ruffled, ready for attack.

"Over here!" yelled the attendant, as he waved and they ran behind two large rocks. Nearby a gate opened. "You damn nuts!" shouted the attendant, who hustled them out, then slammed the gate. "I'm calling my supervisor and then the police!" bellowed the red-faced attendant.

"Yes, do that," replied the out of breath Pritchitt.

"That won't be necessary," came a woman's stern voice. Lt. Lori Bordeaux stood but five feet away, her hands placed firmly on her hips.

"Round up those birds, Joe," ordered Mae Whitehead, the zoo director as she stormed up the sidewalk.

"These maniacs, fools, c-c-crackpots," stammered the attendant, "they almost got ripped to shreds."

"Dad, what's going on?" Terry gasped at the sight of her father, caked in dust, his expensive suit shredded. "All Loretta said was to get over here."

"Have to admit, we did a little bit of panicking," said Wiseman with embarrassment. "We just couldn't wait, believing there was another dead body to be found."

Bordeaux poked him soundly in the chest. "That's my job."

Mae Whitehead stepped between them. "My job is to keep the zoo a tranquil and joyful place. Look what you've done."

The crowd had grown beyond the stone fence. Mothers with worried faces and fearful children all gazed in their direction.

Wiseman handed the faxes to Bordeaux.

She and Terry pored over the message.

Bordeaux gazed upwards. "I apologize, Dr. Pritchitt. And ma'am," she said, looking to Whitehead, "we do need to dig up your Ostrich Pit."

"Wait just a damn minute!" Miss Whitehead was alarmed. "You can't just do that. I'll call the mayor."

"Don't have a minute, ma'am. I'm telephoning headquarters for authorization," explained Bordeaux.

Within a half hour a forensic team was carefully probing the sandy pit, while the big birds were locked in an adjoining pen. The mushrooming crowd had been pushed back by the police but still held a curious vigilance.

Lt. Bordeaux stood near the pit. She paced nervously.

A camera crew and reporters arrived on the scene.

"Here comes your boss," Bordeaux said in a warning tone as she turned toward the pit.

"Have you found anything yet, Lt. Bordeaux?" Nash hastily grunted, barely acknowledging her presence.

"Not yet, but they're still digging." Bordeaux handed the fax to Nash.

"Look at this place," he fretted, observing the roaming reporters and camera crews. "This is a damn three ring circus. We better get some damn answers, and quick. Everyone with a T.V. will know what's going on here by the late news," he fussed, lighting a half-burnt cigar. "We better find more than bird shit in there or this whole damn case will turn to shit," he fumed.

Terry looked to her father, hoping that something would be found with the public spectacle they had caused.

Within an hour the workers had stopped for a break, stretching their sore backs as the deputy police chief and zoo director huddled together. After a long conference, they walked briskly toward Lt. Bordeaux, who sat apprehensively on a park bench beside Justin Nash.

The deputy chief began a slow boil. His frown was more of a child's pout as he approached. "Lt. Bordeaux, Miss Whitehead and the mayor are rightfully concerned about the frivolous waste of time and money going on here. We'll keep looking for one more hour, and that's all."

"Wait a minute, Pete," interrupted Nash. "Dammit, this was a viable lead. Lori did the right thing. We're just as anxious as you to resolve this thing, but let's don't fly off the handle. There's a lot of things the public can't know," Nash scolded.

Deputy Chief Billings waved his hands. "All right, Mr. Nash, keep it down." He nodded in the direction of the media where video cameras ringed the Ostrich Pit. "I'll meet you in

Miss Whitehead's office in one hour." Nash nodded his head. The deputy chief and zoo director stalked away, trailed by a throng of reporters.

Nash walked to the rear gate where Pritchitt, Wiseman and Terry congregated, observing the workmen digging in the sand.

"I just don't get it," Wiseman said with disappointment. "He's never mislead us before. Now what's in it for him to screw with us like this?"

"Remember what I've often told you. A —"

"I know." Wiseman quickly answered Pritchitt. "A depraved mind yields not to organization but to chaos and confusion."

"But how do you know he's mislead us?" Nash asked.

"He's a vicious, merciless killer," Pritchitt blurted with disdain. Frustration clenched his teeth and furrowed his brow.

"Why has he led us on a wild goose chase with this fax?" Wiseman asked in a puzzled voice.

Wiseman was thinking, studying the fax again. Pritchitt strode away, toward the parking lot with his daughter. Terry gave her father a hug, along with an admonition. "Dad, please promise me that you'll stop running around like this. Remember, this guy is a killer and no one to mess with, and that goes for Wiseman, too. The next time you could be attacked by more than an overgrown pigeon."

Wiseman shook his head. "You're right and wrong, Terry. This Simon admires your father and to hurt him would be his last thought. Remember, it's your father who's to send this Simon from . . . hold on." Wiseman interrupted his own soliloquy. "Maybe he didn't mislead you after all," he drawled. He waved the fax message. "I mean, we interpreted the message wrong the first time," offered Wiseman hesitantly. "Maybe it was not the Ostrich Pit."

Bernie studied the sheet and squinted as he read it again in the rapidly fading sunlight. "It's a little farfetched but this makes some sense. In his message he keeps talking in three's. He mentions three which includes himself: Simon, Dr. Park and

Dr. Overton. And also, the Father, Son and Holy Ghost. Even a triangle has three points."

"A little far fetched. But, okay, so we have a message of threes, so what?" Terry asked.

"At the very end, he says if you're up to par. Par is used in what sense here?"

"Par means average or equal to," Pritchitt defined in a less than enthusiastic voice. "It's a golfing term."

"Dammit, think!" commanded Wiseman. There was silence. Eye brows raised in doubt and no one seemed to follow Wiseman's faulty analysis. "The sand!" Wiseman loudly mumbled, his eyes buried in the fax sheet.

Pritchitt watched the young doctor's intensity. His mind unable to extract the same enthusiasm. He stared at his daughter then Bordeaux.

"I've got it. It's been here all along. Too simple," exploded Wiseman.

"I'm glad someone does," a bewildered Terry mumbled.

Wiseman gasped. His eyes wide with excitement. "The par three hole, and it's damn sand traps!" Wiseman yelled out, a reborn spirit in his shriek.

"You think so? God I hope you're right," Pritchitt remarked in a disbelieving tone.

Terry reached for her cell phone. "What the hell. What do we have to lose?" she said. "I'd better clue in Nash."

"Sounds a little too crazy to me," said Bordeaux.

"No crazier than its author," answered Wiseman.

Receiving Terry's call Nash hurried from the parking lot. "We're going to need shovels, people." They hurried toward the golf course club house with the fading light their enemy.

Wiseman emerged from the club house with a layout of the nine hole golf course. He sat in the golf cart next to Pritchitt and pointed to the rear of the score card, indicating the only par three on the course.

Inside, Nash hammered the counter. "Now where can we get a shovel or two? And I need the quickest way to the par three?"

"There are some shovels in the work shed out back," the greensman told them. Nash reached in his wallet and flashed a twenty.

"We're with the District Attorney's office. We're looking for something. This is very important."

"I'll get the shovels," said the greensman, rushing outside. He grabbed the twenty. "It's gonna be dark soon and the layout of the course through the woods ain't that easy, mister. If it's gold you're looking for, then maybe you'll cut me in on the deal," he joked. But seeing Nash's stern face, he grew serious, then reached for a large flashlight. "I'll be glad to show you."

Justin Nash walked briskly from the club house. "Let's go," he said, jumping into the cart beside Terry.

The greensman took the wheel in Pritchitt's cart as Wiseman jumped onto the back.

The fading rays of the setting sun filtered through the treetops as the caravan moved along the green fairways and around large sand traps, then onto a dark trail lined by dense woods.

The greensman hand signaled. The carts struck several bumps, then nose-dived down a steep hill. Nash knew it was near their destination, as did Wiseman, who turned and pointed triumphantly to the hole ahead. Light was fading fast as the sun's dimming rays lingered amongst the highest branches of the tall trees. The carts came to a stop.

Wiseman began to shift through the mounds of white sand, assuring himself that he had seen it all, and fear was alien to a physician. The greensman quickly tilled through the whiteness. Pritchitt watched carefully. Terry stood near the golf cart, her arms folded tightly as Nash searched a trap across the green.

"I've struck something." The beam of the flashlight brightened the greensman's shovel. He plunged his hand into the deep sand and yanked out a dark object. It was a weathered school binder. Fear and relief were replaced by disappointment and Wiseman returned to the frantic digging.

Pritchitt remarked, "We've got maybe five minutes of light left." He kicked at the mound of sand before him. "We can't be that far off," he said excitedly.

Wiseman moved the sand in rapid stroking motions, as if his very life depended on success. The greensman righted himself. "Ain't nothing in this pile of sand," he grumbled.

Wiseman suddenly froze, his shovel held motionless at shoulder level, his muscles rigid. Then he probed gently, removing the camouflaging sand. He suddenly jerked backwards. "My God! It's here!" he shouted.

The flashlight beam traced his shovel until it rested on a face swathed in plastic. Both eyes were wide open, as if fixed by a paralyzing fright. The mouth was wide, choked with sand. No one spoke. Wiseman regained his lost composure and continued to remove the sand from the young woman's upper body. Unveiled before them was a stilled hand, and then an arm, as the sand was swept away by the nervous stroke of his shovel.

"Dear God in heaven," Terry prayed as her voice broke. "That poor girl!" She wept softly as Nash and Pritchitt seated her in a golf cart.

There was a retching sound. The greensman lifted himself. "I'm sorry," he apologized. "I ain't never seen nothin' like that before."

Nash got on his phone outlining his location, reporting the finding. The ignition was turned and a small headlight lit the grass. The cart moved up the hill toward the woods. Terry leaned unsteadily on Nash, holding tightly to his coat. "It's all right, Terry," he whispered. "Everything will be fine, I promise. Simon won't hurt you or your father."

"Dear God, I hope you're right."

Pritchitt watched the tiny red lights move over the hill.

"Son of a bitch," said the greensman, still holding the flashlight on the terrible sight. "You guys are after that serial killer. Now I know."

"I'd say she's not a day over twenty-three," said Wiseman.

The gruesome image vanished as the greensman turned off the flashlight.

Overhead the crescent moon cast its white glow. The tiny headlight of the golf cart reappeared. Nash was alone.

"That stinking, goddamn murderer," the greensman cursed. "I'd like to rip him to pieces."

Nash lit a cigar. "This is tragic. An unfortunate girl whose only reason for dying was that she chose the wrong thing to do at the wrong time."

"Can't argue with that," said Wiseman.

"In the old days we'd just shoot 'em like a mad dog," the greensman added. He handed the flashlight to Wiseman, jumped in the cart and drove away.

Nash looked at the starry sky above. "It did seem to be a better world back then," he commented. Walking in the dark grass he puffed from his cigar. He heard the low roar of a helicopter overhead. A van stopped at the edge of the green. Darkness exploded into brightness. The helicopter's powerful beam shone on them. Men in white jumpsuits emerged from the van.

The deputy coroner, a mask resting on his forehead, slipped on a pair of gloves. "So it wasn't a wild goose chase after all?" he remarked.

Nash turned to the sand trap and its concealed corpse. "Unfortunately not," he whispered. "Unfortunately not."

CHAPTER EIGHTEEN

Police cars lit the darkness. Their strobes created an eerie blue light over the sand trap. A team from the coroner's office surrounded the body. In the woods, officers with powerful flashlights shot beams through the darkness and search dogs barked excitedly. Lt. Bordeaux and Detective Caffey walked up to Wiseman and Nash. Bordeaux shouted orders to the uniformed officers who searched the grounds for clues. "Well, Dr. Wiseman, I was beginning to think you were slipping."

"Or maybe our killer Simon was just having fun and playing mind games with us," offered her partner Det. Caffey.

"These are deadly games," said Justin Nash, staring at the busy forensic team. The body was being lifted into a large body bag.

Lt. Bordeaux turned. "All right, Caffey, there goes the victim. We can let the reporters into the crime scene for no more than five minutes, then get them the hell out. We got the area roped?"

"Yep," said Caffey, who then moved swiftly away. Police cruisers led the coroner van from the golf course.

"There's not much more we can do now," said Bordeaux. "Come daylight we can go over these grounds without a damn seeing eye dog. You guys ready?"

Reporters swarmed the club house. From the rear of Bordeaux's cruiser Pritchitt and Wiseman watched as the greensman spoke before bright lights.

"That fellow's gonna make the evening news," observed Nash.

Lori Bordeaux turned. "When I call them over to make a brief statement, you guys head for your cars." Bordeaux sauntered over to the line of video cameras. Flashbulbs flickered and Bordeaux was quickly encircled by the story hungry reporters.

"Go on home, gentlemen," said Nash. "You've had enough at playing detectives. No response was needed as Pritchitt and Wiseman quietly hurried toward the parking lot.

Though not yet nine, the streets of Memphis were vacant. On the radio, reports broadcast the latest gruesome murder. At a traffic light Nash pulled behind an automobile with a recognizable city seal on its rear window. It was Jesse. Her car continued down Poplar Avenue, as Nash fell behind. She turned onto a side street, then stopped in the parking lot of a women's clinic and headed for the entrance. Nash tapped his horn lightly as he pulled beside her. Shock registered on her face. "Mr. N- Nash, what are you doing here?"

"I might ask you the same."

"Were you following me?"

"No, of course not. Please get in." He reached to the passenger side and pushed open the door. "Please," he urged.

Jesse sat beside him, huddled in her overcoat, fear on her face.

"Jesse, I'm very worried about you."

She turned to meet his eyes. "It's just that we . . . my boyfriend and me —"

"Jesse, something like this is not as simple as it appears.

It's not clear cut. There can be many emotional after shocks from this. Please, believe me."

She said nothing.

"If I had a little sister, I'd want her to be just like you. So, if you're not doing anything, why don't you make a lonely guy happy and let me buy you an ice cream sundae?"

A faint smile crossed her lips, then disappeared. "I am doing something."

"Take more time to think." He took her hand. "Please, come on and let me take you for an ice cream. There's a place a few blocks from here." She nodded.

"I'm a good listener," said Nash.

They drove off.

Nash paid the cashier, then put two large banana splits on the table. Nash began eating his sundae by licking whipped cream from his spoon.

Jesse laughed. Her face suddenly froze. Tears began streaming down her cheeks. "I don't know what to do," she cried. "I'm so torn."

"Have you told your boyfriend about tonight?"

"No," she wept quietly. "He would probably marry me but I don't want a marriage like that. And . . . and I think I'm too young to be a mother." Nash moved his chair beside her.

"When I was younger my girlfriend became pregnant." His voice trailed off. "She made the wrong decision."

Jesse said nothing more. After a few mouthfuls of ice cream, she spoke. "I will go home tonight," she said softly. "You're right. I have to think about this more."

Later in the car she turned to Nash. "Do you think . . . if I do this, God will want my soul?"

Nash slowed the car as he turned in the clinic parking lot. "I do know one thing."

She looked at him wide eyed. Nash took her hands. "I do know that you'll never have another ice cream with that child again, if you end its life."

A security guard flashed a light on the vehicle. The watchman stared curiously.

Jesse hurried from the car. "I'm all right. I'm just reconsidering."

The guard nodded. "Happens all the time."

He walked away. Jesse smiled, waved, and drove off.

The Pritchitt residence was dimmed by night's black backdrop. There was a repeated knock at the front door. After a few moments the porch light came on. Terry opened the door, pulling a silk bathrobe around her neck.

"Just checking on you," said Nash.

"This is a surprise. Come on in," she beckoned. "Dad and the kids are in bed. I'm just stepping from a long hot bath."

She led him to the den and turned on the television. "The late news is coming on." She placed her fingers to her lips and spoke in a low tone. Her voice choked with emotion. "It was a bad evening. I was so upset. I was yelling at the children." She retreated to the bathroom and closed the door. Nash removed his overcoat and sat on the sofa beside a small pile of clothes. He pushed aside Terry's dress and underclothes. He stroked the smooth white slip, then held dainty panties in his hands, just as Terry came into the den.

"Oh," she said with embarrassment.

"Quite sexy," said Justin. "I didn't realize you have such a tiny waist."

"A tiny waist and a tiny brain."

"No, Terry, I didn't —"

"You've always been critical of me." She brushed the clothes to the floor and sat beside him.

Nash smelled the alcohol.

"I'm sorry," she said with emotion. "I'm not in such a great mood. The golf course, and that . . . well . . . that poor girl." She began crying. Nash tried to console her but she pushed his arms away and jumped from the sofa.

"I need a drink."

Terry returned with a half-consumed bottle of white wine

and goblets. She placed the wine glasses on the coffee table and leaned forward. A round breast slipped from her silk robe. Their eyes met. Terry buttoned her robe and sat next to Nash.

"Did anything turn up?" she asked.

"No," sighed Nash, "maybe tomorrow."

The television's low volume was heard from across the den. A news announcer headlined the girl's death. "Another body was discovered around six this evening." Lt. Lori Bordeaux appeared on the screen. "Did she have an abortion like the rest?" asked the reporter.

"We'll have to wait for the autopsy report," Bordeaux answered.

The scene cut to smiling news anchors. "In other news the Tigers are ready to play a big game at Liberty Bowl Stadium tomorrow night."

Terry emptied her glass and slammed it to the table. "You bastards!" she growled. "A dead girl gets two fucking minutes! Now it's time for ten minutes of football scores!" She snatched the bottle from the table and poured.

"A little heavy on the booze tonight?"

"No, I haven't had nearly enough." Her glass slipped from her hand and shattered against the floor.

"Here, let me help," offered Nash.

Terry pushed him to the couch. "I'll clean it up."

She returned with a broom and dust pan, sweeping up shards of shattered glass. Nash traced her shapely figure beneath the silk robe. He heard the tinkle of glass as it fell into the waste basket in the kitchen.

In the den Terry placed her hands on her hips and glared at the television. "More sports?" The TV screen went dark and she tossed the channel changer on the table. She lowered her eyes and folded her arms.

"I can understand your anger, Terry."

She looked at him. "No, my total frustration," she corrected.

"We all have problems," Nash said in a soothing voice.

"Oh, no, not like mine." She began pacing the room. "My

father is going to trial for assisting suicides, my mother is hospitalized for major depression and alcoholism, there's a murderer out there I can't catch, and an ill-advised second marriage that has ended in total humiliation. My poor kids." Her voice trailed off.

"None of that is your fault, Terry."

She grimaced. "Dammit! That's one piece I missed." She collapsed onto the sofa, searching for the glass shard in her foot.

"Let me take a look," said Nash. He placed her foot on his lap. Blood trickled from a small cut. He squinted, then removed a small piece of glass. "That got it." The robe slipped open revealing her firm porcelain legs and thighs.

"Do you find me attractive?" she asked hesitantly.

"I'd have to say that one would be foolish not to. You are very lovely," said Nash.

She leaned over and held his hand. Her wet lips kissed his cheek. She stared into his uneasiness. She tried placing his hand to her breast. He resisted.

Justin pressed his lips to hers for a moment. He pulled back.

"Terry . . . I'm sorry," he whispered. He stood. "I should go," he said, turning toward the door.

Terry's embarrassment showed. Sobering reality returned. Her composure regained, she straightened her gown and walked him to the door.

Pritchitt's eyes opened. He squinted against the morning sun. His only peace was disrupted by the intrusive blast of the door bell. He grabbed a robe and rushed down the stairs not wanting everyone else to be awakened this early. It was just 7:00 a.m. Through the peephole he viewed the unkempt appearance of Niles Mercer. Benjamin stood back from the door wondering what to do next. He decided to unlock the large front door.

"Thank goodness, you're home, Benjamin." Niles folded his hands as if in prayer. His speech was garbled and broken, his eyes wide and bloodshot. There was a bandage on his forehead. Pritchitt looked at him with growing uneasiness.

Niles' head twitched and his breath was foul. His eyes darted back and forth. Pritchitt's unease grew. "Niles, just what can I do for you?"

"You don't know what it means to me that you've opened your door and want to help. Someone who has been there and explored his own soul. Someone prepared to lose everything because of his beliefs. We're no different, Dr. Pritchitt. I thank God for you, sir."

Pritchitt looked through his distorting face and saw mental illness with its fleeting ideas and disorganized thoughts.

"You're a person whose soul controls his destiny," Niles continued.

Pritchitt observed the total confusion of scattered thoughts that escaped any meaning.

Pritchitt pointed. "What happened to your head?"

"Oh, that. I kept hearing someone calling me. Boom! I had to hit my head to make them stop. And it worked, Ben, it really worked."

"Niles, are you taking your medication?"

"No sir, I'm not. It affected me badly. It's the reason Terry has run from me, sir. I knew you would understand and talk to her.

"Niles. I don't think this is the right time or place for this discussion."

"Oh, but it is, sir. It's the most important talk you'll ever have because it involves the happiness of your only daughter and the welfare of both Claire and Benji, who I already consider as much mine as hers."

Pritchitt stroked the stubbles on his chin. "Niles, please go back to your doctor. Let him try something else. Let him put you in the hospital. You need help."

The talking continued, Niles ignoring all pleas to get help. "Niles, I have to go," Pritchitt tried to close the door. A foot held it open.

Agitation changed Niles' fractured cadence. Anger grew

from his frown. "Tell Terry that I can perform my marital duties."

"Son, I've got a lot to do today and I'm already running late." Pritchitt turned.

"Oh, but I've already washed your car," Niles announced proudly. He pointed to the sparkling Cadillac in the driveway. "You can now ride in your crystal clean chariot like the knight you and I know you are."

"What do you want? Money?"

"No, sir. I just wish to discuss my marital problems with my father-in-law."

"Niles, your marriage to Terry is finished! You must get that through your head."

"Never! No, you're wrong." His voice grew angry. "The Bible says that once you marry, it's forever or until death do you part. I'm her husband!" he screamed. He turned and kicked a flower pot off the porch, then stared at Pritchitt with a vengeful hostility. "You're no different than the others." He ripped the flowers from the broken vase and threw them toward Pritchitt. "I looked up to you. I thought you were a spirit from God. I thought we heard the same voice of destiny. I was arrested for defending the unborn and you, you're a compassionate hero for the dying. He ascended the steps, standing a few inches from Pritchitt whose heart raced. He ranted as if preaching to the fallen. His hands gestured skyward with each point.

"Niles get a hold of yourself. You're making no sense."

"What God has joined together, let no man put asunder."

Pritchitt watched in silent shock. Niles was worse than Terry had described.

"Benjamin, she fucked another man."

Pritchitt remained restrained. "Get help, Niles."

"You didn't know your precious daughter could be evil, huh? I must save the children. You had no idea what you helped create could be so wicked."

Pritchitt grabbed Niles and urged him down the steps. "Listen and listen well because there'll be no second warning.

You cause one bit of trouble for my daughter or my grandchildren, or for that matter anyone of my family, and I swear to you by all that is holy you'll have no further need for medicine or therapy. Do you understand?"

A newspaper boy paused on the sidewalk. He witnessed the altercation as he approached. Hesitantly he backed his step.

Niles saw the boy's frightened face. "Did you see what he did? He pushed me and threatened me." Niles yelled to the boy. "This is Dr. Benjamin Pritchitt, the murdering angel of death."

The teenager stopped in his steps. Niles ran to the flower bed and scooped up dirt. He threw it onto the gleaming Cadillac.

"Get help, Niles!" shouted Pritchitt.

Niles turned with a vile glare. "I don't need help. I have God on my side," he shouted, throwing his arms toward the sky. He ran past the frozen boy and down the drive to a beat up automobile.

The boy watched as the old car screeched away. "He's kinda like that ostrich, sir," yelled the boy.

"What do you mean?" asked Pritchitt. The boy held up the newspaper. *Girl Found In Overton Park*. A color photograph was below the headline. Benjamin stepped forward as the boy approached and saw himself at the zoo — *Dr. Pritchitt Attacked By Angry Ostrich*. "Yes," smiled Pritchitt. "Guess you can say he's like the ostrich."

"Except for one thing, sir."

"Yes, and what's that?"

"He doesn't seem like the type that will go and hide his head in the sand, sir."

"I'm afraid you're right, young man. I'm afraid you're right." Taking the paper he retreated to the quiet walls of his home. Terry was standing in the foyer. Resting his head against the closed door he could not erase the insanity seen in Niles' eyes.

"I heard it all," Terry said.

"I think we should call the police," he suggested. "Get an injunction so he can't come near you and the children."

"You're right, Dad."

"He made no sense, even saying you had committed adultery last night." There was a long silence.

"He must have been looking in the window?"

"I don't know. Did . . . ?"

"Justin was here last night. Niles must have —" She began to cry.

"Terry, call the police. He is a very disturbed individual. His actions are totally unpredictable, sweetheart."

"I can't," she sobbed. "I'm too ashamed. I made such a poor choice."

"Get hold of yourself, Terry," he reprimanded. "Shame is no longer in this family's vocabulary. A family fighting for its survival does anything. Now you call the police or I will, and do it now!" Pritchitt slowly climbed the stairs.

He paused before his reflection in the mirror. The last few months had aged his body and soul. "Dear God, when will this all be done?" he prayed. He bowed his head and closed his eyes.

It was noon when Nash pulled into the nearly deserted parking lot at the police station. Still, a small group of reporters, armed with cameras, pounced.

"You guys are just like vultures," he snapped.

"Hey, we're just doing our job," said a reporter. Microphones were pushed in Nash's face. "Any closer and I'll bite them off," he said angrily. *"The Memphis Clarion* made a fool of Dr. Pritchitt."

The reporter laughed. "He should know better than to try to ride an ostrich."

Nash cast a contemptuous glare and wagged a finger at the media. "It was Dr. Pritchitt's perseverance that led to the girl's discovery in Overton Park." He saw their faces grow serious. His hand dropped, realizing he had said too much. Video cameras were turned on and filming.

A dark hand waved for his attention. It was Connie Jackson from Channel Six. "What does Dr. Pritchitt have to do with the serial killings?" she yelled as microphones crowded his face.

Nash quickly backed away. "I have nothing more to say," he blurted with anger.

"Why are you here on Saturday?" someone shouted out.

"I'm always working, didn't you sharp reporters already know that?" he answered sarcastically pinning his I.D. badge to his lapel.

A female reporter shouted a question as he moved toward the entrance. "Is it true that Mayor Daniels and the city council demanded a meeting for today, to express their lack of confidence in your investigation of the serial murders? Is it also true, Mr. Nash, that District Attorney Jeremy Bates might remove you from the case and take it over himself?"

Nash ignored the question and pushed a microphone from his flustered face. He hurried up the steps. He felt a tug from behind, and turned angrily. His silent rage halted their questions. His face flushed. Seeing his surging emotion the encircling band backed away from their prey. His eyes fell on Connie Jackson.

"Young lady," he called out in an even tone, "you already know that the mayor is waiting for me. In fact, I'm sure you bugged the hell out of her the same way you're bugging me, so why ask such a dumb question?" His sudden attack left her speechless and she lowered her microphone. "And, to answer you, I don't care who the hell lacks confidence in me as long as I have confidence in myself." He turned to Eddie White. "And print that in big bold fucking letters, okay?"

"The women of the city are terrified," shouted Connie Jackson.

"Well, the only women who should be concerned are those stupid enough to be leaving abortion clinics unaccompanied late at night." He turned and vanished through the front door.

Nash rounded the corner for the elevators knowing of his dilemma. The growing tension in the community and now the political pressure of this unsolved case had been dumped in the mayor's lap. Anxiously he awaited the elevator. The meeting with Mayor Daniels would be anything but pleasant, he thought.

Police Director John Roberts opened the door; looking at his watch, he said, "You've kept us waiting almost twenty-eight minutes. This meeting was for noon sharp."

Nash scanned the room, seeing Detectives Bordeaux and Caffey along with Tim Bauers, Terry Mercer and various other city officials. "Mayor Daniels, you'll have to excuse me," said Nash, "but the foursome in front of me was late teeing off and most of my shots were played out of the rough." He casually walked to his desk, without looking at anyone, and placed his briefcase on his desk.

Nash saw Lori Bordeaux was chuckling.

"Ladies and gentlemen, please," Mayor Daniels interrupted, standing from her chair. "Speaking of foursomes and golf, Mr. Nash, I'm glad your escapade at the zoo wasn't a flop, considering we did save face by finding that poor girl's body buried in the sand trap. We've gained some ground in the public eye, at least. But speaking of you playing from the rough, Mr. Nash," she lectured, "I feel like I've been left in the rough in this case. And this being an election year, Mr. Nash, well . . . it's time for us to get this case back in the fairway, onto the green and in the fucking cup, if you'll excuse my language."

"Excused," said Nash.

"Gained ground, my ass," Director Roberts ripped. "All we gained is another unexplained body for more people to worry about," he barked. "Now we'll have citizens afraid to play golf at Overton Park. Dammit, Nash. They're scared if they swing at a ball in the sand a hand will pop up."

"Director Roberts, that'll be quite enough," the mayor ordered, stepping between Robert's glare and Nash's tense stare.

"Where's Dist. Atty. Bates?" asked Bauers. "I thought he was supposed to be here, too?

"And who are you and, no, he wasn't asked," said the mayor.

"Tim Bauers, one of my valued assistants, Mayor Daniels," Nash offered.

"Well, I hope he still has a job, like many of us, when the dust settles on this case," she replied. "And, no, Dist. Atty. Bates was not asked to this meeting. I told him I'd give him a call after meeting with his trusted top executive assistant." The plump mayor took a seat.

Daniels was the city's first female mayor, elected with a narrow percentage of votes. She had seen her marginal popularity plummet with the unsolved serial murders. She found herself under pressure from advisors and supporters to solve the case before the killer buried her career in a political sand trap.

Nash took a cigar and waved it in the air. "Ms. Mayor, I just want to say one more thing that needs to be said."

"And what is that?

"That I take back everything I've ever said about your administrative skills. I truly have to hand it to you. To do the job you've done while handicapped by the likes of the people you surround yourself with is a credit to your ability, Mayor Daniels." Nash shook his head as he leaned back and puffed on his cigar.

"That does it!" shouted Roberts angrily. "I'm not going to sit in this room and take crap from this poor excuse for a —" He jumped from his seat heading quickly for the door.

"You're going to stay!" screamed Daniels. All eyes shot toward her. "And you, Mr. Justin Nash, with all your arrogance, you will shut the fuck up." Her large body pulled itself lose from her chair. She began pacing the room. "I'm not happy and neither are the citizens. But we've got a job to do. Do you understand, gentlemen?" She walked over to Nash and grabbed the cigar from his hand. She paused and looking him straight in the eyes placed the cigar to her lips and took a long draw. There was no motion or sound as she exhaled smoke into his face and returned to him his cigar. "You're not any tougher than me, Top Gun. And don't you ever forget that!"

The room filled with quiet tension. The mayor's aides stood silently behind her, waiting for her next command. Her voice returned to an even tempered tone. "We've got a very big problem and have no time for personal bullshit squabbles. Okay. Lt. Bordeaux, do you have any leads?"

Lori looked at Nash. "I'll allow Mr. Nash to disclose what he wishes."

Nash clenched the cigar between his teeth. "Yes, we do have leads, mayor. I plan to hold a news conference later in the day."

The look on Bordeaux's face was one of surprise.

"That's great, absolutely wonderful." Mayor Daniels applauded lightly, looking around the room, as her two aides smiled.

Director Roberts looked at Bordeaux. "You didn't say anything about this to me. Bordeaux, why don't we know anything about this news conference?" he blurted in embarrassment. Bordeaux remained quiet and looked to Nash.

"That's my fault entirely, sir," Nash responded. "There are some very touchy issues at stake here. Some that don't need to be made too public, if you get my drift. The entire investigation can be jeopardized if as much as a small leak were to surface."

Mayor Daniels looked skeptical. "Wait a minute. I smell baloney. The people of Memphis desperately need to know that their mayor is on top of this investigation and that we finally have something tangible to follow." She walked over to Nash. "But if you're by any chance playing me for a fool on this, I'll have your head in my file cabinet. Do we understand each other, Nash?"

"Quite well, Your Honor."

She waved to her aides. "I must attend to other problems. I await this press conference with eager ears." She walked briskly from the room as her aides shuffled off behind her.

Police Director Roberts stood. "Bordeaux, all I have to say to you is remember what it was like handling jail drunks if you mess up. And remember, Lt. Bordeaux, you work for us and not the D.A.'s office."

Bordeaux slumped in her seat. "I can still smell the wino's vomit."

Terry posed the question that had electrified the meeting.

"Is this press conference something that has just come up?"

Nash was quiet as he walked to the window and puffed his cigar.

Terry circled Nash. "Come on. What the hell goes? We're a team, aren't we? I remember that not too many days ago you dragged me across the coals because Wiseman, Atway and I found a body in a garbage truck and you weren't told. We're not playing some kind of double standard here, are we?"

"Of course not, Terry. I'm not sure, but I have a hunch. I do want to say this — before coming inside I was ambushed by the press, and in the heat of the moment I announced that Dr. Pritchitt was the one responsible for locating the body in the park. The reporters had seen him at the Ostrich Pit yesterday. Maybe it's time to inform the public of Simon, and that he has been communicating with your father about the murders."

"Are you crazy? Jeremy Bates will destroy him. The media will butcher him and this less than two weeks before his trial," argued Terry.

"Won't that make him a suspect?" asked Bauers.

"No," said Nash, blowing smoke rings.

"Bullshit! The hell it won't. It will scare Simon away from our only connection with him, too." added Bordeaux. "Bad idea."

"Maybe . . . or it may bring him closer," Nash added.

"Or Simon may grow angry with my father disclosing this to the police," remarked Terry with concern.

"Simon knows Pritchitt's tight with the cops," said Bauers.

"Yep," agreed Nash. "It is time to risk everything. Now everybody out, except Lori," he ordered in a disgruntled voice. He sat at his desk.

"Okay, what do you have, Justin? And it better be good. I don't want to go back to walking a beat."

"I've got a solid source."

"Who?"

"Don't interrupt me!" Nash exploded, slamming his fist to his desk.

"Okay, okay, Mr. Top Gun," she begged off as he straightened himself, leaning toward her as if ready to pounce.

Nash calmed himself. "Lori, I'm sorry. I apologize," said Nash contritely. "My nerves are ragged."

"Accepted," said Lori quietly.

"Two men must be detained for questioning for their possible involvement in these killings." Nash turned back to the window. He tapped his knuckles against the window. "The two you must bring in for questioning are Rev. Milton James and Niles Mercer."

Bordeaux's mouth dropped open. "Terry's ex-husband?"

"No. Terry's husband. They're not divorced yet."

"Are you sure about this?"

"You heard me."

"Terry is going through hell as it is now. This will push her over the edge."

Nash breathed a worried sigh. "I know. We'll just have to be there and catch her. She's a strong person."

"The Titanic was a strong ship," answered Bordeaux.

Nash had no answer, only a glare. He pointed to his briefcase near the bookshelf. Lori handed it to him. He removed a key and opened it. He placed a small cassette recorder on the desk. He pressed the button. "Justin?" Bordeaux recognized the voice. Her eyes widened. "Niles was at the house this morning. He's out of his mind, ranting about abortions. Milton James — he's threatened all of us." Terry's voice choked, as she suppressed a sob. "Me . . . my children. My Dad insists on a restraining order. I am frightened. He spied on us last night, Justin. I'm so afraid. I'll be at that meeting with you this afternoon. Justin, could Niles be Simon?" The message ended.

Concern registered with both as there was silence. "I understand now," said Bordeaux. "You and Terry?"

No answer was heard as Nash looked away. "Nothing happened," he mumbled. "She was upset and I was just being a friend, okay?" He handed Lori some papers. "These are surveillance reports. Niles and this Milton James character are mixed up with some sure-fire lunatic fringe groups. These groups have been known to threaten the lives of abortionists."

Bordeaux glanced through the papers. "There's motive."

"For right now, that's enough. And it's the only thing we've got to go on, too." Nash shrugged. "I could be wrong. Kinda hope I am. But bring them in, just for questioning. I have the press conference scheduled for six. Maybe you can squeeze something out before then."

"Hey, Justin, I'm a damn good cop, not a magician."

CHAPTER NINETEEN

The parking lot was filled to capacity. Many cars double and triple parked as Pritchitt anxiously sought an open slot. Pritchitt looked at his watch. "I can't believe they don't have enough money to build another garage," he mumbled, finally settling on a strip of unused lawn adjacent to the lot. He hurried from his car. Terry and Tyler waited anxiously inside the hospital. There was a 4:00 p.m. appointment to discuss Ruth's condition and he was already fifteen minutes late.

"I wish Dad would hurry," Terry fretted. "Justin Nash is holding a press conference at six and I need to be there."

"More important for you to be here," lectured Tyler.

The door opened and Blanche Tucker entered with a warm smile. "Isn't your father here yet?"

"He should be here any minute," said Tyler.

Pritchitt rushed into the lobby of Memorial Psychiatric Clinic and darted into a closing elevator. To his surprise, he came face to face with Dr. Peters. The eye contact was icy. "My goodness, it seems that the esteemed Dr. Benjamin Pritchitt has come for his therapy, Peters sneered. The elevator door opened letting Pritchitt out. He quickly turned into a nearby conference area.

"Sorry I'm late," he apologized bursting through the door. "They need more parking spaces. See if you can do something about that, Dr. Tucker. God knows I've tried."

She smiled. "Don't think the board would listen to me on that issue."

Terry greeted her father with a kiss, and Tyler gave him a hug.

Dr. Tucker removed her latest evaluation from her briefcase. "Mrs. Pritchitt is making wonderful strides and should be coming home soon," she began. The family lit up with joy.

"Thank God," said Pritchitt.

"That's right," came a voice at the door. "We can all be a family again." It was Niles Mercer, dirty and disheveled. Shock spread through the room. "Hi, Terry," he said joyfully. "Sorry I missed you this morning?" Terry could only clutch her father's arm. Niles smiled. "I'm going to be your husband tonight." His hand fell to his groin and he rubbed it. Everything is going to be all right, I promise." Pritchitt rose from his chair in anger as Tyler grabbed his arm.

"I told you to stay away," said Pritchitt with a harsh growl. "I'm going to break your neck if you bother her anymore than you already have." Tyler held tightly to his father's arm.

"I need to tell her mother how evil she is!" Niles shouted. "It's room 202, isn't it, Dr. Tucker?"

"I warned you to stay the hell away from my family!" Pritchitt said in a threatening tone as he pulled Niles's unshaven face within inches of his own.

"Fuck you, Doc," he slurred. "I'm going to tell Terry's mother she raised a whore." Niles turned and bolted from the room. Pritchitt shook free of Tyler's lose grip and hurried through the door in pursuit.

"Dad, wait," Terry yelled. Staff and patients were brushed aside by her fast moving father. With each stride, the fury of Pritchitt's charge brought him closer to the clumsy foot speed of Niles. At Ruth's doorway Niles stopped. As he turned Pritchitt jumped him and both rolled onto the floor as people scattered and screamed. Startled onlookers scurried away as they wrestled on the floor. They rolled on the cold floor. Arms and legs flew wildly in the air. Groans and moans spirited the fight as both cursed the other. An older woman with a walker was knocked to the ground, then pulled away by another patient. Terry, Tyler and Dr. Tucker pushed through the growing circle of shocked bystanders. Terry jumped into the fight, pounding Niles' back, and Tyler yanked him from atop his father. Security guards intervened, pulling Niles away from the hateful anger of Pritchitt. Both children struggled to contain the unleashed emotion of their father.

"I still do love you, Benjamin. But not you, Terry," Niles yelled, then turned toward Ruth's room . . . her door long since closed. "Mrs. Pritchitt, your daughter is a whore. Ruth Pritchitt, did you hear me!" he screamed.

The security guards pulled him away but he broke loose and began making strange signs in the air. The guards looked at one another.

Pritchitt broke from Tyler's strong hold. He approached Niles. Silence blanketed the corridor. Terry stood with tears of both anger and pity. Pritchitt voice was stern. "Why are you here? Why did you come to the hospital, Simon?"

"Simon? Simon, you say?" Niles laughed. "Am I a Simon or a Niles? I think a Niles, dear misguided Benjamin. I'm your son-in-law, remember?"

Dr. Tucker came forward. The guards held Niles tightly. "Simon?" she whispered. "Do you really think —? Get him out of here," she ordered.

Pritchitt held her arm and whispered, "Let him go. Jail won't do him any good."

"Escort him to the front door and make sure he leaves."

Ruth suddenly appeared from her room. She ran to her husband. She eyed Niles.

"I'll be back," yelled Niles. "I love Benjamin and Ruth. I love all of you." His words echoed through the halls.

"Ruth, has Niles visited you here?" Pritchitt asked.

"No, not that I recall," she answered hesitantly. "What's going on, Benjamin? I was sleeping and with all the yelling and screaming was afraid to open my door."

"I'm glad you didn't, Mom." said Tyler, who gently led his mother back into her room.

Dr. Peters passed with his entourage of house staff. He smiled cuttingly at Pritchitt, then turned to a security guard. "Call the police and call them now! They need to be updated on the goings-on of the infamous Dr. Pritchitt. I do believe the District Attorney would appreciate the call."

Rows of folding chairs were neatly arranged in the church recreational center. In the foyer of the large church a young woman handed entrants a sheet of paper. Pastor Bivens walked up with a brisk step. "Milton, I was misled about this meeting. I had no idea you were involved. This is the very last time you will be allowed on these premises."

A church board member stood at Bivens' side. "I scheduled this meeting a month ago and now I'm very sorry. You said it was a youth event."

"It is," responded Milton James. He sighed. "There is so much hypocrisy in your voice, Reverend Bivens. What are churches anyway, but shrines shrouded in greed?"

A dark look crossed Bivens' face. "Save it for the listeners," he countered. James smiled. He faced the fifty or so gathered. He rang a small bell for silence. The meeting started with a short prayer but was soon followed by yells and chants. Milton James gave a fiery speech denouncing social ills, especially abortion. Shrieks of support punctuated the sermon.

Reverend Bivens looked glum. "I understand their message," he said to the board member beside him, "but these people have nothing in common with the peaceful pro-life organizations spread throughout the country. What I'm hearing is unleashed hatred condoning the use of violence to achieve their aims."

"Reverend Bivens," a voice called quietly from behind. It was Lt. Lori Bordeaux. "I'm here to pick up Reverend Milton

James for questioning," she said, showing her badge. Her partner Det. Caffey watched carefully.

"I hope they'll be no violence," he said softly.

"Only if he starts it, Rev. Bivens. Only if he starts it, sir," Bordeaux repeated as she and Caffey stood together, staring at James, addressing those in the room.

"What do you want him for?" asked Bivens.

"I can't comment on that. But I assure you, the matter is a serious one."

"God have mercy on him," whispered Bivens as the board member responded with an *Amen.*

Milton James' rantings came to a sudden stop. His eyes widened. From the hushed silence came murmurs as heads turned to see what had so captured his attention. James stood down from the podium and marched to the back of the crowded room. "What do want?" he asked defiantly.

"Milton James, I'm Lt. Bordeaux and —"

"Did you call them, Rev. Bivens?"

"He has nothing to do with our being here," said Bordeaux.

"I'm here to accompany you downtown for questioning."

"Questioning, about what?"

"We'll discuss that downtown."

"And what if I refuse?"

"Then I'd have to arrest you and take you downtown, handcuffed like a criminal. It's your choice."

James looked perplexed. His eyes fell on Bivens. "You did this."

"No," said Bivens. "I promise, Milton. I have no idea what this is about."

James was escorted from the room as a humming murmur grew over the packed meeting room.

Outside, Niles frightened face peered from behind the police cruiser.

The followers poured onto the church square, angrily watching. "This is just persecution!" shouted one man as James signaled thumbs up. "Keep the faith, brother," the man yelled.

"Let him go," screamed an elderly woman. "God will punish you corrupt policemen."

Caffey quickened his step, holding James by the arm as Bordeaux followed. All hurried into the waiting cruiser.

As Caffey opened the door, Niles, handcuffed, began screaming, "They're trying to blame us for the girls being killed. I'm not Simon!" He began to cry uncontrollably.

"This is a frame-up!" shouted a large man who approached Bordeaux menacingly with others. Bordeaux put her hand on her revolver.

"Stop right there! I don't think you want to do that," she glared, a harsh bluntness in her voice. "If you guys want to leave here with your balls intact, then step back or I'll make everyone of you the best singing sopranos in the church choir." The car sped away as shouts continued from the dispersing crowd.

Pritchitt sipped a hot toddy. He switched on the T.V. in the den and turned to the evening news. Justin Nash was the lead story. His interview was brief but more than informative as Pritchitt sat shocked to hear his name mentioned in connection with Simon. "At this moment, police are detaining two suspects in the serial murders. I wish to point out, this is merely for questioning. No one has been officially charged. Also, a message was sent to Dr. Benjamin Pritchitt informing him that a body could be found. A search was made at Overton Park and, unfortunately, this proved to be true."

The telephone rang. It was Terry phoning from the office.

"What's going on, Terry? Yes, I'm watching the news. No, the children are in the game room. Claire is using *Paint It* on the computer and Benji's watching *Nickelodeon*. I thought my involvement was going to be kept secret in this case. My God! Jeremy Bates will butcher me and my trial is less than two weeks away."

"Dad, settle down and let me explain, please. We had to say something. For God's sake, Dad, your picture made the front page of the paper." There was a momentary pause. "Lt.

Bordeaux picked up Niles and Milton James." Her voice tightened. She was too emotional to continue.

"Let's just hope for the best, Terry. I love you."

The ringing telephone awoke Pritchitt. He had fallen asleep in the den. It was his answering service. "Is this an emergency?" he asked.

"Well, no," answered a female voice.

"Dr. Pennington is handling my practice right now," he responded with annoyance.

"Sorry to bother you, sir. We know you're not on call but we have a caller who only wants you."

"Who might that be," he asked, a perturbed yawn interrupting him.

"This person has telephoned seven times tonight. It's about some kind of insurance policy. We tried to explain that doctors don't deal with insurance, but the party kept insisting that you would know what he was talking about."

"It sounds like a crank call," Pritchitt mumbled in exhaustion.

"Yes, that's what we kept thinking. But Mr. Simon was persistent."

The name seared through Pritchitt's lethargy like a hot poker.

"Dr. Pritchitt, are you there? Doctor?" the operator repeated.

"Yes, I'm here."

"He said you were like brothers and to relay this message directly to you. It was about some kind of death policy for a family member. Did we do wrong by calling you, sir?"

"No. Of course you did nothing wrong. You did everything right."

Pulling himself up from his chair he walked to the mantle and dying fire. Slowly he paced the room pondering the call. How could Simon telephone while being questioned by police?

Pritchitt dialed the number given to him by Bordeaux in case of an emergency. The phone rang and rang. There was no answer and he re-dialed. Finally, a man's voice answered the phone. "Homicide, Det. Caffey speaking."

"Det. Caffey, this is Dr. Benjamin Pritchitt. Can I speak with Lt. Bordeaux?"

"Geez, I'm sorry, Doc, but she's checked out for the night. She won't be back until early a.m."

"It's very important, detective. Maybe you can help me?"

"I'll give it my best shot, Doc."

"Are Niles Mercer and Milton James still in jail?"

"You bet. At least for tonight, anyway. Why?"

"Have they made any phone calls that you're aware of?"

"Oh, yeah. They each made one to their attorney and then I took Niles Mercer to make a couple of emergency calls he said were important. I saw nothing wrong with that. Why?"

"Do you have a record of who he called?"

"No, Doc. Is there anything wrong?"

"No. Nothing's wrong, Det. Caffey. Thanks for your help."

"Anytime, Doc." Pritchitt rested the receiver to the phone and sat quietly. He closed his eyes and wondered. Niles and Simon . . . were they one in the same. Leaning his head back, the crackling fire heated the den as he tried to capture a moment's rest.

Pritchitt endured another sleepless night. By dawn he was roaming the house. On this Sunday morning a melancholy sun barely lit the sky. And when Loretta came, Pritchitt was already at his desk, examining patient files. Loretta always prepared Sunday breakfast for the Pritchitts. She had awakened the children and seen to it that they were dressed. "Dr. Ben, I am so happy to hear that Mrs. Pritchitt will be coming home soon." She beamed, pouring him a cup of coffee.

"She's doing very well. I know she misses your delicious eggs."

"The Lord is so very good," praised Loretta, as she hummed one of her gospel tunes walking back to the kitchen. The telephone rang. "Dr. Ben, the call is for you and it's your wonderful wife. She sounds so very fine."

Pritchitt hurried to the phone. "Hello, darling."

"Benjamin, I had a call this morning. It was very early and I was half asleep but . . . the caller identified himself as this Simon person." Concern for his wife's safety was paramount to any concern for himself. Rage and anger drove his rapid pulse.

"What . . . what did he say?"

"He asked how I felt, assuring me everything was going to be fine. He told me that he loved me."

"His voice, Ruth, you heard it, did it sound like Niles?"

"The voice was raspy and hoarse. It seemed almost disguised," she offered. "I just couldn't tell. I'm sorry, Benjamin."

"Nothing to be sorry about, sweetheart. Get some rest and I'll see you soon. I love you."

"Oh, Benjamin. I'm scared for you."

"Don't be, darling. I'll be fine. You just worry about getting better and getting home."

"I love you, Ben."

The West Precinct Police Department was in pandemonium. The media had set up camp at the building ever since Nash's press conference. Television vans from as far away as St. Louis parked outside. Huge antennae stretched skyward. Would the police break the case? wondered reporters.

A block away Nash could see the crowded activity far below. He glanced at his watch, realizing it was time to go.

Gawkers slowed on the street, staring at the police headquarters, hoping to catch a glimpse of the two men brought in for questioning. Reporters wondered, Had they caught the killer? Leaning on his horn Nash bullied his way into the drive. Reaching the sanctuary of the parking lot he grabbed his briefcase and dashed for the building.

Bordeaux and Caffey sat quietly in the interrogation room, when Justin entered, dejection in their faces.

"Nothing?" he asked.

"We've got the wrong guys," answered Lt. Bordeaux.

"How is that?"

"Dr. Pritchitt called me this morning. Simon, or someone identifying himself as such, called his answering service last night, and then called his wife this morning at the hospital. We traced the calls. They're from different pay phones within blocks of each other."

Nash angrily threw his briefcase in a chair. He paced, then raised a finger. "What if there is more than one Simon?"

Bordeaux flinched. "That's a little far fetched, Justin."

He continued. "What if there's a group of fanatics using the name Simon."

"Okay, it's possible, but still a bit out there in left field," agreed Bordeaux. "But we have no such evidence, do we?"

"No," mumbled Nash in a tone of surrender.

Terry came inside. She removed a document from her briefcase. "Well, sure hope this is the beginning of a change in my luck. I officially filed for divorce and these are the precious papers."

Nash nodded his approval, then pulled Terry aside.

"I thought we went over this last night, Terry, you have a conflict, as a family member, you're too close."

"Then I'm finished on this case?"

"No, no," Nash said soothingly. "All I want is that you are not present when I question Niles. For chrissake, Terry. You, an assistant district attorney sitting in on your soon to be ex-husband's interrogation. His lawyer would have a field day. He'd be able to throw everything we might get out the window," Nash lectured with growing impatience. "Go spend the day with children."

Terry turned to Bordeaux. "Has Niles requested a lawyer?"

"Yeah, they've got Mason Stringer."

"He's third rate," said Terry.

"But he's cheap," quipped Bauers.

"Well, I guess I'm out of here," said Terry, flashing a less than agreeable smile.

"Just for now," reminded Nash with relief.

She turned and was out the door.

Niles Mercer and his attorney sat at a table in the interrogation room. Niles was impatient, scanning his bleak surroundings and mumbling to himself. On the far wall was a one way mirror. Above was a small video camera. Lt. Bordeaux entered.

"Sign here, Mr. Mercer. This indicates you wish to answer questions, with your attorney present." Stringer glanced at the document and pointed to where Niles was to sign.

"Are you married?" Niles asked Bordeaux.

"We'll be asking the questions, Mr. Mercer."

Nash entered the room, sitting in a chair directly across from Niles.

"I'm Deputy District Attorney Nash."

"I know who you are," Niles answered. "My lovely wife works with you and you like to fuck her, too," Niles smirked leaning over the table and glaring into Nash's shocked silence.

"That'll be enough of that, Mercer," ordered Bordeaux with disgust, bending over the table, staring not six inches from his face.

Nash spoke. "Did you argue with Dr. Pritchitt yesterday?"

"We had a discussion. I wanted him to help me get back my wife."

"Did you say that you and he were alike? Did you say you were like brothers, too?" Nash questioned.

"Yes, we are both dedicated to our own causes. Both dedicated to alleviate the suffering of mankind. Yes, you might say we're like brothers."

"Are you taking your lithium?"

"I took some this morning."

"Oh?"

"I advised my client to do so," interjected Stringer.

"Yesterday, Lt. Bordeaux showed you the names and photographs of the dead women. Have you ever met them?"

"None of them."

"Did you harm them in any way?"

"No."

"Why did you stop taking your lithium?"

Niles was silent. Stringer whispered to him. Niles shook his head.

"Did it make you impotent?" asked Nash.

"Yes," blurted Niles. "It was my medicine that ruined my marriage. May God have mercy."

"You've been diagnosed with a mental problem?" Nash continued.

"So I'm told," answered Niles. "But I'm a nonviolent person. I want people to stop hurting others."

"So in 1992 when you were arrested for assaulting a male prostitute, that was an act of nonviolence?"

"Just a damn minute," interrupted Stringer. "That was self-defense and the entire incident was dismissed."

"Right," said Niles nervously.

"Were you arrested in a park men's room with judge —"

"This is irrelevant!" shouted Stringer, standing.

"Mason, sit down. You're going to give me a headache with all your damn objections," said Nash, motioning him to sit.

Niles looked terrified. "I'm a real man, all red meat. I don't do those things."

"Your record discloses a sexual battery charge against a minor that was dropped in a most suspicious manner."

"I thought she was eighteen," Niles said. "She was a whore and a temptation. The devil made me sin."

"Did your friend 'the judge' pull some strings?"

Stringer fumed. "That does it, Mr. Nash. My client has answered all of the questions he's going to. Either charge him with a crime or release him."

"I am a good man. I am a good man," Niles began rattling. "I won't be bullied." He slammed his fist on the table.

Nash wiped beads of perspiration from his forehead. "All right, we'll release you. But I'm warning you, don't leave Memphis."

A detective escorted Mercer from the room. There appeared a faint smile on Stringer's lips. He jutted his chin cockily. "You're just fishing, Nash."

The door opened and Milton James was led into the room.

Lt. Bordeaux placed papers before him. "You're represented by Mr. Mason Stringer?

Milton James nodded, his eyes darting from Stringer to Bordeaux then Nash. "Yes, I am."

"Do you know why you're being questioned?"

"Mr. Stringer told me it concerns the young women who've been murdered. For the love of God, I can't understand why you'd want to waste your precious time with me."

"Rev. James, what do you think about these girls?"

"Don't you know, Justin Nash?"

"No. I guess I don't. Why don't you help me."

"Vengeance is mine saith the Lord."

"So you think they got what they deserved?"

"They're burning in hell as we speak."

"You're sure about this?" Stringer whispered in James' ear.

Milton James pulled away from Stringer and leaned forward. "I'm just as certain as I can be about that, Mr. Nash. But I didn't know any of them and have no knowledge of their deaths, other than what we've all read and heard in the news."

"But you think they got what they deserved?"

James smiled. "The Lord works in mysterious ways, Mr. Nash."

"Where did you live before Memphis?"

"At Hope Church in Ludlow, Oregon."

Nash turned. "Lt. Bordeaux, see if anything unusual happened in Ludlow."

"Preacher, have you ever had sex with men?"

"That's got nothing to do with this matter!" Stringer bellowed.

"You ever had sex with Niles Mercer?"

"No, that is opposed by scripture."

"I object to this off beat line of questioning, sir," Stringer protested.

"Niles Mercer has indulged his lust with men. He's your pal, huh?"

"He is my associate, sir. We share a mission."

"You two live together?"

"We share an apartment because we are poor."

"Do you think abortion clinics should be bombed?"

"No, but I think abortions should cease."

Nash closed the folder before him. "All right, you're released. But don't go far."

"Where do you think he's going, Mr. Nash? Paris? Rome?" Stringer retorted.

"Stringer, take him out of here, and take your cocky arrogance, too," Nash demanded.

"My arrogance?" Stringer stood. "If the cops harass my clients simply because they are anti-abortion activists, you'll hear from us in court."

"Get out!" said Nash. "And take your choir boys with you."

With a sneering grin Stringer departed.

"What do you think?" asked Bordeaux.

"I was hoping for much more. I'm the big loser. I'm sure the mayor wanted a lot more than what I'm going to give her," said Nash. Nash picked up his briefcase and walked from the room. In the lobby he took a deep breath, then stepped outside. The news hounds came running. Microphones flew in his face.

"The two men questioned about the serial murders have been released. That's all I have to say."

A groan of disappointment went up from the throng of media as Nash hurried down the steps and into his car.

Nash waited in the red leather booth, sipping his third glass of wine. It was a small Italian restaurant near the university. He watched young students laughing and enjoying themselves. Terry walked through the door, slipping into the booth beside him. "Oh, to be a carefree student again," whispered Nash's depressed voice. "I may be waiting tables at this place tomorrow," he frowned.

"Come on," said Terry. "You lost a battle but not the war. Anyway, I'm glad it might not be Niles."

A disappointing sigh was heard as Nash looked away. "At this point it seems that it's not," he mumbled, gulping his wine. He yawned and rubbed his tired eyes.

"A little strong on the wine?" Terry questioned. He stared at his empty wine glass as she ordered a drink and removed her jacket. Nash noticed the perfume.

"You don't smell like that in the office."

"Oh, yes, I do. It's just your damn cigar smoke is stronger than any perfume a woman can wear."

"Well," he sighed, "we're back to square one." Terry forced a supportive smile.

"The other night you touched emotions deep inside of me," reminded Terry, surprised by her own words.

"I didn't mean to," lamented Nash with an insecure shrug.

"But you did," she whispered.

They sat quietly, each aware of the simmering desire between them. Nash left money on the table and helping Terry with her coat they exited through a side door.

Both cars pulled into his driveway and came to a stop. "What a gorgeous old mansion," she gasped.

"There's a big heating bill that comes with it," added Nash as he walked from his car.

"You live here alone?"

"I've got a housekeeper. She's at church every week at this time."

"Do you go to church, Justin?"

"Not regularly. I worship in my own way."

Terry glanced at her watch. "The sitter is supposed to leave by ten."

"Terry, it's only seven. I don't know why I let you talk me into this? I must really be crazy."

"No. I wanted to see where you live and sleep, and you agreed," she smiled.

Nash unlocked the front door. Terry surveyed the odd assortment of old antiques and furniture. "It looks like time stopped here," she whispered. He grinned.

"I don't entertain much. There are just a lot of memories here."

Terry wandered through the living room then took his hand. "I want to go upstairs."

Nash was hesitant. He looked at the staircase then took her hand and led her up the wide carpeted steps. At the top Terry peered down a long corridor which stretched into darkness. "This place is a little spooky," she remarked half-seriously. "You sure you live up here?"

"I'm the only one who comes upstairs. My housekeeper can no longer make the steps."

"I guess not," said Terry peering down the massive staircase.

"It's not very cheerful. You want to change your mind?"

Her eyebrows raised and she cast an inviting smile. "Now what kind of passion is that? I even wore my sexy stockings." She raised her dress, revealing a shapely leg lined in sheer black.

Nash gripped the bannister. "I feel like such a failure, Terry," he muttered in a response she was hardly looking for. "There's a murderer in this city and I —"

Terry held his hand. "You're doing the best you can." She placed her lips to his cheek. Nash pulled back. "Let me give you a back rub. You need to relax."

"You're right. I'm so very tired." He opened a door. "This is my bedroom."

The room was spacious, high ceilinged, with a four poster bed. It was sparsely furnished, with few personal touches. Terry suddenly felt out of place. This is a monk's cell, she thought to herself, devoid of the outside world.

"Depressing, isn't it?" suggested Nash.

Terry removed her coat. "Justin, it is time you hired an interior decorator."

"It's time I did a lot of things." He laid his tired frame across the bed.

Terry placed her coat on a chair and stared at a phone in the far corner of the room. "Let me call home. I need to check on the kids. I'll be just a second," she promised. She dialed and spoke to Loretta.

Terry turned. Nash slept peacefully. His ego had been dealt a heavy blow. He reminded her of a sleeping lion. Like her, he was emotionally vulnerable. She caught her breath and reorganized her scrambled thoughts. She had almost made a blind impulsive jump into his bed. The passion which had stirred her slipped away. She sighed dejectedly. Her loneliness was painful. Bob was dead, Niles would soon be a bad memory, and she was alone. She admired Justin Nash. He was tough and smart. Beneath his gruff exterior beat a kind heart. Or was she simply seeing him through tinted glasses? A vision blurred by her fragile state. No, Justin was deeply concerned about her father and family. She reached for her coat. Like those who feel they are drowning after a failed marriage, she was clinging to the first life boat that appeared.

Terry turned and stared into a full mirror. She took a deep sigh. Once again she was the sharp, clear-thinking attorney.

She stood at the foot of the bed. "I guess I'll let myself out," she said softly, shaking his foot. A loud snore vibrated his throat. "Okay, fine. I'll let myself out." His eyes never opened. She smiled and placed a gentle kiss on his forehead. Nash moaned and curled into a fetal pose.

Terry quietly opened the door. A long, dark corridor stretched before her. At the landing, she stopped. Below, the front door opened. An elderly woman with a cane entered, along with companions who helped her inside. Terry darted to the other side of the staircase, not wishing to be seen.

The trio discussed the church service. Gently tiptoeing down the hall, Terry noticed a faint light beneath a door at the far end. Cautiously she walked toward it. She opened the door. Inside was a bedroom sparsely furnished. A small lamp shone on a dresser. A dozen photographs decorated a solitary table. Curiosity filled her. She closed the door behind her. Justin Nash, young and smiling, posed with his parents. In a gold frame was the picture of a smiling young woman, inscribed: "Dearest Justin, I will always love you." Terry opened the top drawer. Amidst the clutter were photographs of Justin and a woman dancing, faded matchbooks and letters. There were many more pictures. Pictures of children and families. She took the small lamp and held it closer to the table. An eerie feeling crept her skin. She glanced around the morgue-like room. She walked toward the back of the room. Her advance quickly halted. Her steps froze against the squeaky wooden floors. She heard steps moving down the hall. She caught her breath and closed the drawer. She returned the lamp and carefully cracked open the door. The dark corridor was vacant. She could hear the trio of voices downstairs. She glanced at her watch. She took a relaxing gulp, then summoned her courage. She would act as if she was leaving and not sneaking out. She walked into the hallway. "Good night, Justin," she called out. Looking down the empty hall, she waved, saying, "I do hope you feel better," she half-shouted as she skipped down the impressive staircase. The elderly trio stared upwards at the descending voice. "Hello, I'm Terry. I work with Mr. Nash. I had to help him home. He's a bit under the weather, I'm afraid."

"That's right," yelled Nash, his unexpected voice exploded from the balcony, standing bare chested on the second floor landing. "Thanks, for helping me home, Terry, and good night." His unexpected reply turned her head and missing the last step she tumbled to the floor. Her landing was less than artistic with her arms and legs spread in various directions and the contents of her purse rolling on the floor. "Are you okay?" Nash shouted.

"Yes, I'm fine," she replied. Her hesitating speech showed embarrassment. Her voice barely audible. Staring at Nash's imposing figure, then the housekeeper and her friends, Terry lifted herself and nervously exited the front door.

CHAPTER TWENTY

It was overcast and cold. Where had the time gone? thought Pritchitt, with a sense of depression and disbelief. His life seemed empty and his spirit near beaten.

Grabbing his briefcase, Pritchitt walked toward Memorial Hospital. The hospital lobby was its usual smorgasbord of patients, families, and hospital personnel. There were the usual friendly waves and hostile glares. In a crowded elevator an older nurse smiled a warm hello. Everyone used to be so friendly, he recalled. The last months had changed everything. Now everywhere he went there were murmurs and stares. The doors opened on the sixth floor and the elevator emptied. Walking down the hall toward the Department of Surgery, several student doctors greeted him. He entered the main office. There was Patsy. She gave him a hug. Others in the office were cordial but guarded, wary of becoming entangled in the bitter feud between Pritchitt and Dr. Peters. Though merely suspended, most believed Pritchitt's fall from grace was final and would be fatal to his career.

Once inside his office, Pritchitt remembered the not too distant days when his office bubbled with activity and his life seemed on automatic pilot.

A quick knock came at the door and Bernie Wiseman entered.

"What's the word with the serial investigation?" he was asking.

"It's stalled."

"There is speculation that Justin Nash, is on his way out."

"I don't know about that. I do know city hall and the public want arrests. They want an end to this terror. Niles Mercer's and Milton James' interrogation was a flop."

"So those were the two men," said Wiseman, his eyebrows raised.

"Yeah, the police and D.A.'s office are holding back their names, for now anyway."

A loud thump at the door startled both men. Dr. Peters stormed in with Jack Elliott, the chief of hospital security.

"Nice you could drop by, James. What can I do for you this morning?" Pritchitt stood, his arms folded.

"Don't you have somewhere to be, Dr. Wiseman?" Peters asked, a dictatorial order to his tone.

"No, sir. I still have another twenty minutes on my break."

"Then you will leave us now," Peters ordered. Wiseman cast a nervous frown.

Pritchitt stepped forward. "I'm in conference with Dr. Wiseman, and you're interrupting us."

Dr. Peters sneered at Pritchitt. "Well, you made another spectacle of yourself the other day by chasing your mentally ill son-in-law through the halls of the *crazy* people clinic," he chided, knowing full well his using of the word *crazy* would incite Pritchitt's anger.

"Be damn careful how you make reference to psychiatric cases at that clinic."

"Oh, that's right. Forgive me, Benjamin. I forgot your wife is institutionalized there."

Anger tore at Pritchitt and he started toward Peters, only

to be stopped by the protective arms of Wiseman. Pritchitt regained his composure.

Peters focused his jealous eyes into Pritchitt's angry glare. "You're a disgrace to Memorial Hospital. You're a man who has lost control and can no longer make sound judgments. Your actions have caused your wife irreparable damage and —"

Pritchitt lunged for Peters but Wiseman held on for dear life. Wiseman yelled, "Don't do this," as his small frame was dragged by Pritchitt's force.

Back-pedaling, Peters lost his balance and tumbled to the floor. Wiseman held Pritchitt against the wall, whispering, "Don't do it, sir. Don't you see, he's goading you into this."

"Hold him back, he's trying to kill me!" Peters shrieked in a squeamish voice, lying on the floor. The head of security stood in shock, more by Peters' histrionics than Pritchitt's reactions.

Hearing the commotion, Patsy peered through the door and witnessed Peters graveling on his knees, his usually arrogant face terrified.

"He tried to hurt me, just as he assaulted his son-in-law yesterday. Chief Elliott take his keys. Take his keys," Peters repeated, struggling to his feet.

"I'm sorry, Dr. Pritchitt." Elliot was empathetic.

Pritchitt reached in his pocket and handed the keys to Elliot who took them with regret. Peters grabbed the keys and stormed from the office, leaving Elliott behind. Elliott looked at Wiseman and the stunned Patsy, and then at Pritchitt. "I'll file a report, Doctor. What I witnessed was that Dr. Peters fell, pure and simple."

Wiseman shook his head. "He wanted you to hit him, so he could have you arrested."

"Are you all right?" asked Patsy.

"I'm fine. I'm just sorry I lost control," said Pritchitt.

Pritchitt patted his young resident doctor on the shoulder.

"I've been coming here for twenty years. I do my best thinking here." His voice trailed off. "I've got court dates soon." His eyes dropped to the floor. A proud man now humbled. "Sometimes I just need to sit in this old chair and remember what it was like before my living hell began," he mumbled. Patsy fought back tears as he stuffed files in his briefcase and started for the door.

Wiseman accompanied Pritchitt. The department buzzed with the news that Peters had demanded Pritchitt's keys and thrown him out. Employees throughout the department stood quietly, staring with respectful faces, their eyes waving good-byes to the chairman they wanted back.

In the parking lot Bernie bid Dr. Pritchitt farewell, and watched his drive away. A middle-aged woman who had been sitting in a nearby automobile, watching, leaned out the window. "You *are* Dr. Bernie Wiseman," she said with a hint of sarcasm. "I'm Dorothy McCormick. My friends call me Dot. We spoke on the telephone the other day." There was resentment in her tone.

Wiseman remembered the odd call and her wish to die. He had best get away, he told himself. "I'm on duty in a few minutes. So —"

"You look afraid, doctor. Your fear is the same I see every morning. But guess what? I've thrown out all the mirrors from my home so I see no more fear."

Wiseman backed away. "I'm sorry about your problems, ma'am. But I really have to go."

"You're not sorry. Don't lie to me," she screamed out, drawing attention from others in the parking lot.

"I am sorry, ma'am. And as to our conversation on the phone, neither Dr. Pritchitt nor myself would help someone die who can live and get well."

Her eyes widened. "Get well?" She spat the words out with distaste. "Who are you to stand there and tell me that I can get well. You don't know what I've been through."

She got back in her car, backed up, and pulled beside him.

"You doctors are the same. You claim you help the sick but all you want are the big homes and country club memberships."

Wiseman pointed to his yellow scooter.

"Don't worry, you'll have a big fancy car soon enough."

He shook his head.

"Do you remember the story of Snow White?" she shouted, "that's how I want to be. I want to lie in peace. Peace without pain."

That's a bit of a fairy tale, Wiseman was thinking, but he said nothing.

"Prince Jesus will awaken me with a kiss."

"I don't think it works that way. If you kill yourself, won't Satan be doing the kissing?" Wiseman reasoned.

"You've ruined everything," she cried. "How could you destroy such a beautiful dream. You disrespectful bastard!"

Wiseman stared into her hysteria. "Mrs. McCormick, I live in the real world. You really do need to see a psychiatrist and not Dr. Pritchitt."

She cast a hateful scowl, then revved the motor. "You're just like the rest. A hypocrite who took the Hypocritical Oath instead of the one God intended for doctors." Tires screeched and she sped away. Wiseman jotted her license number. He nodded with a disbelieving sigh.

In the District Attorney's Office Dorothy Cohen flashed her media identification. "Channel Eight News," smiled a young secretary. "I watch you every night. I'll let District Attorney Bates know you're here."

Bates stood from behind his desk and he and reporter Cohen exchanged forced smiles and shook hands. She removed a cassette recorder from her purse and took a seat.

"Put that away," demanded Bates. "There's not going to be an interview."

"I don't understand. Why did you call me?"

Bates sat in his plush leather chair. "I'll tell you and then you'll have the big picture."

"I'm listening."

He extended his hand. "Could I have your recorder?

"You don't trust me?"

"No."

Cohen slid the recorder across the large desk. Bates checked to make certain it was off. "All right. Now I'm going to

give you information about the serial killings." She leaned
forward. "It may benefit your television station and you. My
executive assistant, Justin Nash and Lt. Lori Bordeaux are in
deep trouble." He paused.

"Sounds interesting, Mr. Bates. You've got my undivided
attention and without a tape," she smiled.

"Mayor Daniels is holding a press conference this
afternoon. Her administration is crumbling under some pretty
condemning popularity polls because of this unsolved serial
killer case. Key advisors want her to fire Nash and Bordeaux.
She's undecided." Bates passed her an envelope. "Here are
some questions to ask which may get a . . . response at her
conference."

Cohen slipped her fingernail beneath the fold of the
envelope.

"Not now," cautioned Bates.

Cohen tossed the envelope in her purse and left.

Bates pushed the intercom button. "Miss Davis, find
Billings and send him to my office. You do have the documents
prepared?"

"I typed them last night at home."

"Fine. Dr. Pritchitt's court hearing is just an hour a way.
Have the car sent around now. I want to be there with plenty
of time to assist the worthy members of the press with the
facts."

The city hall conference room was packed. Local
reporters and crews vied for space near the podium. From
the hall Terry eyed the banks of lights and stream of media
personnel. She stepped back in the office. "It's a damn zoo
downstairs."

Nash sipped a cup of coffee. "This is mighty nice. This is
where all the taxpayer money goes, to city hall for gourmet
coffee."

Lt. Bordeaux looked nervous. "Do you think she's going to
dump us?"

Nash shrugged. "How the hell do I know? I mean, can

anyone trust or much less read a politician's schizophrenic mind? Hell, I'm not her speech writer."

"Well, I'll be damned, Justin," fumed Bordeaux. "You seem mighty upbeat considering we flopped with our *big suspects.*"

"Right!" he exclaimed. "When my back's to the wall, I come out swinging. Relax, lieutenant, this is a regular weekly press conference. You know that."

"Yeah," Bordeaux shot back, "but the major news this week is another girl dead and we haven't any suspects."

"If we're questioned we'll buy some time, just like Santa does it," Nash confided. "He tells the children what they want to hear, and it makes them happy, right? So, that's what we'll do."

Bordeaux looked shocked. "You mean lie?"

"Of course not," responded Nash. "We'll just sing a few Christmas carols." A commotion was heard in the hall. There was a knock on the door. An aide peered inside. "The mayor is headed downstairs. Let's go."

Mayor Daniels exuded cheerfulness. "November has barely started and I am proud to announce that the good citizens of Memphis have donated $300,000 toward the Christmas fund." Her fist swept the air. "I just know we're gonna make it to a million." There was a smattering of applause from her staff. Nash, Terry and Bordeaux stood with the mayor's administrative aides and a handful of council members. The reporters were poised, ready for action. But Mayor Daniels droned on about mundane city matters.

She glanced deliberately at her watch and rolled up her notes making ready to end the conference.

"Wait a minute!" shouted a reporter, "we've got questions." Daniels smiled widely. "Sure, I've got a few minutes." An audible groan of derision came from the media group.

"They're like hyenas," whispered Nash to Terry, "ready to swoop on any carcass."

"Fred McEvoy here," came a voice. "We need more than a few minutes. My newspaper receives dozens of letters each day from frightened citizens. What's the status of the serial murder investigation? How many more dead bodies are we going to find before your administration is able to protect the people of Memphis."

"The investigation is going ahead at full force," she answered. "Next question."

Hands shot up. Daniels pointed. "I'm with the Little Rock *Eagle*. The District Attorney's Office announced that two suspects were being questioned this past weekend, then it fizzled. Why?"

"I wasn't present at the interrogations. The police and the D.A.'s Office do that. Ladies and gentlemen, that's all. Thank you." Murmurs of disappointment swept the room.

"Hold it! One more question." A woman in the first row shouted as she stood below the podium. "Dorothy Cohen, ma'am." There was a pause. "Is it true one of the men questioned yesterday was Dr. Benjamin Pritchitt's son-in-law and Asst. Dist. Atty. Terry Mercer's husband?" Startled gasps were heard.

"I can't answer that," said Daniels, caught off guard. "I'm-I'm . . . "

An elderly journalist in the first row waved his hand at Daniels. "What's going on? I demand to know. Our citizens are fed up with these murders. Give us some straight answers." Daniels looked to Nash.

Justin Nash appeared at the podium. There was dead silence. "Citizens, sir, are entitled to information but not when such disclosures will jeopardize the entire investigation." Mayor Daniels recognized Nash. "No one wants to solve this more than me," he said emphatically, "except perhaps Mayor Daniels. She is too modest to recount how many evenings she has stayed up the entire night, consulting with police investigators, prodding my office for results. We're all working very hard. But we need the public's help, too. If someone out there knows something, please telephone the police."

Dorothy Cohen waved her hand. "Neither of you has responded to my question."

Nash faced her squarely. "It is no secret that Dr. Benjamin Pritchitt's former son-in-law is opposed to abortion. Prof.

Mercer has made himself a public figure by his involvement in numerous protests. He is entitled to his right of peaceful assembly. Let me state, many people have been questioned, not arrested or booked, but merely questioned. The two men interrogated yesterday were merely questioned with capable legal counsel present." He cleared his throat and looked toward the satisfied grin of Mayor Daniels. There were more hands but he had said enough. Nash stood down from the podium, the reporters on his heels.

"Then you're not denying that Niles Mercer is a prime suspect?" shouted Cohen.

An elderly couple blocked Nash's path. "Why don't you close the damned abortion clinics?" asked a white-haired woman.

"Ma'am, abortion is legal. I don't like it or support it, but the Supreme Court has ruled."

They continued to hurl questions but Nash refused to comment. Terry Mercer stood close by. Dorothy Cohen stuck a microphone in her face. "Were you present at the interrogation? How do you feel about your husband's involvement?"

Terry pushed the microphone aside. "Mr. Nash speaks for the D.A.'s investigation. As for Niles Mercer, go talk to him."

"I'll do that," smiled Cohen.

Cohen exchanged sharp stares with Lori Bordeaux. "What's your comment, lieutenant?"

"You're looking old. Get a makeover," was Lori's response. Cohen whirled and walked away.

Nash and Terry Mercer convened with Mayor Daniels in her chambers. "Thanks, Justin. You handled that very well, not to say how you bent over and kissed my shaky ass."

A slight grin fit Nash's face.

Daniels continued. "I'm giving you another week, then if this case isn't solved I'm going to replace your butt, got it?" She gestured in Terry's direction. "That means you, too, Ms. Mercer and Lt. Bordeaux."

Nash's smile vanished.

"I'm playing hardball and I'll clean house if I have to. You can take that to the bank," she said before turning and quickly departing. The door slammed hard behind her.

On the plaza outside City Hall reporters stood before cameras, broadcasting the latest news. Nash, Terry and Bordeaux crossed nearby on the square. Bright lights shone on Dorothy Cohen. "The mayor just concluded a press conference. The progress in the serial killings case is the first concern of the outraged citizens of Memphis. Channel 8 has discovered shocking information, to the effect that one person questioned is related to a staff member of the D.A.'s Office. Whispers of cover-up are spreading through city hall. It has also been disclosed that the serial killer goes by the name Simon and has directly communicated with Dr. Benjamin Pritchitt. Dr. Pritchitt, as all know, will soon go on trial for his aiding of suicides. He is also the father of Asst. Dist. Atty. Terry Mercer. The web grows around this family and it's preoccupation with death, whether by murder or aided suicide. Disturbing? Yes. This is Dorothy Cohen, reporting live from city hall."

"Whispers of cover-up, bullshit!" shouted Nash. "There's no one whispering but you, Ms. Cohen," Nash said aloud.

"That's the way I see it, Mr. Nash. Prove me wrong."

Nash turned and caught up to Mercer and Bordeaux. The trio walked off. "That bitch," fumed Bordeaux. "I have never liked her. She'd sell her mother for a tip."

Nash spoke angrily. "Someone gave her a direct pipeline to privileged information. Someone who wants this case all fucked up." He stroked his chin. "I wonder who that sorry bastard is?"

"That Cohen is going to push me one day to the point where I'm going to knock the shit out of her," Bordeaux fumed.

"You've tangled before?" asked Terry.

"When my husband died, she was poking her nose around, trying to see if he used drugs."

"Lt. Bordeaux, believe me, you don't want to strike a reporter. Snakes come with the territory. We did what we needed to diffuse criticism," said Nash.

Terry stopped, her eyes downcast. "I hate that Niles' name will be plastered in all the newspapers."

"He's a leading suspect," answered Nash. "Makes good headlines. You're his estranged wife. His father-in-law is Dr. Benjamin Pritchitt. What do you think? Doesn't matter that we haven't identified him as a suspect. The press can say what they want. After all, this is America."

"We've got a week to solve this thing," said Bordeaux, "if not, then I'll be back in the drunk tank, processing winos."

Channel Eight's television van passed by, Dorothy Cohen eyed the trio curiously. "She really gets to me," Bordeaux scoffed.

CHAPTER TWENTY-ONE

A fine mist clouded the windshield. Benjamin
Pritchitt glanced at his watch as he drove his car close to the
front door. Terry hurried from inside, umbrella in hand,
children in tow. They crowded into the car just as a cloudburst
let loose. A torrential rain pounded heavily against the car's
roof. "You just made it," said Pritchitt.

Pritchitt asked about school. Benji said he was going to
sing in a play.

"I sing better," chided Claire.

"We'll have a recital," said Pritchitt.

The rain continued heavily as they approached the school.
Claire poked her umbrella outside, then said, "Good luck, Papa.
I know you'll be okay. I love you."

As the kids splashed their way to the door, Ben could
hardly speak. "She knows about my problems," he sighed.

Pritchitt and his daughter hurried through a side door of
the courthouse to avoid the frenzied circus atmosphere
gathered on the front steps. A security guard waved them

through, and they managed to avoid a nest of hungry reporters. Only a small media contingent had been allowed in the courtroom, where there were no cameras. Tim Bauers summoned Terry to a front row seat where Tyler Pritchitt was waiting. Pritchitt took his place behind the table beside his lawyer and friend. "We are ready to proceed," said Todd Bohannon.

Judge Mary McLaren turned to the prosecution. "And you, Mr. Bates?"

"We are ready, your honor."

Prospective jurors were led to seats. A white-haired woman was first to take the stand.

"Do you believe in euthanasia?" asked Bates.

Bohannon stood. "I object to that term. My client has been charged with assisted suicide."

Judge McLaren removed her glasses. "That is a prejudicial term which we will avoid in questioning, Mr. Bates. You may, of course, under the agreed guidelines, dismiss any prospective juror, numbering twenty, without challenge from the court."

Tim Bauers leaned toward Terry. "Bates wants the seniors out. They'll be more sympathetic to Pritchitt's claim that he is simply ending pain."

Each side was allowed a certain number of peremptory challenges.

A petite woman who described herself as a homemaker was questioned at length by both sides. She was genuinely undecided about the issue. She was asked to remain.

A college student seated himself nervously. "I can't be on the jury," he immediately said. "He's been my doctor since I was a kid."

Bates made a sour face. "Is there is anyone else who is a patient of Dr. Pritchitt?"

Hands shot up. "Thank you, you are dismissed."

A young black man was queried about aided suicide. "It's wrong and the Bible says so," he stated.

Bohannon thanked the man, then dismissed him.

So it went. One by one, the jurors who would decide the fate of Dr. Benjamin Pritchitt were chosen. Curious faces glanced at the distinguished physician.

It was late afternoon when Jeremy Bates summoned Justin Nash and Tim Bauers to his office. Bates' cool demeanor belied the pent-up tension he kept within during the long hours in court.

"How did it go?" asked Bauers.

"This is an open and shut case," Bates asserted. His thumbs tugged the suspenders which stretched across his large stomach. "Even a moron jury must convict, because the law of the state has been violated."

"It's your case, Jeremy," said Nash with a feigned indifference.

Bates leaned back and flashed a cruel smile. "I hear the mayor's office is preparing resignation statements for you and Terry Mercer."

Nash removed a cigar. "You can't wait to see that, eh?"

"Is it four years? You've grown stale, Justin. It's time for private practice." He snapped his fingers. "Criminal law, that's where the money is made. Get a few dope dealers, and you can retire." Bates laughed.

"Why did you call us in?" asked Nash, suppressing his disdain.

"I'm going to appoint Tim Bauers interim chief when you're gone. I may even pick up the case myself after Pritchitt is convicted. It'll be a feather in your little cap, Tim."

Embarrassed, Bauers glanced toward Nash.

Bates flashed a gloating grin. "I surmise that Pritchitt and his fruitcake son-in-law are working together to dice up these women. I think our top gun has a soft spot in his heart for this Pritchitt clan."

Nash leaned forward. "Your little stunt of feeding worms to Dorothy Cohen failed."

"The meeting is over," said Bates snidely. "Why don't you start cleaning your desk out now?"

An intrusive noise disrupted the silence in Pritchitt's office. Wiseman rolled off the sofa and to his feet. His heart raced. The fax machine printed another message. He lit the desk lamp. It was 4:00 a.m. "Will you look at this?" He retrieved the fax sheet. "Hello, Simon," he whispered. He read with trepidation. "Simon says, Dr. Insurance, this is Dr. Assurance and I haven't heard from you as yet. I need to know, Dr. Insurance, if there is a problem with the policy?" The message was most confusing. It made little sense as did the others. He reread the fax. "What the hell? Assurance for insurance," he muttered.

Wiseman's pager sounded with four repetitive beeps. He carefully placed the fax sheet in his pocket and left to prepare for early morning rounds. The message was of a more terminal nature and Simon's serious tone was most distressing. The message was evil as if spoken by a demon. This was a very frightening time, he thought. Wiseman's worry for Pritchitt grew and his concern deepened. He would finish rounds and contact Pritchitt. Goose bumps rose from his skin.

The halls were quiet. The hospital seemed asleep. Dr. Blanche Tucker stepped from her office, and walked down the long hall to Ruth's room. She knocked on the door and entered, smiling. "You've made excellent progress, Ruth," she assured. "I'll let you go home this weekend. By then you'll be ready.

"Home," said Ruth emotionally, "that word sounds like a symphony to these old ears."

"Old? I hope I look half as good as you when I'm your age. But going home is only part of the reason for my visit. I came to invite you to a special poetry and play writing session tonight. It's rather experimental, designed to touch deep hidden emotions in people."

Dr. Tucker noticed the bouquet of flowers on the small table near the window. "They're beautiful. Are these from Dr. Pritchitt?" she asked. There was no answer. Tucker turned and faced the quiet anxiety on Ruth's face.

"No. No, they're not, Dr. Tucker."

"Oh, I'm sorry. Of course, it's none of my business."

"No, but it is your business. They're from Simon."

A hushed silence prevailed. Tucker pulled a chair up to the bed. "You'd never heard about Simon before coming here?"

"No. At least, I don't think so. My memory is a bit fuzzy from all I've been through, but you know that."

"Of course, that's normal, Ruth. We've discussed that."

"But I do recall someone being in this very room the first night I was here telling me everything was going to be all right, but I thought it was a dream."

"As you would with all the medicine you had pumped in you that first day."

"I remember a voice in the room and a gentle hand touching my shoulder. There was a warm raspy voice."

"Would you recognize it?"

"It was very distinctive."

"Remember anything more?"

"That's all I recall. But one thing's for sure."

"What's that?"

"I can remember more today than I could then."

Tucker's face was washed of color. Her stare distant.

"What is it, Dr. Tucker?"

"I just wonder where the men of those dead girls are, the men who made love to these women, then left them alone for Simon. It's pretty callous."

"I guess you could be right. If the men really loved them, they should have married them or supported them."

"My exact sentiments."

"These poor girls get pregnant, then kill the baby," whispered Ruth, "then Simon kills them."

"A vicious cycle orchestrated by a tormented soul," Tucker remarked, stepping to the doorway. "Now get some rest. Another long and hopefully better day awaits you."

Pritchitt drove into the parking lot of the Memorial Psychiatric Clinic. The day had been unkind to him. His thoughts were filled with depression and loneliness. His mind played to a melancholy melody as he walked across the near vacant lot. He cursed the recent events of his troubled life. The afternoon sun was fading. Pritchitt kneeled to tie a loose shoe string. Looking up he caught a glimpse of a shaded figure blending amidst a row of trees, nearly camouflaged by the hurrying sunset. He raised himself and stared at the figure of a long-haired man peering into first floor windows of the hospital. A gust of wind stirred and the man's long hair cast an eerie trail as he moved between growing shadows. Encouraged by his curiosity and absurdity of his wild thoughts Pritchitt continued an uncertain approach.

The man walked to a window. His movement stalled as he looked inside, then seemed to search the area around him.

Pritchitt was struck with a terrifying thought. "That's Ruth's window," he gasped. "My God," he called out. His pace quickened. His age all but forgotten, he lengthened his stride. His mind raced and heart pounded. Losing his footing, he slid down a small embankment. He righted himself quickly. The man stood without movement, his back to the fast approaching Pritchitt. "Hey, you! I want to talk with you," screamed Pritchitt. It wasn't until Pritchitt physically grabbed his shoulder that the long haired man turned toward Pritchitt.

The frightened man fell before Pritchitt and from his mouth came odd moans of near hysteric proportions. Pritchitt leaped his tired frame onto the slightly built man. They rolled briefly in the grass. The man continued with his loud curious sounds.

"What the hell is going on?" shouted one of two security guards, rapidly descending upon the two tangled bodies. One guard stared at Pritchitt as the other pulled the whimpering man to his feet.

"Like I said, what's going on here?" the officer repeated.

"Bobby, are you okay?" asked the other guard, still holding the arm of the terrified long haired man.

Pritchitt stood frozen in confusion.

"You know him?" panted Pritchitt, his chest heaving with short breaths. "I thought . . . "

"You thought what?" one guard asked.

"You've scared him to death," added the other guard as both gave comforting looks toward the near hysterical man.

"Bobby?" asked Pritchitt. "I thought . . . "

"What? That he was some kind of villain or something," said a guard.

"Yeah," uttered Pritchitt's confused voice.

"Hell. Bobby's our ground's keeper. He's a deaf mute. He couldn't hurt a flea," said a guard as his flashlight blinded Pritchitt's sight in the fallen darkness.

"I'm terribly sorry. I thought he was someone else," Pritchitt mumbled in embarrassment.

"Someone else?" a guard laughed. "Bobby ain't nobody but himself . . . a kind, sweet man."

"You, and what's your name, sir?" asked one guard, while the other pulled a pad and pencil from his pocket.

"I'm so sorry," answered Pritchitt. He turned and with a hurried trot rounded the building and was out of sight as the guards continued to console the still hysterical Bobby.

Pritchitt roamed the ghost-like grounds trying to retrieve his lost composure. How could he tell his wife the reason he was late is that he had mistaken a poor deaf grounds keeper for Simon? He couldn't, and he knew it. Having grounded his fleeting thoughts he made his way into the hospital and through the crowded lobby for a much needed visit with Ruth. The visit was shorter than he would've liked. His mind was garbled. He tried to cover his doubts and fears with the joy of her soon to be triumphant home coming. He found it hard to explain to himself the ill-fated chase of the harmless deaf mute. To burden her with his mounting problems would be his worst nightmare, he thought. While he'd prayed for Ruth's homecoming, how would she handle his crumbling world? His discomfort with himself grew. He needed to go. With his visit complete he leaned over and gently kissed her forehead. Pritchitt turned at the door and forcing a smile waved good night. The door closed and Ruth saw in her husband's premature departure an unusually beaten spirit. "God, please help my husband," she whispered.

Pritchitt's night was another sleepless one. His turmoil was more potent than the sleeping pill he'd swallowed hours before. He tossed and turned as demons wrestled his tiring mind. Praying to escape night's depressing loneliness, he would look wishfully to the window and morning's redeeming light. His repeated notion of failing his family haunted his every waking moment. With his struggle for sleep hopelessly beaten he raised himself from the crumpled bed sheets. He stood and opened a nearby window. The outside air was frigid but invigorating. A puttering noise disturbed the quiet. Pritchitt looked out the window and down the street. Wiseman's yellow scooter grunted to make the slight incline of the front driveway, where Bernie brought it to a stop and removed his helmet. He walked toward the front door while pulling a cellular phone from his pocket.

"What is he doing here this early?" mumbled Pritchitt. The phone rang. "Wiseman, what the heck are you doing here? Do you know what time it is?"

"Good morning, sir. How'd you know it was me?" answered Wiseman.

"The window, Bernie. Plus, the sound of that sewing machine you call transportation is enough to give you away wherever you go. Now, what is it?"

"There was another fax."

"And what's so unexpected about that?" an unenthused Pritchitt answered.

"Can we talk?"

"That's what we're doing, Wiseman. And I'm warning you, I've not had a good week and am in no mood for any earth shaking revelations this early. So talk! What's so different about this fax that brings you to my door before the rooster crows?"

"Simon wants you to acquiesce. In other words, assurance

that you'll be the insurance plan he's depending on to leave this world. You know, agree to kill him."

"I thought I'd made it plain to you, Wiseman. I'll agree to nothing that will feed this maniac's frenzy."

"But, sir, just maybe, if you agreed to assist in his suicide he might stop the killings."

"Never! You're trying to predict the dementia of a madman. You're smarter than that. Go home, Wiseman. Let me be rid of this, at least for today," said Pritchitt. Resting his exhausted mind, he sat on the side of the bed.

The puttering sound of the scooter faded and there was quiet. Achy fatigue filled Pritchitt's legs as he stood and walked across the room. He closed the window and had one less chill for his tired body to deal with. Just to make it back to bed and fall asleep, he thought. Sprawling his body across the bed, his eyelids closed. A piercing ring threw open his eyes. Pritchitt grabbed the phone. It better not be Wiseman again, he thought. His body raised up in agitation. His emotions calmed.

Todd Bohannon was calling. He had been pleased with the previous day's jury selection, but his call was really one of concern for his good friend and client. "Stay at home, Ben. Relax. God knows you need to take it easy. We'll need all your faculties in sharp order when the trial begins." Pritchitt said nothing. He mentioned Wiseman's visit and the newest fax. He spoke of the incident with the deaf mute and apologized. "The grounds keeper didn't press charges but for the love of God, Ben, please stay home and out of trouble. At least, promise me that you'll try. Remember, your trial, Ben. Two weeks, Ben. Be good for two weeks."

"I'll try, Todd."

CHAPTER TWENTY-TWO

Though it was a very bright afternoon, the drawn
curtains shut out the sun. A torchiere lamp lit the high ceiling
and a small brass lamp illuminated the antique desk. A white
bearded Dr. Lindsey sat in silence, his glasses positioned at the
very tip of his nose. Spread before him were medical reports,
psychiatric evaluations and notebooks crammed with
scrabbling. There was a knock on his door. "Come in," he said.
He removed his glasses, squinting. "Blanche, how good to see
you." He stood and clasped her hand with both of his. "Well, Dr.
Tucker. A colleague, now of course, but I can't forget you as my
resident. I seldom see you."

"I've got a very busy practice, Dr. Lindsey," said Blanche,
taking a seat.

"Good, that's good. So you've heard I'm retiring?"

"Yes. Who will be taking over your practice?"

He shrugged. "I don't know. Dr. Harkman considered it,
but we couldn't come to terms. I'm not asking much. I still have
at least two hundred active cases."

"He can't hold a candle to you, Dr. Lindsey. You are the

most distinguished psychiatrist in Memphis."

"That's very kind."

"I admire you, Dr. Lindsey, you were most helpful to me."

"On the telephone, you mentioned certain problems, anxiety attacks?"

"Yes, these serial murders and the circumstances bring back memories."

"So you have recurring thoughts about your sister?" He pushed the lamp toward her. "I hope this isn't the misplaced guilt we dealt with years ago?"

"It's not the same," she replied. Dr. Lindsey studied her as she spoke.

"So there is something entirely different in that mind of yours wanting to come out?" He reached for a notebook. "Blanche, what has it been, seven or eight years since your sister's death?"

"Eight years. And I was suicidal because of guilt."

He nodded his head. "I remember. I have your file upstairs, along with thousands of others. I'll get it to refresh my memory."

"That won't be necessary. I'm dealing with my problem. I just thought I would mention it to you."

"Blanche, you mentioned it for a reason. So that we would discuss it."

"I suppose you're right, but I also want to discuss taking over your practice."

"One thing at a time," said Lindsey.

"Can you listen now?"

He smiled. "Can I listen? My dear, that is one of my best attributes. I'll get your file, if you wish."

"No, that won't be necessary."

"Let me recount what we covered," Blanche said, stretching her long legs and crossing them at her ankle.

Dr. Lindsey leaned into the light. "I was so vain about my memory, but it seems I've suffered from tiny strokes, *T.I.A.'s,* which have brought about memory lapses, so that's why it is time to step aside," he said regretfully.

"Oh, I'm so sorry."

"But I distinctly recall your case. Christy was your sister."

"We shared a room while we were university students. I was a medical student and at night for extra money . . ."

Dr. Lindsey interrupted. "You both worked as dancers."

"Strippers, Dr. Lindsey, cheap strippers."

"Why do you say cheap?"

"Because I'm ashamed that I had to expose my breasts. I was too lazy to get a real job. This job paid so well for so little time."

Dr. Lindsey made notes. "You made a great deal of money?"

"Yes, often times five or six hundred a night. Christy was very beautiful. She became romantically involved with a regular customer.

"And she became pregnant?"

"Exactly. She had several admirers, a few became boyfriends, but only one was really special. It was so sudden. They were passionately in love."

Dr. Lindsey stared at Blanche. Tears rolled down Blanche's cheeks. "She didn't want a child, so you suggested an abortion. She wasn't certain who the father was. Am I correct, Blanche?"

"Yes, she suspected that it was the child of an older man, her previous lover, but her new boyfriend believed he was the father, and he was elated. He proposed marriage. Then Christy confessed what she had done, that she ended her pregnancy. He lost his mind." Blanche sobbed.

Dr. Lindsey leaned back in his chair and lit a pipe.

Blanche's breathing became irregular. "He tore up our apartment. He had brought roses. He slapped Christy in the face with them. He called her a murderer and left in a rage."

"That's when she got the sleeping pills."

"I had gone to the club, to explain that Christy and I needed time off, and when I returned . . . my sister was dead."

Blanche buried her face in her hands. She could only sob. Her wet eyes stared upward. She sighed. Her voice grew somber. "The boyfriend . . . " She paused with a brief look away.

"Yes. What about her boyfriend?"

"He would always play a game with her in bed during sex. The game was a children's game. A children's game called, Simon Says."

Lindsey's fatherly jaw protruded and with a long draw from his pipe gave his former student an understanding nod.

"Seems an appropriate mix, if you think about it. A man who plays children's games in bed is a man who finds it hard to be anything more than a child, especially when faced with a problem."

"You've heard about the serial killer?" asked Blanche.

"You would have to be blind and deaf not to have. Must be a pathetic human in a tremendous amount of pain."

Blanche dried her eyes and the sadness retreated from her now serious scowl. "I have discovered that the messages sent by this killer all start the same way, with Simon says."

"And this is what has upset you?"

"Yes. Because I wonder could it be?

"You mean, could it be that man?" Dr. Lindsey, pipe in hand, leaned back in his chair. He began to rock slowly, deep in thought. He finally stopped. "Blanche, it may simply be a coincidence. Everyone hears of this game in childhood. Or this man could be involved in these terrible murders. If you suspect him, then you must go to the police."

"At Christy's funeral he became so distraught that he had to be escorted away. Weeks later in the hospital where I worked, I saw his name on a chart. He had suffered an emotional breakdown and I did the unthinkable."

"You probably did what any normal person would do considering the circumstances," Lindsey said in comforting support. "You pulled his chart and read it."

"His admitting doctor was you, sir." Silence invaded the dimly lit office. Lindsey held his chin and nodded his acceptance of her message. His silence was her answer. She knew that to him the doctor-patient confidence was as sacred as the Hippocratic Oath. The seconds of silence seemed like hours as they looked to one another. "I would just like to . . . "

"Much time has passed," interrupted Lindsey. "Some people change and some don't, my dear Dr. Tucker." Lindsey leaned forward tapping ashes from his pipe into a small tin can.

"You're right, as usual, Dr. Lindsey."

His look was serious and his eyes fixed. "Remember this, Blanche, go from here in a way that does not put you in jeopardy. This person, whomever it is, could be very dangerous. If he is who you think, then may God watch after you and have mercy on his sick soul." Dr. Lindsey stood slowly and reached for a cane. Blanche seemed shocked by his frailty. "Shocked at how I've aged? I'm nearly eighty. And this arthritis has worn-out my knees." He placed a gentle kiss on her forehead. "Let me help you in any way I can. Remember, caution."

She paused at the door, then turned back. "And the other matter, sir," she mentioned. "I will send you a letter detailing my price for your practice, if that's okay?"

"That would be fine," said Lindsey, his eyes framed by his gentle smile.

"Thank you, Dr. Lindsey," she said. She quickly turned and exited the front door.

Wiseman sensed someone's presence. He quietly turned his tired body on the sofa. He heard distinct footsteps. His heart beat faster. Someone was near the fax machine. "Who's there?" he shouted. A tall shadow raised against the dimly lit wall as Wiseman sprung to his feet. His anxiety calmed. It was Dr. Pritchitt.

"Wiseman, you scared the hell out of me."

"You scared the hell out of me, too."

Pritchitt walked slowly into the light. "You look like hell."

"It was a hectic night in the ER. I think I flopped on that sofa about 3:30 this morning," answered Wiseman.

"Not bad. In my days of training we hardly caught a wink when we were on night call."

"I know and you probably got up to milk the cow and walked ten miles barefoot just to get to work, too, right?"

"How'd you know, Bernie?"

The fax machine came alive. It was 6:00 a.m. "Just like I thought, Dr. Pritchitt," grinned Wiseman. Pritchitt snatched the sheet.

"What does it say?" Bernie asked.

Pritchitt read: "'Simon says, Does Dr. Assurance feel good about the treatment plan? Or does Dr. Insurance need to perform a surgical procedure to save a failing bond of brotherhood? The prophecy of I, the Alpha, to protect unborn innocence and you, the Omega, to protect suffering of the aged in a failed society, must go forward.'"

Wiseman whistled in surprise. "This guy is telling you that either you're with him or against him. He's going to have to do something to insure this bonded brotherhood you are supposed to have. It's that something that scares me to death, sir. We can't bluff him anymore. He wants an answer, and he wants it now!"

Pritchitt paced back and forth. "Yeah, and then what, Bernie? Then what do I do, kill him? There's no damn way I'm going to go along with this madness." He seated himself at the computer. He began to type, only to stop. "Maybe you're right. What if I go along with him, just to buy time? What if I try to set him up? You know, arrange a trap, so maybe the police can nab him."

"Now you're thinking like a damn chairman, sir. But what changed your mind?"

"The something . . . the threat. My own life is valueless. I've lived. But my family, I can't risk them. I've done enough to them already. They need suffer no more." Pritchitt's voice choked.

"Now you're using a Yiddisha kupf. I like it. We'll bait the trap and catch a fat rat. And we'll kill it."

Pritchitt locked eyes with Wiseman. "What if we trap him? Should he get a trial and years of comfort in prison, fighting his death sentence like they all do or should we —"

"I say give him the same chance he gave those girls. As if he were a snake, we'll cut his head off."

"I agree. I'll suggest a meeting, so we can talk. That's it."

Pritchitt began typing. "That's my one stipulation, that we meet so I can verify he wishes to die."

"Right, put down that there are copycat Simons, so you'll need proof."

Wiseman rubbed his hands together. "If he brings proof, he puts the noose around his neck."

"Or, if we fail, he takes us out." Pritchitt looked around the dark room. "What if he's got this place bugged? What if he's eavesdropping as we talk? Or maybe Peters has this placed tapped. We try to double-cross Simon and he kills us."

"Whoa, wait a minute, Doc."

Pritchitt unscrewed the telephone mouthpiece. Wiseman examined the fax machine. Suddenly, they were searching every inch of the office. For the next hour they were seized by blind panic, a desperate search for the ubiquitous Simon. They were trying to think like a madman.

Finally Wiseman called a halt.

"Sir, there's nothing here."

Pritchitt paused, lowering his head on his desk. The drawers were overturned, their contents spilled on the floor. Pritchitt's fist slammed the desk. "The bastard has taken control of my life. I'll rip him to pieces with my own hands." He sat down again and typed the response.

In a vacant telephone booth in South Memphis, a portable fax machine began purring. The gloved hands held tightly to the machine. Ecstasy and satisfaction filled the small booth as the message was sent, then the line to a small portable fax machine was hastily disassembled. The black mouthpiece dangled helplessly. There was a tap on the glass door. A snub-nosed pistol poked it's nose inside. The door was yanked open. Two teens with gang graffiti on their jackets smirked. The long-haired figure fell to bended knees. "Please, please, don't hurt me," came a garbled plea."

The portable fax was yanked away. Hands invaded pockets of the kneeling person. "There's a thousand dollars in the car," he pleaded. They pulled the whimpering figure of a man from the booth. They dragged him to his car, banging his head against the car door, laughing at his pain, longhair shaking as he sobbed. The teens taunted him, placing the gun inches from his face. A heavy foot kicked at their victim. "On the seat is the money," he moaned. They flung the door open, and fought over a paper sack. One pulled out a thick wad of bills, along with a packet of cocaine. The other yanked the sack and strode backward. "It's mine!" he shouted, as they grappled over the loot.

Both failed to see the swift hand of the kneeling victim slide beneath the driver's seat. From behind a voice spoke. "Simon says you're dead." Bullets exploded. A head split open like a ripe watermelon. Blood spattered the sidewalk. The fax note, dotted with warm blood, was picked up. The surviving assailant began crawling in the dirt, bleeding from his side and screaming for mercy. The gun was held point blank to his head.

"Oh, no. Please, God, don't." Pop-pop-pop.

"Tell me once again," insisted Lt. Bordeaux.

"I've told you," snapped Pritchitt, pacing the room at the police station, "exactly as it happened. Simon sent this fax to me. And I sent *that* one."

"To this number?"

"To that telephone number."

Lt. Bordeaux looked to Caffey. "That's the number of the telephone booth that was electronically changed."

"What's going on?" asked Pritchitt angrily.

Lt. Bordeaux studied the report before her. "We've got two bullet riddled teens at this booth on South Belmont. They've got petty criminal records. It looks like they picked the wrong guy to rob. Seems Simon was held up as he was getting your fax."

"So that's it," said Wiseman. "Any evidence at the scene?"

Lt. Bordeaux made certain her door was closed. "Yeah, he left a portable fax and some kind of gizmo he used to tap into the telephone receiver.

"Fingerprints?" asked Pritchitt.

Bordeaux shook her head. "Not one. We also found a hundred dollar bill with trace marks of cocaine."

She picked up the fax message Pritchitt had sent. "You're playing a dangerous game, Dr. Pritchitt. A game that if you lose might make Mrs. Pritchitt a widow." She lowered her eyes and read: "'We have bonded in a courageous fight against sin. But, to be certain that you're who you say, I must meet with you. Meet my brother as ordained by God.' I'm telling you, doc, you're feeding a crazy mind with this shit. I can't tell you how uneasy I am about this."

"We're going to get him," said Wiseman confidently.

Bordeaux leaned into Wiseman's face. "That's what those punks thought at the phone booth, too. Now they're in the morgue."

Wiseman was without response, only nodding his understanding.

"I'm buying time," offered Pritchitt. "It's obvious the mayor's going to dump you. And me, I may be in prison soon, so we've really got nothing to lose except time, if we don't move fast."

Bordeaux tossed down the fax sheet. "You're a straight shooter, Doc, and well meaning, but let the police handle this."

"We've got to stop this maniac somehow," continued Wiseman, "so let's play by his rules. By yours we're not doing so good."

There was frustration in Bordeaux's sigh. "You're right," she finally agreed. "And we did turn up something, two strands of long brown hair, entangled in the portable fax."

"That's Simon for sure," beamed Wiseman.

Caffey interrupted, "Two strands of synthetic hair."

Pritchitt and Wiseman exchanged glances. "Then . . . it's a wig!" exclaimed Pritchitt.

"Well, what do you know," mumbled Wiseman.

"Whoever it is, he's smart. He's been altering the numbers of the telephone booths, for fear we'd trace them," said Bordeaux.

"We don't even know if he really has long hair. He's always one step ahead of us," moaned Wiseman.

"Yeah, but he nearly made a fatal mistake last night," said Pritchitt.

"When is his next message supposed to come?" asked Bordeaux.

"It was supposed to be this morning, but it never came. Now we know why."

Wiseman laughed. "Yeah, you've got his damn fax machine."

Pritchitt paced the small room. "Bernie, call the office." Wiseman reached for the telephone.

"Patsy, this is Wiseman. Have any faxes come in?" Nothing? Oh, all right. What? A mailgram? Read it." The attentive listeners moved closer. "Holy shit! This is it. He sent a fucking mailgram," blurted Wiseman.

"Well, what does it say?" said Pritchitt.

"Wait. Quiet, Patsy's reading it to me," answered Wiseman, holding a hand to one ear the receiver tightly to the other. "He says, 'I am overjoyed. We have truly bonded as the Alpha and Omega of all that is righteous. The illness and the medicine will meet. Simon.'"

"What the hell did that mean?" Bordeaux asked as her face lit up. "Hey, we just may trap this scumbag after all. We'll get a plan."

"Is there anything I can do?" Bernie asked.

Pritchitt turned. "Yes, there is. You can pray damn hard and don't stop until I tell you."

"Mama Wiseman, will get the whole synagogue to pray. You'll have more prayers than you'll know what to do with."

There was a worried hush through the room as all considered what was about to happen and how close it could be to the time Simon was finally confronted.

The telephone rang. Lt. Bordeaux reached for it. Her jaw dropped in shock. "When was he brought in? I don't believe this. Thanks, Charlie." She hung up the telephone. She turned. "There's been an arrest."

"Simon's been caught?" asked Pritchitt hopefully.

"No, Tyler was jailed last night."

"Tyler, Dr. Pritchitt's son?" gasped Wiseman.

"What? That can't be. What the hell for?" erupted Pritchitt angrily.

"I'll go right now," Bordeaux mumbled, her emotions showing.

"Not the hell without me. And what's the charge?" added Pritchitt.

"The charge is possession of cocaine." Bordeaux hurried from the room with Pritchitt racing behind.

Within thirty minutes Todd Bohannon had arranged bail for Tyler Pritchitt. In the release room Tyler huddled with Bohannon and his father. "I went to the gym last night to work out, Dad. That's where I was arrested. As I walked to my car all these police jumped out with guns raised. Scared the hell out of me, and that's for damn sure," he fretted, staring off at the disbelieving face of Bordeaux.

"It's a pitiful frame-up," said Bohannon, waving the police report in his hand. "Seems that vice was tipped off to Tyler's car by an anonymous caller. They were told what the car looked like and where it was. How damn convenient for them."

"I've never used drugs in my life," asserted Tyler. "Not even marijuana in college when everybody else in my fraternity was."

"The report says the police got the tip and found the bag of cocaine in your bumper. Hell! It wasn't even in his car, Benjamin," Bohannon balked, staring at Pritchitt's frightened frown.

"Anybody could have walked by and planted that stuff inside the bumper, then called us," said Bordeaux walking to Tyler's side.

"Exactly," nodded Bohannon. "This stinks of a frame-up. Don't worry, with your clean record and your position, I'll get it dismissed."

"It's more than that, Todd," said Pritchitt.

"More than what, Ben? It's clear cut. Tyler was framed."

"It has to do with an insurance policy, I'm afraid." All were quiet as heads turned and waited for what they feared. "Simon did this to my son."

"Why did I know he was going to say that?" said Bordeaux pacing.

"And why is that?" asked Bohannon.

"It's a message. Simon pulls the strings and if I don't dance now, this happens. Happens to my family, just as I feared."

"I've been blind-sided, and that's the fact. I'm sure everyone in Memphis will know after the nightly news. And the university, damn what can I tell them?" complained Tyler.

"We'll tell them the truth, Tyler. You were framed," Bordeaux explained, her hand to his restless shoulder. "The police will back you. I'll see to that, if it's the last thing I do before I get my ass fired."

Pritchitt seethed. "Simon wants to die. Then he will! Damn it!" he shouted.

CHAPTER TWENTY-THREE

Jesse Matthews awoke in a daze with a throbbing head and parched throat. She was seated on a creaky, metal chair. She was naked and cold. Her body shivered. Her wide eyes surveyed the shadowy, candlelit room. An eerie evil was present, she thought, as tears flowed from her cheeks and she struggled to free her mouth from the gagging cloth that made it hard to breathe. She kicked and squirmed but did little to free herself. Metal cuffs were tightly clasped around her ankles. Is this a nightmare? she wondered. Her neck was sore and stiff. Feeling faint, she slumped forward. On the floor was her dress and underclothing. Her fingers moved to try and release her bound hands. She grimaced in pain, a wound in her scalp dripping blood. Her beautiful long hair highlighted in red. She cringed, feeling the pain of a lump the size of a small egg on the back of her head. The wound was clotting with matted hair and dried blood. Ten feet away was a small casket, surrounded by candles. Her heart raced faster. She tried to rise but around her waist was another chain attached to the chair. Unable to turn, she reached behind her. Her head tapped against something.

Craning her sore neck as best she could, she realized she was against a large fireplace grate. Panic swept over her. She tugged at the cuffs on her ankles but they were linked to circular steel rings in the bricks which fronted the fireplace. Thoughts of the previous night returned. She had driven to the Women's Health Center, left her automobile, then felt something strike the back of her head. A plastic bag was placed over her head, then her memory faded. She again looked around. She knew she was alive. This was no dream. She had been kidnaped. "Help me, please," she tried screaming but only moans were heard beneath the tightly stuffed gag. A telephone rang. But where? The sound was right at her feet. She leaned forward, the metal chain pressing painfully against her delicate skin. With great effort she strained and with her toes brushed her dress to the side. Beneath it was the ringing telephone. With a pained effort she managed to knock the receiver free with her bound foot as she scooted the chair forward. "Help me," she shouted into the receiver. There was only silence. "Please!" she cried with hysteria mounting.

"I will help you, Jesse. This is Simon," came a strange voice from the phone.

Her crying eased. Her focus on the floor and phone. "Who?"

The voice suddenly became high pitched. "Siiimmon!" shrieked the voice.

"Call the police! Help me," she panted.

"There's no help for you, Jesse."

"Why?"

"You aborted one of God's innocents. You murdered your own blood."

"No, no!"

"Are you cold, Jesse?"

"Yes. I'm cold and I feel sick."

A sudden whoosh was heard from behind her. Tiny gas flames warmed her back. The orange flames created eerie shadows across the room's dusky walls as she watched in horror. She fought the urge to give way to hysteria.

"How do you know who I am?" she shouted.

"Simon knows everything," came the terrifying voice. "Repeat that, Jesse."

"Simon knows everything," she cried loudly.

"You live with your mother, don't you?"

"How do you know?"

The voice laughed. "Your purse is right before me."

"My mother needs me. I want my Mama," she yelled, bursting into a rhythmic cry.

"Simon says, 'Jesse wants to kill babies.'"

"No, you're wrong." The flames behind her suddenly fired higher and hotter. The nape of her neck felt the fiery heat, as did her back. She tried desperately to escape the chair. "Please turn it off. You're hurting me." Her body began beading, trickling with moisture.

"No more than you hurt your unborn child. I am God's avenger, Jesse. You are now experiencing a taste of what hell will be like for you. You will burn mercilessly for the killing of your own child."

"You — youuuu're the one who killed those girls," shouted Jesse, as tears streamed freely and sweat from the fire's heat oozed from every pore.

"I had to," answered the voice. "That is my mission. But how would you, a common person, know my mission."

"But I didn't do anything wrong," she choked.

"Don't lie! I saw you enter and exit the clinic. And I knew that you were with child. You committed murder, didn't you?"

"No, I swear. It was all a mistake. Look in my purse. You'll find a letter. I was never pregnant. Last night I went to the Center to get my medical records and a refund check. I had already decided not to go through with it. Then I learned I wasn't even pregnant. They got my test confused with another girl and told me that I had just missed my period because of stress. Please, believe me. If you are who you say you are, then God will let you look to make sure of this righteous mission you're on," she shouted, her crying uncontrollable.

There was a long silence.

"But you first *considered* an abortion?"

"Yes, but a close friend convinced otherwise."

The flames lowered, then extinguished. Immediate relief came to Jesse and to her scorched skin. "Thank you. Thank you. God bless you," she whimpered in a tiring effort as her head dropped forward. The door before her creaked open. A dark silhouette of a man with long hair and a long overcoat entered the dimly lit room. The telephone was yanked from the floor below, then dragged across the room and through the closing door. Jesse was bathed in sweat. Terror stricken, her heart pounded. Heavy steps sounded as the long-haired figure walked past her to the small casket.

"Soon! Very soon!" shouted a twisted voice. Jesse clinched her jaws to suppress a scream. She began reciting The Lord's Prayer to calm her fragile nerves.

"Please let me go," she begged. One by one the candles were extinguished. The room now was with total darkness. A door opened and closed. There was horror in the room's silence as she cried a prayer. Her voice was sobbing.

"Simon says . . ." came the strange voice through the darkness.

"Please, please, mister, please don't hurt me," her voice barely audible, and weakened by the terror of the moment. The footsteps stopped. A hand held tightly to her shoulder and Jesse screamed.

The early morning sun dappled the tall oaks and elms. Multi-colored leaves elegantly graced the trees. Squirrels scampered in Overton Park, scurrying for acorns and pine nuts. The club house came alive as the first golfers drove off in carts. The elderly men were in high spirits, filled with joy by the sunlight and deep blue sky. After the second hole they returned to the cart. The men playfully bantered back and forth. The driver climbed behind the wheel. "Pete, after all this damn rain I'm rusty," he said to his pal.

His front seat companion grinned. "Rusty? Man, you're flat out corroded." They both laughed.

The driver slowed. "This is the third hole where they

found that poor girl dead in the sand trap."

His companion shook his head in disgust. "When they catch him, they ought to put him in the electric chair."

The driver nodded. "I'd pull the switch."

The cart slowly approached the sand trap. "It was right down there," pointed the driver. The cart suddenly jerked to a stop.

"Oh, my God," cried the men. They hurried down the slight incline. Stretched on the sand was a young girl. She was naked. A city hall I.D. was tied around her neck.

"What animal would do this?" asked the driver as he draped her body with his coat.

The girl's eyes opened.

"She's alive!" cried his friend. They threw another coat over her pale body. "Get the cart, Pete!" Her mouth gaped wide, opening and closing, but words were hard to come. She mumbled in a barely audible whisper as both men bent down to listen.

"What'd she say?"

"I don't know. We better get her to the hospital and quick," one said with urgency as they lifted her limp body onto the cart.

Justin Nash ran to Terry's office. He was pale and upset. "I just got a call," he gasped. "They found Jesse in a sand trap at Overton Park."

"My God! Is she —?" asked Terry in shock.

"No. No, she's not dead," said Nash with relief. "She's alive. But all she can mutter is one word."

"Don't tell me, Simon?" guessed Terry.

Nash nodded. "She's at Memorial. Let's go," he said. The drive was frantic but quiet. Their mind's crowded with concern and terrifying thoughts.

Justin and Terry hurried down the long hospital corridor as Lt. Bordeaux and Det. Caffey stood protectively by the door.

"Dr. Previn is with her now," said Bordeaux. A doctor emerged.

"I'm Justin Nash, from the D.A.'s office." Nash flashed his I.D. "How is she?"

The physician removed a chart from the door.

"She was found in a state of shock, close to hypothermia. Actually, she was near dead from exposure. She's sedated now and sleeping."

"Any sexual trauma?" asked Bordeaux.

"No. Not that we can tell. But she had a deep gash in her head that needed a few sutures. There are minor skin burns on her back and a few abrasions. Physically, she'll be fine, but emotionally, these kind of things can take their toll."

"Did she say anything to you?" asked Terry.

"Not at first. But she did keep calling for her mother. We got her mother right away." There was a pause as the doctor reviewed the chart. "And yes, there was something else. She kept calling for a friend of hers, a Simon. If so, we might want to get him here."

Silence fell on their drawn faces, for what they already suspected had been proven.

Nash was the first to speak. "Thank you, doctor, but I don't think we need him here."

"I think we can forget that friend," added Bordeaux.

"Okay. She's sleeping now so you'll have to come back later," said the doctor, turning away.

"Who is with her now?" asked Nash.

"Her mother and a nurse," answered the doctor. "She needs rest. She'll be coming around in seven or eight hours. Come back then."

Bordeaux nodded for Nash to follow her. In a private office she opened a briefcase. Carefully wrapped in clear plastic was Jesse's city hall identification. In another clear bag was a white envelope. Nash's name was scrawled on the front. "This was with her," said Bordeaux.

"Did you read it?" asked Nash.

"Not yet."

"Then give it to the police lab."

Terry entered the room. "Mrs. Matthews, Jesse's mother,

wants to speak with you, Justin." Terry led the way.

In an adjacent room was an attractive woman dabbing her eyes. "I'm so sorry," said Justin. He extended his hand for Jesse's mother to take.

"I've never met you, Mr. Nash, but Jesse has spoken so highly of you. She told me you had counseled her about not having the abortion."

Terry and Bordeaux stood to the side, listening with interested ears.

A young man poked his head in the room. "How is she now, Mrs. Matthews?"

"Bill, she's resting." The young man came inside.

"This is Jesse's boyfriend, Mr. Nash. Bill Jones."

Nash's face clouded with an angry frown. His arms reached out and grabbing the young man pinned Jones against the wall. "How could you let this poor girl go through this, and even consider an abortion? How irresponsible!" he shouted angrily.

"Justin, let him go," ordered Bordeaux. She struggled to force Nash to release his strong grip on the boy.

"Justin, for God's sake, let him go," Terry shouted as the mother hurried toward the door.

"Wait a minute. She wasn't pregnant!" shouted Jones, his head pressed against the wall.

"You liar!" Nash drew back his fist, as if to strike.

Terry grabbed his arm.

"She told me herself!" shouted Nash.

"Justin, please!" Terry, again pleaded.

"Justin, you're making a big mistake here," Bordeaux strongly suggested.

Suddenly, Mrs. Matthews went to the boy's aid. "He's right. Jesse thought she was pregnant," she explained, "but that damn clinic had given her the wrong test results. I should sue those bastards. They say she missed her period because of stress," she half-screamed through a soft cry.

Nash stepped away. He turned to Terry, then Bordeaux. His face filled with confusion and anger. He looked toward the boy. "I'm sorry."

"No problem. Damn, you're one strong dude," Jones mumbled, straightening his shirt.

"That's why Simon let her live. She was never pregnant and had no abortion," Bordeaux announced.

"What are you talking about?" the mother asked.

"Yeah, who the hell is Simon?" begged Jones.

"Nobody," said Bordeaux.

Nash signaled for Terry to leave with him. In the corridor Bordeaux caught up with them. "I'm keeping a guard on her door, just in case."

"Not needed," said Nash matter-of-factly.

"And how do you know that for sure? What are you now, a damn fortune teller? And what's this about you counseling Jesse about an abortion, anyway?" asked Bordeaux as Terry looked on with equal interest.

"She's of no use to Simon. Don't you understand?" said Nash. His glare was impatient. "I'm coming back later when she's awake and taking visitors," he said and hurried off. Bordeaux and Terry stood staring and wondering.

"What was that all about?" Terry whispered.

"You got me," said Bordeaux. Terry sighed as both turned down the hall.

The crime lab was nearly empty. The staff had gone, except for assistant Jerry Richards. He looked up. "What's going down, Lori?"

He crossed the room to the reception desk, searching a pile of folders. He glanced up.

"I hear the mayor and director want your head on a platter because of this serial killer case. Hear Dist. Atty. Bates might even be behind some of it." Richards was an African-American in his late 30s, clean shaven with a broad smile.

"Jerry, everybody wants results. That's what life's about, isn't it? Along the way some get stepped on and others stepped over."

"Here it is." He handed her a white folder. "Dr. Patcher prepared a preliminary report."

"He's not around?"

Richards' eyes darted from side to side. "Nope. He's butt smooching," he whispered.

"He's what?"

"He's having lunch with the mayor. He leaks everything right to her. He's a real butt kisser."

Bordeaux frowned.

Jerry leaned closer. "Dr. Patcher has his sights on higher ground, if you know what I mean. And Mayor Daniels is single, like him." He winked.

"From what I've seen of her, she'll always be single. That's one lady with a hidden dick. "

She took the report in hand. "I owe you one, Jerry."

"Yes, ma'am. You certainly do."

Bordeaux hurried from the lab. In her small office, she slipped off her jacket and removed the report from its envelope. There wasn't much to go on. "No traceable fibers on underclothing," she read. But she found what she really wanted. There was a note sent with Jesse. She read the color photocopy of the note. It was from Simon, written in pencil in a childish scrawl. *"Dear Mr. Nash: I return Jesse to your incompetent hands. Remember, I am but God's medicine for the sickness of our world. I only administer my cure to the guilty. She is innocent. Sincerely, Simon."* Bordeaux reached for the phone.

It was early afternoon when the luncheon ended. Loretta brought three custard desserts. Tyler moaned, his stomach full from the large late meal.

"Looks good," said Todd Bohannon, "just like everything else."

"Thank you," beamed Loretta. She disappeared into the kitchen.

"Todd, I want to thank you for helping my son. I know you must be wishing you never heard of the Pritchitts."

"Nonsense, Ben."

Tyler shook Bohannon's hand. "Ditto that for me."

Bohannon wiped a linen napkin across his lips. "They had no case. That's why Judge Montel dismissed the charge. It was an obvious frame-up."

"It was humiliating," said Tyler.

Bohannon jabbed his spoon in the air. "Everybody considers themselves law abiding, upright citizens, assuming they'll never be arrested. They can't imagine that given a certain set of circumstances they can suddenly appear very guilty."

"Thanks again," said Tyler. "I've got to get back to work. I've got a class to instruct at three and a reputation to win back." He leaned in the kitchen. "It was a great lunch, Loretta."

After Tyler's departure Benjamin and Todd moved to the privacy of the den. "There's been a postponement in the jury hearings," said Bohannon.

"Why?" asked Benjamin with dejection.

"They pulled the judge to another case."

Pritchitt shrugged. "It really doesn't make any difference. They're going to find me guilty . . . and then prison," he said, his head down.

"That's one hell-of-an attitude. Need to be more positive." Bohannon paused. "You may have to serve some time, Ben. This serial killer publicity hasn't helped us, either. I mean, some people think you're a little . . . well, off, because of your pen pal, Simon."

"Can't hardly blame them."

"Assisted suicide is a Class D felony. If convicted, the law stipulates not less than two years nor more than twelve."

"So I could get twelve years."

Bohannon nodded. "Yes, one could venture to say that is a possibility, but I believe remote, at best."

"And at worst?"

"It will be apparent to the jury you have deliberately performed these actions. It is not the single situation of a dying family member, performed on impulse."

"You're preparing me for the worse."

"I always do that, even when they're one of my closest and dearest friends. You've been lucky."

"How so?"

"There haven't been any civil suits filed by the families. They're are obviously supportive of you."

"Except for Danny Lavender. Have you forgotten?"

"Well, he can't sue you from where he is and that's a given." Bohannon picked up his briefcase. "Well, we did have a fine lunch. Tyler's a good boy. You're blessed with a wonderful family, Ben. Give my love to those wonderful grandchildren. Hell, that little Benji is your spitting image. Gotta go. I've got clients this afternoon."

As Pritchitt waved him off, the telephone rang. It was Terry. She told him about Simon's note which was found with Jesse. Pritchitt listened attentively.

"Dad, Simon wrote that he was the *medicine?* Justin and I will speak with Jesse this evening."

He pressed Terry for details of the kidnapping and Jesse's release, but Terry had few answers. "The media frenzy is building, Dad. We think it best if you kind of disappear from view until your trial."

Pritchitt was stunned. Simon could have killed her but chose not to — it was puzzling. The doorbell rang. A medical supplies truck was in the drive. The man waved an invoice. "Dr. Pritchitt?"

"Yes?"

"I've got a delivery for you."

Pritchitt signed the paper. "Bring it around back to the garage, please." With a small dolly the boxes were stacked in the garage. After the truck pulled away, Pritchitt opened one. Inside were small metal canisters. He rummaged about then removed a suitcase from a shelf. For the next hour he assembled a new machine, a "death machine," as the press called it. He connected the canisters to a tube and added the mask. These would take Simon back to hell, where he belonged.

Lt. Bordeaux sat quietly next to the hospital bed. Jesse

tossed and turned, then her eyes opened. She stared at the woman in blue, then her eyes scanned the room. "Where am I?" she asked.

"You're in Memorial Hospital. I'm Lt. Lori Bordeaux."

"I know you. You've been to our offices before." Jesse's eyes widened. She raised to a sitting position. As if awakening from a dream, she eased back in the bed. She closed her eyes. "It was horrible."

"Relax. I know it's been an ordeal. Jesse, did you see this Simon? The person who kidnapped you."

"Yes, well . . . not his face. It was so awful." She covered her eyes. "It was like hell itself. There was fire and darkness," she cried. "My back hurts."

"You've got burns to your back, Jesse."

"Oh, yes! God, do I remember," she whimpered holding her eyes shut as if trying not to remember. Bordeaux was soothing in her questioning and Jesse calmly recounted what had occurred. "That's all I remember until the park," she whispered, concluding her scanty details.

The door to the hospital room opened. Nash entered.

"Mr. Nash!" cried Jesse.

He gave her a hug.

"How's the world's greatest secretary?" said Nash, a calming voice soothing her anxiety. Jesse slumped on the pillow emotionally exhausted.

Lori Bordeaux called Nash into the hall. "She didn't get a good look at Simon's face." Bordeaux shook her head. "Sometimes I wonder if this bastard even has one."

Nash grimaced. "So close, and yet so far away," he uttered in disappointment.

"Close doesn't cut it. Not while there are still girls out there at risk. He's a maniac, but a very shrewd maniac."

"Why a maniac?" Nash observed. "Does he have to necessarily be mad? Can't he be emotionally disturbed without being mad?"

"What's the fucking difference, Justin?"

"Makes a difference in profiling potential suspects, that's how."

"For chrissakes, Justin, I'll take any suspect right now. We've got a big zero when it comes to leads." The strain of the investigation was getting to Bordeaux. A frustrating hush filled the air. Tempers were short and patience gone. Her mind couldn't rest as she mentally tried to piece anything into meaningful clues. "Jesse said it appeared to be an older house. The floors creaked. And the radiators ancient," she recounted aloud. "There were dozens and dozens of candles, pictures in frames and a small coffin. How eerie and evil," Bordeaux murmured.

"Eerie and evil, maybe ... but mad ... I think not," lectured Nash. He turned with brisk pace and was gone. Lori stood in silence, her mind disrupted by strange thoughts and unanswered questions.

CHAPTER TWENTY-FOUR

A chill breeze ushered in a winter day. The low leaden sky brought signs of an early snow. Benjamin puffed heavily, his breath frosty. Tomorrow Ruth would be home. The park at Shelby Farms was nearly empty. Pritchitt continued his routine jog around the lake, exhilarated by a forgotten feeling of freedom. His mind recovering from its troubled thoughts with the rest he'd needed. His muscles were tired, but he was less tense. Across the rolling fields two young boys sailed a silver kite in the gray sky. He slowed his run staring off at a nearby woods, then suddenly stopped.

At the edge of those distant woods was a solitary figure. It was a man wearing a long overcoat. "Not again," he mumbled. Hold your composure he told himself. It's just a man with rather long hair and an overcoat, he thought. Another test of his sanity, he was sure. He resumed a slow jog. The man lifted his hand in a slow wave. His hair was long and face darkened by shadowing trees. Pritchitt stared; his heart raced and his mind wandered. Pritchitt raised his arm in a wave. The two communicated their hello. Pritchitt's thoughts were racing.

Pritchitt shivered as the cold wind whipped his soaked body. Should he pursue him? Perhaps he had a gun. Don't be a coward, he chastised himself. No, the moment wasn't right. This man wasn't Simon, but Simon's attempt to control his mind was real. There was a method in Simon's madness. A two-fold madness, Pritchitt thought. The first, was to accomplish his own death, the second, was to share his madness with his new-found brother, Pritchitt himself.

There was a grisly ritualistic ceremony being enacted, both by Simon and in Pritchitt's tormented mind. Candles and caskets, said Jesse of her kidnapper. "That's it!" shouted Pritchitt, his legs jogging faster, his mind momentarily with an answer. Simon wants to be a sacrifice against the evil of a dismal world. That's why he won't kill himself. In his warped mind, then he would be as Jesus, sacrificed for the sake of fighting sin, thought Pritchitt in dismay. His jog abruptly stopped and he spoke aloud, "I will sacrifice you I swear," vowed Pritchitt. He resumed a quickening pace with an energy born by that promise.

Blanche Tucker pushed the door open and quietly entered Dr. Lindsey's study. It was well past six and darkness had fallen.

Dr. Lindsey was asleep, resting his head on his desk. He suddenly stirred. "I thought I heard someone knocking." Then recognizing Blanche he gave a slight wave of his hand. "I wasn't sleeping, Blanche, just resting my eyes," he said. He looked downcast. "I'm just an old man," he sighed. "The golden years! What a lot of nonsense."

"The housekeeper let me in. I'm sorry to disturb you." Blanche removed an article from her briefcase. "This will be published next month."

Dr. Lindsey eyed her happily. "Wonderful. Now I know why you're so busy. I will read this." He placed the article in his desk drawer. "So, Blanche, I understand you have taken over my position with the Police Department. I am pleased. The real

estate broker tells me you might want to buy my practice and
the building as well."

"I am considering it. I believe I will qualify for a mortgage,
since I'm a veteran."

Lindsey's eyes opened wide. "Really, Blanche? I had no
idea."

"Yes. I served one year in the army during the Gulf War.
I'm still in the reserves." She sat facing Lindsey. "Wartime
stress can destroy the soul," she remarked. "The desert had a
way of reducing humans to insignificant animals. The absence
of normal life was traumatic."

"You know, Blanche, before my war, I considered myself a
pacifist. Then we began learning of Hitler's vicious destruction
of the million Jews and the myriad of others he counted out
because they did not measure up in his mind." He reached for
his pipe. He puffed deeply. The sweet aroma of tobacco
permeated the room. "By the war's end, I supported the atom
bomb, and I consider myself a rational man." He shook his head
in disgust. "We have to end the impulse to kill."

"It is our job to penetrate those mysteries of behavior," said
Tucker. "Humans eliminate psychological problems by
murder."

"And that is our job to help those poor souls," he added.

Tucker nodded. "Well, Dr. Lindsey, would you mind if I
took a look around? You know, to see the house I may be
buying."

"By all means, Blanche. I rarely go upstairs my knees are
so bad, but you go."

Dr. Lindsey's office was a beautiful old brick residence
which had been converted into a small clinic some years ago. On
the lower level was a study for patient interviews, a library, the
kitchen, and a former bedroom which Dr. Lindsey used as an
office.

"I'm going upstairs," she said.

"I'm sorry for the dust," Dr. Lindsey apologized. "I need a
maid," then he smiled. When you get to be eighty, you need
everything."

The upper rooms, once bedrooms, contained closed patient files, alphabetically arranged. Some files were thick, some were thin. All were bound in notebooks with names along the spine. She walked slowly down a row of files and stopped. She removed a file and slipped it in her briefcase. She turned to see if his arthritic knees had allowed him to follow her upstairs. He hadn't and she continued her walk along the next row. She removed another file finding what she wanted. She placed it in her briefcase.

Lindsey waited at the foot of the stairs, "It is perfect," said Blanche, descending the stairs. "It's really a beautiful home. How many patients have you seen over the years? You have so many files."

He linked his arm in hers. "Many, many, yes. I must throw some away when the home is sold." They walked toward his study.

Blanche produced a file from her briefcase and sat down. "I took the liberty of bringing one down, hope you don't mind," she said. "Would you look this over again? Maybe there is something we've overlooked that could help me with my grief."

"I'd be happy to, but I believe your scars have all but healed. It's just loneliness that tugs at your memory, and that only you can cure. I do know loneliness and with it comes a depressing hypnosis. There's more to life than your patients. They can't keep your life fulfilled. Without sharing of the heart, one might say, there is no real life. No love, no life?"

He glanced toward the stairs. "I used to go up those stairs ten times a day, now it wears me out to make one trip." He tapped his chest. "I say it's my knees but I think it's my heart." He leaned back and closed his eyes.

"I know a good cardiologist," she said.

"No, my time is coming." He snapped his fingers. "I want to go like that. I've stopped driving. I'm getting ready."

"What does your family think?"

"My wife is dead. We had no children. Even my two dogs have passed before me."

Tucker glanced at her watch. "I must go. I'll make a bid on the practice and property."

He pulled himself up awkwardly. His stiff body seemed to totter. "It's dark outside. Let me see you to your car. This serial killer has every woman in Memphis looking over her shoulder in fear," he lamented.

"That's why I carry this." Tucker withdrew a small handgun from the briefcase.

Lindsey's eyes widened. "You know how to use that?"

"Oh, yes. The Gulf War was training enough."

"Good night, sir," she said and she walked securely into the night.

Bauers, Terry Mercer and Bordeaux met in Nash's office.

Terry spoke first. "We've checked the public health records to determine if any lawsuits were filed against a clinic or a physician for a botched abortion. There's nothing."

Bauers was next. "I tried the hospitals, to see if any woman came in the emergency room. I came up empty-handed, too."

Nash puffed his cigar. "I've got to call Mayor Daniels, and tell her we have another fucking zero. Can't we do anything right in this case!" he growled in angry frustration glancing out the window into the dark night. "The hour glass is running low for this investigating team."

There was a knock on the door. Someone from the police lab poked his head inside and handed Jesse Matthews' report to Nash. "It's not much," he said. "No fingerprints, fibers or leads of any kind."

"Nothing at all," said Nash. "We may as well adjourn this meaningless meeting."

Nash blurted, "What happened to Jesse's clothes?"

"Her dress, stockings, underclothes, shoes, coat and purse weren't with her." Terry tapped her pen on the yellow pad before her. "Now that's interesting. With the dead girls, their possessions were with them. But with the girl he's released, he keeps her personal effects."

Bauers nodded. "That's either an interesting point or no point at all."

"Bravo, maybe it's some kind of fetish," added Nash.

"Maybe we've got something," interjected Bordeaux. "Maybe he's kept them to remind him of something."

"Like what? This is really reaching, you guys. I think he didn't want to dress her so he threw the damn clothes away," said Bauers. "What we have is a sick mind who's killing while disguising himself and his voice. What we don't have is a clue as to who he is, excuse me, and that sucks." Frustration was palpable in the room.

Finally, Lt. Bordeaux spoke. "Maybe it's someone all the girls knew? We have an updated profile from our police psychiatrist, Blanche Tucker, of a man who's lost someone close and is hurting and possibly —"

"Small world," Nash interjected. "Dr. Tucker's the police psychiatrist? As of when?" Nash's disturbed voice was evident.

"Since last month; she's replaced Dr. Lindsey. He's retired."

"You got a problem with her, Justin? She's a damn good doctor. I can vouch for her. Look what's she's done for my mother," said Terry.

"No. No problem with Tucker," he answered. "I hate to say it, but we're still at ground zero, people," he fumed, his voice an unsettled tone.

Bauers rose to leave. "I might as well pull the classifieds because City Hall is going to have our fading careers on a chopping block." There was no laughter as the room emptied.

The bar was dim and a jukebox played a depressing melody. "It's been a long day and I can barely keep my damn eyes open," yawned Nash.

Terry nodded in agreement. "You're right. One more sip of wine and you'll have to carry me to my car. But I really appreciate the support you've given to me and my family. "

A cold wind swept the near empty parking lot as both

walked from the bar. Into the emptiness of night they walked, loneliness stalking both as easy prey.

Terry turned to Nash. "I don't want to go home," she confessed. Nash paused and stared into her confusion. "I don't know what I want, Justin, but I know I don't want to be alone," she repeated. "Call me crazy but I think I just need to be held."

"I don't know, Terry. We're both exhausted."

She frowned. "Well, can I at least drop by your house for a nightcap and hug?"

Nash hesitated. "All right. You follow me in your car. A hug and drink," he reaffirmed.

At the bistro, Terry had telephoned her father. "I've already said good night to my kids, and told Dad I would remain at the office. He knows I have much work to do."

Nash nodded. "Was all that necessary?"

"I don't know. There are a lot of things I'm not certain of right now." Terry hurried to her car and followed Nash as he pulled out of the parking lot.

The house was dark as Terry followed Justin into the massive entry hall. "Emma usually goes to bed early," he said. "But I'll introduce you as a good friend if she's awake."

Terry made a pouty face. "A good friend?"

"A very close friend," said Nash.

"That's better."

He gave her a kiss, then another. The passion between them was evident. Terry was torn.

Should she leave? She took his hand.

A warm nightcap and the loneliness of night led both up the impressive staircase. In the bedroom, Nash handed her a pair of pajamas. He undressed hurriedly. Terry admired his muscular physique and broad chest. He donned his pajamas and got beneath the covers. Terry slowly removed her clothing, allowing his eyes to feast on her toned body. She stood before him naked.

"Terry, you are lovely, but . . . not tonight." He turned away. She sat on the bed.

"What is it with you, Justin? Is it me?" He sat up and stared into her wanting eyes.

His voice struggled, then he whispered, "I'm impotent. I'm no good anymore." She caressed his naked shoulder.

Nash clenched her hand. "You've confused a man who thought his love life was over forever."

"Maybe all you need is some medical help?"

He raised his tired body. "I don't think so. I've seen doctors and more doctors."

"You can work this out, Justin. I do have feelings for you."

"Feelings? Only because you need something in your life other than pain. If it wasn't me it would be someone else. As soon as you're divorced and your father's ordeal is over, your whole being will change. You don't need me, Terry. You need love. A love that will help you forget your pain." His words mirrored her thoughts but she felt rejected.

"And what are you, a psychiatrist?"

"Maybe not, but the mind and its complicated functions are no stranger to me."

"Maybe your impotency can be treated."

Nash smiled feebly. "It's not physical with me, Terry. A psychiatrist has told me that. My libido was destroyed."

"Were you married? What happened? Let me help you like you've helped me."

He rose from the bed. "I was in love. She's dead now."

Terry grew sullen. "Justin, the father of my children is dead. The only real husband and love I've really known. I'm trying to get over it, too. We can help each other."

"Yes, and you tried to get over him with Niles. You're trying to get over Niles with me. And now, you're here only to forget all the problems in your life, right? I know you women. Everything with y'all is deep emotion and true love." Nash grabbed Terry and spun her. She clasped the pajamas tightly against her naked body and faced the long oval mirror. "Look at us, Terry. Look at both of us. Two people trapped in the emotional basement of their lives. And you want to pretend we're in some kind of honeymoon suite and none of this bullshit is really happening in our lives?"

Terry stood stunned, quieted by his outburst. Trembling at the sight of his tense face she turned from the mirror and began to dress.

"I'm sorry, Terry. I am just physically and emotionally exhausted." He slipped beneath the covers and turned away. Tears glistened in Terry's eyes as she sat on the edge of the bed. Confusion reigned. A shiver swept through her as she reached for the lamp's switch. Darkness filled the room and surrounded her emptiness. She quietly wept. It would be hard for her to sleep . . . her thoughts were self-condemning. She was angry with herself. She had nearly made a wrong choice, once again.

In the pre-dawn hours, Terry awoke with a parched throat. She slipped from the bed. Justin slept soundly. In the hall she found a bathroom, letting the cool water soothe her thirst. In the dark hall, she paused. She glanced inside a small room. It was an office with law books in glass bookcases. The next room was a bedroom where time had stopped. The furniture was shabby and covered with dust. An old television set with a broken antennae was on a dresser. On the fireplace mantle were two brass urns. Charles Nash and Edna Nash were the names inscribed. Both parents had been dead over a decade. This was their bedroom, she surmised. How dare I pry like this, reproaching herself. She clicked off the light. As she was about to reenter Justin's bedroom, the door swung open. Nash stared.

"You startled me." She caught her breath. "I was in the bathroom."

"I had a dream," said Nash. Terry moved as if to enter but he blocked her way, then took her hand. He led her to another room. In the dark she felt uneasy. A old lamp cast light on the dresser and photographs. "That's her," said Nash. "And those are my parents." The light of a match flashed. Nash lit candles on a dresser.

"You don't have to do this, Justin."

"Mom and Dad died young, just a year apart. I was a hotshot lawyer and when they died I had money to burn." He pulled Terry toward him. "Your body reminds me of her. She was a lot like you, Terry." His hands began fondling her. His grip was smothering.

"You're hurting me, Justin," said Terry, pulling away. "What's wrong with you?" she half-shouted, backing away from his advancing steps.

"Isn't this what you wanted?"

"You're looking for a dead woman in me?"

"She was wild. You're more intelligent."

"You mean you weren't impotent with her?"

"I was madly in love with her."

"How did she die?" Terry backed away and her breath grew short.

"I had nothing to do with it," he said defensively.

Panic brought tingling to Terry's hands and feet.

"I was so happy." He looked at the photograph he held of a young woman. "She had an abortion. My world came crashing down." His knees weakened and he clung to a table as Terry backed herself to the wall. "I was rejected and my child *destroyed*." His voice cracked and with it a moaning sob spread despair.

Terry straightened herself. She walked toward him unknowing of his next impulse. Fear swept her heart and it raced. "You were both young?" she offered.

Nash straightened himself. His voice exploded in anger. "Get out! Go home, Terry. Leave me!" His eyes filled with pain as Terry backed from the room. "Get out!"

A depraved tone filled his voice. Shock froze Terry's retreat. She hesitated. What madness had enveloped him? "You need help, Justin," she said in a sympathetic whisper.

Nash's head turned. "For God's sake, Terry, we both do. You said you wanted to help me, then leave me!"

Terry stared into his pleading eyes. Reluctantly she turned and left.

The morning sun was bright as Ruth pulled the shades on

the large window. There was a light tapping. Dr. Tucker entered.

"Good morning, Ruth."

"Morning," she answered, as if there were something on her mind. "Dr. Jerome said you had another productive session in group therapy this morning?"

Ruth said nothing.

"Is something wrong?"

"Yes," she said excitedly, as if a great weight were unburdened.

"What is it?" asked Dr. Tucker.

"I'm afraid to go home."

"Why?"

Ruth sat on the bed, her eyes lowered. "I'm afraid of failing. I mean, I do so much want to see my family and home but . . . " Her voice faded.

"You feel safe here and assured of yourself?"

"Yes," Ruth agreed. "But at the same time I want to go."

In Dr. Tucker's assessment Ruth seemed terribly ambivalent. "But Ruth, seeing you on admittance and the way you look now, well, it's like seeing two different people. However, we don't want a relapse and if you need more time . . . Well then, let's delay your release for a few days, until you feel certain."

Ruth looked relieved. "One of the nurses told me that this Simon person had released a girl unhurt. Had she had an abortion, like the rest?"

"Don't know, Ruth." Tucker seemed ill at ease and disappointed as she walked toward the door. "I'll telephone your husband about the delay." She forced a smile.

Pritchitt stared at the photograph in the morning newspaper. Niles and Milton James had led a protest march down Poplar Avenue, distributing leaflets. Marchers held banners and signs aloft. The article stated that another protest march was planned for today. Benji and Claire were already in the den, watching the Saturday morning cartoons. How their presence brightened the house, so dreary since Ruth's absence. But soon everything would get back to normal.

The telephone rang. He was certain it was Terry calling about the kids but it was Dr. Tucker.

Pritchitt was disappointed at her news. He had already stocked the refrigerator and was about to order flowers to welcome Ruth home. Tucker assured him it was simply slight nervousness on Ruth's part. He slumped on the sofa, dejected.

The doorbell rang. There was an overnight Federal Express truck in the drive. Inside a thin envelope was a postcard of downtown Memphis. The hand scrawled block letters read: "Today. Beale and Third. Telephone Booth. 1:00 p.m."

Within an hour Wiseman arrived. Pritchitt led him to the garage. At the back was a spacious storage room. "Ahh!" said Wiseman, eyeing the green canisters. "You've got quite a supply."

Pritchitt nodded. "As a doctor, I can simply order these from an out of state medical supply store." From behind an old gasoline container Pritchitt withdrew a shiny handgun.

"Wow," said Wiseman. "You're going to shoot Simon? That's what he wants now?"

"No. You're going to cover me, if he shows."

"What?"

"You heard me. You're going to be my back up."

"But I've never shot a gun. I don't even know which end to hold."

"God willing, you won't have to." There was the sound of an automobile in the driveway. Through the garage window Pritchitt observed his daughter. "You'd better wait here," he told Bernie.

"Dr. Tucker called. Your mother is nervous about coming home. She's afraid she'll fail," Pritchitt told Terry.

She looked perplexed. "She wants to stay in the hospital?"

"Just for a few more days."

Moments later the children and Loretta came out of the house and bundled into the car.

He bent to kiss them.

"I promised I'd take the kids to the park today," she said. "You'll be okay, Dad?"

"Of course." He hugged his daughter.

Terry drove away with the kids and Wiseman emerged from the garage. Inside the house, Pritchitt looked for a needed distraction from their immediate problem and he turned to medicine, as Wiseman discussed the night's activities at the hospital. "Good diagnosis," said Pritchitt, hearing of one case. He listened to Wiseman's treatment of patients. They finished lunch in the kitchen, still conversing. Pritchitt glanced at his watch. "It's nearly noon. Time to go." Wiseman wiped his mouth and both men stood and walked from the room.

CHAPTER TWENTY-FIVE

Pritchitt sped down Union Avenue, heading west for his rendezvous downtown with Wiseman, lying in the back seat, a blanket pulled over him. He heard Bernie's muffled voice. "Don't move because I'm the police."

A fleeting smile lit Pritchitt's serious face. "How many times are you going to say that?" he asked.

"Until it sounds right," Wiseman shot back. "I'm practicing in case I'm needed to bail you out."

At the intersection of Union and Cooper eastbound traffic was snarled.

Ahead Pritchitt saw banners. "Hey, Bernie, you won't believe this," he uttered in disbelief. Wiseman rose from the rear seat. Blocking westbound traffic were Niles Mercer and Milton James passing out leaflets. There were supportive shouts, and angry ones.

A dozen followers held signs and banners which rippled in the strong wind. Singing and chanting, the group conveyed their strong views against abortion. Milton James and Niles preached and prayed together. They were united in a holy cause. Pritchitt's car raced by the protesting group.

A slight drizzle began as Milton James passed out leaflets to those who took them. Suddenly a hand shot from a vehicle, grabbing the white sheets. There was a loud ridiculing jeer from the car. The driver flung them into the street. James tried to retrieve the leaflets but the wind swept them away. A sweet-faced young girl from his group ran to help. She darted into traffic. She leaned across the yellow divider lines in the center of the street. Her hand stretched for a few swirling sheets. A horn blared, tires squealed on the wet pavement, then a thud. Niles turned. He dropped the pamphlets he held. Horror filled him as a head sailed into the air. It smashed into the windshield of an approaching car. The car swerved out of control, and bounced onto the curb and over a fire hydrant. Water exploded into the air. Milton James stared in shock at the headless torso of the young girl laying in the gutter. He fell on his knees, weeping and praying for his young follower, as the water-filled gutter ran bright red with blood. The group of followers began wailing and screaming. Drivers stopped in disbelief. The crowd grew as did the followers' hysteria. Approaching sirens blunted the rising murmur of cries of shocked bystanders. Niles turned and ran as Milton knelt over the blood stained torso. Niles yelled for him to follow. But Milton James was frozen with only muffled bursts of pain heard from his covered face.

It was nearly 1:00 p.m. Pritchitt emerged from his car. Three teenagers carrying boom boxes passed. Beale Street was tranquil, the night spots closed until evening, then music would bring the famous street alive. Pritchitt scanned the area and walked slowly toward the phone booth. His heart thumped and his palms began to sweat. Wiseman peeked from the back seat to check on Pritchitt. From a distant park bench an unkempt, downtrodden man approached the phone booth. Pritchitt was leaning against the glass when a man tapped him on the shoulder. He swung his body around. He stood face to face with a greasy long-haired man in tattered clothes.

Pritchitt froze . . . unable to speak. Finally, words seeped from his dry lips. "Are you Simon?"

The man stood in silence, then slowly raised one hand while the other reached beneath his heavy overcoat. Pritchitt nervously backed into the phone booth.

Wiseman's stared nervously. His eyes widened and he fumbled beneath the blanket for the gun. He jumped from the back seat of the car and ran toward the booth. Pointing the gun with a nervous tremor, he shouted, "I'm the police. Don't you move, or else." His voice was fractured and barely audible and he shook visibly.

The man was terrified. "Don't shoot," he yelled. His hands fluttered wildly in the air.

From across the street came a shout. A woman emerged from a door. Pritchitt and Wiseman turned in surprise. It was Lt. Bordeaux racing across the busy street.

"Put the damn gun down before you shoot yourself, Wiseman," she ordered, catching her breath as she made the curb. "That's not Simon, you idiot amateur detectives. For God's sakes, that's Eddie, the Beale Street beggar," she exclaimed. Dropping her head to catch her wind she nodded in disbelief. Det. Caffey ran to her side.

"Give me that gun," said Bordeaux. "No, no. Don't point it at me. Hand it to me by the barrel. Here, give it to me."

The disheveled man looked about in total dismay. Lt. Bordeaux walked over to console him. The man's hands moved rapidly. He cried aloud. "Everybody knows Eddie. He's kind and harmless. He's been down here doing odd jobs and begging for spare change all his life."

"He's scared to death," Pritchitt said apologetically.

"Well, he scared me to death, too," said Wiseman. "He was reaching under his coat. It might have been a gun or knife." Bordeaux asked him to show what was in his coat.

"Here's your weapon, Dr. Wiseman," said Bordeaux, handing Wiseman sheets Eddie pulled from inside his coat. They were flyers advertising a nightclub dance. Wiseman looked at a sheet, then turned looking for a place to hide his embarrassment.

"We're very sorry," Pritchitt told the trembling man. He reached in his wallet. A wad of green was handed to Eddie. "For the party. Have a nice time at the dance."

Lt. Bordeaux eyeballed Wiseman. "The only thing you would have done with that gun is shoot Dr. Pritchitt or blow your balls off!" she fretted. She looked to Pritchitt for better judgment.

"Lt. Bordeaux," said Pritchitt, "I've got a permit to carry a gun."

She gestured to Wiseman. "In his name, Dr. Pritchitt?" Her face pouted. "And he's supposed to be a brilliant young doctor?"

Wiseman's pride was hurt. "Just think, someday I may be operating on your brain."

Bordeaux winced at the idea.

"Lt. Bordeaux, how is it you are here?" asked a baffled Pritchitt.

"No. I'm the cop and I ask the questions, remember? What are *you* and your side kick doing here?"

"I really think he wants to know what you're doing here, too," Wiseman said to Caffey and Bordeaux. "You two show up like Batman and Robin."

Bordeaux leaned toward Wiseman. "I don't think you're in this conversation, Wiseman, so shut the fuck up."

"That's just great," Wiseman went off, "but first I have to say something." He raised his hand like a school kid. Bordeaux and Caffey barely feigned attention.

Wiseman began. "We've gathered here on historic Beale Street, the birthplace of the Blues for this invigorating conversation. But if you wouldn't mind," said Wiseman, speaking to Lt. Bordeaux with a conspiratorial tone. "I'd like to give birth to the following question. What the hell is this beggar doing here at this phone booth, at the very time Simon told Dr. Pritchitt to be here? Now I'll shut the fuck up," said Wiseman. Bordeaux grinned as they stared vacantly at one another.

"We'll have to take Eddie to the station for questioning," Bordeaux agreed. Det. Caffey ran after Eddie. Lt. Bordeaux tapped Wiseman's chest. "In fact, I'm going to have to ask you all to come down to the station."

"That's fine. But tell me something. How did you know to be here?" Pritchitt asked.

Bordeaux hesitated. "Nash suggested a tail on you a few days back. So we follow you and find you and the brilliant Dr. Wiseman threatening a homeless beggar on Beale Street. I'd say we out did ourselves with this tail, wouldn't you, Caffey?"

Wiseman shuffled nervously, then looked to Pritchitt and Bordeaux. "I think we're missing the point.

"And what's that?" asked Bordeaux.

"Looks like Simon has just set us up. Instead of us doing the hunting, we're now his prey. He knows the police were here and he's probably watching us right now."

"Just follow us to the station," Bordeaux repeated.

Suddenly, Caffey gave a frantic wave to Bordeaux from the cruiser. Bordeaux hurried to the police car. "There's a report of a traffic fatality on Union. Seems one of Milton James' groupies was decapitated in an auto accident while handing out pamphlets protesting abortion," said Caffey.

"The station," she yelled to Pritchitt and Wiseman from the window as the tires squealed and the car sped off, siren wailing.

"Doc, he thinks you set him up. You do know that, don't you?"

"Yes. I know, Bernie. He'll never believe I didn't know the police were following me. His instructions were to come alone, or else. It's that or else, I'm worried about.

Pritchitt and Wiseman turned toward their car. The telephone in the booth began to ring. Pritchitt glanced first at Wiseman, then to the booth. Wiseman nodded. Pritchitt hesitated. "Dr. Pritchitt, you have to answer it, and now!" pleaded Wiseman.

Pritchitt sucked in his breath and hurried to the phone. His hand froze, then released as he picked up the receiver.

There was an eerie silence. Pritchitt held the receiver to his ear. The sound of heavy breathing on the other end of the line matched his own. He began to feel the light headedness of hyperventilation rush his body. He turned to Wiseman who was standing not four feet away.

"Say something, for God's sake," whispered Wiseman.

"Doctooor," the eerie voice stretched the word. Its deepness filled with a haunting hoarseness. "You brought the police. You shall be punished."

Pritchitt looked to Wiseman, his face telling of the threat. "I knew nothing about the police being here. You have to believe me."

"I saw you jogging, but made no effort to hurt you, did I? But you would hurt me, my supposed brother?"

"What's he saying? What's he saying?" came a whisper from Wiseman's anxious lips.

"Please, I'll meet you anywhere," Pritchitt was saying. There was silence. Beads of sweat poured from Pritchitt's brow. Wiseman moved closer.

Then came the voice of evil. A voice that sent spine curdling chills through Pritchitt's soul as his breath cut short and he gasped deeply. "I am hurt; therefore, you must feel my pain. Simoooon says, sooooon!" There was silence.

Pritchitt and Wiseman arrived at the downtown police station quite shaken. Lt. Bordeaux paced the office. She turned and paused before the pair. "It seems that a boy on a bicycle gave our Eddie twenty dollars and told him to be at the phone booth at 1:00 p.m. sharp."

"Is that it?" asked Pritchitt.

"No. That is not it, doctor. Tell us what the hell is going on. You know, we *are* the police," pleaded Bordeaux with a sarcastic sigh. "Why were you there?"

"That was where Simon told me to be."

"I'm sorry, Dr. Pritchitt, I don't think my ears heard you right. Let's see, some psychotic serial killer calls you up and says, 'Hey, let's meet on Beale Street for a beer,' and you jump in your car and head down there, right?" Bordeaux asked.

"It wasn't like that. I explained to him that I would have to meet him to make sure he was who he said he was."

"Oh? And meet him for what reason?"

"Before I'd help him with his own suicide, of course."

"Of course! How fucking stupid of me," she snarled. "Did you get that?" She turned to her partner Caffey who was taking notes.

Caffey looked confused.

Closing her eyes, Bordeaux nodded repeatedly. "I just can't believe what I'm hearing from supposedly two smarter than average men," she called out, her voice rising an octave with each spoken word.

"Not too smart, Doc," added Caffey.

"And you weren't going to tell us?" Bordeaux asked. She tilted her head and rolled her eyes.

"He said to come alone with no police, or else. I had Wiseman as backup."

"Oh, that makes you safe with Sherlock Holmes, Jr. toting a gun. My God, Doc, what were you thinking?"

Bernie waved his finger. "Can this Eddie identify the kid with the twenty?" he asked.

"And what are we gonna do, Wiseman? Line up every kid with a bicycle and have Eddie pick him out. Then get that kid to draw us a sketch of the person who gave him the money. Get real!"

The West Precinct station was bustling in chaos as Bordeaux made her way through a zoo of human degenerates. Entering her office she leaned against the closed door. With her head back and eyes closed she relaxed, shutting her problems out, if only for a moment's time. A startling knock and the opening door pushed her away before she had a chance to react.

"Damn. What are you doing, leaning on the door to keep people out or something?" asked Justin Nash, pushing his way through her surprised stare.

"And to what do I owe this uninvited visit?" said Bordeaux, recovering from a few seconds of peace.

"I've thought this out and it all comes to the same conclusion."

"And what same thing is that, Mr. Nash?"

"That Niles Mercer is our Simon."

"Oh, is that all," she mused.

"What do you mean, is that all?" said Nash, his scowl deepening.

"What I mean, Justin, is that it's nice to know that the number two man in the D.A.'s office has made up his mind. You've solved the case," she chided, flopping into her chair. She sipped a cup of coffee and puffed on a cigarette as Nash paced and thought.

"You don't believe me. You sit there and have the audacity to question my resolve of this case," said Nash. "You ridicule me with your glaring silence." His face sprung a growing contempt.

"Listen to me, Justin. I have no ridicule, or any other thoughts right now, only fatigue and monthly menstrual cramps, okay? I have no reason to run out and pick up Niles Mercer or his weird pal, Milton James. The last time we got more egg on our face than answers, remember?"

"That was last time. This time will be different."

"Bullshit!" Bordeaux rose. "I'm tired. The only thing I'm thinking about is the time we're wasting with this conversation. If you don't mind?" Bordeaux nodded toward the door.

Nash's frown wrinkled with disturbing anger. "Oh, but I do mind, Lt. Bordeaux."

Bordeaux noticed his irritated countenance. "Okay, Justin. You win. After a short nap I'll think about it, but not now." The door opened with an explosion as Det. Caffey burst through. "You, too?" she said with exhaustion and collapsed back into her chair.

Caffey handed Bordeaux her coat. "What do you say about our paying a visit to a certain professor and preacher?"

"See, Bordeaux?" Nash chided.

"Can't a girl take a break . . . drink a cup of coffee . . . smoke a cigarette, please!"

"Don't have time," prodded Caffey, placing her purse in her hand.

"Christ! What's with you, Caffey? What the hell is it with you two? What makes it different now? Before we got nothing from them. What's changed?"

"The young girl that got decapitated working their protest, that's what. This might break the ice. Make one talk. You know, rustle their feathers."

"And what, Mr. Nash, if I may be so bold, is probable cause for bringing these two fanatics in for a second round of questioning?"

"The death of that young girl. She was a fourteen-year-old runaway. A minor who was living with them and very, very pregnant."

Bordeaux looked at Caffey, then to Nash. "Good enough reason." She paused. "Why the hell didn't you tell me that?" she asked, gulping her coffee. Dousing her smoke, she grabbed her coat and hurried from the office with Det. Caffey on her heels.

CHAPTER TWENTY-SIX

Only a glimpse of light penetrated the faded and dingy curtains. A naked bulb from the entry hall shed light on Niles Mercer who lay on a ripped couch. Bordeaux, Nash and Caffey crouched beneath a broken window pane, as Mercer mumbled incoherently.

Bordeaux peered through the window. A bathroom light showed from beneath a partially closed door at the end of a darkened hall. In a filthy kitchen mice nibbled on a dirty table. Caffey and Nash rose to peak into the dusky interior. The room was dimly lit by the flickering bulb of a small lamp. On a distant wall in an adjoining room was a large cross. A cluster of candles with their fluttering light wrapped the cross in a dismal hue. "Burning candles and a cross? What else have they got in there?" Bordeaux whispered, turning to her two companions.

"Looks like some kind of altar in that room. But I don't see anyone," whispered Caffey, peeking above the peeling paint on the weathered window ledge. Nash stared quietly. Suddenly, Mercer's voice roared and an echoing madness filled the walls of the small room. Their eyes widened.

"Why did you leave me, Milton?" he cried out. "I really did need you. We had plans, remember? Why did you go?" he repeated in an eerie rhythmic chant. He continued in a sobbing cry. His words strung together and his garbling made it difficult to understand. Nash moved his ear closer to the broken pane as Bordeaux grabbed his shoulder and motioned him to stay down.

"This was to be our holy crusade. Our bond, Milton. A bond born by God. Don't leave me, Milton." His cry deepened and grew with an impassioned plea.

"He's talking of a bond," whispered Nash. "Isn't that what Simon talks about, bonding with Pritchitt?"

"Yeah, you're right," Bordeaux nodded.

"We live among the outstretched arms of Satan," moaned Mercer, rising from the couch, his arms reaching to the ceiling. He turned on a lamp and began pacing, his arms flailing as if in charismatic preaching. Bordeaux signaled, telling Nash to stay put as Caffey circled around the back of the building.

Niles stared into a dirty mirror. His face was hollow and unshaven. His eyes red with worry. "I don't understand God. Why do you allow these things to happen to me, your trusted servant? Was it supposed to be this way?" His deep hollow-set eyes darkened, then widened as he looked upwards. "God! You are right! How could I be so ignorant? Please, forgive me, Lord. Now I understand." Niles turned toward the window. Nash ducked his head.

Reverently he walked the darkened hall toward the lit bathroom. The wood floor panels creaked with each shuffling step.

Bordeaux was at the front door. She waited, giving time for Caffey to reach his position. Mercer's voice trailed off. Bordeaux took a deep sigh, then rapped repetitively at the front door. "Niles Mercer, it's the police." She could hear fast approaching footsteps from the other side of the door. Bordeaux lifted her gun.

"Who's there?" Niles hollered with a frightening cry cracking his voice.

"It's Lt. Bordeaux, Niles. Now please, don't make this any

harder than it already is. Just open the door and step back. We want to talk with you, that's all."

"That's not all. You're messengers of Satan and all that's sinful in this world. Go away. Leave us alone." There was a dreadful hush as Niles's heavy breathing could be heard. "Milton, they've come, just as you said. I didn't believe you. You said they'd never give us peace."

"Niles, I'm gonna count to ten and by then you'll have to let me in, or I'll knock the door down," shouted Bordeaux. Nash watched Mercer's frightened stance from the window.

"You told me there was only one way for peace, didn't you, Milton? I didn't believe you. I wish you were here. But you've gone. Gone to be with God. Waiting for me, aren't you?" he cried out. "Milton, ask God. Tell me what to do," he loudly prayed.

Nash's impatience hurried him around to the front door with Bordeaux.

"Damn, I'm not believing this shit," mumbled Bordeaux, her head nodding as she checked her gun. Nash returned the nod in anxious anticipation. Mercer continued with his ranting, half, in chanting-like prayer, the other, in a gospel humming voice. Then it stopped. "Niles, we're coming in. Caffey, are you there?"

"Yeah. Just say when," he yelled. Again, a moment's quiet. A strong but calm voice broke the silence.

"Are you sure about that, God?" Niles called out. Bordeaux banged once more at the door.

"He's lost it," said Bordeaux turning to Nash.

"Niles, we need to ask you some questions about the accident with the young girl, today," yelled Bordeaux as Caffey echoed a similar message from the rear door.

"Go away!" Niles shouted.

"The guy's lost it . . . gone totally out of his gourd," huffed Nash with an impatient glare. "Are you going to go in, or not, Lt. Bordeaux?"

A horrible wail came from within the apartment.

"That does it," Bordeaux mumbled. She tapped a cracked pane in the door, it shattered. She reached in and lifted the latch. The door opened and she rushed in, her gun raised. Nash followed behind. The back door crashed open as Caffey joined her, his gun raised. "Niles Mercer?" she called out. She and Caffey met in a small room. Their silhouettes shadowed against the peeling wallpaper by flickering candles. Nash watched from the front room.

"Spooky as hell in here," said Caffey. He shouted, "Where the fuck did he go?" His adrenaline was pumping and his eyes were wide. He pointed his gun anxiously at every darkened corner. "This place smells like a damn garbage dump."

"Take it easy. He's here," said Bordeaux.

Nash stared down the darkened hallway. The bathroom door opened and a gaunt face glared through the dismal corridor.

"I'm right here," spoke the calm voice of Niles Mercer who was standing in the lighted bathroom. Niles' face cast a haunting pose. He glared at the two pointed guns aimed at his peaceful stance.

"Come on out, Niles. We just want to talk to you," ordered Bordeaux.

Niles walked slowly into the cluttered room and without a word he sat on the broken down sofa, a dazed look in his eyes.

Caffey lowered his gun. "Where's Milton James?" he asked.

"With God. Isn't that wonderful?" Niles answered calmly.

Bordeaux walked beside him. "You mean he left town?"

"No, he's gone to heaven to be with Lisa. That's where he wanted to be. To be with a loved one rather then stay here without love. I can understand that, can't you? To go on living when your love has gone from this existence called life?"

"Lisa? Lisa, who?" said Bordeaux.

"Yes, Lisa. You know, the girl who died today. The sweet angel you came here to question me about." Niles smiled. "She was so devoted to Milton and he to her. They talked of marriage."

"Marriage?" sneered Caffey. "She was fourteen. That's crazy and against the law."

"Whose law? Not God's."

"I thought you and Milton were a couple? Weren't you?" asked Bordeaux.

"Absolutely not! Milton never had such desires."

"But you have?" acknowledged Bordeaux. Mercer raised his head, then stared at the floor.

"Yes, I've sinned. But haven't we all in this vile existence we call life?"

"That's why you do what you do, isn't it, Niles?" Nash asked.

"And what is that? Who are you to judge anyone from your glass cage?"

"Niles, did you see the accident today?" asked Bordeaux, lighting a cigarette from a candle.

"Yes. Yes, I did." His head turned with the painful memory. "Her head . . . " He began crying.

Bordeaux comforted him, glancing up at Caffey. "That driver accidentally killed Lisa . . . Have you, Niles, ever done anything like that?"

"Anything like what?" His voice was barely audible . . . his head turned down.

"Killed anyone by accident?"

"I've never hurt a soul in my misfortunate life."

"Why misfortunate?" Bordeaux asked. "Are you misfortunate because of that voice that keeps telling you to kill those girls who've had abortions . . . abortions you believe so sinful as to be worthy of death as their punishment."

"They are wrong! But I've not killed."

"What about poor Lisa?" asked Nash.

"She ran away from an abusive home. She was a beautiful girl. Milton was helping her."

"Did she live here?"

"Yes," shouted Niles. He raised his head. His eyes moistened.

Caffey stepped up. "Milton James has skipped town, hasn't he?"

"We need to take you downtown, Niles," said Bordeaux as Caffey pulled him up by the arm.

"May I please use the bathroom," pleaded Niles, his voice sad and fractured by the whimpering of a soft cry.

"I think we have our Simon," whispered Caffey.

"I think we have nothing right now," said Bordeaux. Niles stood and stared into Nash's face.

"And what are you looking at?" barked Nash.

"A face of sadness and loneliness. A portrait of my own misery, kind of like peering into a mirror and seeing my tormented soul."

Nash stood in silence as Niles turned away. "What bullshit is that?"

"Go on and pee if you gotta pee," blurted Bordeaux, puffing a cigarette.

"Let's get out of this creepy place. Hell, pee in your fucking pants," said Caffey. "Damn, this place smells like he's peed all over the floor anyway."

"It's all right, Niles," said Bordeaux quietly. "Go ahead, then we'll go downtown."

"Thank you and may God bless you, Lt. Bordeaux." He walked down the dark hall to the bathroom, where they observed him.

"Leave the door open and don't try anything," she shouted, then lowered her voice. "It looks like this Rev. James was quite a cradle robber."

"Two real fucked up people if you ask me, this guy and his reverend pal," added Caffey. "This place gives me the heebie-jeebies. Something's just not right and you can book that."

Niles turned at the bathroom door. His lips moved in a silent conversation. "That guy is one flipped-out head case. He's gone off the deep end," repeated Caffey. Niles smiled and waved.

"Hurry up," shouted an impatient Nash.

"Milton says everything is going to be all right," shouted Niles.

Bordeaux looked alarmed. She turned to Caffey, then to Nash. "The fucking bedroom? Did you check it?" she asked. Caffey shook his head. They hurried quickly toward the back bedroom. Nash turned and looked to the hall bathroom. The door was almost closed.

Nash hurried down the dark hallway. Pushing the door open he stared beyond Niles' frozen stance.

There, dangling from a rope tied to an overhead beam in the shower was Milton James, his tongue swollen, his eyes bulging. Niles sighed deeply and with dilated eyes turned toward Nash then back to the swollen cadaver "Satan is in charge of the world we live in, Milton. Just like you said he was. In fact, he's in the next room. He's come after me. Just like you know he would?"

"For God's sake!" gasped Nash.

Niles fell to his knees in prayer and surreptitiously lifted a razor from the back of the toilet. "I'm coming, Milton, I'm coming, Lord," he chanted incoherently.

Caffey flicked on the switch in the bedroom. On a dresser was a note. *I have failed everyone.*

"Son-of-a-bitch!" Caffey shouted.

Nash screamed out.

Bright red blood spurted from Niles' slit carotid artery on the side of his neck. The tile floor puddled with his blood. His body slumped against the bathtub, his head rested on its edge. His open eyes, now fixed, stared upwards into the swollen face of James, dangling above. His hand flopped against the tile floor, a razor tightly in its grasp. Bordeaux burst through the door. There was no word spoken as she and Nash stepped back from the bloody spectacle.

Calls were made and the bodies taken away. The apartment was roped off with the yellow ribbon of a crime scene. Nash gave his account as did Bordeaux and Caffey. "Looks like a case of a pure and simple double suicide," Coroner Patcher concluded.

Nash folded his arms, deep in thought.

"There isn't a damn thing plain and simple about what happened here," said a miffed Bordeaux.

"Your autopsy will be complete by morning?" asked Nash.

"If it's that important."

"It's that important, Dr. Patcher," nodded Nash.

"Then, you'll have it." The room cleared as the bodies were rolled from the apartment.

"I knew there was something weird about this place, the moment I stepped into it," mumbled Caffey, following the rest and closing the door behind him."

To Justin Nash, the morgue always felt like an extension of hell. Dr. Patcher entered the room. "Did anything turn up in the apartment?" he asked, removing his white lab coat.

"Not yet. But it's still a crime scene and the police are examining everything."

"That was a very peculiar place, a sort of cult chapel, wouldn't you say?"

"Don't know much about cults or their chapels, so I'll have to pass on that."

Finally, something the astute Justin Nash knows little about; how humbling, Patcher thought. There was a less than flattering exchange of glances.

"Thanks for performing the autopsies so quickly," Nash said, taking a copy of the autopsy report from Patcher and placing it in his briefcase.

"I usually sing in the church choir on Sunday morning," remarked Patcher. "But this was more important."

"I know the mayor will want the report."

"You can be certain of that," smiled Patcher. "We're having brunch later. I'll tell her."

Nash raised his eyebrows. "I hear you two are quite friendly."

Patcher smoothed his thin moustache. "I'm sure you hear a lot of things about people, Justin." He straightened his tie. "I hear them, too. Even heard some about a certain executive assistant to Dist. Atty. Jeremy Bates, but that's another story, isn't it?"

"Another story I'm sure I have little interest in hearing about. Good day, Coroner Patcher."

"Good day to you, Mr. Nash."

In the outer lobby Benjamin Pritchitt waited for Nash to review the report. "No drugs were found in either body," he remarked to Pritchitt. "And thanks for officially identifying Niles."

Pritchitt seemed at a loss for words. "Terry couldn't have done it. I wouldn't have wanted her to. She's already been through so much."

Nash gripped Pritchitt's arm. "And understand this, Dr. Pritchitt, she's not to blame for Niles' suicide. It would've happened sooner or later. The man was mad."

"Niles, Simon? I just find it hard to believe." fretted Pritchitt.

Nash shrugged. "They were both suspects. At this point we have no direct evidence of their involvement. But I do have my suspicion."

Pritchitt looked in Nash's face and saw a hint of relief. "I guess you're right. Niles was simply unstable, like Milton James."

"No, doctor. He was mad, sir, not just unstable. You should've heard him at the end, but then again, I'm glad you didn't."

Pritchitt was exhausted. He walked from the morgue into the parking lot, pausing to remember where he'd left his car. He spotted a woman standing nearby. He suspected a reporter, and lowered his head, purposely avoiding eye contact, and hurriedly fished his pockets for his keys.

"Dr. Pritchitt, please wait." The woman came closer. She was a middle-aged woman, stylishly attired. Then he recognized Dot McCormick.

"We've met. I used to be married to —" she began.

"I know who you use to be married to, and I know who you are," Pritchitt said curtly. "And I know what you want."

"Please help me," she pleaded.

Pritchitt shook his head. "I can't help you. I would never consider such a thing. You have no physical illness."

McCormick grabbed his arm. "Dr. Pritchitt, illness of one's mind can be more devastating than illness of one's body. I'm suffering, doctor, and I beg you to help. Please, for the love of all that's good and merciful, have mercy on me. Save my family. For the love of God, help me!"

"I can't."

"I'm hearing voices to kill my family. I love my husband and children. Please Dr. Pritchitt," she cried with an impassioned plea, holding tightly to his arm.

He pulled away and turned to face her squarely. "No. You need help but it's not the kind I can give you," he repeated emphatically. "Don't you understand? I can't." He paused. Frustration filled his frown. With a deep sigh he took on the needed energy to combat her aggressive pleas. "I wouldn't if I could. How did you know I'd be here?" he asked, opening his car door.

"I read the newspaper. I heard about your son-in-law."

"Please, Mrs. McCormick, I advise you to call your psychiatrist."

Dot McCormick's expression turned from upset to anger. "You're not the man I envisioned," she screamed as Pritchitt drove off.

It was late Monday morning when Lt. Bordeaux arrived at work. Niles Mercer's and Milton James' deaths were unsettling but it came with the territory, she kept reminding herself. She wondered if Simon was to be heard from again, or had the serial killer case come to an end. While fetching a cup of coffee she lit her third morning cigarette. Out of the corner of her eye she saw a young woman approaching. Bordeaux turned. "Yes, and what can I do for you?" she asked.

The young woman stopped and stared. "They told me over there," she gestured toward a desk across the room, "that you were the person in charge around here."

"Well, that's a bit of an over statement, but I'll give it a shot. What can I do to help?"

"My name is Ann James, Mrs. Milton James," said the girl.

Bordeaux looked shocked, choking on a sip of coffee.

"You were married to —"

The woman removed a document from her purse. "I am Milton James' legal wife," she said, handing a copy of her marriage certificate to Bordeaux.

"Follow me," said Bordeaux. They walked to her office.

"I came to claim his body and all his personal belongings." The girl looked no older than 19. Her eyes were steely.

Bordeaux made a copy of the marriage license. "Take this original to the coroner's office. They'll help you with the arrangements there. I'm sorry about your husband."

"Oh, really?" she sneered with sarcasm. "I really doubt that you are. You police hounded him to his death. You hound all of us to death. Just because we fight for a just cause in an unjust world we are prosecuted by the long arm of the law in an immoral world."

Bordeaux raised her hand. "Just a minute. We did nothing to push him over. He may have done it all to himself. It's not my place, but what the hell. You need to know. The good reverend was living with a runaway teenager."

"He was merely helping Lisa."

"So you know? Helping her how? She was pregnant. Did you know that?"

The girl barely flinched. "Of course, I did. And so am I," she said proudly. "Reverend James had a grand plan. An idea given to him in prayer. A gift of life. To replenish a uterus with life for every uterus aborted. Milton, Niles, all of us had a mission."

"So let me get this straight, just for my slow brain. You were married but he was out there sharing his sperm and you, you accepted that?"

"How could you understand? You couldn't know. You'd only think of it as wrong. She leaned into Bordeaux's face. "Some have fallen, but the war continues."

"What war?"

"The war against abortion," she said emotionally.

Bordeaux saw the woman's fierce determination. "The

coroner's office can help you, Mrs. James. I think it's time for you to leave, ma'am. And, ma'am, as long as you're in Memphis, enjoy your stay but be a law-abiding citizen. Because, Mrs. James, if you're not, then I can promise you that you'll see my sunshiny face again, got it?"

"It's been my pleasure, Lt. Bordeaux."

It was mid-morning and the hospital was abuzz with the death of Dr. Pritchitt's son-in-law. It was the main story of all newscasts and the link between Pritchitt and Mercer highlighted in every report. The link between the deaths and the serial killer case were expounded. All Memphis was alive with gossip.

"Maybe that Niles Mercer *was* involved. Maybe he *was* Simon and that will be one less concern for Dr. Ben," hoped Patsy.

"Wouldn't that be great, but I don't think it's Niles Mercer," Bernie Wiseman was saying. "He was too unstable. Too tightly wound to have the organized mind of Simon. No. Simon is still out there somewhere."

Patsy glanced at the newspaper and pointed to a photo of Milton James. "What about this one?"

"No," Bernie replied. "Milton James was a fanatic but not a cold blooded murderer."

"You're supposed to be a genius, Dr. Wiseman, but I sure hope you're dead wrong about this."

"I wish you wouldn't use dead wrong. How about just plain wrong. I do believe that Simon could be a member of a radical group. A group like the one Milton James was involved with. And that group still may cause some trouble."

"Trouble?"

"Yes, with the abortion clinics here in Memphis."

"In my day," said Patsy, "abortion was simply wrong."

"It's still wrong," asserted Dr. Peters, overhearing Patsy's comment as he approached Patsy's desk. He snatched the newspaper. "The hospital isn't paying either of you to read and gossip. If you haven't noticed, this is a busy place."

"I'm off duty," said Wiseman defensively.

"And this is my ten-minute break, every day at 10:30," was Patsy's retort. "So, may I have my paper back?"

Peters fumed. He knew that both Wiseman and Patsy were a direct pipeline of information to Pritchitt. I won't forget it when I'm the permanent chairman of this department, he thought.

Neither Wiseman nor Patsy uttered a word. They were watching Ben Pritchitt get out of the elevator and head toward them.

"You're a disgrace to medicine," Peters snapped when Pritchitt approached. "Our lawyers will file suit very soon to throw you out."

"Then you won't begrudge me if this reprobate of a doctor leaves your holier-than-thou company. See, Dr. Peters, I need to duck into my old office to check my messages before checking in with my probation officer," said Pritchitt sarcastically.

"That's fine, make light of this matter, but remember, that is your old office and the past tense needs to be understood by you. Because as soon as your trial is over another name will be on that door."

Heaven forbid, it isn't yours. Peters had already assumed his guilt, Pritchitt thought. If I'm innocent my name stays. I wonder where his will be, Pritchitt wondered as he gave a departing nod and walked into his office.

Wiseman followed behind. "I'm off duty, sir. Need to talk with Dr. Pritchitt," Wiseman said, notifying Peters his talk with Pritchitt was not on hospital time.

"There's no way he'll be found innocent," Peters growled unconvincingly.

Patsy simply shrugged her shoulders without uttering a response.

The elevator door slid open and a woman barged through the outer office.

"Is Dr. Pritchitt here?" she was saying.

"Well, are y'all deaf? Is Pritchitt here?" Her voice grew

louder and more demanding, yet she seemed nervous and upset.

"And who might you be?" Peters asked sharply.

"You're not Pritchitt. I need to see Dr. Pritchitt," she shouted.

"I'm Dr. James Peters," he huffed. *"Chairman* of the Surgery Department. Dr. Pritchitt is not. Now, ma'am, I think you should depart these premises before I call security and have you thrown out in a very unlady-like manner."

Patsy watched the woman's eyes and saw her agitation grow with Peters obnoxious retort.

"You're not going to throw me out of anywhere, mister. I've asked Dr. Pritchitt for help numerous times but he refuses."

"That's understandable," said Dr. Peters. "There are others here who can help you." He turned, sporting a gloating grin, content someone else was upset with Pritchitt.

"You must be his secretary," said the woman. She stared at Patsy, Patsy at her. Peters exchanged glances with Patsy. Both were uneasy with the woman's demanding voice and a seemingly possessed scowl. A chill trickled Patsy as she recalled the voice and realized the woman's identity.

Suddenly, the door to Pritchitt's office opened and Bernie backed out slowly. "Yes, I'll do that Dr. Pritchitt. And you have a good day, sir." Bernie bid farewell, then turned with a shocked frown in recognition of the agitated visitor. He looked to Patsy. They both knew. "Mrs. McCormick, what are you doing here?" said Bernie.

"If it isn't Dr. Wiseman," she snarled. "He wouldn't help me either. I pleaded and he turned his back as did Pritchitt."

"Wiseman, is that true? I'm terribly sorry, ma'am. I'm head of the department and he will assist you. Won't you, Wiseman?" Peters face filled with an ingenuous power. A naive satisfaction spread across his face thinking he'd righted a wrong of Pritchitt's.

"Excuse me, sir. You don't quite understand," Bernie and Patsy simultaneously blurted.

"A concerted duet," said Peters. "You must have practiced that." Peters turned with a fraudulent smile.

"You lied to me, you bastard," shouted McCormick.

Every head in the department turned and Peters retreated from her forward advance. "Excuse me, ma'am. I will not be addressed in that manner."

"You told me he wasn't here."

"Who?"

"Pritchitt, you fool!"

"Oh, well, he's here only physically and not professionally."

She laughed loud and uncontrolled, as if possessed. Fellow workers started their quiet exit through a side door. An ominous cloud filled the room.

"Patsy, call security. Enough is enough," ordered Peters. Pritchitt heard the commotion and walked from his office. "What's going on out here?"

"Well, well, if it isn't Dr. Benjamin Pritchitt. The humanitarian who says he'll help, but won't. He must be a fake. A publicity seeking fraud," she spat with anger.

"Dr. Peters has told her that he will help her," announced Patsy.

"Oh, he has . . . has he," said Pritchitt. "That will be very interesting, indeed it will." McCormick moved closer to the grouping around Patsy's desk.

"Dr. Peters, now that you're the new head of the department, you are in a position to help me more than anyone. I see you're a person with a true concern for the patient. You're a different man than Pritchitt."

"I should say so."

"Not one who would deceive and degrade your great Hippocratic Oath."

"Absolutely," Peters beamed as the others stared in disbelief at his blind naivete. "I certainly try," he said with a slight bow. "Do you have a complaint against them? And how may I assist you, ma'am?"

"You'll assist me?"

"Certainly." He stared haughtily at the others.

"I wish to end my life. I wish your assistance in my suicide, sir."

Dr. Peters arrogant demeanor vanished. He managed an unsure grin. "You're kidding?"

"No. I have come for you to put me to death, to deliver me from a mental anguish that threatens the safety of those I love."

"If this isn't a joke, then you need to see a psychiatrist and not me. On the other hand, maybe it is Dr. Pritchitt you should confer with," mumbled Peters with growing discomfort.

"No. You're doing just fine, Chairman Peters," offered Pritchitt.

"Mrs. McCormick. That's your name, isn't it?"

She nodded.

"I believe you're mentally unbalanced, my dear," said Peters in an attempt at a caring voice.

"Oh, that's tactful. Great bedside manner," whispered Wiseman.

Dot McCormick's scowl was tinged with anxiety and bitterness.

Peters backed away as she approached his anemic glower. "Call security, Patsy. Ma'am, I suggest you leave," he ordered nervously as Pritchitt stepped up and interrupted her intrusive advance.

"Enough of this, Mrs. McCormick. We've told you that we can't help you, ma'am. I feel for your problem, but this is not the way to solve anything. You need help that I cannot and will not give to you. You need counseling and medicine, not suicide. We've talked. I know your psychiatrist. He's great, but only if you give him a chance."

"Enough of your bullshit!" Suddenly she withdrew a gun from her purse. She waved it in the air.

"Please put that away," begged Pritchitt. Peters quickly backed behind Wiseman who stood in shocked silence. Patsy fell to her knees in prayer behind her desk. Pritchitt stood motionless. His hand extended to receive the gun. All remaining workers in the large working area fled. Panic swept the department. Hysterical screams were heard as workers darted for safety.

"It's my time," she said calmly. Her voice changed and her scowl transformed into a gentle smile. "You know I've prayed for your help. I'm truly a nice person with a terrible problem. I wish you could've known me before," she cried.

"But I want to help, but not in the way you ask. Let me try to help you in other ways. I know we can work this out, Dot," said Pritchitt in a soft and caring tone, his voice trying to reach through her frightened desperation.

"You know, I do believe you, Dr. Pritchitt. I take all those bad things back I said about you, sir. But it's too late. There are voices talking to me. And they're becoming more talkative," she smiled painfully. "They're waking me in the black of night. They're telling me to get up and go to each of my three children's rooms and kill them. Last night I walked to the room of my sweet daughter. I stood at her door with this gun in my hand. I put it to her head, but thank God the voices went away."

Patsy cried out, hysteria filling a muted scream as she tried to quiet herself with both hands and rocked her head in disbelief. Wiseman went to her side. Peters remained frozen with fear. "I appreciate your effort and apologize to all of you," she offered in a soft voice. "I realize that an assisted suicide was a remote option and truly knew you wouldn't do it, sir."

Her eyes bled pain and despair.

Surging anxiety swept Pritchitt as he stared into her hopelessness.

"I have no other choice. I'm truly sorry." She lifted the gun barrel into her mouth.

"No! No!" screamed Pritchitt. He lunged for her arm. There was a violent blast and the back of her head disintegrated. Blood sprayed onto the surrounding floor and furniture. Blood soaked tissue spattered a nearby wall. Eyes wide and fixed, she tottered, then hit the floor with a thud. The gun still tightly clasped by her twitching hand.

Patsy screamed, her head shaking from side-to-side. Wiseman tried to comfort her. Peters ran toward his office. He turned at the door, his mouth trying to form words. His face blanched by the horror of the event. "You-you-see-see where all of this has taken us. All this has taken us to hell!" Peters shouted, slamming his door.

Pritchitt slumped to his knees, staring at McCormick's involuntary seizures, his head bowed over in disbelief, his eyes captured by the painful vision of her jerking extremities. Security guards rushed in. They turned with nauseous shock at the grotesque scene.

Pritchitt covered his eyes from the painful scene. "My God. My dear God. What has happened?" he prayed. "What will her family say? What will her children do? What have I done?" From his knees he rocked in pain as Bernie led the teetering Patsy away. A single tear ran down Pritchitt's cheek as the guards pulled him to his feet.

CHAPTER TWENTY-SEVEN

In a state of shock from Niles' suicide, Terry had remained at home. She was sitting in her father's den with Lori Bordeaux. She tried not to blame herself for Niles's tragic ending. "I didn't want this for him. I mean, it wasn't that I hated him, Lori. I hated that he wasn't right for me and the children."

Bordeaux offered comfort. "Terry, Niles wasn't right for himself, sweetheart. No one is blaming you. It was his tangled mind that led him down that road. And that road was going to end in a dead end, sooner or later."

"I'm not going to tell the kids, not just yet."

"You'll know when the time is right."

"They hardly knew him as it was."

"Terry, you don't have to convince anyone. He chose his own ending when he refused any kind of therapy. Niles did this, you didn't."

"Yes," Terry agreed wistfully. "You're right."

"Now, go and get those kids and enjoy the evening with your father. I have a feeling that you both need each other's company and love tonight."

Terry nodded with a sad expression. "Yes, you're definitely right about that."

"And, Terry, you're lucky," Lori said, with a hint of jealousy. "When I lost my husband, I lost all my family. With family you can make it through many things where adversity would normally sink you." Lori winked and the two embraced.

A full moon illuminated the Mid-City Female Center. The young woman walked from the front door. She buttoned her coat. A flashlight momentarily blinded her. "Can I escort you?" asked a guard.

"A-All right," answered the woman nervously. She walked along the street, keeping her head low, followed by the guard. Arriving at her car, a look of relief swept her face.

"It was a hard decision?" asked the guard.

"If you only knew," she said quietly. She slid behind the steering wheel.

"Then you'll need this." The guard reached into a long overcoat and removed a bottle of clear fluid. She looked puzzled.

"What's that?" He poured the fluid onto a cloth, then suddenly covered her face. The woman struggled but the chloroform worked fast. "Please, stop. I must telephone —" She moaned weakly before lapsing into a deep sleep, falling to the seat. The guard removed his cap and long hair fell over the sloping shoulders. He pushed her over and sat behind the steering wheel.

"Simon says, you're out of your pain, my dear simple-minded fool." The car sped off, the soaked cloth pitched from a closing window.

Walking down the hall Terry could barely hear Benji's voice until she approached the bedroom door which stood ajar. She peered into the dim room. Her father knelt with Benji and Claire in prayer.

"Oh, I almost forgot something," Benji said softly. "God, be sure to watch after my mom. If you've forgotten, her name is Terry Mercer."

"And please watch over our Daddy," added Claire. "You probably know him. He's with you in heaven. Tell him how much we miss him and love him."

Terry choked back tears as she listened to her children and realized they were her only stability in an otherwise self-destructing life. From the door she bowed her head in prayer.

"And, God, bring Granny Ruth home real fast," added Benji, "so she can take care of Papa and make us cookies, and be with my Papa, too. Oops, you better watch out for my sister, sometimes she hits me, but I do love her. And let me think."

"I believe you covered everything that God needs to know about for tonight," Pritchitt said, hugging his grandchildren. From the hallway Terry wiped her eyes and headed for the den downstairs.

The room was warmed by the fire. Terry felt safe and snug with her father on this cold fall night. She poured a glass of wine and had just sat on the sofa when her father walked into the room. He poured himself a drink.

"Dad, I don't know. Maybe I could have done something more to help Niles," she related, her voice touched by guilt. Though he heard her voice, Pritchitt's mind was far away. "Dad, did you hear me?" He looked distant. "About Niles, could I have handled it any differently?"

"Absolutely not. He had lost touch with reality. He would have taken you down with him and possibly the children, too."

She nodded, pleased to receive her father's absolution and sound reasoning. "You look so tired, Dad. You're still thinking about that McCormick lady. Aren't you?"

"Yes. And I ask myself — what more can happen to this family? Here we are, two peas in a pod. Depressed ones at that. You asking what you could've done more for Niles, and me asking the same about Dot McCormick. You know she had three young children," said Pritchitt, turning from the bar, his eyes ringed by deep circles, his face hollow. "I called the hospital a little while ago. They admitted Patsy for twenty-four-hour observation. She was like I've never seen her before. But then she'd never seen anyone blow the top of their head off, either. I guess that would be enough to send anyone into shock." Pritchitt sipped his scotch. "Bernie said that Dr. Peters was his typically obnoxious self by late afternoon."

"Peters, that flaming idiot, or should I've said asshole!" Terry said with disdain.

"Peters told the police that I was to blame. He was denouncing me in his usual tirade, that I should be in jail and so on. He suggested my aided suicides precipitated McCormick's death." Pritchitt sat, swirling his scotch and looking wistfully into his glass. "He might just be right."

"Wait a minute, Dad. Don't blame yourself. Remember, I tried to pull the same self-pity routine with Niles, and you wouldn't let me. Well, I'm not allowing you to do what you wouldn't let me do," Terry half-scolded. "I remember how you helped that first dying patient."

"Mrs. Epstein?" recalled Pritchitt.

"You had to do something, you said. She had lost 50 pounds in two months. Her bodily functions had gone. She was taking up to fifteen pain pills a day, but still crying every waking moment. Am I right? You told me the stench of urine and stool had permeated her skin she had laid in it so long, never cleaned and no one to help."

"Yes," he remembered, feeling the warmth of the flames from the hearth as Terry talked of the warmth she saw in him.

Terry came to sit beside him. "Doctors are not only supposed to heal but to allay the pain of their patients. Many doctors just write a prescription, then jump in their fancy sports car and head to the club, but not you, Dad. So do me a favor. I'll kick my guilt if you kick yours. Is that a deal?"

"I'll try to, baby," he whispered in a less than convincing tone, his eyes fixed on the flickering flames in the fireplace, as if it were the hell he was living. "It's just . . . from Mrs. Epstein, to your mother, to this sick soul today. Who knows?" He shrugged.

"Have you talked to Tyler today?" he asked, still transfixed by the burning embers.

"Yes, I have, Dad, but since that arrest and frame-up he seems withdrawn."

"That's understandable." Ben walked to the grate, took a steel poker and stoked the logs. "Goddamn Simon!" he cursed bitterly.

"I want you to promise me something, Dad."

"And what might that be, counselor?"

"That when your trial is over and you're found innocent on all counts, which you will be, you'll promise to take Mother and go on a much-needed vacation and forget about all this."

"If I'm not on my way to prison, I promise to do just that." The expression on his face was distant and devoid of emotion.

Terry's heart was breaking for all her family's troubles, but especially this man who was her hero for life. It was agonizing to see his good soul being devoured by his own conscience. She knew it was far from over and worried how much more her hero could endure. "Daddy, I love you so much," she said, hugging him tightly. "Now, I want you to get a good night's sleep and I'm going to my old bedroom to do the same."

Alone in the den, he stretched on the sofa. His greatest fear still gnawed at him. Would Simon strike at his family, as he had hinted. What was to be Simon's *prescription*? A prescription to cure Pritchitt's infidelity toward their supposed brotherhood? Please, God, don't let him hurt my family, he prayed. If it has to be someone, make sure it's me. I should have done it already, he told himself. I should have put the bastard to death when he wanted. He was torn, depressed that his hesitation to put Simon to death would cause the death of another person, even a loved one. This was his recurring nightmare, a terrifying vision that robbed him of sleep and destroyed any hope for peace. Sitting by the fire he rested his head and with closed eyes tried to escape.

Bernie was fast asleep on the sofa when the fax machine came alive. He awoke and rubbed his eyes. "I know it's you, Simon." He snatched the sheet from the tray. He read aloud, "Dr. Trust has become Dr. Deceit. Another betrayal and heaven's prophecy will prove untrue. Are you a Judas? Our destiny has been ordained. The innocent will be set free, but the guilty must die. Dr. Summer tell Dr. Parkway what you have done.'"

So Niles Mercer and Milton James may have been innocent, after all, of any wrong doing in connection with the serial murders, concluded Wiseman. Simon's alive, he thought. As Wiseman studied the message a distant explosion rattled the windows. He ran to the window. "What the hell?" He ran through the door. A sick feeling gripped him as he hurried toward the ER. It was there he knew the answers about the explosion would soon be answered.

A sleeping neighborhood had been awakened by the tremendous blast. The Mid City Female Center was aflame or what was left of it. Sirens wailed as fire trucks arrived on the scene. Police kept the crowd behind barricades. Firemen discovered a dead security guard in bushes near the burning foundation. The growing crowd stirred with anxiety and shock. Police searchlights scanned the trees. Debris and mangled body parts were strewn in the branches. A girl began screaming as blood dripped on her head. The rubble smouldered. On the ground a ripped torso was spread upon a rug of blood stained grass. Someone shouted about a body under a collapsed wall. Flashlights swept the grounds as policemen and firefighters searched desperately for life. "There's a leg!" yelled a policeman. He motioned a fireman to bring a ladder.

Lori Bordeaux found Fire Department Chief Raymond. "It was some kind of blast all right. We'll have to wait until morning to figure it all out," he shouted.

Bordeaux stood helplessly as the fire was extinguished on the lower level. "Survivors?" she asked.

"Only a receptionist. She had just walked out of the clinic. She was taken to Memorial in an ambulance. She was conscious."

Wiseman was the resident physician on trauma duty. The

receptionist was awake when brought into the Memorial Emergency Department. A pack of reporters hovered near the entrance, eager for information. The young woman, about 35, was alert but groggy. Fright sprinkled her anguish. She had overheard the paramedics discussing the bombing of the clinic. The force of the explosion had thrown her against a car, banging her head. "I think we should get a skull series. It'll be a few minutes before anyone can see her," said Wiseman, motioning to security to corral the media back towards the waiting area.

"Did anyone make it out?" she asked weakly.

"You're the only one here," said Bernie evasively.

There was a light knock at the door. It was Lt. Bordeaux. "We're getting ready to run some tests," he said. Bordeaux pushed by him, introducing herself to the woman. Wiseman pretended to busy himself but couldn't help but eavesdrop.

"There was a young woman. She said she was a student. She had a backpack. I recall she removed a book," mumbled the receptionist.

Bordeaux jotted notes. "What did she want?"

"Just to talk to a doctor about pregnancy termination."

"Did she have any type of treatment?"

"I don't think so. She went upstairs but got into an argument with another patient about something."

"Did she leave the backpack?"

"I'm not sure." Nurses arrived with a stretcher. "Are there any survivors?" she asked hesitantly.

"Doesn't look like it," said Bordeaux. The girl began sobbing.

Wiseman spoke in a low voice. "Dr. Pritchitt got another fax from Simon. It looks bad."

"How bad?"

"At Summer and Parkway I think you'll find a body."

She thought for a second. "That's at the corner of Overton Park near the clinic," Bordeaux remarked.

"Do you think Simon blew up the clinic?" asked Wiseman.

"I don't know." A scowl of frustration swept Bordeaux's

face. "It seems like all we ever have are questions and never a fucking answer."

Rain and sleet added to the gloom of the morning. Jeremy Bates' staff assembled before the federal prosecutor. Vance Watkins was the U.S. Attorney. A former football star, he was a black hero to the South Memphis community. Standing over six feet tall, and admired by all he was a new face for the media. He stood somberly, as the room quieted. "Investigators are still sifting through the rubble but it looks like a couple of sticks of dynamite were used. The FBI lab is testing debris for explosive traces. This is now a federal crime scene. It's your case. But I'm here to assist in anyway I can." He was to the U.S. Attorney's office what Jeremy Bates was to the District Attorney's office with one big exception, he was a team player.

Tim Bauers raised his hand. "You're telling us the security guard was shot?"

"Yes," said Watkins. "With a small caliber, probably a .22 with a silencer."

Atway Jackson came into the room. He signaled for Nash to step outside as Bates glared at the two. "The police just found another body. It's a young girl. She's at the morgue." Nash folded his arms. "This Simon's gone super berserk," commented Atway, "now he's setting off bombs."

"I'm not so sure," said Nash pensively. "Go to the morgue. Call me as soon as you hear anything." Atway looked uneasy.

"I'm supposed to be filing legal documents in the office." Nash looked cross.

"A good lawyer's got to be part-detective, Atway. You may as well start now. You're all I can spare. Get you butt over there and find out something."

Group therapy was about to begin. The room was nearly filled. One chair remained vacant. Ruth Pritchitt was a no-show. Dr. Tucker waited impatiently for Ruth to walk through the door. Tucker's wait turned into disappointment. When the session ended, Tucker hurried from the room. She found Ruth lying in bed, staring aimlessly at the rain beating incessantly against the window panes. "Ruth, are you okay? You weren't at our group session."

"There was a call earlier. It was him," whispered Ruth loudly. "He told me something very bad was about to happen. He wanted to warn me. He wanted me to know that nothing would happen as long as —" She hesitated, searching for words. "As long as Benjamin filled some kind of prescription and did what he was supposed to."

"It was Simon, wasn't it?"

"I think so," answered Ruth. She sat up in her bed. "But I don't understand what he wants." A terrifying anxiety punctuated her every word. "There was an uncomfortable cadence to his voice. It was more than creepy. It was evil. It was as if the devil himself was telling me what he wanted. The voice was impatient and very angry, saying that my Benjamin had betrayed him."

Tucker sat on the side of the bed. "I don't understand," she said.

"How can I say it . . . like everything was revolving around a dwindling timetable with no time left," said Ruth, her face drawn and depression resurfacing. Perspiration formed on her forehead. "I'm terribly afraid for Ben."

"Did you try calling Dr. Pritchitt?"

"Yes, Loretta said he had just left."

Dr. Tucker gave her a smile and took her hand. "He may be coming to see you."

"God knows I hope he is. I need to hold him. I have a feeling. He needs me," mumbled Ruth. Her hands held tightly to Tucker's and they embraced.

Atway Jackson stood uncomfortably in the Shelby County morgue. A side door opened and blasting through were Lt. Bordeaux and Det. Caffey. "Damn reporters," she fussed. "Damn good thing they aren't allowed back here." She continued to bitch having had to wade through a rude group of media on the way to the morgue. "Well, Atway

Jackson, have you learned anything for your boss?"

"No, ma'am. I'm still waiting."

"That's what I like about you young lawyers, manners. Haven't had anyone from the D.A.'s office call me ma'am in years. They still in there?"

"As far as I know they are. Still running tests on the remains of those who died in the explosion, as well as on that unknown girl they found a couple blocks away."

"Curious about her myself," added Caffey. The double doors opened and Jerry Richards emerged from the main autopsy lab.

"Jerry," said Bordeaux. "What gives with this girl?"

"Thought I'd find you and your straight man out here, Lieutenant."

"Very fucking funny," said Caffey, knowing he was the partner to whom Jerry Richards referred.

"Rather be straight than like you."

"Cut the crap, both of you," yelled Bordeaux as Atway stood and watched the bantering.

Richards lacked his usual charm. "It's pretty gruesome in there. They're still trying to match the right arms and legs with the right torso."

"Excuse me, I've got to be going. Is there anything I can take back to Mr. Nash?" Atway asked.

"Yeah, what do you have for me?" said Bordeaux, her eyes quickly darting from side to side.

Richards lowered his voice. "I'm not supposed to tell until it's official, but this is just for you. The female victim near the park was shot with the same small caliber gun that shot the woman's clinic security guard." He discreetly opened a notebook showing Bordeaux and Caffey as Atway looked on. "And here is her picture." Bordeaux stared at the distasteful image of a dead corpse.

"I know her," shouted Bordeaux. "Where do I know her from?"

"Let me correct you, Lieutenant, you *knew* her. I have her name." Richards fumbled, looking for a piece of paper he'd stuck in the notebook. "Yes. Here it is. She was Ann James. Ring a bell?"

"Of course. Milton James' wife. She was pregnant."

"The hell you say?" blurted Caffey as Atway drew near.

"And how did you know that? That was the next thing I was going say," asked Richards.

"I owe y'all big time," Atway jotted it all down and hurried from the room.

"I hope I've helped you, Lieutenant," said Richards.

"It sure can't hurt us. It's given us food for thought and that's for damn sure," said Bordeaux as Caffey pinched Richards' cheek and hurried to catch his fast departing partner.

"I love you, too, sweetheart," yelled Richards as the doors closed behind the scurrying detectives.

Justin Nash sat in his office. Terry sat across the room, uncomfortable with the cigar smoke. His feet were propped high on his desk and he looked across the room at his assistant. "Are you okay, Terry?"

"Can we get on with it, if you please? You think Simon killed the girl and bombed the clinic?" she asked.

Nash shrugged his shoulders. "I don't know. What do you think, Asst. Dist. Atty. Mercer?"

"I don't know about the clinic. Dynamiting? That's not —" The door burst open and hurrying through was Atway Jackson.

"Well, well. If it isn't my messenger from the morgue," remarked Nash, puffing his cigar. Atway rushed in, telling them what he'd discovered. The door snapped open again. This time it was Bordeaux and Caffey, following not far on the heels of the fast-moving Jackson.

"Well, well. If it isn't Memphis' finest detective duo," bristled Nash.

"Damn, Atway!" said Bordeaux.

"What?"

"You could've gotten speeding and reckless driving tickets the way you drove over here. Hope the hell you don't drive like that all the time," bitched Bordeaux, appearing in anything but a good mood.

"We were just discussing some information that my driving fool brought to us."

"Well, Justin, let me cut to the quick and save you a bunch of time. Ann James, Milton James' wife, blew the clinic," Bordeaux announced.

Terry's eyes widened. "Ann James. Are you sure, Lori?" she asked.

Lori snapped her fingers, then pulled a cigarette from her purse. "She did it. As I am Lori Bordeaux, she's your bomber."

Terry looked perplexed. "She was a fanatic, too?"

"I met her at the station. She had come to complete some paperwork to claim her husband's body. She was very hostile. Much more hostile than her husband, Milton James. A very militant personality. She got right in my face and said there was more to come. That it wasn't over. And guess what? She was right. But I don't think she wrote the script to end the way it did."

"My God! She planted the bomb, left, and was killed," said Atway.

"It's gonna take more than that to convince me that this was just a random-type killing," said Terry.

Bordeaux continued. "It wasn't random in a sense. She was pregnant. Try this on for a crazy quirk of fate. She was like all the other girls but she didn't end up in a garbage container or sand trap. She was simply in the wrong place at the wrong time. She walked into the clinic and walked out. Bingo, there was Simon. Unbeknown to him she had just left a fucking bomb. She's murdered by Simon, the clinic blows and our maniac's still out there."

Nash looked stunned. He sat up and placed his cigar in an ash tray. "Simon doesn't know it, but he killed an unborn baby. That my friends is exactly what he was killing to prevent. I'd say our madman has lost it even more, if that's possible, and that makes him even more dangerous. He thought that she had just had an abortion."

The door pushed open with a thud. Dist. Atty. Jeremy Bates and U.S. Atty. Vance Watkins sauntered in. Behind them was Asst. Dist. Atty. Bauers who looked nervous. Watkins folded his arms with a menacing stare. Bates approached Nash. "Justin, did you visit the Mid City Female Clinic on the night of October 22?" The room took on a morgue-like silence. Nash looked up.

"Why do you ask?"

"Just answer the question, Mr. Nash."

"It's possible. I can't remember dates."

"We found this list in the glove compartment of the dead security guard. Under 'suspicious license numbers' he had jotted yours, Mr. Nash. I believe that Lt. Bordeaux had instructed the guards at every clinic to keep an eye out for suspicious persons or suspicious cars stalking the clinics."

"Oh, yes. I remember. I can explain. That's the night I saw my secretary Jesse at that clinic."

Bates confronted Nash with a glaring stare. "And pray, Justin, share with us why the both of you were there."

"At the time Jesse thought she was pregnant. And, well, she was going for an abortion."

"Did you follow her there, Mr. Nash?" asked U.S. Atty. Watkins in an explosive voice.

"Absolutely not," Nash balked defensively.

"So, Mr. Nash, we can assume you were just cruising by the clinic and spotted your secretary? Who were you really looking for that night, sir?" asked Watkins, his face inches from Nash's. "Is it a habit of yours to drive by these clinics? Did you report your presence there to anyone?" Watkins' demeanor was slightly more restrained.

Nash leaned back in his chair, an arrogant sneer spread his face. "No, I did not, Mr. Watkins."

"Her pregnancy was brought up in front of myself and Lt. Bordeaux," interrupted Terry.

"It was Ms. Mercer? And to you, too, Lieutenant?" queried Bates. "And you thought nothing strange of this, Lieutenant?"

"It was right after Jesse had been found in the park. It

came up then. It really didn't seem like much because it was a one time thing. And Mr. Nash had seen her turning into the clinic from his car and followed. At least, I believe that's how it went down," Lori explained.

"You *believe*? You didn't check it out?" questioned Watkins. "Now, Bates, I'm getting a clearer picture of why this case has gone unsolved."

Bates produced yet a second list. "Police surveillance has spotted your car circling two other clinics that specialize in abortion. Can you explain that, sir? Lt. Bordeaux, if you had checked it out, you would have discovered this too."

Again, the room was quieted. A silence so great one could've heard footsteps of an ant upon on the hard wood floor.

"I counsel kids on Saturday mornings. And I do a lot of things I don't discuss with co-workers."

"We're finding that out, Justin. We're definitely finding that out," remarked Bates. "Including counseling girls not to undergo abortions."

"So what? If I can talk them out of it, all the better, right?"

"Does abortion bother you to a great degree, Nash?" asked Bates bringing his face within inches of Nash.

"If you're asking me does it bother me to the point that I would go around killing girls who've had them, then the answer, Jeremy, is no!"

"Okay, that does it," shouted Bordeaux, separating the two with the help of Bauers.

"Now excuse the language, but what the shit gives?" Bordeaux blurted. "I know we've been more or less deaf and dumb bystanders but now we're standing here with thumbs up our butts. I want to know what gives, and if I am reading this correctly. Do you suspect Nash is Simon?" Her disbelieving glare awaited an answer.

Bates regained his composure and Nash slumped into his chair.

Bates held up a folder. "Have you ever undergone psychological counseling, Justin? Counseling that talked of tremendous anger that you had with regard to an abortion.

That at one time you even threatened to kill the doctor who performed a certain abortion." Bates approached Nash's desk and stood in wait of a response.

Nash eyed him coldly. "That was a long time ago. And that, Mr. Bates, is confidential and very personal."

"It's not personal now! Is it Justin?" Bates lowered his face, eyeballing Nash. "It seems you neglected to inform the D.A.'s office of your treatment when you were hired. And you know there's a section on every application that deals specifically with emotional stability. Lawyers in this office are entrusted by the people of this commonwealth to be mentally competent. And you, Mr. Nash, according to this," continued Bates, holding high the folder, "would have great difficulty separating your emotions from this case. One could even imagine you having empathy for a Simon-like killer."

Nash stood abruptly. He grabbed for the folder, but Bates held it back. "Where did you get that?" snapped Justin, furious over Bates gloating.

"Let's just say it came by mail. We didn't solicit it. In fact, we have no idea who the doctor was. We can't read his signature," chuckled Bates. "But who can read a doctor's writing. Good thing he dictated his notes or we wouldn't have a clue of your dark side." Bates flashed a vindictive smile. "I've consulted with the powers that be, including U.S. Atty. Watkins, and you're fired, Justin." Nash said nothing. "Mr. Bauers is now replacing you as my executive assistant. Clear out your desk." Bates gloated. He turned, spotting Atway Jackson.

"What are you doing in here?"

"I —"

"He ran an errand for me," blurted Nash.

Bates looked suspiciously at the quiet group, then turning departed with U.S. Atty. Watkins.

Bauers looked embarrassed. The room was in shock. No words were spoken. Each person waiting for the other to break the ice. "Justin, I'm sorry," Bauers spoke apologetically. Nash stood and grabbed his briefcase. "Don't apologize, pal. I was already on the scaffold. But I would like to know how that folder got to him." He picked up his coat.

"I knew nothing about that folder until I got in here," defended Bauers.

"Just throw all my personal crap in a box and send it to me." His eyes met Terry's stunned face. Then he hurried out the door.

Todd Bohannon handed the telephone to his client. "It's Ruth and she sounds upset." Pritchitt listened attentively, then asked, "You're sure he said *medicine?*"

Bohannon saw the concern in Benjamin's face.

"I love you, dear. Don't worry about me. I'll come by later." He handed the telephone back to Bohannon. "Simon called her. He talked of my betrayal." Pritchitt glanced at his watch. "I've got to pick up my grandkids. I'm late."

"We need to have about four more meetings like this one before we go to trial, Benjamin. Be damn sure to make time for them. Promise me," hollered Bohannon as Pritchitt scooted out the door.

"I promise," shouted Pritchitt. The drive that usually took a few minutes took twice as long in the sudden downpour that fell and with the tentative navigation of Memphians on the slippery streets.

"Damn this rain," Pritchitt muttered, as children and parents passed him. A thicket of umbrellas sprouted before the school entrance. Pritchitt parked his car and made a mad dash to the door. Claire waited inside. "Where's Benji?"

"Out there, Papa." She pointed outside. Benji played with little boys, unconcerned about the chilled rain, splashing in puddles, pushing each other and laughing. He ran to his grandfather.

"You're soaking wet," said Pritchitt, slightly annoyed.

"We were having fun," Benji beamed.

"We'd better get you out of those clothes as soon as possible or you'll catch a good cold." Pritchitt wrapped him in his coat and held him in his arms. They hurried to the car and drove quickly home.

After the children were changed and warm Loretta fixed cups of hot chocolate and sat them on the kitchen table. She patted Claire's cheek and rubbed Benji's head.

Pritchitt donned a raincoat and grabbed an umbrella. "I'm going to be with Ruth."

"Dr. Ben, I've got to leave by six."

"I'll be back by then. Be good kids." Benjamin kissed each on the cheek.

"Don't worry, we'll have a good time," said Loretta.

"I want to go for a swim," said Benji.

"You've already been," laughed Claire. They all laughed.

"It's too cold," said Loretta. "You were wet enough when you got here. Aren't you afraid of catching pneumonia?"

Benji smiled broadly. "I'm not afraid of anything with my Papa being the bestest doctor in the whole world."

"Not anything?" whispered Loretta in a teasing mood.

"Well, maybe the boogie man and the dark, but just a little." They laughed.

CHAPTER TWENTY-EIGHT

Ruth Pritchitt looked lovely, thought her husband. They sat together in the downstairs lobby of the clinic. It was the place where Pritchitt often relaxed before driving home. He held Ruth's hand. A frantic couple came through the front door, the wife waddling with nine months of expectancy.

"Good luck," said Ruth. "Boy, does that bring back memories," she mused.

"I'll say," he smiled, remembering. Then he turned to Ruth. "We all need you at home. The grandkids really miss you. Terry and Tyler need you. I miss you."

"I know I'm disappointing everyone," she apologized.

"Dr. Tucker says you are ready to be released."

She wet her lips, swallowing with difficulty. "It's just that I'm so afraid of failing. What if I start drinking again?"

"Then we start from point one."

"You're right, Ben. I've got to face the world some time."

"Soon?" Ben asked hopefully.

"All right," she said resolutely. "I'll . . . I'll leave here."

He kissed her lips. "I need my wife again. And —" His voice

broke off. He summoned his strength. "My trial is in a few weeks. It looks bleak. I know I've broken the law. But the law is wrong and there is the chance we may not have much time together, Ruth." She stroked his cheek. "I'll be with you in a few days, and forever more."

"Loretta's got to leave at six." He looked to his watch.

"And Simon?" she asked with fear in her voice.

"As I explained to you, the police and I are going to work together. We'll get him."

"There's no 'we'll' in that, Benjamin Pritchitt. You'll be no bait. You hear me? They'll catch this maniac and not you. Not a 60-something man with bad knees and no experience with playing real life cops and robbers, do we understand each other, Benjamin Pritchitt? Tell me now!"

"I promise to let the police do what they do best. Don't worry about me. I'll be fine. You just worry about getting home to us, and that's all." He kissed her lips and held her hand as he walked her to her room.

Sleet and rain impeded the drive home. Intersections were flooded. There were minor traffic accidents. They drive too damn fast in this city, he thought, rain or shine, everybody's in a hurry.

Twilight had fallen and darkness was creeping over Memphis. Even through the rain he could see the red and green Christmas decorations in the shop windows, and it was not yet Thanksgiving. The yard man, Riley, promised to have the Pritchitt residence decked to the hilt for Ruth's return. Home would be home again with her back. He admired Ruth's bravery, but worried about her insecurity in leaving the protection of the psychiatric clinic.

He pulled into the driveway. Loretta's car was in the front drive, where she always parked. He thanked God for having her. His raincoat dripped water on the kitchen floor. "Loretta!" he called. "I'm back." But the home was strangely silent. Uneasy, he hurried to the den. "Kids!" But there was no answer. In the living room, near the door, was an overturned basket of flowers. Pritchitt began searching the house. He went from room to room, calling out for Claire, for Benji. But the house was empty. He went to the pool terrace, standing in the icy, driving rain. Then he saw the trail of toys. He picked up Claire's doll. There was a tiny spaceman near the steps leading to the garden and into the woods. "Benji! Claire!" he shouted.

Then from the terrace he saw Claire's frightened white face peep from the woods. He ran through the garden. Claire shivered, clutching herself to keep warm. He tossed his raincoat over her and lifted her in his arms. Her lips were blue and she was frightened.

"Claire what happened?"

"A-a-a mm-m-man came with flowers. Bo-o-oo-g-g-i-i-e mm-m-man. We-we-we were in the — kitchen." Claire was cold and in near hysteria. He cradled her tightly and ran toward the house.

"Benji!" he shouted over and over. There was no answer. Ben rushed her shivering into the house. Grabbing a kitchen towel he dried her and quickly wrapped her in a blanket. "Tell me, Claire, what happened? And think, sweetheart." Her lips were regaining their color and when her shivering quieted she began to cry.

"Loretta began yelling. They were fighting. He was calling us. Benji and I ran outside. We were scared, Papa. Then he came outside calling us. I hid and Benji hid, Papa. It was the man with the long hair. It was the boogie man from the hospital."

Horror gripped Pritchitt. Rain fell harder against the window panes. His worst nightmare had been born. Simon had made the dreaded house call.

Pritchitt hugged Claire tightly and told her to stay put and that he'd be right back. Claire cried for him not to leave her. He had to find Benji. The thought of being too late chilled his soul. He rushed onto the back terrace. He called out for Benji, but only Claire's distant cry disturbed the dismal silence. His eyes rushed the limits of the property and seeing movement he ran to the outer fence. It was a rabbit running for shelter from the rain. The rain fell harder but he hardly noticed. It pelted his body. He ran from bush to tree, but there was nothing. He looked to the dark sky above and screamed out, "Benji!" He glared into the wet darkness above and thought it was surely God spilling his tears upon his cursed life. "Please, God. Not Benji." Again, Claire's cries could be heard from the house as he scanned the elaborate landscape. He turned back toward the house . . . his mind spinning. In the pool, tiny rings sprang from the thousands of heavy droplets splattering the rippled surface. Amidst the leaves, something floated. He ran to the pool's edge. It was a body floating face down. "My God! Benji!" he screamed and jumped into the chilled water. Pushing the leaves aside he turned the body. "No! God!" he cried out. It was Loretta. He held her head from the water. He pulled her from the pool. His emotions overwhelmed him. He waved for Claire to get back in the house as she stood crying on the covered terrace. He knelt at her side and began mouth to mouth resuscitation. Nothing helped. Claire watched from a window, tears flooding her cheeks as Pritchitt looked toward the house. Fear stamped on her face and Simon had changed their lives forever.

Pritchitt's tears mixed with the falling rain. He heard an automobile. He looked up from the woman who was part of their family to see Terry. She opened the side gate, umbrella in hand. Her run halted on the pool deck. She saw her father kneeling over the lifeless body.

"My God! Dad, the children?" she screamed out. Pritchitt rose to his feet. Loretta's body lay motionless — her eyes open — face bloated and blue. He grabbed hold of Terry's arms as the rain fell with more force, as if to douse their pain that burnt within. They stood in silence. Claire burst through the back door. "Mommy! Mommy!" she yelled as Terry lifted her into her arms throwing the umbrella to the ground. Pritchitt wrapped them in his arms and pushed them toward the house.

"Benji? Where's Benji, Dad?" shrieked Terry, her voice near hysteria.

"The bbbo-o-ogg-ie mm-a-ann, Mommy. The bbbo-o-gg-ie mm-a-nn!" cried Claire.

Terry stared into her father's torn face. "Benji's gone!" Holding Claire in her arms she turned back toward the pool. Her eyes scanned the icy water. "Benji!" she called out. She wept uncontrollably as Pritchitt led her into the house.

"It'll be okay, Mommy, I promise," Claire cried touching her mother's face. Pritchitt placed a blanket around Terry. She sat holding tightly to Claire while Pritchitt phoned Lt. Bordeaux.

The police were on their way as he stoked the fire. He sat at his daughter's side and placed his arm around her. She dropped her head to his shoulder. Nothing was said. The three simply sat and waited.

It took but a few minutes for the police to arrive. Terry carried Claire upstairs to her bedroom and tucked her in bed, drained by fright and cold. "I can't say my prayers so good without Benji," Claire whined.

Terry fought to hold back the hysteria she felt raging within. "Benji will be home soon, my darling. Mommy promises."

Claire shook her head. "That man took him." Tears filled her eyes. Terry lay down on the bed beside her little girl.

Pritchitt spoke with homicide detectives as the coroner took Loretta's body off, covered, on a stretcher. Bordeaux and Caffey talked with other detectives. "We've searched every inch of the house and property," said Caffey. "The boy's not on the premises."

"He's been kidnapped!" shouted Tyler, entering the den. Pritchitt tried to comfort his son, but it was Bordeaux's comfort that stilled his rage, if only for a moment.

Det. Caffey nodded with a hint of embarrassment at their ineptitude in handling the case. "We agree, we've called in the FBI," said Caffey.

Pritchitt took Tyler to the living room. "I've already called Loretta's son. He's devastated." Filled with self-deprecating guilt, Pritchitt broke down. Tyler put his arms around his father, whose grief had a sobering effect. Tyler regained his sensibility, thinking Mother must be warned. Simon may try to contact her and she must be aware of what's happened.

Terry walked into the room, she said nothing, but squeezed her father's hand and looked toward her brother. There was no need for words. Taking charge of what needed to be done, Tyler left the room. Terry pulled away from her father's hold. "Justin Nash was fired today," she said. "It seems there are psychiatric records that have just turned up, the sum of which is he's carrying an obsessive love for a dead girl. She ended her life after having an abortion. They're starting an investigation."

Pritchitt listened, then shook his head. "Bates has been targeting him for some time."

Then her voiced choked but she continued. "We've been together. There is a candlelit shrine with photographs of his parents and this girl."

"Do you think . . . no way . . . couldn't be . . ." Pritchitt was astonished by his thoughts. He couldn't complete his sentence. He paced the room, then turned back to Terry. "Didn't his secretary, Jesse, say that Simon had hundreds of candles burning?" Pritchitt's eyes burned.

"There are closed rooms upstairs. I've never seen them," said Terry. The second floor is so very large. The whole house is huge and the housekeeper, Emma, is too old to climb the steps."

"So no one ever goes upstairs but Nash, and you," said Pritchitt, his thoughts racing.

"I've left a message but he's not at home. Emma answered and didn't know where he was, but she did say he was very upset."

"Let's keep this to ourselves for now," said Pritchitt.

Terry went to Claire's bedside.

Tyler suddenly rushed into the room. "They say she's not there, Dad. Mom's not at the hospital. She's gone!" Tyler half-shouted.

Pritchitt leapt forward. "What are you saying? This can't be. There were supposed to be security guards watching her!"

Caffey knocked on the door frame before he entered the den. Two FBI agents and Bordeaux were with him. "We've a team on it. We haven't figured how she disappeared," Bordeaux was saying.

Pritchitt clenched his fists and walked toward Bordeaux. "We can't afford a mistake," he whispered. "I made one before. You do better. Simon has my grandson and now he has my wife." His voice choked with fear, then rage. "You know what I have to do?" he said coldly.

"I know," answered Bordeaux.

"We've tried to trace the calls without luck," Caffey added.

"The calls are being routed through a portable fax line that can be hooked into any phone, even a pay phone," explained an FBI agent. "Tracing the calls is futile because some kind of electronic device is blocking the calls, scrambling the numbers. This Simon left part of it at the telephone booth where those two teenagers were found dead. We think it is similar to a scrambler machine our embassies use to disguise telephone lines."

"He's going to send a fax to the office," insisted an expressionless Pritchitt.

"Wiseman's watching the fax machine at your office," said Bordeaux.

Claire slept peacefully in her bedroom. Pritchitt, Tyler and Terry linked hands. Pritchitt spoke solemnly, "Please, God, watch out for Benji and Ruth."

"He's so afraid of the dark," wept Terry. "I can't believe this is happening."

Tyler's hands fell from the circle. "Enough praying. Let's kill the bastard."

It was after ten when the house emptied of the last investigators. The shattered family was left alone.

Pritchitt could not contain himself and around midnight he backed his car out of the garage. He informed the officers on guard that he would be at the hospital.

Terry sat alone. Her son was gone. For God's sake, where could he be? Her mind danced with horrifying thoughts.

The telephone rang. With fear, Terry reached for it. It was Justin Nash and his voice was slurred. "What's up?" He

admitted he had been drinking. He sounded truly astonished by
the double kidnapping.

"Justin, I need to see you. I need to talk. My brother will
watch Claire."

"Sure, come on over."

Her drive was filled with confusion. From candles to
abortions, her mind played out anger and fear. Where were her
son and mother, and who was Nash?

The house stood as if an abandoned castle, its towering
roof spiraling into the black of night. Only a small lamp lit a
front window. The front porch was dark. Terry stepped from the
car. Her respirations quickened in the chilled night air. She
barely tapped the door and it quickly opened. Nash stood
before her. She could smell the scotch on his breath. The
downstairs was dark, lit only by a single lamp. He offered
her a chair.

"What a fucking miserable day," he said, pouring himself
a drink.

"What's going to happen?" asked Terry.

"I don't know. I've failed. It looks like the pig was smarter
than the farmer."

"Do you have any ideas who did this?"

"Not a goddamn one. But all your father has to do is kill
Simon. Simon will be happy and he'll release your son and
mother."

"So you think he has them?"

"Come on, Terry. Who else would do it?" Nash turned and
stumbled into a chair. Terry stared up the steep staircase. She
took a deep breath and clinched her teeth. Her thoughts were
confused. She had to be certain. She paced the room.

"I'm at my wits end," she sighed heavily. She walked to the
foot of the staircase. She needed to go upstairs. She turned to
find Nash asleep in the chair. The drink in his hand had slipped
to the carpet.

Terry removed her shoes. Slowly she ascended the wide
steps with an occasional glance at the sleeping Nash below.

As usual, regardless of the hour, ambulances blended with other emergency vehicles in the hectic traffic surrounding Memorial Hospital. Pritchitt's car dodged an oncoming ambulance, then he quickly pulled to a stop and got out of his car. He cut across the lobby and rode the elevator to the tenth floor. He stopped outside his office, his eyes drawn to Dot McCormick's blood stains still evident on the carpet.

Inside the office Bernie sat next to the fax machine, a medical textbook in his hands. He stood when he saw Pritchitt, searching for words. "It looks like he's still calling the shots," said Wiseman. "How did it happen? Your wife, sir, how'd she disappear?"

"We don't exactly know," offered Bordeaux as she walked through the door.

"Following me, Lt. Bordeaux?"

"Let's just say, Dr. Pritchitt, that brilliant minds often travel the same path. I just came from the psychiatric hospital. Someone reported a gurney being wheeled through a service elevator. It was being pushed towards your wife's room, Dr. Pritchitt. Amazingly, no one paid attention to the person pushing it, or to exactly where the hell it went," said Bordeaux.

Pritchitt slammed his fist to his desk.

Wiseman held up a newspaper. "Today the newspaper was filled with articles about the bombing of the clinic and the coincidental murder of Ann James who, by the way, is a known radical activist from the West Coast, with a police record," he added. "Seems she was pretty busy out there doing what her husband was doing here. She was definitely a more violent person from the reports. But one thing's for sure, Simon now knows he's killed two innocents, Ann James and her unborn child.

"I think he's more than ready to die and this will only hasten that desire," said Pritchitt.

Lori Bordeaux took a seat next to the fax machine. "So you will assist Simon in his death?"

"Absolutely. My hand is forced. And with what he's done to

me . . . well, I may just really enjoy it. And, Bordeaux, I can't afford for the police to screw it up, either."

"It is going to be a long night," Bordeaux said matter-of factly.

Nash's bedroom was lit by a small lamp. Terry moved quietly across the room. The dresser was covered with mementos of the doomed romance. She returned to the hall, cautiously she explored each dark room. Her thoughts ran wild. A roach passed before her. She imagined hearing its footsteps above the eerie quiet. She suppressed a desire to scream. Calming herself, Terry inched her way along the wooden floor. It creaked slightly. At the end of the long corridor she stealthily opened another door and entered another dark hall. She slowly turned a doorknob. It was pitch black inside. "Benji," she softly called. She pressed the wall seeking a switch. The room lit up. Within were file cabinets and dozens of boxes labeled "Smith & Nash Law Firm." She turned off the light. In the hall she moved to the next room. Again, she called her son's name. There was a rustling sound. "Benji," she loudly whispered. There was the sound of unintelligible words. "Who's there?" she asked, her voice expressing fear. Her hand nervously searched the wall for the switch. There was a high-pitched squeal. Terry gave a muffled cry just as she found the light switch. Near her was a parrot in a cage, surrounded by plants. Her heart raced. But there was no sign of her son. Her nerves were frail as she quietly opened a door to avoid the squeaking of rusty hinges. With a jittery calm she turned back toward the main hall and staircase. At the top of the staircase she sat. She brushed a tear from her cheek. Despair and anxiety mushroomed within her thoughts. She had searched for her son in Nash's home. What game was her mind playing? Justin had an odd past but she felt as if she had betrayed him. She stood and gripping the bannister quietly made her way down the steps toward the still sleeping Nash.

It was after 3:00 a.m. when the fax machine began its

much anticipated chatter. The trio, Pritchitt, Wiseman and Bordeaux, hovered over the sheet of paper sliding into the tray. Then the machine was silent. No one moved. Pritchitt turned to Wiseman. "Read it."

In a breathless voice, Bernie carefully read aloud. "'Simon says, You have been unfaithful to our brotherly bond. I, too, have now made a terrible mistake. I did not bomb the abortionists, but I did take the life of one who was carrying life. You and I, Benjamin Pritchitt, are parallels. Truly a brotherhood paralleling death at life's beginning and end. It is death's parallel that has brought us together. It is a divine calling we share. My time here is over. You have painfully forced my loving hand against your family. Our bond shall be consummated by your medicine. Go to the Penguin Club now!'"

"The Penguin Club?" asked Pritchitt.

"It's a weirdo bar, past South Main," responded Bordeaux. "Every deviant type hangs out there."

"I'm off," he said. "And, Bordeaux, there has to be no police. Understand! I've got the carbon monoxide in the trunk of my car. That's it!" Don't either of you interfere," he said emphatically.

Pritchitt drove into the dark night. He headed past the bright lights of Beale Street, beyond South Main, to a neighborhood he'd never ventured into. Women sauntered beneath street lamps and drivers slowed to look them over. On a side street he glimpsed a pink neon penguin. The parking lot was crowded.

Inside it was dark. Loud music blared. The air was stale with smoke and the stench of spilled beer. Pritchitt sat at the small bar next to a clean-cut man his hair slicked back. He greeted Pritchitt with a smug smile. The bartender came over. "Beer," said Pritchitt. He felt a knee press against his leg.

"Say, would you care to hang out together?" smiled the sweet smelling man.

Pritchitt was unsure. "Maybe," he said quietly. Could this be Simon? he thought. The man slid his hand along Pritchitt's thigh. "I've got something you might find interesting. What's your name?"

"Ben. What's yours?"

"Charley."

"You're not Simon?"

"If you want me to be."

"Did Simon send you?"

The man leaned closer. "Bennie boy, I'll be whoever you want me to be. If the price is right."

A distinguished elderly man in a suit approached, frowning. He tugged at Charley's suit coat. "The price is right," he said. Charley grinned.

"Too bad, Bennie. Next time."

Pritchitt nervously took a sip of the bottled beer. His eyes had grown accustomed to the dimness. At small tables patrons were clustered. Elegantly dressed women kissed at the end of the bar. Men danced together on a small dance floor. At another table men were dressed as women, with unflattering results.

He waved the bartender over. "I'm looking for a man."

The bartender smiled. "Who isn't, pal. Help yourself."

"The man I'm looking for is named Simon. Do you know him?"

"So you're that weird dude's brother? Strange dude, that Simon."

Pritchitt nodded. "Yeah, he can be really weird when he tries."

"Well, this was left here for you." He placed an envelope on the counter. Pritchitt reached for his reading glasses and pulled a small lamp on the bar closer. In a whisper he read, "For my brother Benjamin from Simon.' He left this himself?" Pritchitt asked the bartender.

"Naw, a messenger service dropped it off, with a twenty dollar bill."

"Do you know who he is?"

"Hell, he's your damn kin, don't you?"

"It's been years since I've seen him. I need to find him."

"Yeah, I know him. A long-haired guy, a loner. Seldom

speaks. Usually sits at the end of the bar, or at that corner table. His head is always down," he said, gesturing toward a darkened corner. "But when he did talk it's usually about you. You know, family shit."

"Like what?"

"I don't remember, man. I'm not no damn social worker. I get so many pity parties in here. Open that envelope. You're turning me onto you. Let's see what's inside it," said the bartender as he leaned over the bar. "I'm kinda like Charlie. I love older men, too," he whispered.

"Yeah, I can see that." Pritchitt tossed a bill on the table. "Now what does my brother usually talk about?"

Across the room skin-headed bikers in black leather sat staring at him. A woman at their table came forward. Ben put the envelope in his pocket. She smiled. "You're new around here."

"I'm from out of town," Pritchitt lied.

"Oh, baby, let's make friends." She moved closer to his ear, and whispered. "You name it, we got it. Boys, girls, whips, dope. If you just want to watch, we can arrange that. Name it."

"Maybe some other time." Pritchitt stood and hurried from the bar. Outside he breathed the sweet cold air. Once in his car he flipped on the overhead light and ripped open the envelope. He began to read the note. "'Simon says, you have passed this test of trust. You came alone. Your final prescription for a dying soul will come, and you will fill it.'" Was this it? Was this why he'd come to Memphis' version of hell. He was anxious and angry. He wanted to kill Simon and do it now! He felt like a puppet on a string, yanked and made to dance as his master wished. His wife and grandson were his prisoners somewhere in this city. But where? He was desperate to find them and he knew the only way would be through Simon. He wanted him dead and them back, alive and well. He would have to wait for the next message. He prayed it would come soon. He started his car and headed home.

It was nearly 5:00 a.m. when he arrived home. Terry, fully

clothed, was asleep on the sofa in the den. Pritchitt gently shook her. "Baby, are you all right?" he whispered.

"Dad," she mumbled rubbing her eyes. "Oh, Dad," she cried, hugging his neck. "I went to Justin's home tonight. But I saw nothing of Benji. The house is so big. Dad, we have to find Benji and Mom." She began to cry aloud. She calmed herself and stared into her father's quiet suffering. "Where have you been? I paged Lori to ask her, but she wouldn't say much. She promised me you'd be okay. I have this bad feeling that you went off on your own to play hero, again. Tell me that's not true, Dad?"

"That makes two of us who went off on their own to play hero tonight, doesn't it?" Terry nodded. "Simon sent a fax. As a result I had to go to a part of South Memphis I didn't know existed." She sat up straight, her eyes now fully open, her attention his. Pritchitt handed her the envelope. "This is pure torture," he said. Anger and defeat disrupted his beaten tone. She eagerly read the message.

"Dad, at least he's still in touch with you," she said with renewed hope. "If Justin is Simon, then I'll kill him myself, with my own hands if necessary." She cursed him as she buried her head in her father's arms and sobbed. Pritchitt held her tight. "We'll be okay, baby. I promise. This family we'll be okay."

Dawn broke in glorious splendor. Too pretty a day for what was happening in their lives, thought Pritchitt. The newspaper blared the previous days's misery: *Pritchitt Housekeeper Dead In Pool. Wife and Grandson Missing.* The telephone began ringing around seven. Pritchitt did his best to dissuade callers, even those with the best intentions.

Around nine Dr. Blanche Tucker rang the doorbell. Tyler showed her into the living room. Her eyes were weary with dark circles. Tucker sat. Two plain clothes detectives carrying equipment passed them. "They've taken over the house with line taps, you name it," said Tyler, referring to the FBI and police who had set up a monitoring room for all incoming calls.

"They're hoping Simon will call. He won't," said Tyler, frustration in his words.

"I feel so terribly bad about what's happened," she apologized as Terry and her father entered the room. "I feel personally responsible for Mrs. Pritchitt. She was under my care at the hospital" Tears swelled her eyes. "She's such a wonderful human being."

"Don't," said Terry. "You have helped her so much. You're so special to us all."

"Any news? Have they got any leads?" Tucker asked.

"Nothing of any substance," said Pritchitt.

Tyler paced the room. "I feel so damn helpless just sitting here. If I don't do something to occupy my mind, I'll snap. If I just drive around looking, even knowing I'd never find them, I'd feel that I was at least doing something, for God's sake!"

"I understand, son. We all feel that way. But we have to work with the police and FBI." Pritchitt grabbed his overcoat.

"And where do you think you're going?" asked Tyler.

"I'll be at my office. I can only pray Simon will send another fax soon. Wiseman's camped out there. Think I'll keep him company."

Unlike her usual calm self, Dr. Tucker seemed jittery. After a long silence she spoke. "Wait, Dr. Pritchitt, before you leave. There is someone I suspect. And have all along. I even went to talk to his psychiatrist." Terry and Tyler sat listening intently. Tucker looked their way. Pritchitt turned away from the door and walked back into the room.

"Who is this person?" asked Pritchitt.

"It's only a suspicion, mind you, but I believe a strong one."

"Who? For crying out loud," barked Terry.

"Justin Nash. I know it sounds crazy, but —"

"No, it doesn't," interrupted Pritchitt. His eyes met those of his daughter. "Why? Why do you say that, Dr. Tucker?"

"Justin Nash and my sister were lovers. This was years ago, mind you. She became pregnant. She didn't think the child was his. But Justin was sure it was. My sister had an abortion. Nash went berserk. He became enraged.

"Please, go on," Terry frantically coached with her hands, waving to continue.

"He upset her so that she took an overdose of sleeping pills and died."

"Good grief!" said Pritchitt, walking deeper into the room.

"My sister told me he liked to play kinky games in bed."

"Games like 'Simon Says'." Terry looked to her father.

The pain of recalled memories reflected in Blanche Tucker's face.

Tucker went on, "Christy was the great love of his life. It's all in the files. He had psychiatric treatment."

"Then it was you who sent his psychiatric file to Jeremy Bates?"

"I was hoping something could be uncovered to help. I didn't want to ruin him, especially if my hunch was wrong."

"You did end his career. He was fired yesterday."

Tucker was silent.

"This is total bullshit!" yelled Tyler. He paced the room. "Shit! If Nash is responsible for this, and I mean in any way, then I'm going over there and make him talk . . . if I have to beat him!" Tyler hurried from the room with Pritchitt close behind.

The doorbell rang. A police officer stood with a mailgram. "Federal Express has a truck at the driveway. We stopped him." Pritchitt stood at the door with Tyler. He took the envelope and returned to the living room. His fingers fumbled with it and he felt his nerves unraveling. Pritchitt read: "'A husband's love should never be parted from his wife's nor a grandfather's from his grandson's. Your pain is for your betrayal. Your pain shall leave as wounds heal where the Rolling Tide of our destiny crosses the Fallen Shadows of this life's sinful ways. Sin finds refuge in life's garbage.'" Pritchitt looked up.

"Wish Wiseman was here. He's good at these damn rhymes," said Pritchitt.

"That's just fucking great! Rhymes from the memoirs of a madman," fretted Tyler.

Terry gasped. "Rolling Tide? That's the street I'm about to move to, 1123 Rolling Tide is the house the kids and I are going to live in. My God! Fallen Shadows is the street that dead ends at the corner of the house."

"Son-of-bitch," said Pritchitt, stuffing the message into his pocket and hurrying toward the door. Terry followed.

"Tyler, call the police. Tell them to hurry to Terry's new address," shouted Pritchitt.

Pritchitt swerved in and out of the traffic. His car might as well been on automatic pilot. His mind was on the message and not the traffic ahead. Cars and pedestrians alike crowded the streets, oblivious to the turmoil within the speeding car. "Terry try the cellular phone again," shouted Pritchitt.

Terry grabbed for the phone. "Lori, please meet us at 1123 Rolling Tide. It's the address of my new home. You've been there with me. It's an emergency. My Dad and I are on our way. Please, it's an emergency!" she cried into the phone, her palms slick with sweat.

Pritchitt's car roared past the stately homes of the Central Garden district and into a more modest neighborhood. He brought it to a screeching stop next to one of two police cars with blue lights flashing. Another police car skidded to a halt behind them.

Jumping from her car was Lt. Bordeaux and her partner Det. Caffey. "What the hell's the emergency? We got an urgent call from Tyler," Bordeaux yelled. An anxious and puzzled frown plastered her face.

"Hurry! It's Simon." Terry called out, trying to keep pace with her racing father up the driveway. Pritchitt sprinted toward the garage. A uniformed police stood and watched his frenzied pace.

"Has everyone gone mad?" mumbled Bordeaux as she and Caffey ran to keep up. Pritchitt came to a stop at the top of the driveway. Terry rested at his side until Bordeaux and Caffey caught up. Other officers stood in the front yard poised for action.

"I've got to start working out," gasped Bordeaux, bending to catch her breath.

"It's those damn cigarettes," Caffey admonished.

"Now, what's the reason for all this?" huffed Bordeaux.

Pritchitt surveyed the house and then targeted a large garbage container sitting in front of the garage. He'd rethought that message during the harried drive. He understood. He glared at the closed container.

Terry looked at her father, then at the container. "Da-a-a-d-d," she stuttered. "There was no garbage container here before."

"I know that, sweetheart," he whispered anxiously. They stared nervously at one another, then back at the container afraid to move, afraid of what may be inside.

Impatiently Bordeaux walked to their side. "One more time, what's going on?" Pritchitt handed Bordeaux the mailgram. "Wait a damn minute," Bordeaux's eyes spoke volumes as she walked to Pritchitt's side. "I haven't the faintest idea what I just read. So, I'll open it."

Pritchitt and Terry stood with unchanged expressions as she approached the container.

"What about explosives? Are you just going to open it without the bomb squad?" yelled Caffey as her hand touched the container. She jerked and stood back from the still closed container.

"Perfect fucking timing, partner, to scare the shit out of me," she scolded, then backed a few steps farther away. Other officers in the yard backed toward the street.

"Remember, the clinic?" reminded Caffey.

Pritchitt stepped forward. "He wouldn't do that. He doesn't want me dead, at least now. There'd be no one left to fill his prescription of death except himself. He's too much of coward to do it himself. He wants me to do it. This is all about my punishment. There's no bomb," Pritchitt repeated, his eyes unflinching, the container his focus. Bordeaux walked to the container.

Terry buried her face in her father's chest. Bordeaux withdrew a handkerchief and covered the handle of the green container. She opened the lid slowly. Caffey walked to her side and both stared into the near full container. The air was fouled by a rotting aroma. Bordeaux looked to Caffey, and he at her. She gingerly placed her hand into the container and hesitantly pulled out a small bloodstained sweater.

Terry felt her father jump. Terry turned. "That's Benji's!" she screamed. Terry collapsed, sobbing. Pritchitt knelt at her side. Hysteria reigned. Bordeaux and Caffey tilted the overflowing garbage container. The stench worsened as officers near the street covered their faces and approached.

"I see it," shouted Bordeaux.

Terry's wail escalated. She cradled the ground. Bordeaux looked to her fallen friend.

Pritchitt ran to the container. Inside was the bloody carcass of a dog.

"I'll kill that son-of-a-bitch," swore Pritchitt.

He turned and screamed, repeating his desire to the crowd of curious bystanders collecting across the street.

"Is it . . . Benji?" screamed Terry from her knees in a praying pose.

"No, baby," said Pritchitt kneeling with his daughter. She stood with his help.

"That no good bastard!" said Pritchitt. "You did this on purpose, didn't you?" he shouted in a shrilled pitch that filled the air, as if hoping it would carry to the ears of Simon, himself. Hate was Pritchitt's message knowing Simon had smeared the dog's blood onto the boy's sweater. "You did it just to see my face and hear my response," he shouted. "And you call yourself my brother?" Pritchitt's body swirled in anger as he made his way down the driveway. He'd lost it and Bordeaux knew it as she rushed to his side. He pushed her away. Terry held her son's sweater, crying at the sight of her father's growing hysteria. His wife and grandson, it had been too much, thought Bordeaux, hurting for the man. "Here, take a little more of my heart." He patted his chest.

Caffey withdrew his gun; a sudden anxiety coursed through his body. He felt as if Simon was close by.

Pritchitt cursed, spinning in a circle, as he made his way to the street. "Show yourself! Tell me where and when!" he shouted, walking into the street. His eyes scanned the curious neighbors, searching for Simon. "I'll be there to put you to death, three, even four times, if you want, you worthless piece of garbage." His voice ricocheted through the tall trees. An echoing hate stirred the still air. An officer held Pritchitt back from the shocked bystanders. Terry gathered herself and ran to his side. She tried to calm his rage. Caffey signaled for Bordeaux from the top of the driveway. Caffey held a small note found taped to the underside of the container's lid. Bordeaux read the note, then stared at Caffey. She motioned a uniformed officer to keep Pritchitt and Terry from following, then both ran to the rear of the house. Turning the corner with guns pulled, they were in a full run, then suddenly stopped. They stood paralyzed by what lay ahead. Caffey looked to Bordeaux; neither could manage a word. Slowly they skirted the patio, guns raised, pivoting in circles as if waiting for Simon to emerge from the wooded surroundings. They turned and in shocked stances, stared at what appeared to be the body of a bloodied infant wrapped in a small blanket. Caffey froze, unable to move. Bordeaux searched her partners face. She shook off a revolting chill, then walked slowly toward the infant body. Her body flushed with horror and relief. Her spiraling emotions settled. "That fucking maniac," cursed Bordeaux. "What kind of a person would —"

There was a scream as Bordeaux and Caffey turned to see Terry drop to the lawn. "My baby. My baby," she cried.

"I thought I told you to keep her out!" screamed Bordeaux at the officer. "Terry! Terry!" shouted Bordeaux quickly picking the large doll from the ground and waving it in front of her. "It's a doll, Terry. It's a fucking doll!" she repeated with anger aimed at Simon. Terry cried uncontrollably. Her father knelt at her side.

"That sorry animal," said Caffey as he walked onto the patio. He took away the bloodied doll. "What a sick bastard," he growled.

"My God," gasped Bordeaux. Caffey glanced in the

direction of her shocked stare. Both glanced upward. From a distant tree in the backyard, a dummy painted in red swung from a branch. "Guess that's supposed to be Ruth Pritchitt. No need for them to see that," said Bordeaux angrily. "I believe they've seen enough. Simon's made his perverted point."

Bordeaux led Terry and her father from the back yard. I got your message, you low-life murderer! thought Pritchitt as he glanced back.

It was late as Oscar Maple sat on his front porch. A car slowly approached — dodging craters in the dirt road. Maple rose — arthritic knees shortened his stride as he cautiously descended the steps. He shook hands with Benjamin Pritchitt. From the automobile Terry, Tyler and Claire emerged. Benjamin motioned Claire up the wooden steps.

"Hi, this must be Claire," said Oscar Maple. "Tomorrow we're going to milk the cows."

"You have real cows?" asked Claire.

"They're *real* and the best cows around," laughed Maple.

"Uncle Tyler's going to stay, too?" Claire asked.

Terry kissed her daughter. "He sure will."

After Ben and Terry returned to the automobile Oscar Maple stood at the car door. "Like I said on the phone, I owe a big favor. She'll be safe here and —" he wiped his eyes, "she'll be like my own little girl."

CHAPTER TWENTY-NINE

The door flung open. A solemn figure cloaked in a long overcoat walked into the darkened room. Weeping, he bent before a mirror. "I have killed the innocent and I must die." He smashed the mirror into hundreds of pieces and stared at his fragmented reflection. There was a moan. Blindfolded with her mouth taped, Ruth Pritchitt lay strapped to a hospital gurney. The tape was yanked from her mouth. She winced in pain "Where am I?" she weakly muttered.

The figure poured clear liquid onto a cloth. "Time to sleep," whispered the hoarse voice.

Sunset blanketed the river, and splintered rays slipped through the shaded window. The dismal room's silence was broken by the whimper of a small child lying on a makeshift bed. There was but one window, covered by a torn shade. In the room, only a radio at low volume kept Benji company. A bedside toilet was a few steps away. Wrappings from the food were strewn on the floor. Benji didn't know where he was. Through the cracked shade he had seen the river far below. He was so high and the door was locked. He cried for his mother, for Papa, but no one came. Why had he been brought here? His mind was too young to process thoughts through all the confusion. He felt a fear no one his age had the right to feel. It was dark and that's what he feared the most. Most of his sounds were a low pitched whimper. When could he go home? He turned his head into a small pillow and cried.

The day was quickly slipping away and neither the police nor the FBI were any closer to finding Ruth or her grandson. Despondent, Pritchitt sat alone deep in thought.

"How about a fresh cup of coffee?" asked Wiseman.

Pritchitt nodded. He sat at his desk and stared aimlessly out the window. His thoughts were with Benji, recalling the look on his little face and the tremble in his slight voice when he was left alone in the dark. Pritchitt's heart wrenched with pain and his jaws clenched in anger at the thought of Simon being near his grandson. And Ruth. Would her fragile nerves break being abducted by the serial killer? Could she recover from another fall into major depression? Maybe they were being held together, thought Pritchitt, then they could comfort one another. Like a dormant volcano his thoughts erupted into anger. "Damn, why doesn't that bastard called me? I've told him I'll do what he wants, if not with the carbon monoxide mask, then with my own hands." He raised his clinched hands in a show of violence.

Wiseman polished his glasses. "He knows. He's just making you pay for betraying him. In his own sick way he's getting back at you. Your wife and grandson are fine. He's paying you back for that fuck up at the phone booth."

"Fine! Fine, you say?" Pritchitt agonized. "How can you say that?"

"I'm sorry. I meant physically fine, sir. I know they're hurting."

"I apologize, Wiseman. Sorry I jumped on you, of all people. You've done more than your share to help me," said Pritchitt, his tone repentant.

"That bastard just wants to make sure that when he finally tells you to jump, you'll jump right through his hoop. That's why this insane punishment," said Wiseman, sipping coffee.

"God forgive me, but if he were before me now it would be so easy."

"I have no doubt of that. You'll get your chance. You just have to wait and that's the hardest part," said Wiseman. "But maybe not too long," he uttered in the same breath, acknowledging the fax machine had begun to print. Pritchitt stood from his chair, spilling his coffee.

"Is it from Simon?" asked Wiseman, straining to see over Pritchitt's shoulders. A nod from Pritchitt gave the answer. His eyes devoured each word. He walked slowly back to his chair, his head never raised from the sheet. Wiseman hesitated to interrupt the intensity of Pritchitt's concentration.

He handed the sheet to Wiseman. "Read it aloud, Bernie."

"'Simon Says, what was once just in society is now gone. Society has lost sight of the true path. As it was with Jesus, we have been dismissed as fanatics. History will confirm what you and I have done are righteous acts. Like the alpha and the omega, we have been anointed to watch after the unborn and dying, as brothers ordained by God. We have sacrificed our lives for others, as did God's beloved son. But now we've arrived at our long awaited last act, the final scene we shall call *Simon's Departure From A Living Hell*. You must be outside the Orpheum Theater when the clock strikes midnight. And, my brother, be alone or we shall both lose . . . I, my final scene, and you, your Ruth. Oh, and let me not forget, Terry, her Benji. I love you, my brother. I await your painless mask and my painless departure.'"

Wiseman sat, quieted by the message. "So you really think it's Nash?"

"It all fits. His obsession with abortion and his desire to depart a tortured life to be with Dr. Tucker's sister and unborn child . . . the child he believed to be his. And his mention of Terry. I'm going to prepare my suitcase," said Pritchitt.

Ruth awoke in eerie shadows. She was dressed and sitting in a leather armchair. Hundreds of candles glowed in the dusky room. Flickering evil was cast throughout. Crackling flames lit a fireplace behind her. Her silhouette was a portrait of terror against the flaming hearth. She tried to rise only to discover a leather strap attached to her ankle. A short link of chain led to a steel ring in the floor near the foot of the hearth. She screamed out in fear. On a table six feet away lay a small casket. She shouted. Her screams went unanswered as she struggled to pull the steel ring from the floor. A ringing telephone broke the dead silence. Ruth searched and beneath a table was the phone. She grabbed the cord and pulled the phone toward her. She paused in terror before answering.

"Hello, my dear Ruth," came the chilling voice. "This is Simon, my dearest. Don't be frightened. I called to say good-bye. I'm going to miss you most of all. Your strong but fragile innocence has given me strength."

Ruth sat muted by the wicked insanity of the voice. "I'll be leaving for good tonight. Benjamin, my brother, will assist my departure. It will be painless and humane. But most of all, it will unite me with my family. You, Ruth, you'll be back with your family and I with mine. What a sweet ending. A true love story, don't you agree?"

"Let me go, please. I haven't done anything to you," she cried.

From the frightening voice emerged a mesmerizing horror. "Oh, but you have, Ruth. Your whole family has been important. You all have shown me the love I've missed in my meaningless existence. I feel part of your family. I've envied that love for quite some time. If all goes well the letter on the far door will explain everything. If my brother betrays me, you will die just as little Benji will. We'll have all lost."

"Benji?"

"I'm taking good care of him. I only wish he were

mine."

"You monster! You touch a hair on that child's head and I'll —"

"You'll what? Kill me? But your loving husband is already going to do that, remember?"

"Please, for the love of God —"

"Oh! Didn't I tell you? God's the author of this entire play. I must hurry to catch the final act. I am the star of this climactic scene."

"Don't hurt my Benji," she cried, dropping her head in anguish. "Don't hurt my Benjamin."

"Isn't it ironic, Ruth. I go to be with your family and leave what's left of mine in my life's casket. What a glorious ending. A truly wonderful love story."

The raspy voice breathed a satisfying sigh, then exhaled with an evil hiss. The telephone went dead.

Ruth struggled, desperately trying to free herself, but the link chain kept her movement to a few feet. She yanked at the chain with repeated tugs. In the shadows a door creaked. Something rolled slowly along the floor until hitting at her feet. She picked up a bottle of scotch. "No, no!" she screamed. "I won't! Please, God! Benji! Benjamin!" she cried. Suddenly, from the depths of her despair came an idea. She reached for the chain. She looked back at the flaming hearth, then to the note left on the distant door.

Pritchitt was at work in his storage room. Terry suddenly appeared. "Dad, what are you doing?"

"Tonight is the night, Terry. It's time." He loaded two canisters into a suitcase. Then he handed her the fax. "It's Nash," said Pritchitt, continuing his work.

"Are you sure?"

"Terry," said Pritchitt in a condemning voice, "The man has been obsessed about abortions, and has kept his prurient depravity hidden."

Benjamin continued loading the trunk of his car. He placed the green canisters carefully into a suitcase, He covered them with a heavy quilt. "I drove by Nash's house on my way home. It took every ounce of strength left to keep from driving right through his damn front door." Blind rage ran through his body as a crop of goose bumps appeared. Quickly he refocused. "His mansion is huge, Terry. Ruth and Benji could be hidden anywhere in there. From the basement to the third floor ballroom."

"I'm coming with you," Terry declared.

He pushed her away. "No! I'm following his instructions to the tee. They'll be no screw up like the last one. The screw up at the phone booth cost us dearly. We can't afford a mistake. He's got your mother and son. You will stay here; and for God's sake, stay near the phone. You never know what Simon will do."

"Dad, should I call the police?"

"No!" He slammed the trunk closed. "I've betrayed him once. I'm afraid he'll—" His voice cracked. He pleaded with his daughter, knowing he would be unable to bear life without Ruth and Benji.

The thousands of bulbs normally illuminating the old Orpheum Theater were dimmed by a low fog. There was a wet chill in the air. Pritchitt's breath revealed his anxiety. Hurried puffs of mist floated as clouds before his mouth. He waited beneath the marquee, his collar turned up to buffer the cold wind. He gripped the suitcase tightly in his hand.

It was midnight. A light shown down the dark track. A faint bell acknowledged the approaching trolley. Pritchitt scanned the few passengers. Justin Nash peered through a window. Their eyes met. Pritchitt's heart raced as he prayed for self-control. The trolley stopped. Following instructions, Pritchitt stepped aboard. The conductor clanged the bell and the coach regained its speed.

Pritchitt avoided a drooling wino slumped forward in the aisle.

Nash lightly patted his seat. He was solemn. His narrow eyes were distrustful. Pritchitt sat beside Nash. What was the plan? thought Pritchitt. The conductor turned and smiled. Pritchitt returned a forced smile, then stared into Nash's stern face.

"Simon said you would be here," whispered Nash, his eyes fixed straight ahead.

"He did . . . did he?"

"Yes, he did." Nash held out his hand. It was one of Benji's favorite toys. "This came with my invitation to this late night party."

Pritchitt's face grew ashen.

The trolley moved down the track, past dilapidated buildings on South Main. It paralleled the river, high along the bluff. A distant whistle of a river barge sounded. The next stop saw three drunken passengers stumble off, vanishing into the fog.

The conductor turned to Pritchitt. "And you, sir, must be getting off at my last stop, the old 1890 brewery?" he asked.

"And how do you know that?" said Pritchitt.

"Because he told me so."

Pritchitt stared at the quiet and expressionless Nash.

"No, not him," corrected the conductor, seeing Pritchitt's misinterpreting gaze. "This spooky as hell guy handed me a twenty note and told me that I'd pick his brother up at the Orpheum and drop him off at the old brewery."

Pritchitt sat forward with a quick glimpse at Nash's calm face.

"Anything else?"

"Yeah, that he'd be carrying a suitcase. And that narrows the field to you, doesn't it?" he chuckled, then spat a wad of tobacco out the window. "He told me to make damn sure you got there. I said no problem."

"Nice to be wanted, isn't it?" whispered Nash, his grin strange. Pritchitt sat back. His hand frozen to the handle of the suitcase.

They rode deeper into night's black mystery, as if hell was their destination. The trolley moved through dark streets littered with broken bottles, past abandoned warehouses.

Pritchitt stared into passing alleys. Rats scurried through the trash filled gutters. Only inches separated him from Nash but they were strangers. The conductor stopped his whistling. Silence wrapped the trolley. Surely death had come aboard, thought Pritchitt.

"Simon has to die," whispered Nash.

"Yes, Simon will die tonight," agreed Pritchitt, his lips dry and eyes wide, fearful he would give away his feelings and rip Nash's throat.

The trolley stopped in a decaying neighborhood. Passengers exited. The conductor helped the unsteady wino to his feet and out the door.

The trolley chugged away, past cheap bars and dead factories.

"Next stop," yelled the conductor. Pritchitt surveyed the coach. Only two people remained near the back: a teenager, and an older man. Both were of street gang appearance. The trolley slowed and the boy stood, tapping his fingers nervously against the trolley's brass handrail. His eyes met Pritchitt's, then surveyed the cabin. He stood not four feet from Pritchitt. Tattoos covered his skin. An unnerving agitation spread across the teenager's face. Pritchitt gazed into his drug-fed scowl. The trolley slowed to a crawl. Pritchitt looked to the rear. The older man stood. He readied for his exit. Pritchitt began to button his coat.

"Bluff stop," the conductor called out.

His coat buttoned, Pritchitt reached for his suitcase. A sudden tug pulled at his arm. He looked up to see his suitcase in the grasp of the tattooed boy who jumped from the trolley.

"Stop him," yelled Pritchitt.

The older man in the rear flew out the door.

Pritchitt bolted after them, hurrying through the door and into the cold mist. His thoughts exploded in panic. How could this be? How could he fulfill Simon's wish without the canisters? He ran with the strength of his very being but fell behind.

The older man caught the tattooed youth and both

tumbled to the ground. The suitcase flew into the air. Pritchitt gasped as he saw it fall open on the track. He ran harder, his breath shorter as he approached the exposed canisters.

"Oh, no you don't," yelled the older man, handcuffing the teenager. A bag of cocaine was pulled from the boy's pocket. "I've been after your drug selling butt for weeks, asshole. You have the right to remain —"

"Fuck you, pig," screamed the boy.

"Is that any way to talk to me?" The youth's arm was twisted and he screamed in pain. "Besides, tough guy, now I can add a charge of theft." The handcuffed teenager lay on the ground, squirming beneath the officer's booted foot on his neck.

"Sorry about this inconvenience. I'm with vice. I've been following this drug sucking parasite all night."

"Fine, officer," panted Pritchitt nervously, his side splinting in pain, his anxious eyes on the open suitcase. He moved quickly to close it.

"And sorry about your suitcase," said the undercover cop. "Here let me help," he offered, closing the suitcase.

"I'll get it," said Pritchitt. The two stared at one another, both gripping the suitcase.

"You're all right?" asked the cop.

Pritchitt cleared his head. "Yes! Of course, I'm fine. I'm sorry. I guess I was in a state of shock," said Pritchitt. "It's not every night you're robbed, is it?"

"No, it's not, but in this area, and at this time, what do you expect? I'd be more careful if I were you."

"You're right. I'll be more careful. Thanks," said Pritchitt, eager to leave.

"Hold it a damn minute," screamed the handcuffed youth. Pritchitt slowed his step. "Aren't you gonna check his fucking suitcase. It's probably filled with drugs and money."

Pritchitt's pace quickened. He dared not stop or look back.

"When are you going to learn, not everyone is a criminal like you," the cop yelled.

Pritchitt heard a moan as a swift kick struck the teenage thief.

Out of breath, he boarded the waiting trolley.

Nash and the conductor stared at the flashing squad car that roared by.

Benjamin tightly clutched the suitcase to his chest. The bell clanged and the trolley pulled away.

"Almost lose something important?" asked Nash.

"Yes. But I didn't," gasped Pritchitt as the trolley continued its dark trek. His composure regained, Pritchitt stared at the lights of a distant bridge. He wondered if his family would survive the night.

"There it is," said Nash. Before them, illuminated by the trolley's spreading beam, loomed the abandoned brewery. A Gothic structure with *1890* carved over an arched entrance. The castle-like tiers and arched windows spiraled high into the black hole of night.

"Last stop, gentlemen. The old Brewery," the conductor called out. He turned with a curious stare.

"End of the line," whispered Nash. "Did you tell the police about this?"

"No," said Pritchitt.

Nash patted his coat. "I've got a gun. I'll be ready." Distrust reigned as Pritchitt looked to Nash, then at the eerie old brewery.

"Let's get this over with," said Pritchitt. They stepped from the trolley. Both stared at the towering fortress rising before them. A bell sounded and the trolley departed. They were alone. Not even a breeze or rustling of leaves interrupted the terrible silence. It was as if nature knelt fearfully before the haunting structure. Pritchitt gazed upward in anxious awe of the deserted building.

Nash withdrew a small flashlight. He aimed the low beam onto the chipped brick of the gray walls. The abandoned Memphis landmark breathed a disturbing evil. The massive building hovered as an unburied corpse of years past. Pritchitt followed the light against the imposing walls.

The large windows were boarded and filled with concrete, others held broken panes. Foliage grew around the lower floor. *Beware* and *Condemned* signs guarded the arched entrance and warned the curious to stay away.

"I do believe he's expecting us," whispered Nash, shining his light upward. Pritchitt's eyes followed the light. There, on the fifth floor, light filtered through the jagged wood of boarded windows. They stood staring at their dimly lit destination. Pritchitt wondered if Ruth and Benji were somewhere inside. They hurried toward the arched entrance with Pritchitt following Nash's determined lead. Once through the arch Nash came to a sudden halt. He glanced about nervously. He probed the overgrown shrubbery and found an open door half-ajar. It creaked open. "After you," said Nash.

Pritchitt hesitated. "I don't think so. You're doing quite well, after you."

"Then follow me, doctor." Nash grinned.

The air in the room was foul. The flaming hearth previewed hell's own kitchen, as if death had come to visit. Ruth managed to reach the bottle of scotch beneath her feet. She tore at the wrapping. Then slowly, she managed to unscrew the top. The fragrance of scotch was overpowering. She mentally savored the taste. "I can't," she wailed. She sealed the bottle and summoning her surviving strength shattered it against the wall. She stared at the small casket resting on the table six feet away. "You bastard," she screamed as she strained to reach a poker sitting at the side of the fireplace. Her fingers were but inches away. Tears came to her eyes and she cursed Simon. With a painful thrust her outstretched fingers brushed the poker. She winced. The pressure on her ankle brought sharp pain. The poker fell and rolled toward her. As she reached for the poker she saw her ankle smeared in blood. She gave a pitiful moan, then angrily banged on the table. She repeated the angry jabs. The table rocked and the casket fell to the floor. The top flew open and strewn at her feet were photographs. Her tears halted. Her anger simmered into pained curiosity.

The firelight illuminated faces. She strained to see who the woman in the picture was. She recognized an ultrasound of what appeared to be an embryo in a uterus. She knew these from having seen them with Terry's pregnancies. She studied the images; a haunting shadow of a fetus and a beautiful young woman, both left in a casket. She understood. This was Simon's family. His reason for wanting to die. But what did this have to do with her family? Ruth sobbed. She wept. Her pain reflected the thought of finding her family in a casket, lifeless pictures of what use to be. "Let me go, now!" she screamed. There was no answer. "Damn you, Simon. I won't let you do this. You hear me, you bastard from hell?"

She dropped the handful of photographs, trying to hurl them into the fire. Her fury grew. She pulled at the binding chain, her ankle now numbed and swollen. She wished for a miracle of strength. "Please God," she prayed. Blood dripped from the ankle brace. She cried in pain. Her struggle seemed futile. Her strength diminished as she stared back into the raging fireplace. Two pictures burned at the fringe of the flames. Images of the fetus and the young woman ignited and disappeared. Her head dropped wearily, tears falling onto her lap. Depression commanded her thoughts. Was this her final omen? Was she to be like Simon . . . never to see her family again? She glared into the flames. Perspiration bathed her face. She thought herself a prisoner in hell with pain, chains and fire. "I won't. I won't allow this," she shouted, her words determined, her strength returned. Her crying ceased and she grabbed the chain and recited a prayer, her eyes fixed on the fire.

The corridors were black as midnight. The stench of mildew and rotting wood was smothering. Only a narrow beam of light guided their steps around broken glass and large holes. They walked through massive rooms filled with rotten grain and lost memories. The archaic building was destined for destruction. Nash pushed opened a partially boarded door.

"Know exactly where you're going, Nash?"

"For both our sake, I hope so, Benjamin. I truly do hope so."

A single bulb lit a large hall which smelled of urine and mold. Cobwebs and dust covered broken pieces of furniture. *Jenkins Brewery* was printed in faded gold letters along a peeling wall. Beneath it was a hand lettered sign. "Elevator to 10th floor." Nash's eyes darted from side to side. The small flashlight's beam barely illuminated the path ahead. Nash opened another creaky door. They made their way down yet another dark corridor. The air was damp and cold. The overwhelming mildew and dust triggered Pritchitt's asthma. A paroxysm of wheezing coughs slowed his step.

Nash looked back. "Are you okay?"

"I'm fine. Just keep going," said Pritchitt, clearing his throat.

A haunting echo filtered down a nearby shaft as an ancient freight elevator descended, groaning and creaking. It was doorless, an old platform elevator used to haul supplies. Mesh wire served as walls. Pritchitt took a deep breath and stepped onto the rickety elevator. "Seems we're expected. Even sent us our transportation," coughed Pritchitt. He stomped at the elevator's splintered wood flooring. "Damn considerate."

"It'll all be over soon, Benjamin," mumbled Nash, his eyes carefully searching as the elevator began its slow ascent.

Yes, it will be, Pritchitt prayed.

Nash's gaze was somber and resolute. The freight elevator went past floors filled with rotting grain and scurrying rats. The decaying aroma was a reminder of death. Pritchitt's heart pounded as the elevator creaked upwards. He clutched his suitcase tightly. He glanced at Nash whose face betrayed no emotion. Nash's flashlight tracked the floor numbers painted in red. Just after the fourth floor, the elevator lurched to a sudden halt. A disturbing hush followed the silencing of the elevator's grinding motor. Nash drew his gun. He rotated in a circle with his gun pointed high.

From the floor above, a dark silhouette moved between the shadows. Pritchitt froze. Both men stared and waited.

The extended muzzle of a gun spit orange flames from the

blackness. Two successive blasts rang out in the elevator shaft and a resonant echo reverberated in the vacant building. Pritchitt felt no pain. The flashlight fell and rolled. The light illuminated Nash. His face wrenched in pain. His gun dropped to the floor. His knees buckled.

"My God!" blurted Pritchitt.

Nash looked to Pritchitt, then tried to raise himself. Pritchitt grabbed him and pulled him to his feet. Pritchitt cast a frightened gaze upwards. The grinding motor hummed and the elevator inched upwards toward the shadowed silhouette.

"This isn't how I planned it, Doc," gasped Nash with a painful sigh. Pritchitt held him tightly. Confusion scattered Pritchitt's thoughts.

The elevator came to a stop. Nash groaned, his legs weakening as Pritchitt prevented him from falling. Pritchitt backed the two into the far corner of the elevator as footsteps approached. A gurgle stirred as Nash's breath passed through his thickening secretions.

From the darkness emerged a long-haired figure. It was Simon.

With a swift motion a wig was thrown to the floor. A rubber mask peeled off. A contemptuous smile was revealed and a gratifying sigh heard. The person stepped closer. "Too bad, Justin, but you had to pay."

"My God! Blanche . . . Blanche Tucker? Why?" Nash gasped in pain, gaining enough strength to pull away from Pritchitt's hold.

"Why, Justin? Why, you say? You killed Christy! Don't you know? You might as well have handed her the fucking pills," she ranted.

"No," he managed. "I loved her . . . it was my child. It was you. You told her to kill our child. She told me. You were the one."

"Shut up! Enough of this!" Tucker raised her gun. "I have atoned for my sins," she said, her voice shameful. "I'm resurrected in the eyes of God!" she screamed. She took aim at Nash.

"No!" pleaded Pritchitt. "For God's sake, don't. Let me help you. I brought the suitcase, see?" implored Pritchitt. He lifted the suitcase with one hand while the other struggled to support the weakening Nash.

Tucker moved closer. She chanted a prayer-like verse. On her face was a depraved scowl. "Maybe it could have been different, Justin," she hissed. "If you had only loved me, the way you loved Christy, then we could have regained our lost child. God would have overlooked our sin."

"You're insane," shouted Nash, blood soaking his shirt, his eyes barely open. He clung to Pritchitt and his knees buckled.

"Please don't," pleaded Pritchitt.

"God be with you," she said quietly.

"No!" screamed Pritchitt.

The thunderous blast was deafening. Nash's body flew backward's against the wire mesh.

Pritchitt reached to cradle him then turned in anger.

Tucker wore a triumphant grin. "Amen!" she whispered. She gazed at Nash's limp body. "Pick up the suitcase and follow me, Dr. Pritchitt. Now!" She waved the gun for him to follow. He gently rested Nash's body to the floor and stepped from the elevator.

CHAPTER THIRTY

Tucker stood at a worn table in a dimly lit room. She rested the gun in front of her. "The suitcase," she ordered.

Pritchitt placed it on the table next to the weapon. He watched her pull off a padded overcoat, then the leather gloves she wore.

Pritchitt grabbed the gun. "Where's Benji?"

She smiled a devilish grin and held up a key. "In a grain room, third floor. Right below that room." She pointed toward an adjacent room. Pritchitt aimed the gun at her head.

"You can do that and take a chance on freeing Benji before he's buried alive by a mountain of grain but you'll have lost Ruth. Do it my way or lose."

Pritchitt lowered the pistol, uncertain of his next move.

Her glower was sculpted by madness. "This is our destiny," Tucker reminded. "I will be with Christy and her baby . . . my family. You'll be with yours. And poor Justin, well, he's where he needs to be." Her face was cold and unforgiving, her voice harsh. "I do love you, Benjamin."

"You're insane."

An evil sneer spread across her face. "Insane? Remember, Benjamin, you killed Nash, your fingerprints are on the gun you hold. You thought he was Simon, remember? Think hard. You've been under such stress. Don't you *remember,* you've come to aid in the suicide of Dr. Blanche Tucker, a suicide requested because of my terminal illness. And Simon follows you here. That's what Bates, the police and everyone else will believe."

"You're crazy. No one will believe that."

"I've left records telling of my illness."

"What illness?"

"I agree, Benjamin, the world is a mad place. But there is an illness I was born to die with, as was my sister and her baby. My legacy is Huntington's Chorea. You know all about that, don't you?"

"Huntington's Chorea?" said Pritchett — his thoughts, for the moment, on a dreaded degenerative neurologic disease. It was a disease genetically transferred that left many a victim, in mid-life, praying for a merciful and quick end.

Tucker's expression was intense and her eyes constricted. "Christy should never have become pregnant. We had agreed to remain childless," she cried out. "But the baby, God have mercy. The poor baby." With a sudden calm she stared at Pritchitt. "Our parents both died from the disease. We lived in anticipation of the humiliating death we saw torture them in their last years."

She began pacing. "My attorney, neurologist, and Dr. Jonathan Lindsey have letters outlining my plan at your hand, here tonight. The plan was interrupted by Nash, I mean Simon." She turned and faced him squarely. "Now how crazy am I, Benjamin?"

Pritchitt's thoughts swirled with disbelief and confusion. Absorbing the cleverness of her scheme, the impact was devastating. Pritchitt stared through the doorway at the fallen

Nash, then to the adjacent room which led to Benji, captive in a room below. Tucker had him outfoxed.

She removed the flashlight from the table. "My medical records are extensive. I really do wish you could see them, Benjamin." She directed the flashlight's narrow beam to a near corner. Pritchitt turned toward the light. He gasped. "You know, I just may have an extra copy of that medical report for you to see. I don't think my esteemed mentor will mind if I borrow his copy, do you?"

In the dark corner was Jonathan Lindsey propped upright, his back against the wall, open mouthed, his eyes lifeless with a vacant stare.

"Poor old fellow," she said with pity. "He was too nosey. Found out too damn much." Her voice grew angry, then calmed. "So brilliant in his time. He followed me here. When I confessed, his failing heart gave out. I loved him, like I love you, Benjamin. I only hope your luck is better than his, but that's up to you, isn't it. This can be all so simple."

"Blanche, please, give this up, and I —"

"Show me the suitcase, Benjamin."

Pritchitt hesitated, then opened his precious suitcase, displaying the canisters.

"Once I'm gone there are instructions for Ruth's release. If I'm betrayed, you will never see her again." Tucker's voice grew impatient. "The other way, with a bullet in my brain, we all lose. Justin will be Simon. You'll be a hero. But," she gritted, "Ruth will be dead and Benji buried alive. Your life destroyed unless you do exactly as I say."

"You've thought of everything, haven't you?"

She gently took the gun from his hand. Her lips brushed his cheek. "I have a suicide note in my pocket, detailing my illness. They'll be no need for an autopsy." She flashed a key. "Benji's freedom," she said, stuffing it into her pocket.

"All right, but I want to see him first."

Tucker nodded. "I can understand that. A reasonable request." She turned and walked toward the elevator. She softly sang a gospel hymn as Pritchitt followed. The humming motor helped drown her annoying melody. Pritchitt tried not to look at the motionless Nash lying sprawled on the floor. The elevator trembled to a stop.

Naked light bulbs lit a cavernous room piled high with grain. A worn conveyor belt ran into a large tubular cylinder which snaked high above them, then passed through the floor to the storage room below. Pritchitt studied the mountain of grain and the cylinder encasing the belt. It was a conveyor capable of dumping tons of grain every few minutes.

"Benji better be all right or —"

"He's fine. Look down there," she sneered with a pointing finger.

At the base of the cylinder was a large hole widened by years of wear-and-tear on the rotting wood. Pritchitt knelt. Suddenly, his heart lifted. Through the opening was Benji asleep on a makeshift bed. The cylinder's large spout opened above Benji's bed. He watched Benji's chest move with gentle breaths.

"All right, Simon, or whoever you want to be, let's get this damn thing over with."

Tucker nodded in agreement. They turned toward the elevator and made their way back to the floor above and the waiting suitcase.

Pritchitt emptied the suitcase and began his work. Tucker watched from a chair. Two canisters were connected to rubber tubing. Pritchitt flipped a switch. A purr began. Tucker hummed peacefully as a mask covered her face.

"Ready?" Pritchitt asked.

Tucker's eyes lifted. Her stare intense. "Benjamin," she warned, "you become a Judas and the grain will come tumbling down. Heaven's angels won't be able to dig fast enough to save Benji." Her head dropped . . . her eyelids slowly closed.

Let's do this, Pritchitt anxiously thought. He fixed the mask tightly to her face. Her humming of a gospel tune and the purring machine combined in a unnerving duet. Pritchitt paced. His fragile state was near hysteria. He thought only of the key and instructions in her pocket. He measured her drifting consciousness. He dare not blunder, unknowing of any safeguard she had, not wanting to risk the mountain of grain spilling onto Benji.

What was but minutes seemed like hours. Finally, Tucker's movements stopped and her humming was no more. Standing at her side he lifted her arm and gently reached his hand deep into her pocket.

Distant voices were heard from the ground floor, interrupting the hypnotic hum of Pritchitt's machine.

"Benjamin Pritchitt," cried a voice.

Frantic voices filtered up the elevator shaft spilling through the abandoned building. Pritchitt flipped off the machine. The voices magnified ten fold against the opposing silence and then they were gone. Sweat poured from Pritchitt's brow with a sense of urgency. His hand pushed deeper into the pocket. No longer did the distant voices disturb the quiet. Where did they go? Whose voices were they? His anxiety boiled. He knew he needed to hurry.

Pritchitt glanced at Tucker's closed eyes then back toward the elevator shaft. His hand fumbled for the key. Suddenly, a chilling shock ran his spine. A strong grip clasped his wrist. His eyes met hers.

Tucker's stare was enraged. She lashed out. "You Judas," she screamed, inflamed, her eyes furious. She pulled the mask from her face and struggled to her feet. "How could you?"

Pritchitt's stance was of shocked paralysis as fear flooded his confusion.

Tucker lifted the canister. "Nitrous oxide?" she screamed. "Nothing but fucking laughing gas, you miserable Judas," she shrilled, her thunderous voice overpowering.

"You won't get what you want from me," shouted Pritchitt. "No way I'll give you that pleasure. I'm no killer. As much as I want you dead, I can't and I won't," he repeated. His thoughts were frayed. His plan to anesthetize her long enough to get Benji and call the police had failed. Had he killed his family? He couldn't bear the thought.

"You betrayed me," she shouted, pulling the key from her pocket. "You've killed your grandson, and wife. This key is to Benji's tomb." Tucker turned and ran to a small box on a far wall. Pritchitt chased her. She placed the key into a slot and gave a quick turn. Pritchitt pulled her away, knocking her to the floor. A terrifying sound was heard. A motor roared and the conveyor belt began its deadly roll. The belt was alive, carrying grain through the cylinder to the room below . . . Benji's cell.

Pritchitt turned in terror watching the towering grain spill onto the conveyor. "No!" he yelled as a child's piercing cry came from below. "Benji!" he screamed. He frantically searched the panel but found no key. No way to stop the smothering flow. Again, Benji's shrieking cry was heard. Pritchitt ran to a large crack in the floor next to the conveyor and saw Benji standing in terror. The grain swarming at his feet. "Benji!" he screamed above the roar of the conveyor.

Benji raised his tear stained cheeks. "Papa!" he cried above the howling noise. Pritchitt raised up and pushed at the steel tubing of the conveyor but it was hopeless. Pritchitt turned toward Tucker. "Give me that fucking key, or I'll kill you with my bare hands."

"So now you want me dead," she howled, her voice a wicked background against the raging motor and Benji's distant screams. Tucker ran to the belt. She dangled the key over the moving grain. Pritchitt ran and lunged. His fingers missed by inches as the key vanished beneath the grain and into the tubular cylinder. The cries from below stopped. Pritchitt knelt to see the room filling fast.

"No! Please, God. No!" he screamed. He raced toward the open elevator shaft. He had to get below. There he'd have a chance to reach Benji. He stood at the edge of the open elevator shaft. His temples throbbed. He peered down. The elevator was on its way up, a floor below. He jumped, unable to waste the valuable seconds. He landed on the open platform and raising himself reversed the elevator's direction. Horrid thoughts raced through his mind. He prayed to hear Benji's cry but he didn't. "Benji hold on," he cried out. Was he too late?

In his frenzy he stared at the elevator floor. His eyes found Nash's gun. Nash was gone. Only blood stains left. He reached down. Suddenly, a disabling weight fell onto his back and his wind was lost. He struck the floor with a bone rattling thud. He gripped the gun. Blanche Tucker lay beside him, her stare filled with insanity.

She grabbed for the gun and they wrestled. They rolled across the moving platform. Voices were heard shouting from the ground below. The elevator continued its slow descent. Pritchitt's aging strength was no match for Tucker's conditioned body. She stood and landed two staggering kicks to the side of Pritchitt's head as he tried to raise himself. His body lay sprawled against the floor. His vision blurred as she stood over him, the gun pointed above his head. He staggered to his knees with his body drained. He tried to shake the grogginess. Tucker was a haze before him.

"How does it feel to have killed Benji and Ruth?" She backed away. He pulled himself to an unbalanced stance. He could struggle no more. The gun exploded and Pritchitt fell to the floor grabbing his left leg.

"You animal," he cried, wrenching in pain. He held tightly to his bloodied pant leg.

Tucker's demon face gloated. "None of this had to happen, Benjamin. All you had to do is what God wanted you to do," she screamed angrily. She kicked his wounded leg. He grimaced in pain, rolling to his side. Again, voices and shouts calling for Pritchitt echoed through the elevator shaft from far below. Tucker pushed the dangling elevator switch. The elevator's direction changed. Slowly they ascended the shaft. She raised the gun. The motor sputtered. The elevator jerked and she lost her balance. Pritchitt threw his wounded body against her unbalanced stance. The blow sent Tucker from the moving platform onto the floor below.

Anger and hate reduced Pritchitt's painful wound to a numbing nuisance. He stared at her motionless body. He pulled himself to his feet and grabbed at the dangling switch, stopping the elevator. He limped from the open platform and onto the floor above Benji's room. Suddenly, there was a deathly quiet. The clamoring conveyor belt was silent. He hobbled to the large opening in the floor Tucker had shown him. A burlap bag lay on the floor, he quickly wrapped his leg while he watched through the opening. The room below was filled by a mountain of grain. Where was Benji? There was no movement in the grain . . . no muffled sound. "Benji!" he cried, tightening the tourniquet around his bleeding leg. "What have I done?"

A bullet ricocheted off the steel conveyor next to his head. Blanche Tucker stood across the room, her back to a pair of open doors overlooking a room filled with grain. She took aim and pulled the trigger but the gun jammed. Forgetting his pain, Pritchitt, raised himself and ran toward her. His leg gave way and he fell before her. She raised to fire again. Another blast exploded. Pritchitt flinched and in a blaze of sparks the gun flew from Tucker's hand.

"Freeze!" shouted Lori Bordeaux standing in a far door.

Tucker held her wounded hand. She stared wide eyed at Bordeaux then at the kneeling Pritchitt. "Bitch!" yelled Tucker.

"I said freeze, lady!"

Tucker ignored Bordeaux's command. She edged slowly toward the open doors and the pit of grain below and jumped onto the massive mound of grain. "I'm coming, Christy. I'm coming," she shouted. She twisted and turned as if splashing in water. Her depraved laughter filled the building. Pritchitt limped to the edge of the floor where he and Bordeaux stared some six feet down onto the crazed motions of Tucker waist deep in the grain and sinking fast.

Blanche Tucker halted her frolicsome play. She cast a triumphant glower at Pritchitt. "I win. You lose. I'll be with my family and you . . . you've lost yours."

"The hell you do!" he shouted as he jumped onto the grain and grabbed Tucker's arm.

"Are you crazy?" shouted Bordeaux quickly looking for something to throw the sinking Pritchitt as he and Tucker struggled in the giant sandbox.

"Let me go!" Tucker screamed as she clawed at his arm.

She flung grain into Pritchitt's face. They wrestled. Her strength was tremendous against his failing grip.

"Dad!" shouted Terry who had joined Bordeaux at the edge of the flooring above. They stared down helplessly as they watched the two sinking in the quicksand-like grain.

Bordeaux quickly knotted burlap sacks into a tattered rope and handed an end to Terry. "Hold this!" she shouted. Bordeaux tossed the burlap rope onto the top of the grain. "Grab the rope," she ordered.

Tucker pulled back Pritchitt's outstretched arm. "Never!" Tucker shouted as both she and Pritchitt sunk deeper with increasing movement.

"I can't," Pritchitt gasped. His fingers were inches from the rope's end as Tucker lunged at his flailing arm. Above the struggling Pritchitt was the opening spout of a large tubular cylinder. Bordeaux's eyes traced the cylinder. It was attached to the ceiling beams high above. It projected down from the roof to within six feet of the grain it had delivered from the room above. The vessel that had delivered the grain could serve as a conduit to safety for the flailing Pritchitt, thought Bordeaux.

Bordeaux grabbed Terry's arm. "I can make it," she shouted to Pritchitt's ignoring daughter.

Terry, straining to reach her father with the tied burlap sacks, looked up with shock as Bordeaux leaped from the floor's edge. "What the hell are you doing?"

Bordeaux's body banged the medal tubing of the projecting cylinder. She slid down and grabbed hold of the chute's spout. Her body swung like a chandelier above the unaware Pritchitt and Tucker, whose struggle had submerged them to their upper chests. Again, Terry, heaved the tattered rope but it fell apart and far short. There was a loud wrenching noise.

The dangling Bordeaux looked to the tearing ceiling above. "Oh shit!"

"Watch out!" gasped Terry.

Bordeaux's weight pulled the chute free from its ceiling support. She dropped onto the mound of grain still clinging to the metal chute. She reached and clasped Pritchitt's wavering hand. Straining, she pulled. Pritchitt's grip began to slip.

"Hold on, Dad," Terry shouted. Blanche Tucker's head sunk beneath the grain.

"No!" shouted Pritchitt. He released his grip as his daughter's pleas fell on deaf ears. With his chin barely visible, he reached deep for Tucker. Terry screamed as she saw her father sink beneath the surface.

"Son-of-a-bitch," shouted Bordeaux a few feet away. She swam through the grain a strong arm anchored to the metal chute. She strained, pulling the tubing with her. The cylinder, still connected above, was her life line . . . the only thing keeping her from being swallowed, she thought. How long would it hold? She concentrated only on the spot where Pritchitt sank beneath the grain. Bordeaux dug deep and with surging adrenaline pulled Pritchitt to the surface, his hair matted with grain, he gasped for breath. With a grunting heave he pulled up Blanche Tucker, flailing and spitting grain from her mouth. She was too much for his fading strength. Bordeaux's fist smashed into Tucker's face, knocking her unconscious.

Terry knelt at the floor's jagged edge, staring down at the floundering threesome, her hysteria quieted. Grain again filled Pritchitt's mouth. He spat trying to clear his throat. His eyes looked toward his daughter.

A tearing sound shifted all eyes as the cylinder's ceiling support ripped away from the beams above. Bordeaux looked to Terry. Her lifeline was in jeopardy. The cylinder now tenuously fastened by two flimsy cords. "Just don't stand there, dammit. Find a stick, pole, anything," she shouted realizing that any second they could be like three fish floundering in mud. Terry disappeared from the edge of the flooring above.

"Hurry!" pleaded Pritchitt, his breath wheezing from aspirated particles. Bordeaux hugged Pritchitt closer as he struggled to hold Tucker's mouth from the swarming grain. A crashing sound vibrated above as Bordeaux and Pritchitt looked up to see the cylinder tear free from the ceiling. The tubular chute tumbled onto the grain and their lifeline was gone. Bordeaux looked up to the floor's edge. There was no Terry. Bordeaux looked back to Pritchitt's half-buried frown. He coughed grain, still holding onto the nearly hidden Tucker. Suddenly, a hard blow on the head turned Bordeaux. The end of a pole lay before her. She grabbed hold and looked up.

"Hold tight," shouted Ruth Pritchitt. With Terry at her side, Ruth and Terry strained to pull the trio to a ledge on the side of the large pit. Bordeaux, Pritchitt and the waking Tucker were hoisted where they could climb from their would-be tomb.

A fleeting joy warmed him as he stared into Ruth's consoling smile. They embraced. He sat upright. But his warmth suddenly vanished. How could he tell them about Benji?

"Thank God, my darling," Ruth cried.

"Let me die. You promised me!" Tucker angrily shouted as Bordeaux gripped her tightly.

Pritchitt stared into Tucker's depraved rage. "No way, Dr. Tucker, or should I say, Simon. You lost. There will be no good ending for you. Your last act has just been rewritten."

Tucker erupted into a destructive laugh. "No, Brother Benjamin, you're the big loser, aren't you? Isn't there someone you forgot to pull from the grain?"

Pritchitt lowered his head . . . tears swelled and he felt his heart stop. He looked into the queried frowns of his wife and daughter. How could he tell them? How could he live with himself? Ruth and Terry spoke but he couldn't hear. He wiped a tear from his cheek and looked toward Terry.

Tucker was ranting. "My goodness, tell them, Benjamin. If you won't, let me," she taunted. Cruelty filled her laugh.

Lt. Bordeaux yanked Tucker's arm and they started for the elevator. "Come on. I've had just about enough of your insanity," said Bordeaux.

"Wait, bitch, they need to know," shouted Tucker, pulling free from Bordeaux's grasp. Tucker swirled and was face-to-face with Pritchitt. "May I tell them how you murdered your own —"

A bubbling voice exploded from the far corner of the expansive room near the elevator shaft.

"Papa, Mommy!" Benji hurried toward his stunned family. Pritchitt dropped to his knees. Benji ran into his arms.

"No, this can't be," shouted Tucker, disbelieving. "Shoot me. Kill me, please! But how? How can he be alive? This was not God's plan, not in his plan for us at all!" screamed Tucker. Bordeaux led her across the room toward the elevator. "I have to die. I want to be with Christy." The motor of the freight elevator started and drowned out Tucker's moans.

Pritchitt knelt with Benji. "How did you get out, my little hero?" he whispered.

"A man, Papa," said Benji. "He came and got me, Papa," his chattering excitement contagious as Terry lifted him into her arms. Pritchitt was puzzled.

The elevator halted. "This can't be!" Blanche Tucker screamed wildly.

A man stepped from the elevator's platform.

"That man, Papa!" cried Benji.

There in the shadows, a man walked from the elevator. Bordeaux pulled Tucker onto the elevator. "It can't be. It's not fair. This is not God's plan," screamed Tucker. The elevator descended as it's motor squelched her cries.

"He pulled me from that sand, Mommy. He stopped me crying," blurted Benji who was cradled in his mother's arms. Ruth placed a kiss on her grandson's wet but happy cheeks. Pritchitt limped forward. Can it be? Pritchitt wondered. A heartfelt grin spread across Pritchitt's face. The man walked into the dim light. A soft laugh was heard from both men. It was Justin Nash. His shirt bloodied and his arm limp at his side. The two men clasp hands, then embraced.

"I thought you were —"

"Dead? I would've been if it hadn't been for this," Nash said, opening his shirt. "It stopped two bullets, but their impact knocked me out."

Pritchitt's eyes strained. "A bullet proof vest. Well, what do you know."

"Looks like both of us are going to have some mending to do," Nash sighed.

"Let me start," grinned Pritchitt. "How can I tell you? There are no words."

"None needed," whispered Nash. Terry hurried to his side, her joyous face was all Nash needed to see. "To be honest, it was Benji's screams that woke me. I just followed his voice, slid down a conveyor duct, although a bit clumsy with one arm. Once in the room, I couldn't open the door with already several feet of grain piled against it. From there the little guy took charge. He stood on my shoulders and reached up an old heating duct. He climbed in, found a long burlap sack and lowered it. He anchored the sack around a bar in the duct and held on for dear life. I grabbed hold and rode the rising grain while pulling on the sack to keep me from sinking. Then I climbed into the duct and here I am. Hell! That little guy saved me."

Ruth held her husband. "I always wanted to see the inside of this building, but now that I have, can we please leave?"

Pritchitt turned to Terry as they made their way out toward the elevator. "How did you and your mother —?"

"Benjamin Pritchitt, that's a whole different story, too long for now," interrupted Ruth.

Pritchitt examined his wife's wrists. She flinched. There were burns. He noticed a metal handcuff on her bloodied ankle. His limp halted. "What —"

"Like I said, darling," she repeated. "It's a long story. Let's just say I've been to hell and back and now I really want to go home."

Pritchitt nodded. "Anything you say," he agreed, leaning on his wife and relishing the moment.

Ruth suddenly stopped and turned. "Where's Claire?" she blurted.

Pritchitt smiled. "On a farm with a dear friend of mine. A very dear friend. That's where we all need to go . . . to the country."

Pritchitt limped toward the elevator. Nash, Terry, Ruth and Benji huddled beside him.

Simon had seen a parallel in death, one orchestrated by a merciful angel; the other by an avenging angel. Were they that much different? Pritchitt pondered. He prayed so. He turned and staring back into the dying building, he was glad to be alive. A hand was extended and with a tight clasp Nash pulled Pritchitt onto the platform of the elevator.

The elevator motor rumbled. A sound trumpeting Benjamin Pritchitt's answered prayers and his wished-for ending . . . a family together . . . a family safe.

CHAPTER THIRTY-ONE

The judge took her seat and waited for the return of the jury. Todd Bohannon leaned toward his restless client. "Ben, are you ready?"

Pritchitt straightened his tie. "Not really. This has gone a lot faster than I expected."

Bohannon looked at his watch. "They've been out for six hours. This could be a good sign, then maybe not."

"That's reassuring," said Pritchitt as he forced a smiled at his family who were seated directly behind him. Ruth returned his smile, as did Tyler and Terry. Benji and Claire sat on either side of Ruth, each clutching a hand. Nash sat beside Terry, his arm in a sling. He lifted an unlit cigar and extended two fingers for victory. He and Terry had apologized for their rush to judgment. Justin was receiving needed counseling to deal with his grief and guilt of the past. Lori Bordeaux, seated beside Tyler, gave a confident nod to Pritchitt. Benjamin turned to face the empty seats of the jurors. He thought of all that had happened and wondered what the minutes ahead would bring. Would it be prison to toast his last few months of hell, or would the jury, in some way, find him, as he thought himself, a compassionate man?

Bohannon tugged his client's sleeve. The jurors filed into the courtroom taking their seats. Pritchitt looked into their faces but none returned his glance. The lawyer patted Ben's knee in anticipation and apprehension grew throughout the room. "One is smiling, Ben."

"I don't call that a smile," whispered Pritchitt, studying their expressions. "Here it comes," sighed Pritchitt. He glanced at Ruth. She lent a supportive smile. In the courtroom was Dr. Lane Powers, Sarah Taylor, Atway Jackson and even Dr. Peters. Then Benjamin recognized the appreciative face of Oscar Maples.

"Would the defendant please rise," ordered Judge McLaren. "Mr. Foreman, have you reached a verdict?"

The foreman stood. "We have, Your Honor."

The judge donned her glasses. "How do you find the defendant?"

Pritchitt stood facing the jury. His heart pounded.

"We, the jury, find the defendant guilty of second degree murder." A murmur of disappointment swept the room. Disbelieving murmurs, jeers and applause rose from the spectators. Pritchitt turned to Ruth.

The verdict was handed to the judge. Her gavel silenced the courtroom. She read the charges. Dr. Benjamin Pritchitt had been found guilty on all charges of violating state law forbidding assisted suicides.

Judge McLaren peered over her glasses. Their was a hush and she paused before talking. Her puckered lips seemed to search for words. "You have been found guilty by a jury of your peers, Dr. Pritchitt, a verdict that quite simply would be hard not to arrive at considering the clarity of our state law." She paused and looked at a note attached to the verdict. "I will say this, if I might," she began, laying her glasses to the side and looking over the courtroom. "Even though I find no wrong with the jury, I would hope, as I believe each of them would, that when my time comes there will be a doctor with compassion, to be by my side. You are hereby sentenced to two years in prison." Shouts of disapproval filled the courtroom. People stood with protesting remarks. Jeremy Bates turned with a gratifying smile. The judge slammed her gavel. "However, due to the nature of this so-called crime and the note I possess from the jury your sentence is to be suspended."

Jeremy Bates jumped up in protest. "Your Honor, I —"

"Sit down, Mr. Bates, or I'll hold you in contempt and you'll be the one spending time in jail, sir," ordered McLaren.

"Dr. Pritchitt, you will serve a one-year probation." She lifted her glasses. "I will remind you that your participation in any form of aided suicide will send you to jail. I advise you to use your legal efforts to modify many of our foolish laws, sir. Do you understand?"

"I do, Your Honor," nodded Pritchitt as Bohannon hugged him tightly.

A loud eruption of joy rang through the courtroom. Pritchitt gave an appreciative hug to his attorney. With tears in his eyes he embraced his family. Bernie Wiseman and Patsy cheered the verdict.

Pritchitt kissed his wife. "I think it's time we all went home."

The freshly mopped floor was the only brightness in the barren gray corridor. High windows permitted scant light to brighten death row's cellblock 12. The stench of a clogged toilet filled the unventilated air. A woman's shriek sliced the stench which hung heavy in the air. A matron approached the screaming prisoner with a baton in hand.

"Do something about that crazy bitch!" shouted an inmate.

"I can't sleep," yelled a fat woman. The guard rapped her baton in her palm. Her beady eyes focused on the complaining prisoner. "Crystal, you shut the fuck up. I'll handle this." She slammed the baton against the bars of the cell.

The fat inmate stepped back, cursing the guard.

"You're telling me to shut up? Hell, tell that insane bitch

next to me to keep her crazy talk to herself or I'm gonna slit her fucking throat!"

The matron pointed her baton. "You've done that before, Crystal. You won't get a second chance, that's why you're in here waiting for twelve years to get yourself fried. But instead, you'll just grow old with me," taunted the guard. "

The guard walked slowly to the next cell. The prisoner knelt at her cot, staring at the walls covered with chalk drawings. The guard smacked the metal bars. The disheveled inmate was oblivious, singing to herself, rocking back and forth as she drew on the wall. A bucket of cold water flew onto the haggard woman. The dousing by the guard brought a roar of grotesque laughter along the row of cells. Blanche's head turned. A hostile glare shot toward the guard. She had completed her chalk sketch on the cell wall. It was a small casket surrounded by many burning candles. On an opposing wall was a woman holding a baby.

"Doctor Tucker!" the guard yelled. "Keep the fuck quiet, or I'm gonna let Crystal have a go at ya' for a minute or two."

Another female guard walked up. "What the hell's going on down here?"

"The same old shit on this end of hell's alley. Crystal is screaming about her crazy neighbor."

"So that's the infamous Dr. Blanche Tucker, huh?" asked the second guard.

"Yep, all this nut does is sing, draw on the walls and kiss those damn pictures," said the guard, pointing to a few scraggly pictures resting on a nearby sink. One guard walked off as the other stared at Tucker's constant rocking. With her babbled singing growing louder and more irritating other inmates began to yell for quiet. Shaking her head, the guard walked down the noisy corridor.

"Don't leave me next to this maniac," screamed Crystal.

A sudden shriek pierced the air. "I need to die today!" screamed the voice.

"Shut the fuck up, Doc," screamed Crystal, clinging to the bars of her cell.

"Please, let her kill me." Her continued pleas for death roused every prisoner. They shouted for the guards to silence her.

"To think she was one of the most prominent psychiatrists in Memphis," one guard said with awe.

The second matron lowered her baton. "The Doc's lawyer is appealing her case. She'll be in that cell for years."

"I doubt that. I hear she's going to die from some kind of nerve disease . . ."

"Poor bitch," said the guard as she clanged a door shut behind them.

"I need to die," begged Tucker. A shrill cry filled her cell. She crawled to the cot and picked up two wrinkled photographs. She kissed both. "I'll be with you soon, Christy," she whimpered. "And you, too, my baby," she whispered, kissing the ultrasound of an unborn fetus.

She counted the hours until darkness. The only solace in Tucker's miserable existence was her nightly dream. It was calming and reassuring. She beheld a golden, glowing face that smiled gently. In the dream she caressed his face and kissed his lips. He alone understood. He was the executioner.

ABOUT THE AUTHOR

Oakley Jordan is a Memphis, Tennessee, physician. Despite having a large practice, Dr. Jordan manages to find time to write. "Writing is my passion," says Jordan. "I've always been a storyteller, and I enjoy spinning an exciting tale."

Oakley Jordan is currently at work on a mystery thriller with the title, *Fallen Angel.*